THE GREATEST ESCAPE

Based on the true story of the greatest escape
of World War Two

The Greatest Escape

Steve J Plummer

Cloth Wrap Publishing
2015

First published 2015
2nd edition 2016

The work which follows is based on actual events although certain names and incidents have been imagined by the author. Where those people who were present during the events described have been identified, the author has attempted to represent their part in those events as accurately as known records allow.

ISBN 978-1-326-66721-4

Cloth Wrap Publishing

By the same author

Salamander Dreaming:
The Story of Jean and George Russell

Fin's Judgement

Enlist!
The Story of One Man's
Determination to Serve his Country

A Man of Invention

The Wheelwright Family Story

The Wheelwright Genealogy

The Legendary Lieutenant

Foreword

By Maj. John A Thomas MA, TD**
Director of the 1940's Swansea Bay Museum

In 'The Greatest Escape' Steve Plummer vividly describes how ordinary people on the Homefront reacted to the frontline being brought suddenly into their lives with the mass escape of German officers on their very doorsteps.

He puts us firmly out in the darkened lanes and sodden fields with the locals. But he also highlights the uncertainties that surround the story...

ACKNOWLEDGEMENTS

The author wishes to acknowledge several published sources of information which have been useful in his research and preparation of this book. These include the works of Lieut. Col. A P Scotland OBE, *The London Cage* (Evans Bros., London, 1957) and of Jon and Diane Sutherland, *Prisoner of War Camps in Britain During the Second World War* (Golden Guides Press, 2012).

Much help has been provided by the British Library's archive of local and national newspapers, The National Archives at Kew and Glamorgan County Archives at Leckwith, Cardiff where records are held relating to the former Glamorgan Constabulary. The author is grateful for the assistance given by Archivist, Michael Wilcox and others.

The author also acknowledges the information published, among other places, in Internet websites which relate to Camp 198, particularly *bracklaordnance.co.uk* and *islandfarm.fsnet.co.uk* and the hard work and dedication shown by Richard Williams and Brett Exton, the respective compilers of the above websites. The author has no wish to duplicate the original material contained therein and recommends that readers who wish to research further into the Bridgend Ordnance Factory or Camp 198 should visit the websites.

In particular, the author wishes to thank Maj. John A Thomas MA, TD**, Director of the 1940's Swansea Bay Museum, for his generous contributions, comments and, in particular, for making available notes and drafts compiled while researching for his MA thesis on the subject of Wartime Heritage and Island Farm Camp.

Finally, thanks must go to my wife for her tolerance of my own research notes being scattered about the house, for her patience during the many hours of my self-imposed incarceration and, ultimately, for her proof-reading.

A full list of original record sources is included in the final pages of this book.

"The first casualty when war comes is truth."

> - US Senator Hiram Warren Johnson
> (1917)

"Among the calamities of war may be jointly numbered the diminution of the love of truth, by the falsehoods which interest dictates and credulity encourages."

> - Samuel Johnson, *The Idler Magazine*
> (11th November 1758)

"In war, truth is the first casualty."

> - Aeschylus (Greek tragedian & playwright)
> (525 BC – 456 BC)

February 2005

The two men stopped briefly, standing side by side and gazing in silence at the view before them. It would have been, for most people, a bleak enough sight; a rough field, thick with damp grass, overgrown by clumps of brambles and pitted with thick, muddy pools. Fallen trees, long dead and rotting, surrounded them, taller tufts of unkempt grass poking through the grime. They might have been reaching for fresh air and daylight, were it not for the thick blanket of grey cloud overhead. Scarring the natural wasteland, a few tangles of rusting barbed wire lay like industrial tumbleweed, anchored and half submerged in the puddles. Heaped between them, discarded masonry had been piled and pushed high as if by a monstrous mole. It seemed that the giant beast might still lurk, scratching out subterranean tunnels beneath their feet. The rubble, now green with moss and ivy had lain, inadvertently camouflaged, for as many years as anyone concerned with the land could remember.

The object of most interest to the two men revealed itself slowly as they progressed cautiously across the mire and emerged from the shadow of a bank of trees. Half obscured by the overgrown tangle stood a long, low, single storey building. Over a hundred feet long by twenty wide, its once grey walls were now decorated with patches of mud green lichen brought by sixty years of neglect. A gently pitched roof of tiles, engulfed in tentacles of thick foliage, had collapsed at the far end. Thin timber battens, bent and blackened with age and weather, lay exposed like charred ribs. The same chill elements now seemed more determined than ever to stamp their control and an easterly wind picked up as rain started to fall.

The older of the two men shook his head; his only discernible communication since their slow walk through the trees had started. The other held up his hand, arresting their progress again. He lifted one sodden leather shoe from the mud, looked down, then up at his companion, apologizing in desultory silence for his lack of foresight. The older man, standing firmly

1

in a pair of well used Wellington boots, sniffed before returning his attention to the building he was seeing for the first time in more than half a century.

He had travelled too far and waited too long to be deterred by poor weather, another man's wet feet or the mild infirmity of his own eighty years. He trudged stubbornly on, closing on the building. Slowing only as he reached a wooden door, its flaking grey paint beaten and scarred, he raised the palm of his hand to the rotten timbers. Hesitating, he changed his mind. Moving slowly to one side and bending slightly, he peered through a slot of blackened glass, just visible between the window frame and the rough edge of a chipboard panel that covered the window. Seeing nothing, he moved on, following the line of the wall.

"Mr. Charteris, please, hang on a minute."

The older man ignored the request, resting his hand on the old concrete and tracing a line of soft mortar, flaking easily with the movement of his fingers.

George Charteris, despite his age and a slight reduction in mobility, had lost none of his memory. Time and progress might have altered the surrounding area beyond recognition, clearing the site and placing a modern housing estate to one side and an industrial park on another, but this one remaining building was unmistakable. Six decades earlier he had spent many hours discussing and studying every inch of this building. He had been sure then that he had become as familiar with it as any man could. Certainly as familiar as any man could wish to be with such a place. Since then, he had been reluctantly forced to acknowledge the simple truth. He had made mistakes. Today, a jumble of memories returned in a maze of conflicting emotions. The pride he had once felt had already given way to disappointment. He was not a man who took easily to self-reproach and now he found himself swamped by waves of anger, overpowering the regrets and doubt.

"Mr. Charteris, are you all right?"

George glanced round, sad eyes focusing on the other man's face.

"You wouldn't understand." He looked away again, patting the concrete wall as if petting a faithful old dog. His voice dropped, the younger man's presence seemingly unimportant. "Hut Nine has haunted my thoughts for so long. There hasn't been a week gone by that I haven't wondered about it."

Clive Williams nodded, anxious to engage in the moment.

"Me too."

"You and your newspaper story." The older man made no attempt to disguise his indifference.

"Well, you know. It's the anniversary."

Charteris dismissed his explanation with a brisk wave of his hand. "I'm not bothered about anniversaries any more. I've seen too many of them. I'm more concerned about what happened. I mean what *really* happened."

The younger man frowned. "I'm pretty sure we know what happened, don't we? It's just a matter of getting the story out there."

Charteris' eyes narrowed briefly. "As long as it's the *true* story." He turned, revolving round his walking stick to face the younger man. "You might think you know what happened here, back in 1945." His chin dropped to his chest as if the answer may be buried in the mud beneath their feet. "I'm pretty bloody sure that you don't." His voice lowered slightly. "I'm not sure, even, that I do." He turned away quickly, angrily almost. "And I was bloody well here."

INTRODUCTION

Even the more credulous of Britain's members of parliament were, by early 1939, beginning to doubt the repeated promises made by Germany's Chancellor that he would keep to his promises of a non-aggression pact in Europe.

With a jerk that was almost visible, Politicians emerged into the glaring daylight of the real world. They rose from their opposing benches in the House of Commons, crying their demands that the nation ready herself for war.

A primary requisite for such a war was, and sadly still is, military ordnance: the bombs, bullets and shells deemed necessary to destroy the enemy. Britain's main and publicly owned supplier of ordnance was based on Frog Island; a loop in the River Thames at Woolwich, wedged between Dartford Creek and Thames-Barking Creek.

No factory that was so close to the capital's centre could be regarded as safe, least of all the Woolwich Arsenal; an organisation well known to every major military force across the globe. Situated in south east London, it was also considered too close to the continent to be safe from potential bombing raids.

The original site had begun life as an ordnance storage depot in 1671. This had soon incorporated a factory for the manufacture of gunpowder, shell cases and fuses, obliquely named 'The Royal Laboratory' and, in 1717, a gun foundry (The Royal Brass Foundry). The Crimean War had placed greater demands on the ageing buildings and in 1854 a large open space known as the Laboratory Square had been given a vast roof to create a new munitions factory. To keep pace with changing technology, a new shot and shell factory had been completed on the site in 1857.

By the advent of the Great War in 1914, the Woolwich Arsenal employed 80,000 workers but even this had proved insufficient to meet the war effort. Additional temporary factories had quickly been built but only Woolwich and two others, at Enfield and Waltham Abbey Royal Gunpowder Mills, were still operating in 1939.

The needs of modern warfare, as had been shown in 1914, demanded that greater capacity would soon be needed, particularly for the manufacture of shells. Initially, it was agreed that two overspill factories would be built and plans were urgently drawn up for their construction. They should be as far from London as was practicable and preferably out of range of what, at that time, were Germany's (and Europe's) most advanced bomber aircraft.

Sites throughout England, Scotland and Wales were considered for their suitability until attention became focussed on Chorley in Lancashire and the small village of Waterton, near Bridgend in the county of Glamorgan. The combination of local unemployment and geographical location made both areas suitable.

With unaccustomed haste, a compulsory purchase order for 450 acres of land at Waterton was made. The new factory would be split into two distinct sections; one to be used as a storage facility and the other as the shell filling factory itself. In the small market town, more used to the thunder of its surrounding iron foundries and coal mines, the reaction to the plan was mixed. There were those who opposed the idea on grounds of public safety while the proponents of the scheme stressed the employment opportunities and the area's patriotic duty to support the war effort.

One of the loudest complaints focussed on the assumption that the establishment of such a factory, which later became known locally simply as 'The Arsenal', would provide a magnet for the *Luftwaffe*'s bombs. Strangely, however, the Bridgend Royal Ordnance Factory (or ROF) which followed survived the duration of the war untouched by enemy action. There has been much speculation over the reasons, led by the belief, locally held, that the low-lying site was frequently shrouded by early morning and evening mists which obscured the target from the air. Those theorists were not to know until long after the war that, on 24th August 1940, a perfectly clear aerial photograph had been taken by a *Luftwaffe* reconnaissance photographer. This shows in absolute clarity the town of Bridgend and The Arsenal's location and layout.

It is possible that the buildings in the photographs were never accurately interpreted as being of importance. Another possible explanation is that orders had been issued by the German high command – possibly by Adolf Hitler himself – that the factory was to be preserved in anticipation of his forces' successful invasion of Britain.

1930's Britain was blighted by industrial unrest and high unemployment. In the months leading up to the outbreak of war, increasing numbers of young men, jaded by inactivity and low income, began signing up to join the armed services. Now, a sharp rise in the nation's defence budget meant that military leaders could embark on the largest national recruitment campaign since military conscription had been introduced in 1916.

In 1937 there had been 200,000 full-time soldiers in the British Army. The Military Training Act of April 1939 demanded that all men aged between 20 and 21, who were not in a reserved occupation, register for six months military training. Volunteers swelled the ranks of the Army to 875,000 by September 1939 but even this was judged insufficient to take on Germany's land forces as they spread across continental Europe. One month after war was declared, in October 1939, military conscription was introduced for men aged between 20 and 23 who were not working in reserved occupations. Further, the Government warned that they might soon extend the call-up to include men between the ages of 18 and 41.

The early call-up created a shortage of male labour but it was not until 1941 that women in their twenties were conscripted for civilian war work

Royal Ordnance Factory Number 38 at Waterton was completed in 1939 with the help of employees and managers from Woolwich, despite delays caused by a severe winter and heavy rainfall. By the end of the year, full production was underway and the factory employed an extraordinary total of 39,000 workers. Even this workforce was unable to meet the demands of war and the construction of a further shell filling factory at Brackla Hill, also in Bridgend, was soon commissioned from Sir Robert McAlpine & Sons at a cost of £580,000.

In the absence of male workers, even before the first factory opened, Royal Ordnance managers publicly declared that they were satisfied with their new, mainly female, workforce. Women, they declared, were 'temperamentally suited' to the work and 'manually dextrous', once trained, to fill shell cases with high explosive.

A principally female complement of many thousands of employees, however, presented logistical problems. Never before had a Government department been required to house so large a civilian workforce in such a small provincial town.

Camp 198, as it would later be named, was situated just a few miles from ROF 38 and started life as a group of dormitory style hostels for these thousands of female munitions workers. Originally known as Island Farm Camp because it was built on land the Government had acquired from Island Farm, it was situated on a narrow triangular site adjacent to the main A48 road between Port Talbot and Cardiff. There, the authorities had quickly erected a large camp of temporary buildings to accommodate the expected influx of munitions workers.

The British Concrete Federation obligingly provided an 'off the shelf' solution; a design for a multi-purpose single storey building, constructed from prefabricated reinforced concrete slabs and panels. These could be quickly manufactured off site and shipped in by lorry. Once on site they could be quickly and easily assembled to any number of different configurations, depending on their intended use and the limitations the location presented. The resultant structures were extremely durable with shallow pitched tile roofs. Built on a long and narrow footprint, the accommodation buildings erected at Island Farm Camp were each internally divided into small bedrooms, communal kitchens, living areas and washrooms all accessed from a corridor which stretched the length of the building.

The Ministry of Works and others were quick to declare themselves more than satisfied with the end result. The workers, however, had different ideas. The number of Arsenal employees continued to grow, yet by 1940 many of the huts had been abandoned. The women, drawn from counties spread along the South Wales coast and beyond, had arrived, looked and even tried out their new homes. Almost without exception, they had quickly left, preferring to either find their own digs locally or remain with their families and travel daily to Bridgend, despite difficulties with wartime train timetables and the blackout. The prospect of spending the duration of the war living in cramped rooms within cold and drab huts clearly did not appeal.

The hastily built Island Farm huts remained wastefully unoccupied until 1943 when the planned D-Day invasion of continental Europe made it necessary to house thousands of

American GI's in temporary billets. Supposedly a strict secret, there were few residents of Bridgend who could have failed to notice the American wartime hardware as it rolled slowly and noisily down the A48 or the crowds of smartly dressed and scrubbed young men who herded between the pubs of Bridgend each evening. Only a few more would have been unaware of the VIP visit to Island Farm by General Dwight 'Ike' Eisenhower. Many lined the wire fence between the camp and the main road to hear his rallying speech to the American troops, delivered with characteristic informality from the roof of a truck. The local newspaper, to the dismay of the locally garrisoned British troops (although the Americans didn't seem to mind), published the highlight of Ike's address when he promised his men that with their help, he would "thrash the enemy".

The Americans soon departed for training camps on Salisbury Plain, the Brecon Beacons and the West Country. Island Farm was left deserted once again.

Within weeks, the D-Day landings in Normandy had become the talk of every village and town in Britain, including Bridgend. Much was made in the press of allied advances being made across France and, significantly, the large number of German troops who daily either gave themselves up or were taken prisoner.

Winning the propaganda war was important and, however compliant some of these early prisoners appeared to be, the Allies could not risk the humiliation of captured soldiers wandering out of their sparsely guarded tented holding stations. Rather than using valuable front-line troops to guard them, The Allied High Command and the War Office decided to ship their prisoners back to Britain.

It wasn't long before an announcement was made that Island Farm had been selected once more – this time as one of the new sites for a Prisoner of War camp.

There was an immediate protest in the small town, its neighbours and surrounding villages. The local people had tolerated the significant risk of having an ordnance factory on their doorstep out of patriotism and a feeling that they must be seen to 'do their bit', but having German prisoners as well, in the view of Bridgend's Urban District Council at least, was a step too far. Despite the clear need for such camps – over two hundred in total were planned throughout Britain – there were concerns over the close proximity of so many enemy soldiers to the Arsenal and the valuable docks at Port Talbot and Swansea. Public worries turned to outrage when it was learned that the War Office intended that Island Farm Camp should house up to 2,000 prisoners.

The need, however, was immediate and crucial to the success of the European advance. The protests went unheeded. Camp 198 was born.

In August 1944, however, the prefabricated huts, sited in their open field, presented no security against escape. To the amazement of many, the first German prisoners brought into Bridgend were tasked with the job of securing their own prison.

The majority were junior NCO's and private soldiers, physically exhausted as well as politically and ideologically ambivalent. Most were compliant, happy to have escaped the increasing carnage in Europe and considered to be of low risk. They were set to work with barbed wire and fence posts to erect a boundary round the camp, satisfied at least that the boredom of imprisonment was being temporarily averted. They may have been less happy, had they known, that when their work was completed, the War Office would decide that Camp 198, with its compact bedrooms and modern facilities, was altogether too comfortable for other ranks. Within a few days, all but a few of the prisoners were shipped out and set to work constructing further camps in other parts of the country.

In their place, in November 1944, a large contingent of German officers was brought by rail to Bridgend. These were not from the same mould as the subordinates they were replacing. Although a small number of junior ranks had remained as orderlies for the incoming officers, along with more senior NCO's to act as supervisors, the new intake was chiefly made up of die-hard Nazis, loyal to their Fuhrer and the Third Reich. Most still believed firmly in an ultimate German victory in Europe and regarded their incarceration as both a futile interruption and an indignity.

To add to their rancour, when their train pulled in to Bridgend's railway station, their shouts of 'Heil Hitler' were cut short by news that there was no road transport available and they were expected to walk two miles to their camp, carrying their own luggage. The officers refused starkly to disembark.

It was only the appearance of a smartly uniformed man, clearly in control of the situation, who brought them to order. He commanded them to leave the train and line up on the platform. From beneath his gold braided peaked cap, he ordered them to come to attention, pick up their bags and march.

Had they known he was a civilian employee of the regional railway company, his words would have had no impact whatever. Wilfred Hills, Senior Stationmaster and a former Staff Sergeant in the Royal Welch Fusiliers, had been watching the swelling scene from his office window. The young captain in charge of the prisoner escort, he had observed, was clearly out of his depth. Hills had pulled on his greatcoat, doing up the embossed brass buttons against the cold and wedging his Great Western uniform cap on his head. He had interceded, not to save the officer's embarrassment; he had little affection for officers of any description and even less regard for those who held temporary commissions. The early morning mail train from Cardiff was due at any moment and he would be damned if he'd allow a load of defeated German officers an opportunity to interfere with the Royal Mail.

The prisoners obeyed without a further murmur. They goose-stepped from the platform, waiting until they were outside the confines of the station before bursting into a loud German drinking song. Defiantly and unopposed by their escort, they kept up the impromptu chorus all the way to Camp 198.

The singing didn't stop even after the prisoners arrived at the camp. Every night, complained neighbouring residents, the impromptu concerts became louder and seemingly more defiant. It was as if the Germans were unleashing their hatred vocally, warning their captors of what was to come when (and it was surely 'when', not 'if') the tide turned and the vanquished became the victors.

The local newspaper, always eager to provide a patriotic voice, accused the prisoners of behaving like a badly behaved football crowd, even when there was no trouble within the camp. Trouble, however, there was.

When two German Naval officers were carried to Bridgend Hospital having taken a severe beating, it was learned that their injuries were inflicted as a punishment, spontaneously handed out by their fellow Prisoners of War because they had refused to send Hitler a birthday card.

While other prisoners spent much of their time demanding unnecessarily of the Camp Commandant that their rights under the Geneva Convention be met, a small number tried to force a

German padre to give up his church so they could use it as a gymnasium. The priest, a Roman Catholic, reported them to the Camp Commandant who posted extra guards for his protection. The threats continued to escalate until the padre was moved for his own safety to another camp. The British officers in charge of the camp were only too aware that physical fitness, for any Prisoner of War, was regarded as essential. German officers had standing orders to maintain their physical health in order to improve their chances of escape if captured. Allied officers received the same instruction. Indeed, an entire branch of Military Intelligence, designated as MI9, had been set up with responsibility to provide training and assist Allied Prisoners of War to evade and escape captivity.

Less fortunate than the hapless German padre was a 49 year old Austrian born military engineer named Otto Iskat. Early in 1945, he was overheard to make a passing comment about the futility of war. The remark earned him an immediate and brutal beating from a group of fanatical young German officers. Iskat, although a non-combatant, was no pacifist or conscientious objector. During the Great War he had served in the Austro-Hungarian Army as an infantryman and had been awarded the Austrian Silver Bravery Medal, the Prussian Iron Cross and the Karl Troop Cross for bravery for his service in the front line trenches. He had been taken prisoner by the Russians and served time in a labour camp in Siberia before being released in 1917. Over the course of two years, he had trekked on foot across Siberia to Vladivostok where he had taken refuge at the YMCA. A gifted linguist, poet and artist, he had managed to earn enough money along the way to feed himself. It was 1921 before he landed on friendly soil and in Vienna was released from military service. He was pronounced to have a 25% war disability and, by the outbreak of war in 1939, had been suffering from heart disease for many years. Despite that, he had been called up for military service. By the time of his capture in 1944 at the town of Brest, perched on the north-westerly tip of France, he had attained the rank of *Oberregierungspaurat*, the equivalent to a Lieutenant Colonel, in the construction and building administration.

The sudden and frenzied attack on 26th January 1945 proved too much for his fragile health. Iskat was dead even before the young thugs had disentangled themselves from their assault. It was a heartless attack and a thoughtless one. Iskat's obvious talents and experience could have proved immeasurably useful to his fellows in the months which were to follow.

The camp was, in many ways, fundamentally flawed as a prison. The disinterested junior prisoners who had constructed the three surrounding wire fences and barbed wire barricades had discarded several of their tools and left-over building materials around the site. Whether by design or not, there were small caches of timber, mortar, bricks and nails, left in dark corners beneath the huts and dotted around the parallel layers of perimeter fencing. Although most had been gathered together and made secure by the guards, it seems likely that some were missed, to be found later by the incoming and infinitely more inquisitive prisoners. Why the clearance had not been more thorough was a question which, seemingly, wasn't asked until it was too late. So too were questions relating to the Camp Commandant's repeated requests for more men and equipment. He was denied an increase in complement, even though he had just 150 men under his command. Ninety of these were guards, expected to control and contain over 1,600 German prisoners, most of whom were intent on breaking out. It was calculated that there were just ten guards on duty at any one time for every mile of wire fencing.

Some said the very location of the camp was an open invitation for escape. Within two days march of either Swansea or Cardiff Docks and barely fifteen miles to the docks at Port Talbot, the camp was adjacent to the A48 road linking the largest towns and cities in South Wales. Train stations dotted along the same route adjoined the rail network with tentacles into England's industrial midlands and the capital itself.

The reality was that it would be difficult to find an area of the UK so isolated that escape would be made impossible, although many had advocated the less accessible reaches of Mid Wales, the Western Isles or even the Highlands of Scotland. It seems that the need to provide housing for so many prisoners and the expediency of having a ready-made camp already in Government ownership was too tempting a solution to pass up.

The Camp Commandant, however, was a different matter. Lieutenant Colonel Edwin Darling was a career soldier with over thirty years experience. During the Great War he had been a Prisoner of War in Germany. He had managed to escape, travelling through Holland before successfully crossing the Channel back to England. There were few tricks that potential escapees could pull out of the bag that Darling had not already thought of, or had tried for himself.

Just two months after the prisoners' arrival, in early January 1945, his officers discovered the second of two tunnels. The first, uncovered just before Christmas, had been a primitive, almost half-hearted affair which had reached no more than a few feet into damp and unstable ground. It had been sited dangerously close to a washroom and the soil had been particularly unsuited to excavation, being even more fluid than normal. Nevertheless, after its discovery there had been even more noise than usual, created by prisoners who supposedly were enjoying their recreation hours singing, playing musical instruments or indulging in noisy games of football. Darling had recognized the signs of disguise and had sent two of his officers into each of the huts in turn until, in Hut 16, they found the hearthstone in front of a stove had been disturbed. The officers used iron bars to lift the stone to reveal the mouth of a freshly dug tunnel and a prisoner, oblivious to the search being carried out above his head, busily at work with an improvised spade.

Darling also knew that tunnels were seldom dug in isolation or even in pairs. Prisoners theorized that, on discovering one or two tunnels, the guards would be so pleased with themselves that they would become complacent. Confounding their theory, Darling ordered that regular searches of every building used by the prisoners be stepped up. The result he hoped for was that work on other tunnels, if there were any, would have to be temporarily suspended.

The Germans, however, were nothing if not persistent. Camp guards discovered that several iron bars had been dislodged from one of the hut windows. Colonel Darling ordered that extra guards patrol outside the window until replacement bars could be supplied. Repeated checks confirmed that no prisoners were missing and the Commandant was heard to question why prisoners would remove the bars and risk detection when they had apparently not attempted an immediate escape.

His question was answered within a few days when guards found a pair of crude wire cutters, fashioned out of the missing bars. They were lying next to a hole cut through the outer perimeter fencing. The escape had been made easier by the fact that Colonel Darling's requests for extra barbed wire, searchlights and timber to make raised guard towers had all been turned down. Instead, he had to make do with minimal foot patrols, a few Alsatians and acetylene flares. These couldn't be left in situ for fear that the prisoners would use them as weapons, despite being unreliable, dangerous to use and difficult to move about quickly when needed.

The two prisoners who escaped were recaptured in Port Talbot, making for the docks. It was embarrassing to the authorities that, until that point, their absence hadn't been noticed. At roll-call, the remaining prisoners had repeatedly faked rowdy arguments and continually moved about among their own ranks, frustrating attempts to accurately count them.

Colonel Darling stepped up the number of roll-calls and searches, timing them at random throughout the day and night. The prisoners inevitably complained, but beneath their protestations everyone knew they were celebrating the fact that their captors' resources were being stretched ever further.

Brothers, John and Garfield Davies had more reason than most to be concerned about the proliferation of escape attempts. They farmed at Island Farm and Newbridge Farm respectively, both of which adjoined the camp.

As Garfield was ploughing one of his fields close to the boundary wire, he noticed a row of prisoners lining the fence and watching him intently. Garfield was proud of his ability with the plough and turned skilfully towards the opposite side of the field. Glancing over his shoulder, he was disappointed and puzzled to find they had apparently lost interest, turning their backs on him and smoking casually on a shared cigarette. As he turned from the far side of the field and headed back towards them, oddly, their interest seemed to be rekindled and they watched him closely as he skirted round a large flat stone close to the wire fence. The stone had been in his field for as long as he could remember and it was a matter of routine for him to avoid hitting it and damaging his plough. He puzzled over why he, or it, it should seem to be of such interest to the Germans. It was the morning of Saturday 10th March 1945.

Saturday 10th March 1945, 22:55 hrs.

Four men wandered, apparently with little purpose in mind, along Merthyr Mawr Road. They were travelling north, in the direction of Bridgend town centre away from the main A48 road between Port Talbot and Cardiff. It was a dark, moonless, night and due to black-out regulations the street lamps were not lit. Even in daylight, the men would have attracted little attention. They spoke quietly to each other and were dressed innocuously in dark, plain clothes. Two of the men had their hands pushed into their trouser pockets and one had turned the collar of his heavy greatcoat up to protect against a chill northerly wind.

Had any of the local residents paid them any attention, they might have asked if they required directions as, from time to time, one of the men glanced about as if checking their route.

Steffi Ehlert had first copied, then memorised the map of South Wales drawn on a piece of white cloth torn from one of his fellow officer's shirt tail. That, however, was of little use at present. As a *Luftwaffe* pilot he had more than a passing familiarity with navigation but with no visible stars, no compass and only his small-scale, hand sketched map, he was guiding the group almost entirely from memory. This was part of the route he and his fellow prisoners had taken on their march from the railway station to their camp four months before.

More recently and importantly, however, he had travelled several times, incognito, along the same road. A few weeks earlier he had persuaded a German NCO to smuggle him onto a detail of men ordered to work on one of the local farms. Officer prisoners were not expected to work although other ranks were permitted under the terms of the Geneva Convention to work for the enemy in ways which would not directly aid their war effort.

Ehlert had borrowed a German artillery gunner's uniform and submitted himself to some twenty hours of manual labour over the course of three days. On each occasion, he had made careful note of the roads and farmland surrounding the camp. He had paid particular attention to a couple of wide suburban avenues, mentally taking note of the large homes along the route. These were clearly the property of affluent families and, just as importantly, he had noted that there seemed to be no official buildings which might house military or Police personnel.

Leading the group, he held up one hand and slowed to a lazy stop, leaning against a high garden fence. As the others drew alongside, he nodded across the road. As on his earlier visits, an Austin Ten car had been parked outside a large detached house, set well back from the road and separated from it by a high hedge and narrow garden path. He murmured quietly to Hans Harzheim, a tank officer and the only one of the four whose command of English might be described as fluent. Harzheim nodded and carefully approached the car. He glanced quickly at the number plate, repeating the registration silently in his head. DTG 688. He had been briefed that it was usual for British police officers, when stopping vehicles they suspected might have been stolen, to ask the driver to repeat the number as an initial test of ownership.

The driver's window had been left slightly open and the German was able to curl his fingers over the rim of the glass and with short, jerking movements, edged it down until it opened a few more inches. He threaded his forearm through the gap, reached down and pulled the door handle firmly up until the door clicked open.

U-Boat Commander Oswald Prior joined him and knelt at the rear of the car. He explored the steel petrol filler cap in the darkness. It gave way easily under his grip and, removing it, he lifted himself up so his nose was at the level of the open tank. He inhaled deeply and smiled as the heady aroma of petrol hit the back of his throat. Harzheim, meanwhile, slipped into the driver's seat. He reached into his pocket and pulled out a handful of metal strips. He and the other men had spent several days collecting and hiding surplus nails, left discarded in the soil around the camp huts. Over time, they had hammered these flat and then filed them until they approximated the teeth of car keys. Now, one by one, Harzheim tried each of the nails in turn by inserting it in the car ignition and gently trying to turn it, experimentally moving it slightly in and out of the lock. On the fifth attempt, the nail turned and the men all heard the distinctive click of the car's magneto as the ignition was switched on.

Another turn of the makeshift key and the engine turned over. It was sluggish but noisy, the sound echoing off the surrounding walls. All four men winced at the din as Harzheim tried a second time without success. Prior beckoned to the remaining two Germans from his position at the back of the car. Conscious that the sound could alert the vehicle's owner, the three of them starting pushing the inert Austin down the road towards Bridgend.

It was then that Harzheim, staring through the windscreen saw, strolling along the pavement towards them, four infantry privates. They swayed slightly as they walked and the German judged, accurately, that they were returning home from a night at the pub. He hissed an instruction through the open driver's door at the three officers behind him. Drunk, off duty and unarmed they may be, but there was no escaping the obvious fact that they were enemy soldiers – and they had seen them.

Harzheim cleared his throat and smiled ingenuously.

"Good evening you chaps." He waited for a reaction which might indicate his accent had been detected. None came. "You couldn't give us a push could you?" Another smile.

The four men nodded as one, grinning back. The motorist's voice was cultured and they had him immediately marked out as an officer home on leave. Officers in distress were always worth a few moments of fun. The foremost private spat on his hands and placed them firmly against the rear window of the car. The others joined in and between them they pushed the reluctant vehicle down the street. Harzheim jerked the gear lever into second, released the clutch and the engine sparked, coughed and sprung to life. Quickly and wordlessly the other three Germans piled into the car and the driver waved cheerily through the window.

"Thank you chaps. Goodnight fellows." More quietly, to his passengers, he muttered "For you, Tommy, it will be the glasshouse." His three companions understood enough English to grin silently as the car accelerated gently down the street.

The soldiers waved back as the car disappeared into the darkness. They nodded at each other, satisfied with a job well done and shoved their hands deep into their trouser pockets. They continued their sloping walk home. As newly posted guards at Camp 198 who had been off duty since six o'clock that evening, they weren't to know who the four men were or that there had been an escape. It would be several hours before one of the soldiers admitted their part in the escape, faced by an increasingly tense Police investigation and an embarrassed local GP.

Dr. R Baird Milne of Merthyr Mawr Road immediately accepted responsibility for failing to immobilize his car. So humble and complete was the Doctor's confession that some remarked that he seemed to be claiming responsibility for the entire break-out. It was with a rare rush of conscience that the soldiers finally stood before Colonel Darling and made their statement.

By that time, the exact sequence of events made little difference to the investigation. The Germans had already driven the Doctor's car to Cardiff and, in Ely on the western outskirts of the city, had concluded they were lost. Posing as Norwegian sailors, they asked a passing pedestrian – a tram driver returning from a night shift – for directions to the Newport Road. The man was used to foreigners. In his job he met them on an almost daily basis, especially in the Cardiff Docks area. He decided the easiest way would be to accept a lift to the other side of the city where he lived. From there, as they deposited him close to the end of his street, he pointed them towards Newport, giving them onward directions to the Gloucester Road.

As the Austin rattled on its way along the A48 east of Cardiff the fugitives reflected on their plan to make their way to Croydon. They knew the western suburb of London was home to a large airport and the presence of a capable pilot among their number was no coincidence. Each of the groups which had broken free of Island Farm had been carefully constituted to include an officer who could manage a boat and navigate on land or sea, another who could pilot an aircraft and navigate in the air and at least one who could speak reasonable English. In some cases, an *SS* officer had been added to their number to ensure they maintained a positive attitude to their mission.

Some seventy miles from Bridgend, the car began to falter. The engine coughed and died, coasting the Austin to a stop at the side of the road close to the village of Newnham-on-Severn.

Harzheim tapped the fuel gauge, announcing they were out of petrol.

Sunday 11th March 1945, 02:20 hrs.

Even on his better days, William May didn't like being woken up. Recently, and particularly since his retirement had been involuntarily postponed, he had enjoyed very few better days. He felt his shoulder being pushed and foggily recalled that when he had gone to sleep it had been Saturday. He liked being woken up on a Sunday morning even less. He opened an eye, his gaze resting first on the window. Despite the thick blackout curtains he could tell it was still dark outside. He looked next at the clock on his bedside table. It was a little after three o'clock. His wife's face moved unfocussed into his line of sight and he became more aware of his shoulder being shaken.

"William, dear, please. You must wake up. There's a Colonel Darling on the telephone."

May grunted, a little ungraciously in his wife's view. She was not allowed to know much about her husband's work and was unaware that he had spent several hours in meetings with the Colonel over the previous few months. The demands already placed upon May's depleted and beleaguered officers were severe enough and Darling, through no fault of his own, invariably increased those demands whenever they met. Despite that, he liked the man and had an unusual level of respect for him. It took a great deal to earn the respect of Police Superintendent William May and the fact that the Camp Commandant was calling him at this early hour could only mean there was serious business to be done.

He pushed his feet into the slippers at the side of the bed and thanked his wife quietly as she held his dressing gown open for him. Tying the cord belt, he took the stairs quickly to the hall below and picked up the telephone.

"May." No further questions were required as the Colonel's cultured voice described the events of the last few hours. His language was crisp and succinct, the product of many years in military service. Besides, he knew the man he was speaking to would have no time for casual chat. The finer details could wait until they met again. There had been an escape from Camp

198. It would be classed as a large-scale escape. An estimated fifty or more German prisoners were on the loose and it was likely that the first escapees already had a head start of about five hours.

It had been at Superintendent May's own suggestion, when the two men had first met during the summer of 1944, that in the event of an escape, the local Police should take immediate responsibility for securing the area by setting up road blocks in a cordon three miles from the camp. It had been agreed that the sight of armed soldiers roaming the area would unduly alarm local residents. It could cause panic and even violence by concerned but over-zealous groups of vigilantes. There had been many reports from other parts of the country of civilians who had seriously assaulted, and in some cases even shot, innocent men they had mistakenly taken for enemy spies or escaped Prisoners of War.

A few miles from Bridgend, an airfield in an area known as Stormy Down had been used over the previous few years to train Canadian, Czech, Polish and, more recently, American airmen. Any one of those young men, with a foreign accent or ignorance of local geography or culture, could be mistaken in such a heady atmosphere for an escaped prisoner. May's office had filing cabinets full of reports of enemy agents roaming the Glamorgan countryside spying, apparently, on everything from military manoeuvres to the number of sheep grazing the hill farms.

It had been planned that, in the event of an escape, police officers would stop and question any male pedestrians, motorists or cyclists of military age. The public would be reminded to immobilize their vehicles when they weren't in use and to lock away anything that might be of use to the enemy.

The Superintendent had also pointed out that an escaped Prisoner of War might not attempt to leave the country. Many Nazis sincerely believed that an invasion of the British mainland was imminent and escapees could well be tempted to remain in the vicinity to aid an invasion with sabotage. There were, after all, plenty of potential targets within a few miles of the camp.

Whatever the intention of the escapees, however, this situation called for different measures. Only briefly had they considered their response in the event of a major break-out. Even before the two men had ended their initial telephone conversation that morning, both knew that under the circumstances they now faced, the Army and other armed services would have to be called in.

Within an hour of Darling's 'phone call, Superintendent May, as head of Glamorgan Constabulary's 'C' Division and Inspector Lancelot Bailey of his Detective Branch with responsibility for the Bridgend area, were sitting in the Camp Commandant's office.

Bailey was widely regarded as a bright and relatively young officer for his rank with a promising future and his superiors had worked hard to keep him from the draw of the call-up. Despite being excused compulsory military service due to his Police work, he had been keen to answer the call to arms and only the strongest encouragement and a promotion to his current rank had persuaded him to remain in post. He was given command of a small team of detective officers and responsibility for the areas of Port Talbot, Neath, Bridgend, Gowerton and Aberdare. Despite this large geographical area, the art and science of detective work was still relatively young and he had no more than a handful of officers to call upon. Even after the war ended and available manpower allowed an increase in strength, the Detective Branch for 'C' Division which covered the Bridgend and Porthcawl area would only warrant one Inspector, one Sergeant and two Constables.

Outside the Commandant's room, in an already overcrowded clerks' office, the most recent addition to his staff, a nervous young Detective Constable named George Charteris, waited for his boss to emerge from the meeting.

George had, until a few days before, been stationed in Hampstead, a wealthy middle class suburb of North West London. A uniformed Constable with little more than six months experience, he had been flattered and surprised when told he was to be moved to the Detective Branch. Usually seen as a form of promotion reserved for more experienced officers, he was slightly less happy with the addendum to his orders which instructed him to report to a police station in a town he had never heard of, buried deep in a county he had hitherto been only vaguely aware of and had certainly never visited. Glamorgan, he soon discovered, was some 150 miles west, in Wales – a nation he associated less with the sort of serious crime he had ambitions to solve and more with coal mines, sheep and a curious language which he privately hoped the natives would not insist on speaking.

Early on the third morning after his arrival in Bridgend he had been awakened from his slumbers by his landlady. He had been so busy familiarising himself with his new work that he had managed to do no more than briefly introduce himself to her. He knew her only as Mrs. Williams, a slim woman with a viciously tight bun tied at the back of her head and shrivelled, tight lips that looked as though they had been sucking lemons - had lemons been available. She had hammered on his bedroom door, clearly annoyed, hissing in a badly suppressed stage whisper that a man who claimed to be a policeman was asking for him.

"I hope this doesn't mean you are in trouble, young man." She sniffed, her pursed lips tightening into a blanched raisin. "I don't hold with trouble makers, especially not nowadays, what with... everything." Her voice tailed off as George emerged from his room, pushing his shirt into his trousers. He pulled his suit jacket on as he moved towards the stairs, taking them two at a time and dropping quickly out of sight. The landlady watched the spot on the landing where he had vanished, momentarily unable to put into words her misgivings. She made a mental note to speak with the official at Bridgend Council who had billeted him with her, lecturing that it was her wartime duty to take in lodgers. The front door clicked shut behind the two men and Mrs. Williams sniffed again. Her muttering unheard, she half turned to close her lodger's bedroom door, left ajar in his haste.

Surrendering to an insuperable instinct, she allowed herself time to scrutinize his room. To her frustration, there was nothing immediately suspicious on view. No jemmy or sack marked 'swag'; no boxes of black-market goods or forged ration books. She glanced over her shoulder to ensure none of her other lodgers had been drawn from their beds. The landing was still silent and in darkness as she took a sideways step into the room and gently closed the door behind her.

Detective Inspector Bailey's route to Island Farm Camp had taken him past his newest detective's lodgings and the decision to wake both George and his landlady had required no thought at all. If the current state of war had any compensations, one of them had to be that members of the public no longer questioned a police officer's need to wake them in the middle of the night. Actions which in peace-time would have elicited letters of howling protest to the Chief Constable now drew no greater reaction than a resigned shrug.

As they drove the remaining distance to the camp, the Inspector used the brief time available to relay what little information he had been given. George remained silent, unsure whether he was being put through some sort of test. By the time the Inspector steered his car onto the A48, he was sufficiently convinced to lower his window a fraction and allow a stream of cool air to shock him into full consciousness.

In the relatively warm bedroom George had left behind, Mrs Williams bent low and quickly scanned the space beneath the bed. With surprising speed for a woman in her middle years, she dropped to one knee and reached into the void. Her hand closed over the handle of George's small suitcase. She pulled it towards her and without pausing for thought, pulled the brass clips aside, opening the locks with a sharp double click.

Inside the case, George had packed half a dozen white shirts, each one folded carefully at the waist to form a neat square, the buttons fastened to the collar. She picked up an oblong tin, economically packed in the corner of the case, and prized the lid open. Inside was a smaller, circular container of black shoe polish, two brushes and a clean duster. She closed the lid and carefully returned it to the same corner. She sighed. There was no point in disguising her disappointment when there was nobody to observe her.

Her hands burrowed with practiced attention to detail beneath the shirts, long fingers probing. She found nothing more than a pair of trousers. Another delve produced more disappointment; the pockets were empty. She clicked her tongue, still disapproving despite the lack of incriminating evidence. She closed the case, pushing it back under the bed and turned her attention to the small table under the window. It was clear her new lodger was using this as a desk. Perhaps he had been careless enough to leave some documents out that would prove his culpability. A small black notebook contained a few dozen names and addresses. Many of them shared George's surname and she reluctantly admitted to herself that she couldn't condemn a man for wishing to keep in touch with his family. Other names sat alongside addresses local to Hampstead in London. Despite an instinctive mistrust of the English – especially those from the capital – she remembered the letter of reference George had provided on his arrival. The letter had spoken in glowing terms of the young man's reliability, decency and honesty. It had been written by a Justice of the Peace on headed notepaper with an impressive looking address in the same area of North West London. It would seem normal for a young man away from home to keep in touch with friends from his former neighbourhood. Even more disappointingly, Mrs. Williams found not a single surname in the address book which sounded remotely foreign – unless, that is, one considered the English to be foreign, which Mrs. Williams most assuredly did. Nevertheless, even she couldn't accuse a man of treasonable behaviour on the basis of being born on the 'wrong side of the water'.

Her eyes alighted on a brown envelope. She put the notebook down and greedily scooped it up, peering in the dim light from around the blackout curtains. She could make out the black print clearly enough; *On His Majesty's Service*. Barely containing her excitement, she turned the envelope over and pulled out a flimsy piece of paper, folded double. Fully expecting to read that her mysterious lodger had been discharged from prison or, even better, that he was avoiding the draft, she opened the page and tilted it towards the light. She could see the brief letter was typed but the print was too faint to make out.

She moved silently again to the bedroom door and placed her ear to the panelling. Her household consisted of a further two lodgers and her teenage grandson, sent to her for the duration of hostilities from Swansea by her sister following a particularly nasty series of air raids. The silence on the other side of the door suggested all were soundly asleep and she crept to the bedside table, switching on a small lamp. Squinting uncomfortably, she read the letter. Her eyes opened and she re-read the few lines several times as if unsure she should believe what she had just seen.

Her hands dropped to her lap, still holding the scrap of paper. It was several seconds before she pulled her thoughts together and quickly pushed the paper back into its envelope. She returned it to the table and extinguished the light, leaving the room as silently as she had entered it. To her surprise, she found her fingers were shaking on the handle as she pulled the door shut.

The memo had confirmed her young lodger was a police officer; a detective, no less. He had been ordered by the

Metropolitan Police Commissioner's office to report to a Superintendent of the Glamorgan Constabulary at Bridgend. Mrs. Williams didn't claim to know much of such things, but she was sure a Superintendent and the Commissioner of Police must be extremely important men.

As she settled back into the relative warmth of her bed, squeezed into the back parlour next to her kitchen on the ground floor, she was already formulating a means of dropping into conversation with her neighbours and rival landladies the enviable truth about her important new lodger.

George Charteris would be mildly puzzled when he returned to his lodgings late that evening to be offered an extremely late but large supper of ham and eggs, with extra bread and butter and even an extra egg.

Mrs. Williams' previously cold reaction to his arrival, verging on the disdainful, suddenly seemed unaccountably welcoming. He decided not to ask her reasons.

George Charteris was one of the first people to be briefed on the events of the previous night. After a thirty minute wait in the clerks' office at Camp 198, Detective Inspector Bailey opened the Camp Commandant's door and beckoned to him.

The three senior men were seated round a single polished oak desk which was covered in papers. A map of South Wales had been spread across one end of the desk and George had to suppress a smile at the sight of a small pile of children's coloured crayons that had been used to draw a series of circles, lines and arrows over the map.

Again, the Inspector beckoned to the junior man, drawing him closer.

Superintendent May eyed the younger man over his wire framed reading glasses. He knew only of the newest constable to join his Division that he had recently arrived from the Met., along with a promising report from his former supervising officer. He had been appointed as an assistant to the head of the Detective Branch which covered Bridgend, largely because he could drive a car; a skill Inspector Bailey had acquired but which, in the normal course of his duties, was seen as being beneath a man of his rank. When he spoke, May's tones were low and measured.

"Constable, what you are about to be told is not to be repeated outside this office. You are being given an early briefing because time is of the absolute essence."

George nodded dumbly. Despite having worked in the capital, he was not used to being trusted with privileged information so early in an investigation. So far, all he knew was that the Camp Commandant had reported an escape from the camp.

The Superintendent nodded at the Inspector. Bailey picked up one of the pages scattered across the desk. He cleared his throat, aware that he was under the scrutiny of his Divisional Commander. He chose his words carefully.

"Overnight, Charteris, there has been a break-out of enemy Prisoners of War from the camp. A little after midnight, a guard spotted a prisoner emerging from a hole in the ground a short distance outside the wire. Had he not been holding a light coloured kitbag, he may well have gone unnoticed. He was apprehended and a further thirteen men were brought out of a tunnel which extends under the fence from one of the camp's accommodation buildings. The alarm was raised and a search party was immediately sent out. Shortly afterwards, a further two prisoners were apprehended a hundred yards or so from the fence." He glanced at his senior officer and the Camp Commandant. Already he had slipped into the habit of omitting important details. "In short, sixteen prisoners have been recaptured by camp guards in short order and close to the perimeter fence. Those prisoners are currently being held in isolation and will be interviewed in order to gain intelligence on the escapees and their methods." The Inspector paused, looking up at the junior officer. "You look surprised, Constable."

"Sixteen escaped prisoners, sir?"

"Sixteen recaptured. Fifteen are confined to solitary quarters." He coughed slightly. "The sixteenth is currently receiving medical attention, under guard of course, at Bridgend hospital. The number of prisoners who are still at liberty is still being assessed." He glanced at the Colonel. "Unfortunately the prisoners are making this difficult."

The Colonel coughed incoherently from his position behind him. While the Inspector had been talking he had been watching the quadrangle outside his window. He spoke for the first time since George's arrival.

"The prisoners are doing exactly what I would do in their situation. They are disrupting the roll-call by moving about, pretending to fall ill; feinting and so on." He shook his head and returned his attention to the scene outside. "Excuse me." He flung the window open and barked at a Sergeant. The NCO reached the window smartly and saluted.

"For God's sake man, get a grip on the parade will you. Line your men up in two files facing each other to form a pathway from the parade to the nearest hut. Have Sergeant Hanson, two corporals and half a dozen of the other men direct the prisoners down between the files, counting them as they pass. Make sure they go into the hut and stay there until the roll is completed."

The Sergeant saluted again and turned on his heel, shouting his orders before he had taken his first step.

The Colonel shook his head sadly. His tone was apologetic. "Many of the guards are retired policemen." He caught the Superintendent's raised eyebrows. "No insult intended, but they have little military experience and not much more of containing prisoners. It's become pretty clear that most have no idea of how to deal with the calibre of German officer held here." He turned away from the window and inhaled deeply, his chest expanding. "The remaining men under my command are chaps who, in the main, have been through absolute Hell. Most have been physically or mentally wounded, pulled out of the front lines and shipped off to some God-forgotten corner of Scotland with orders to recuperate. After being fed through the medical examination system, most have been downgraded to B-2 and deposited with us."

He shook his head, privately reflecting on the psychological destruction caused by battle fatigue and shell-shock. It would be many years before the term 'PTSD' would first be used. "It seems the authorities believe camp guards have no need of battle fitness. On the other hand, the detainees here in Bridgend are nearly all front-line professional soldiers; officers who are experienced fighters and tacticians, used to commanding men in the most difficult of circumstances. Several of them also have a history of attempting escapes from other camps."

He took a silver cigarette case from the breast pocket of his tunic. It clicked gently as he opened it and pulled out a cigarette. He offered the case around. Only the Superintendent accepted. "Many of the detainees are dedicated Nazis. They firmly believe their comrades in arms are poised to invade." He lit each of the cigarettes with a heavy lighter from his desk and inhaled again. "We try to educate them, of course; to convince them the Allies are advancing on Berlin." He shrugged apologetically. "Many of them simply dismiss our accounts as enemy propaganda. We even tried allowing them to listen to the news on the wireless but they refused, dismissing the BBC as a cynical chattel of the Allied High Command. To these officers, the very thought of a Third Reich defeat is an act of treason." The Colonel returned to the window and watched his men's progress on the parade ground. "Every one of them has taken a personal oath of allegiance to Hitler. Although we adhere strictly to telling them the truth, it only incites them further." The sun was beginning to rise, casting long shadows as the prisoners were moved slowly and reluctantly along the corridor of guards. Next to the door of Hut Sixteen, a Corporal loudly counted them in as a Sergeant checked and made notes on a clipboard.

Colonel Darling drew his attention back to his visitors. "I'm afraid that some of the guards have been rather in awe of many of the prisoners. One doesn't like to admit it but some of them, particularly the SS men, are supremely self-confident. I overheard one of our young subalterns the other day describe a couple of the prisoners as being quite charismatic." He shook his head. "If only they had the same view of their own commanders."

Superintendent May turned to the young Constable. "And that is *definitely* not to be repeated outside this office."

Inspector Bailey cleared his throat again. "Yes, well, let's hope we get a clear report of the number of escaped convicts we are dealing with very soon."

"They are not convicts, Inspector." The Camp Commandant displayed a hint of irritation for the first time since the meeting had begun. "They are not criminals. They are PW's; Prisoners of War. There is a very great difference. For one thing, they regard it as their duty to attempt escape and for another, they are committing no criminal offence in so doing."

The Superintendent grunted. "Quite so, but that makes them no less dangerous."

"More so, I would say." The Colonel sat in his chair and leaned back, relaxed once more. "They feel their actions are morally justified. They have been trained to be dangerous, after all."

The discussion was interrupted by a rapid knock at the door. A Sergeant-Major entered, glanced about at the civilians present and handed the Colonel a slip of paper. He snapped a salute, did a smart about-turn and left without a word. George observed quietly that the soldier seemed to have been in something of a hurry to leave.

The Colonel's eyebrows rose. He swallowed hard and carefully placed the thin piece of paper on his desk.

"Gentlemen, the total number of escaped prisoners, double-checked and confirmed, is 86. 84 officers and two NCO's."

William May sat down heavily. "Ye Gods and all that's holy." He was a large man and, as his wife occasionally reminded him, was somewhat overweight. Despite the cool weather, he had been sweating profusely beneath his shirt and waistcoat since arriving at the Commandant's small office. He took a handkerchief from his pocket and dabbed it over his broad brow. "Isn't that even more than the escape in Lower Silesia a year ago?"

The Commandant nodded. "I'm rather afraid it is. Seventy six men broke out of *Stalag Luft III*. The seventy seventh man out was recaptured at the exit from the tunnel. Damn shame, but most of the other seventy six were rounded up fairly quickly. Only two made it home and, sad to say, neither of them were British." He glanced again at the flimsy piece of paper handed over by the Sergeant-Major. "My officers are currently establishing the identities, rank and so on, of the missing prisoners."

Superintendent May regained his senses quickly. "You know we can't allow this to get out, don't you?" The other three men looked at him expectantly. "We can't allow the public to know that a greater number of German prisoners have escaped from Camp 198 than allied officers managed to escape from *Stalag Luft III*." He paused to allow his words to penetrate. "The mandarins at the Ministry of Information would fling themselves off their ivory tower if the newspapers got hold of the figures."

The Colonel referred again to the slip of paper, trying to find solace somewhere in the figures. "Of the eighty six escapees mentioned here, sixteen have been recaptured in the immediate vicinity, either in the tunnel or just outside the wire."

The Superintendent slapped the corner of the desk with his open palm. "There you are then. The number of escapees is seventy. Fewer than in Silesia"

"But the count of *Stalag Luft III* escapees has always included the man who was recaptured outside the wire. By the same measure, we've counted 86 here." The three senior men all turned to glare at Constable Charteris. "Sorry. Just an observation." He fell silent.

Without taking his eyes from George's downcast face, Superintendent May spoke through gritted teeth. "If pushed to provide a figure publicly, the number is seventy. Are we agreed?" All four men nodded grimly. "I'll report the full details to the War Office, of course, but will emphasise that we are working on a figure of seventy prisoners currently at liberty. There is no need to give more detail." He glared at Charteris. "Agreed?" George mumbled his compliance and apologised again.

The senior men began to relax, as if the decision had somehow lightened their load.

Colonel Darling opened a drawer behind his desk. "I know it's early, gentlemen, and we're all on duty." He placed a bottle of Whisky on the desk and produced four tumblers from the same drawer. "But I think we deserve a stiffener. We all have a trying and busy few days ahead of us. I imagine the first steps will involve a number of telephone calls." He grinned wryly and opened the bottle. "I'm sure we are all capable of drinking and making those calls at the same time."

The Superintendent nodded. "One thing's certain; none of us will get much sleep until this business has been dealt with."

Behind his senior officers, the young Constable smiled quietly and eyed the Whisky bottle. As the glasses were offered around, he extended his hand.

"Not you, Charteris." Inspector Bailey intercepted the tumbler. "You need to go and see the commanding officer of the local Home Guard."

Darling looked up from his bottle. He politely reminded the policemen that the Home Guard had been officially stood down on 3rd December 1944.

Bailey sipped his drink and nodded. "They haven't been disbanded though. We've been keeping the local CO sweet for the last few months, just in case they are needed." He grinned. "I'm reasonably confident they'll be eager to play their part. If not officially, we can rely on the men to volunteer."

Darling smiled to himself. "The regular Army may not like it but if I'm any judge, this might be just the occasion for which they are needed." The bottle filled another glass with a satisfying gurgle as Bailey turned back to Charteris.

"Ask him if he would be so kind as to accompany you to Bridgend Police Station immediately. When you get there, ask Sergeant Hewlett to call in as many Specials as he can and muster every officer on duty to the conference room. The Superintendent and I will be back as soon as possible to give a briefing." He took a sip of Whisky, licking his lips appreciatively. "In the meantime, not a word to anyone about what has happened." He thought for a moment. "And for the time being, no mention of numbers. All you may say is that a serious situation has developed over-night which Superintendent May is dealing with and which requires an immediate response." He pulled his notebook from his pocket, wrote briefly and tore a page out, passing it to the younger man. "This is the CO's name and address. He's a decent fellow but don't expect too warm a welcome at this hour of the morning." George nodded once and turned to leave. "Offer him a lift back to the 'station will you? He prefers not to drive." The Constable nodded again, turning towards the door. "And Charteris, once you have delivered Colonel Llewellyn you are to stay with him until the briefing gets under way. We'll join you when the list of escaped prisoners has been completed." Another nod. "Don't get too settled, though. I anticipate you are going to have a busy and uncomfortable few days."

The two senior policemen sat as Charteris left the room.

Bailey waited until he heard the outer office door close before he spoke again. "He's very new to the Detective Branch, but we'll have to hope he's competent enough to interview the recovered prisoners and give us some idea of where the others might be heading. I need all my more experienced men to plan and lead the search parties."

The Commandant nodded. "I can provide an interpreter and a couple of officers to help things along."

They enjoyed their Whisky in silence for a moment before the Superintendent reached forward for the 'phone. Instead of picking up the receiver, he pushed the instrument at Inspector Bailey.

"First job for you Lancelot. Let County Headquarters at Cardiff know there's a flap on before they get wind of it from elsewhere. Play it down. If I call they'll know it's serious. The last thing we need is a hundred bobbies from outside the area rushing around and causing a panic." He growled into his tumbler. "I'm saving myself for a discussion with Whitehall."

He looked up at the Camp Commandant, seated on the other side of his desk, silently buried in his own thoughts. "Well Edwin, at least you have the satisfaction of knowing you were right." The Colonel looked up and smiled faintly as if grateful for any form of solace. "You've always spoken of what we should do *when* there was a large-scale escape and not *if* there was one."

The three remaining men knew only too well that bad news behaved like water reacting to a pebble dropped in a stagnant pond. The news of the break-out would radiate from Bridgend towards Porthcawl, Port Talbot and Swansea in the west and to Cowbridge, Cardiff and Newport in the east.

Their first job was to ensure that the authorities, including those responsible for South Wales' many ports were placed on high alert before the first muddy ripples reached them.

Within a few hours, half a dozen county police forces, local units of the three armed services, harbour-masters, railway officials, fire wardens and others, had all been informed. In the corridors of power at Westminster, officials from several departments of at least three ministries were being summoned from their homes.

Sunday 11th March 1945, 03:00 hrs.

Joe and Vi David had at least one thing in common with Superintendent May; they didn't like being awakened in the early hours of the morning. Joe had been working late the night before at his car repair business. Business had been slow, petrol rationing and public disapproval of excessive motoring having forced most motorists to leave their cars alone. Yesterday, however, no fewer than three customers had turned up unexpectedly, each with an apparently imperative reason for the repair of their vehicle to take priority.

When the sound of garbled voices drifted through the thin casement window Joe didn't stir and his eyes remained closed. Muttering his frustration into his pillow, he turned away from the noise and pulled the bedclothes around his ears.

Vi, however, was less inclined to tolerate such behaviour. She lay for a moment, silently listening and trying to make out what was being said.

She and Joe lived in the quiet village of Llanharan, some seven miles east of Bridgend on the road leading to Pontypridd. Five years before, Joe's father had passed away and had left them a small legacy. When a neat little detached house had been advertised for sale, along with a garage and workshop, the opportunity to start his own business had been too much to resist. Joe had given up his job as a fitter with the local bus company and they had moved from Canton in Cardiff to the relative quiet of Llanharan.

Vi could make out that there were several male voices but, leaning half out of bed towards the window, still couldn't hear what they were saying. She concluded they must be drunk. Suddenly aware that Joe's garage and its valuable contents might be at risk, she slipped out of bed.

Pulling on a dressing-gown, she caught sight of a group of six men on the forecourt of the garage. Without pausing for thought, she pushed the sash-cord window up to its fullest extent and called out to them. Fully expecting a tirade of abuse in return, she was surprised when, after glancing quickly in her direction, all six ran down the street and through a narrow alleyway towards the railway which ran through the village.

Vi returned to bed, sitting thoughtfully with her back to the headboard. She frowned and nudged her husband with the sharp bone of her elbow until he grunted to full consciousness. He blinked uncomfortably and shuddered.

"Why's the bloody window open?"

His wife folded her arms. "There were a load of wasters out there, by the garage." She sniffed. "About half a dozen, I'd say. My guess is, they would have been away with those cars."

Joe sat up, suddenly interested. "What do you mean, they would have been?"

Vi folded her arms smugly. "I frightened them off. Scuttled off they did like scared rats."

Despite himself, Joe rolled out of bed and made his way to the window, staring at the garage doors opposite and then each way along the road. "There's nobody about now."

"God alive, Joe, I swear you don't listen to a word I say. I told you I frightened them off. They ran off down the gulley to the railway line."

It wouldn't be until the following morning that the newspapers reported the break-out from Camp 198, and as Vi brought a pack of sandwiches wrapped in paper to his workshop, a small black Talbot car pulled up at the kerb. The driver, a small man known to Joe only as Mr Johnson and who periodically had needed his car worked on, asked that he change a wheel for him. He indicated the bulging tyre, fattening into the gutter. Vi had long ago marked him out as a spiv and not to be trusted.

As Joe obligingly set to work, jacking one corner of the car up as his wife stood guard over her husband's lunch, Mr Johnson leant against the opposite wing. Cigarette balancing on his bottom lip, arms folded, he eyed Vi up and down.

"Terrible news from Bridgend, don't you think missus?" He sniffed. "Makes you think, don't it."

She regarded him sourly. "Makes you think what, exactly?"

"Well", the small man shifted slightly against the car. "Must make you glad you've got your husband to look out for you."

"Look out for what?" Vi was becoming impatient and the fat from Joe's bacon sandwiches was beginning to soak through the paper onto her hands.

"Well, the escaped Nazis, of course. Haven't you heard? There was a break-out from the prison camp down in Bridgend last night."

A metallic rattle from the other side of the car interrupted his revelation. Joe's head appeared above the car wing. He asked the man to repeat himself.

Joe and Vi glanced at each other. He threw his spanner noisily into his toolbox and stood up with unaccustomed haste. He hurried across the road, pausing momentarily only to grab the greasy package from his wife, before disappearing down the road. They had no telephone but the Police Station was only a few hundred yards away.

The motorist gazed after Joe's retreating back, mouthing silently his consternation and waving ineffectually at his car, now reduced to three wheels.

Within a few minutes the details of his Vi David's brief encounter had been recorded, placed on record and reported to officers at Bridgend's Police Station.

Sunday 11th March 1945, 04:00 hrs.

Steffi Ehlert, Hans Harzheim and the remaining two German passengers clambered out of the Austin Ten, casting about for a solution. A lock-up garage presented the most likely source of more fuel but a quick check of the heavy doors and padlocks convinced them that attempting a break-in would create too much noise. The sun was rising above the brow of the A48 ahead of them. They consulted briefly and decided they should lie up for the day. They pushed the car over the pavement and through a gate into a field, manoeuvring it behind a hedge. On foot they made for a thicket of heavy undergrowth and trees on the boundary with the next meadow.

They reached the cover of the trees before the sun had fully risen, their boots now covered in mud, and looked about for a comfortable place to settle. Each had brought a few apples, biscuits and pieces of bread smuggled from the camp guards' kitchen. They had elected not to bring powdered eggs or oatmeal with them on the grounds that lighting a fire to boil water would attract too much attention.

Sharing out the few biscuits they had left, they leant back in the soft bracken. It had been unusually dry over the previous few weeks and they soon slept, sheltered from the wind.

At eight o'clock in the morning, five Land Army girls arrived to start work. Normally, they would have taken Sunday as a rest day but, having spent the previous afternoon at the cinema in Gloucester, they had promised to put in a few back-breaking hours pulling potatoes on Sunday morning. Now, however, they paused to look curiously over the Austin. It seemed to have broken down or, more excitingly, might possibly have been stolen and deserted. In any event, it shouldn't have been in their potato field. Peering through the side windows and finding no obvious clue to the car's antecedence, and still in no rush to start work, their attention was caught by the strenuous noises coming from a herd of cows in the next field. Although all the girls were strictly 'townies', they had become used to the presence of the heifers as they worked and had never heard them make such a fuss. One of the girls, shading her eyes from the rising sun, commented that they seemed to be upset about something.   The other girls nodded agreement, rhetorically questioning why they were crowding round the small copse.

Under the trees, Oswald Prior was the first to wake, aware of something large and heavy, ponderously pushing its way towards him through the shadowy trees. He blinked in the dim light, barely daring to move. Something snorted and he felt a waft of warm pungent air on the back of his neck. He glanced round and, swearing, fell to one side. The commotion woke the other men and together they scrambled, laughing, into the sunlight.

The heifer gazed after them, her curiosity unresolved. She sniffed the ground where the men had been and, finding nothing to interest her further, returned to her herd.

The Land Army girls stood, unseen, next to the deserted car watching the four silhouetted figures pass in front of the cows and cross into a neighbouring field. The shadowed shapes followed the line of the hedge towards the main road before turning towards the car. Silently, the girls retraced their steps, crossed the road and ran to Pebble Brook Farmhouse where they were billeted.

Fifteen minutes later, a Constable at nearby Blakeney had relayed the girls' report to his principle Police Station at Gloucester. The Sergeant on duty had received a report less than an hour earlier that in Glamorgan there had been an escape of Prisoners of War. He looked again at his scribbled notes. He had no idea whether four prisoners had escaped but he picked up the telephone none the less.

A total of thirty eight members of the former Newnham-on-Severn and Blakeney Home Guard Companies immediately volunteered to join the search. With surprising efficiency, five of them were posted to each of four crossroads which surrounded the field on Pebble Brook Farm where the men had been seen. The remaining eighteen, accompanied by a few local constables, fanned out to cross the fields from Blakeney in the direction of the deserted Austin.

Just before midday, a red faced and panting young Home Guard Private careered up Blakeney High Street on his bicycle. He turned right into Bridge Street, swerving and narrowly missing the Rector who had been attending to Eucharist at the parish church.

His tunic jacket awry, the Private flung his bicycle against the wall of the Police Station and almost fell into the small front office. Gasping for breath, he announced that his platoon were still in pursuit of the four escaped German Prisoners of War. They were combing the fields around Blakeney along the A48. The Private tried to compose himself, drawing breath.

"Extra manpower", he said, unconsciously mimicking his commanding officer, "would be most helpful."

The Constable behind the desk called over his shoulder to his Sergeant. The Sergeant, recently promoted from being a volunteer Special Constable, paused for a moment's thought before picking up the telephone. He called his Inspector, a career police officer, based in Gloucester. He raised his hand to the Private, showing more control and reassurance than he actually felt.

Within an hour, another dozen men were combing the fields and woodlands around Newnham and Blakeney. They were still searching as darkness fell. Their torch batteries didn't survive long and before long the muddy soil beneath their boots became a featureless black blanket. Reluctantly, they were stood down, given thanks for their efforts and, after a mug of tea and a bun, were told they could return to their homes. Most found their way to the nearest pub.

Sunday 11th March 1945 09:30 hrs.

Helena Cord-Evans had recently enrolled in the Auxiliary Territorial Service and had returned from her initial training in Aldershot the Friday before. She had spent the last six weeks learning to march, salute and make her bed (something which had hitherto been quite alien to her, despite having passed her twentieth birthday).

As her Platoon Sergeant had told the thirty or so young women who had made up her garrison's latest intake, the Army would be the making of them. Recently promoted from Corporal, she had been transferred to the training branch just weeks before and regarded herself very much as a career soldier.

Helena wasn't so sure that she was cut out for military life and even less so when told she would not be expected to fire a rifle. A country girl from birth, it was one of the skills she had acquired in her early teens and one of the main reasons she had volunteered. She was known in her village as a capable shot, seldom failing to bring home a rabbit or two from the neighbouring hills and fields when out walking with her gamekeeper father. She still lived on the estate where he worked, half way between Bridgend and Porthcawl on the Glamorgan coast. This morning she had dressed in her new ATS uniform, neatly pressed the night before by her mother, in preparation of attending the morning service at nearby St.Tydwd's Church in Tythegston.

After breakfast, she had sneaked upstairs and admired herself in the full-length mirror in her parents' bedroom, smoothing the uniform jacket and standing sideways to admire her figure. There was no doubting that over the last year or so she had blossomed, as her mother said, into womanhood. The uniform certainly showed her new curves off to their best advantage.

She had gone downstairs to the kitchen, flicking an imagined speck of dust from the ATS flash on her shoulder before pushing a final piece of thickly buttered toast into her mouth.

With a glance out of the kitchen window, she stood and prepared to clear away her breakfast dishes.

A movement beyond the neat garden hedge which bordered the estate's lower pasture caught her attention and she put the plate absently into the empty sink without turning the tap. Her father's balding head bobbed briefly into view and the gate flew open. Even at that distance, Helena could tell something was bothering him. Dressed in his Sunday tweeds and calf length leather boots, he pounded heavily up the short path. The back door flung open and red faced, panting, the gamekeeper waved a hand ineffectually at his daughter.

"Whatever's up Dad?" Helena took a step towards him. "Are you ill?"

Pendri Cord-Evans took a deep breath and steadied himself.

"Get my gun, girl. We've got trouble." He placed his hands on his knees, his brow and red cheeks losing a drop of sweat onto the kitchen flagstones.

Without a word, Helena left the room, returning with her father's double barrelled shotgun and her own smaller .22 calibre rifle. In her pocket were several rounds of ammunition for both. "Where's your mother?" Pendri still hadn't looked up from the growing pattern of dark grey droplets accumulating on the flags.

"She's already gone to the church to see to the hymn books and flowers." She hesitated, adding sadly, "There are only daffodils these days."

Her father looked up and wiped his broad forehead on his sleeve. "We may miss the service, girl. We've got something more important to do first." He took the heavy gun, broke it and pushed the two offered cartridges proficiently into the breech. He nodded at the girl's rifle. "You'd better load that pea-shooter as well."

Without another word, Helena pulled on a jacket and pair of Wellington boots, oddly incongruous below her uniform skirt. As they left through the kitchen door towards the estate fields, he nodded again in acknowledgement of his daughter's new uniform. "I never thought I'd say it, but you being in a soldier's uniform may be a good thing this morning."

"I only put it on for church. It itches like mad."

As they walked, quickly and keeping to the edges of the fields, her father quietly told her what he had seen. "I was checking the traps. We've been having problems with foxes and the squire had me set a dozen extras last week. None of them have been triggered." He pulled a handkerchief from his trouser pocket and wiped his brow again. "But I was down by the copse on Newton Meadow when I saw what I thought were a couple of poachers skulking about near Lower Barn." He glanced at his daughter to ensure she was listening. "I shouted at them and they made off up the rise towards the air base at Stormy Down." He rolled his eyes. "Being Sunday, damn it, and only being after the traps, I didn't have my gun."

For the first time since leaving the house, Helena glanced at her father. "It's not like you, Da, to think you need a gun for a couple of old poachers."

"That's it though. They weren't poachers. When they turned and ran I could see plain as day, one of them had a pair of letters sewn onto the back of his coat."

The girl stopped, bringing her father up sharply with a tug on his arm. "Hang on now. What do you mean, a pair of letters."

Her father exhaled impatiently. "Letters, you know, yellow letters: 'PW' sewn onto his back."

"So what does that mean?"

Her father swung his large hands out, still clutching the shotgun, in a wide gesture of disbelief. "Haven't they taught you anything in that Army of yours, girl? PW means Prisoner of War. They're two of those Nazi prisoners they've got up at Island Farm. They must have escaped."

Helena's eyes opened in sudden understanding. "Bloody Hell, Da. Shouldn't we have called the Police or something?"

Her father turned and moved on at a heavy jog, gripping his shotgun more tightly. "The 'phone hasn't worked for weeks." He checked over his shoulder that she was following. "And don't bloody swear. Remember it's Sunday."

Any further discussion regarding appropriate observations for the Sabbath was quickly cut short. The older man's left hand swung out from his side, almost colliding with his daughter and bringing her to a sudden halt. Pendri was well into his fifties and, by virtue of several decades of his wife's good cooking and his own penchant for home-made cider, was not the fittest of men. However, his eyesight was sharper than many half his age and he knew every inch of ground on his employer's estate. He edged into the shadow of a hawthorn hedge, drawing his daughter with him and unaware of the havoc being wreaked on

41

her bare legs by the thorns. He nodded at the horizon ahead of them.

Ignoring the scratches, Helena squinted, adjusting her eyes to the deep brown of recently turned soil. It contrasted starkly against brightening grey cloud which clung to the ridge of the next field. Barely visible, but unmistakeable once she had focussed on it, the slowly moving shadow of a man, more than a hundred yards ahead, crouched low and shuffled from left to right against the dark earth.

"Skulking bastard." Pendri muttered, fingering his shotgun.

"Language, Da. Remember, it's Sunday."

Pendri didn't take his eyes off his quarry. "Sod Sunday. We'll have the bastard, and his bastard pal." He moved cautiously forward with surprising stealth for a large, sweating man. Moving a few feet to their right, they slipped into the cover of some trees and edged forward. Moving diagonally through the copse, they both knew where they would be in relation to the man when they next emerged into daylight. Helena slipped the safety catch on her rifle, moving it slowly so it made the quietest of clicks.

The German was caught totally by surprise. Faced by a large, red faced man and a young, slim, girl wearing a military uniform and levelling a rifle at him, he had no choice but to thrust his hands in the air and surrender.

"Where's your bastard mate, then?" Pendri growled the words, more because his throat was dry after his exertions than from any deliberate attempt to sound fierce.

He was saved further discomfort as a second pair of hands, almost eerily, appeared from the mud a few feet to his right. They were followed by a pair of thin arms, a mud patched face and a bedraggled torso which rose on sodden knees. Eventually and after a brief struggle to untangle a pair of spindly and shaking legs, the second prisoner rose miserably to his full height. A cake of mud dropped from his elbow to the ground with a final, wet, plop.

In some triumph, Pendri marched the two Germans back to his cottage. A satisfied grin spread across his face and he slung his shotgun casually over one shoulder, watching the backs and sloping shoulders of the two prisoners in front of him. Helena kept her rifle stock firmly tucked into her shoulder, the barrel squarely pointed at the nearest prisoner and her finger in the trigger guard.

The men were marched into a stable and the doors firmly closed and bolted. Pendri sat on a small three legged stool outside the door, the double barrel of his shotgun now held vertically in front of his face as he gripped it and leant on his clenched fists. He shook his head. "Thank God that's over." His face was running with sweat and he could feel his shirt sticking to his body, despite the chill of the wind. "Go up to the big house will you, girl, and call the Police to get over here, sharp."

Helena looked again at her father, concerned for his health for the first time in several months. "Will you be all right?"

He waved her away, giving his assurances. "I'll just sit by here now. Your mother will be back from Church soon enough." He jerked his thumb at the stable door. "Those buggers aren't going to give me any trouble."

Helena fetched a pint glass of water from the kitchen before leaving, taking a sip herself and giving the rest to her father. He looked at the glass with some distaste. "I reckon I deserve better than that." Seeing his daughter's reproachful look, he again waved his large hand at her. "Go on, girl. The sooner you're back the sooner I can have a proper drink."

Tythegston Court was, and still is, a large eighteenth century manor house with a grand hall and tower dating from several centuries earlier. Owned and managed by the same worthy family for over two hundred years, it's fine frontage and double doors look down over the surrounding estate with Georgian dignity.

It was, however, the rear of the building which Helena hurried to and one of the household staff who answered Helena's rapid knocking. The young girl who answered the scullery door was wearing a primly starched apron on which she wiped her hands, grinning broadly. She was the same age as Helena and the two girls had known each other and enjoyed each other's company since childhood.

"Well, look at you, all dressed up in your uniform. Have you come for Sunday lunch, then?"

Helena couldn't help smiling. She bobbed a mock curtsy. "Well thank you Miss Jess but I've got more important stuff to do right now than eat. Is Mr Evershott about?"

The other girl shook her head. "He's at Church. He should be back in about an hour. It's his day off, mind."

Helena shook her head and asked to use the telephone. Jess looked uncertain and glanced over her shoulder, catching the moving shadow of the household's cook. She was the senior member of staff available and, once the situation had been explained, quickly nodded her consent.

A little over an hour later, Helena was sitting across her kitchen table from a smart your plain clothed Policeman. He had introduced himself as Detective Constable Charteris and, thought Helena, spoke with a very posh English accent. More importantly, he had nice eyes and throughout their interview she had been trying to coax a few more personal details from him. What, she wanted to know, was his first name? Where was he living? Wasn't he lonely, being new to the area?

Apparently oblivious to her flirting, he had his notebook open and resting on the table. She was flattered that he was carefully recording her words as she explained how she and her father had captured the men. She had barely noticed the older, uniformed policeman seated next to the kitchen range and talking to her father. The two men locked in the stable and now under Police guard were, the Detective had assured her, almost certainly escaped German Prisoners of War.

George, who had been delighted to be released early from the tortuous meeting between his Superintendent and several senior public officials, smiled encouragingly and assured her that he understood she must have acted very bravely. Catching a reproachful glance from his senior officer, he cleared his throat and assumed a more official tone.

"What were the prisoners doing when you first saw them?"

Helena shrugged. "One of them, the first one, was just, well... skulking, I suppose."

"Skulking." George repeated the word carefully and wrote it in his notebook.

To Helena's disappointment, both officers left shortly afterwards having politely declined her repeated offers of tea, coffee, cake and, finally and in some desperation, a pint of cider.

She watched with little attempt to disguise her disappointment as the good looking young detective closed the car door and drove down the lane towards the main road. Her mother placed a hand gently on her shoulder, drawing her indoors. Noting her mother's reproachful expression, she pushed her bottom lip into an exaggerated pout.

"I can't help it Mammy. He just looked so lonely, like he needed a proper *cwtch.*"

Her mother's eyebrows rose. "A *cwtch* is it good girl?" She tutted, suddenly busying herself with kitchen chores. "I don't suppose he even knows what a *cwtch* is."

Helena grinned. "Don't be daft Mam. Everyone knows the English cuddle but only the Welsh can *cwtch.*"

Her mother inhaled, joining her hands primly beneath her bust. "You just be careful who you're giving your *cwtches* away to young lady." She turned away, smiling secretly. There was no doubting her daughter had an eye for a handsome face. She glanced fondly at her husband, still warming his socked feet by the range. The apple, she concluded, seldom fell far from the tree.

Later that morning, and on the instructions of Superintendent May, Inspector Bailey spoke to a freelance reporter known to be reliable enough to circulate a story without too much ferreting about, 'making a nuisance of himself', as Mr May had put it.

By the following afternoon, as expected, several regional evening newspapers had included a brief item confidently declaring that an ATS girl had, single handed, captured two Nazis, the first '*skulking across a field*' near the camp. The second prisoner travelling with him, read the reports, had quickly and peacefully surrendered to her.

Pendri Cord-Evans dismissed the newspaper report as unimportant rubbish, disguising his obvious disappointment that the incident had passed without his name being mentioned. Helena remarked only that she resented being referred to as a girl. If she was old enough to wear the King's uniform, she had declared, buttoning up her tunic and preparing to leave once more for Aldershot, she was old enough to be recognised as a fully grown woman. As if providing evidence, she had pushed out her chest and nodded with finality at her father. Kissing her mother on the cheek, she had turned smartly, stamping her foot in parade-ground style before marching deliberately from the house. Only when approaching the bus to take her to Bridgend railway station did she allow her pace to slow to a civilian stroll, her mind returning to the good looking young detective.

On the upper floor of Bridgend Police Station, William May congratulated his Inspector on his handling of what he chose to call his 'informal press briefing'. The short piece contained all the appropriate elements. A plucky girl in uniform, a tremulous pair of Nazis, a prompt and easy recapture and, best of all, the prisoners hadn't managed to get far from the camp. He smiled generously over the rim of his newspaper.

Sunday 11ᵗʰ March 1945, 10:30 hrs.

Flight Sergeant Jim Thomson had spent the previous four and a half years at various RAF stations across England, periodically flying bombing missions over Continental Europe. By February 1945, however, bombing raids were seen as being less essential to the war effort. Many Bomber Command aircrew were relieved of their more hazardous duties and their resultant free time used to update their training. The war had seen innumerable technological advances in aircraft engineering and navigation, creating for the RAF the logistical problem of constantly re-educating their airmen.

Jim was sent on a training course to RAF St.Athan in the Vale of Glamorgan. Had he thought that the remainder of his War would be spent in the sanctuary of a classroom, however, he would have been wrong.

Hastily briefed about the overnight break-out from Camp 198, he was ordered to round up a group of fifteen members of ground crew, or 'any idle buggers you can find' as his immediate superior had put it. He had purloined a RAF recovery vehicle and with men holding on to the trailer behind him, had headed off at speed towards Bridgend.

A few miles down the road, a ramshackle road block manned by two former members of the local Home Guard arrested his progress. A retired cafe owner in a corporal's uniform and clutching a rifle approached the lorry. He checked it and the passengers' identity cards with the air of professionalism demanded of his wartime role.

Jim glanced at the block-built pillbox standing at the side of the road. Pillboxes had been constructed on the outbreak of hostilities in order to provide cover for defending troops in the event of an invasion. Usually hexagonal in shape, they had a hole, some twelve inches by six, in each of their six sides. At shoulder height, they allowed the soldiers inside to fire out in all directions.

Jim nodded at the stocky little building. "What's up with your mate?"

The Home Guard man's eyebrows rose. "What mate?"

"The one in the pillbox." He jerked his head at the gash in the wall nearest to them. The soldier shrugged blankly. "There's only the two of us." The Private standing close behind him straightened. "We've been detailed to stop all vehicles and pedestrians. There are some Prisoners of War on the loose, you know."

Jim nodded. He knew. He wandered to the back of the lorry, leaning closer to his passengers. He muttered quietly and three RAF men silently slipped from the tail-gate to the road. As they moved to the far side of the truck, he nonchalantly returned to the Home Guard men and offered them each a cigarette. He took one himself and, as he lit them, whispered quietly. "Don't do anything sudden. Just act normally. I think we have company."

Behind them, a sudden babble of voices shattered the calm of the country road. Two RAF NCO's emerged from behind the pillbox, a small figure in an oversized greatcoat being projected on the tip of one of their rifles. He was covered in wet leaves and moss and sneezed violently as he emerged into the daylight. Miserably, his hands on his head, he gazed around. Identifying the Sergeant as the senior man present, he nodded briefly and, unexpectedly, apologised.

Behind him and at the tip of the second rifle, another man, even dirtier than the first, angrily shook his shoulders, trying to shake the rifle barrel away. The Aircraftman jerked backwards with his thumb.

"There's another one in there." He grinned. "Polishing his boots, of all things."

Jim smiled at the Home Guard soldiers, answering their questioning look by simply tapping the side of his nose. The first German seemed to appreciate the question.

"Please, how did you know?"

"Your glasses, Fritz. The sun reflected off them. Through that gun-port. You were flashing away like a bleedin' lighthouse."

The German's shoulders dropped. "We couldn't leave, you understand." He nodded at the part-time soldier at Jim's side. "We did not want to be shot."

The Home Guard man looked away almost shamefully and looked down at his rifle. "That's a laugh, that is. We haven't been issued with any ammunition for this thing in the last twelve months."

Sunday 11ᵗʰ March 1945, 14:45 hrs.

Having recovered from being woken up at three o'clock that morning and a subsequent visit to Llanharan's small Police Station, Vi David was pegging laundry to a line alongside her husband's garage. Joe was once again working, bent into the engine compartment of a Crossley saloon.

Beyond the workshop and the mean scrap of rough land which served as Vi's vegetable garden and space for her washing line, a slow train rattled noisily up the valley towards Pontypridd.

Less than a quarter of a mile north-east, following the route marked out by the railway track, six dark figures moved steadily in the shadow of the deep banking. They walked in line, like a disciplined crocodile of school children, the man at the front glancing down occasionally at a handkerchief sized square of fabric. The map had been hastily drawn, copied from another owned by one of his fellow officers a few months earlier. A few of the place names had been misspelled and smaller towns and villages missed altogether. As far as the men knew, they were following the main line towards Cardiff. The original he had copied his map from had not shown contour lines and, tasked with navigating their route, he had no way of knowing that the steady incline they had been climbing all morning led, not to Cardiff but to the narrowing Taff Valley at Pontypridd. If they continued to follow the same route, they would soon be thirty kilometres north of the docks and potential escape route which was their intended destination. Such was their discipline and faith in their respective training that none of the men had questioned whether it was reasonable that a major artery such as the main South Wales to England railway line should consist of nothing more than a single track.

The man at the tail of the crocodile uttered a single word of warning and the men obediently moved into the overgrown shrubs at the side of the line. They crouched until the old train and its few motley carriages had rattled past. Neither had any of them asked why so few trains seemed to be running.

Later, they were to reason with each other that they shouldn't have expected much traffic on a Sunday; that Britain was believed to be bereft of resources and that coal was in such short supply that train journeys were believed to have been rationed to a minimum. At least three of the men had mistakenly believed that aid being supplied from America was still being effectively blockaded by U-Boats. As for the Americans themselves, everyone knew they had been softened by affluence and dissolute living. They would prove ineffectual and unreliable allies. Their leaders had assured them the Americans would soon withdraw and Britain would be forced to capitulate.

The passing train, however, had woken them up to the obvious fact that six men, if seen travelling together, would undoubtedly provoke suspicion.

From the small woodland rendezvous point close to their prison camp tunnel, the six had originally moved off in two groups of three. Like the rest of the escapees, each group had included an officer who could navigate and an officer who could speak English. The two groups had met up unintentionally some time later and, already unsure of where they were, had decided to join forces.

Now, however, they split into three groups of two. One pair moved west, another east and the third continued to follow the railway line.

Had they paid more attention to the passing train they might well have chosen a different route. The rear carriage had been reserved shortly before it had left Bridgend by the Adjutant from the local Army barracks. It contained a Sergeant, a Corporal and eight other young but enthusiastic soldiers.

At Talbot Green, the next station along the line, the Sergeant instructed the Corporal and four of the men to alight.

Slightly under an hour later the two Germans, following a wide bend in the railway line, came into the line of sight of the five soldiers. The Germans spotted the British soldiers first and jumped for cover. They moved quickly, but not quickly enough and the Corporal, walking down the centre of the tracks with his rifle at the ready, barked an order. His men spread across the railway cutting, suddenly alert. Holding their weapons before them, the five young men broke into a trot towards the patch of undergrowth marked out by the Corporal's pointing finger.

When they were some thirty yards away, the prisoners emerged from their inadequate hiding place, hands raised. The Corporal ordered his men to halt, their rifles aimed at the surrendering officers. The Corporal called out his instructions for the prisoners to advance slowly towards them, their hands raised.

At that moment, a loud metallic clatter shocked the soldiers into breaking ranks. Surprised by the noise of an approaching goods train behind them, they stepped quickly away from the tracks. A siren sounded and the train rattled by, the driver apparently oblivious to the drama he had interrupted. Hidden from the soldiers' view, the Germans grasped their opportunity and scrambled up the railway embankment, through a thicket of trees and onto the narrow road beyond. Hardly believing their luck, they began running down the lane away from the soldiers and back towards Llanharan.

They quickened their pace, sure that the soldiers would not be far behind them. They rounded a right hand bend, hugging the inside edge of the curve and moving closer to the line of heavy trees.

Police Constable Philip Baverstock had not expected to find any escaped Germans when he had set out from Llanharan Police Station earlier that afternoon. Even though he was all too aware that Vi and Joe David had reported seeing prisoners on the loose in the early hours of the morning, he expected that they would be a long way off by now. In addition to that, he had been notified that Army search parties had been deployed in the district so if there were any Germans still around, he could safely leave it to the soldiers to find them. Nevertheless, he had dutifully pedalled his bicycle as far as Talbot Green, scanning the hedges and ditches as he went and was now returning with a view to spending the rest of the afternoon writing his uneventful report.

It came as something of a surprise then, when rounding the final bend on his way back to Llanharan, that he ran into the retreating backs of Karl Ludwig of the *Waffen SS* and Tank Commander Heinz Herzler.

It was, perhaps, fortunate for PC Baverstock that he found himself momentarily and unintentionally out-manoeuvred by the Germans. Losing control of his cycle, he crashed headlong into Ludwig who in turn fell into Herzler's path, tripping him up. Baverstock, landing relatively comfortably on top of the two men and, being used to his bicycle unseating him, was first to recover. Foggily, he identified the curses emanating from beneath him as being of foreign origin. It was enough for him to draw his revolver, despite the fact it had not been fired since the day he had received it. Untangling his limbs from the others about him, he gathered his prisoners together and had them standing upright just as the panting British soldiers rounded the bend.

With one of the squaddies pushing his bicycle, they marched their prisoners back down the valley towards Llanharan.

Sunday 11th March 1945, 15:00 hrs.

Superintendent William May sat uncomfortably behind the hastily erected trestle table. The early success of a few recaptured prisoners now starkly placed in context to the number still on the run. Next to him and possibly feeling even more uncomfortable was Lieutenant Colonel Edwin Darling. On his other flank sat Detective Inspector Lancelot Bailey.

Also sitting at the table was Colonel William Llewellyn, the former Commander of Bridgend's Home Guard. In civilian life, a 'gentleman farmer' but also a trained mining engineer and organiser of the county's mine rescue volunteers. He had served during the previous war, initially as a junior officer in a unit which specialised in bomb disposal and demolition and being promoted to Colonel during the closing months of 1918. He had taken little pleasure from his recent position of authority and was only marginally consoled by the fact that, having been officially 'stood down', his continuing leadership of the Home Guard could be regarded as service beyond the call of duty. While the other men might have some awkward questions to answer regarding their professional conduct, he could claim to be nothing more than a willing volunteer, brought in to help clear up the mess.

The Police had commandeered a classroom at Bridgend Boys' Grammar School and at least one of those present felt even more uncomfortable than most, having spent many painful hours in this same room during his childhood either serving detention or being lectured by belligerent teachers.

At the back of the room, and behind a small but assorted audience, stood Detective Constable Charteris. Thankful to be away from the spotlight, he shared only one thing in common with the journalists sitting with their backs to him. Leaning forward in their seats to gain a better view of the uncomfortable group at the top table they, like George, all held a small notebook in one hand and a pen in the other.

Superintendent May had, much against his better judgement, been persuaded by his superiors at Whitehall to hold a full press conference. It was better, he had been told, that the press be given a clear and concise message which would diminish the damage, than to allow a 'herd of marauding newspaper hacks to roam freely across Glamorgan'. Visions had been formed in the Superintendent's mind of sensation seeking reporters roving from pub to pub, questioning half informed squaddies and random members of the public for their opinions. Subsequent newspaper articles would inevitably scare the wits out of the more timid elements within the civilian population. May had resisted hard but the instruction from Whitehall was clear. The Ministry of Information had enough on its plate at present. The last thing senior Civil Servants and Government ministers wanted, he had been told, was an 'impromptu army of over-excited Welsh miners lashing out with pit props at passing strangers'. The early hysteria of parachuting Nazi spies disguised as nuns had barely been expunged and despite the success of the Allies' advance through France, the spectre of escaped Nazis must not be permitted to raise the Celtic temperature.

May had winced at the aristocratic and pompous English voice at the London end of the telephone line. He had spent his fifteen years in South Wales trying to avoid stereotyping the population it had been his responsibility to police. Nevertheless, he had to reluctantly admit, the man from the War Office had a point.

William May now sat with the Camp Commandant, the town's Mayor, the commander of Bridgend's former Home Guard Battalion, the senior Air Raid Precautions officer and, somewhat incongruously and wearing khaki shorts, the leader of the local Boy Scout troop. They had all hastily written their names and official job-title on pieces of card which were now propped up against glasses of water or matchboxes on the table in front of them. Only the Home Guard man had a wooden desk name-plate on which was painted in neat gold letters, 'Col. W.H.C. Llewellyn – C.O, 3rd Glam. (Bridgend) Battalion, Home Guard'

The Superintendent cleared his throat. He looked briefly to left and right, ensuring he had the support of those sheltering with him behind the table, and rose to his feet. Suddenly aware that he was towering over his audience, seated as they were at miniature school desks, he decided to confine his opening remarks to a few words of introduction.

"We have asked you gentlemen of the press to attend this morning as a courtesy and in order to provide such information as we can, regarding this current..." He searched for an inert description of what he privately regarded as a foul-up of epic proportions. "This current situation." He cleared his throat, playing for time. "There will now follow a statement of the facts which you are at liberty to promulgate, verbatim, through your various publications." He glanced at the men sitting alongside him. To a man, they were gazing stonily ahead at their audience. May sat down hastily and glanced down at a hand written piece of paper. He read out a brief account of what had happened overnight.

His statement was designed to be concise, brief, matter-of-fact and sparse in detail. It had also been carefully checked word for word and approved in advance by the Ministry of Information. The other men sitting with him registered no surprise. They had already been well briefed and knew the statement had also been approved by Glamorgan's Chief Constable and by a Brigadier at the Army's Western Command Headquarters at Chester. They also knew it was quite untrue in several particulars. From Westminster to Chester it was hoped, but not expected, that the information would go unchallenged.

A middle aged man sitting in the front row and wearing a grey Mackintosh moved uncomfortably. His small wooden chair, polished smooth by countless generations of juvenile backsides, was becoming increasingly painful. He raised his right hand, a short stub of pencil lightly held between two fingers. The Superintendent nodded in his direction. "Mr Williams. Are you here for *The South Wales Post* today?"

The man rose with some effort and turned, bowing slightly to his fellow reporters as if in acknowledgement of an envied status. He spoke slowly, his accent broad South Wales valleys. "I am, Superintendent May, I am indeed. I am also here for *The Western Daily Press*, *The Gloucestershire Echo* and any other respectable journal prepared to accept my copy." He paused, glancing about him. "Providing they are prepared to pay for it, of course." There was a ripple of laughter from the other reporters. He removed his spectacles and squinted down his nose at his battered notepad. There was an impatient clearing of throats behind the trestle table. Several of the other men in the room recognised an old hack's habit of hogging the limelight. The man seated next to him scribbled urgently on his pad, wanting his own question to be put forward. Not to be distracted, Dafydd Williams proceeded with customary tardy perseverance.

"You have told us, Superintendent, that seventy men escaped from Island Farm Camp last night, and that sixteen were quickly rounded up from the immediate vicinity of the tunnel where it emerged outside the wire." May nodded. "And were these sixteen immediately returned to captivity?"

May nodded again. "That's correct and, I may say, the Camp Commandant's officers and men performed with great efficiency as soon as the break-out was discovered." Before he could be asked more, the Superintendent turned to Colonel Darling. "The Colonel can tell you more of that operation."

Darling half stood, changed his mind and sat down again.

"Camp guards were alerted when a prisoner was spotted emerging from the tunnel exit. Fourteen men were apprehended in the immediate vicinity. All available camp personnel were turned out within a matter of minutes and an immediate search was organised of the surrounding fields and woodlands where a further two were apprehended. Simultaneously, a role call was taken and checked and the, um, number of prisoners who had taken part in the break-out was established."

The Colonel paused, dreading the flood of questions he was sure must follow. He expected at least an exclamation or two of dismay or shock. None came. Instead, the small audience of local news reporters sat in silence, scribbling notes. Emboldened by the apparent ease with which his explanations were being accepted, Darling leaned forward in his seat, fixing his eyes on the nearest reporter.

"The search continues, gentlemen. The Police and military authorities will persist until all the prisoners have been recaptured. The important point to emphasise is the sterling work carried out by the Police and other services and the speed with which prisoners have been recaptured. Following a thorough search of the woodlands to the east and west of Camp 198 and the surrounding farmland, we had by dawn this morning recovered sixteen of the prisoners. They have all been returned to captivity."

A hand rose from the audience and before being invited to speak, the reporter asked where the recaptured prisoners were being held.

Darling's voice dropped slightly. "All of the detainees are being held under close guard and just one of them is being held outside Camp 198."

In unison, the row of reporters lifted their heads in silent question.

Superintendent May coughed, interrupting what may have been an unguarded reply. "Most unfortunately, a guard was forced to fire a shot when one of the prisoners disobeyed an order to stop and give himself up. Instead, he tried to make a run for it." The reporters leant forward, pencils waggling. "The prisoner received a bullet wound and is now being given proper medical treatment."

The Superintendent stood, leaning forward on his fists.

"I need hardly remind you, gentlemen, but I will do so anyway..." He scanned the room once again to ensure he had everyone's attention. "All matters concerning enemy Prisoners of War and Internees are subject to Defence Notice Number 43." He adjusted his spectacles and read from a typed note at his side. "*'No information should be published without submission to Censorship concerning 1: the activities, interrogation, control, movements, location, or identity of enemy prisoners of war or internees in the United Kingdom or elsewhere. 2: plans for the repatriation or exchange of such persons. 3: the escape or attempted escape of such persons.'*" May inhaled deeply, fixing his gaze on the front row of reporters and glaring along the row of faces. "Your editors will, of course, submit all your copy for proper scrutiny by the Censor before publication."

There was a general mumble of complaint. Press reporters had been all too aware of what they regarded as the blight of censorship since, and even before, the outbreak of war. Now, with hostilities all but over and the enemy on the brink of capitulation, it seemed there was to be no respite from the Official Censor's strict adherence to procedure and his blue pencil.

The Superintendent's clear tones interrupted the quiet hum of dissent. "You will excuse us, gentlemen. You may be assured that you will be kept informed of our progress as we recover the remaining prisoners. In the meantime, you will appreciate that we have urgent work to attend to."

The uniformed men behind the trestle table rose stiffly and left the room, leaving the reporters discussing what they had heard. Behind them, George Charteris edged towards the door.

He ignored the confusion of numbers being repeated round the room as the reporters attempted to make sense of what they had been told.

Sunday 11th March 1945, 15:15 hrs.

When Steffi Ehlert, Hans Harzheim and their two travelling companions were later asked, none of them could provide a rational explanation of how they had managed to evade capture after deserting Doctor Milne's stolen Austin. They knew, after the car had been spotted near Newnham-on-Severn, that they could not risk using it again, even if they had been able to find a supply of petrol.

Each of the men described their desperate run, heads down, through mud-heavy ploughed fields, then thick undergrowth until they reached patches of trees.

There had been no time to take their bearings or calculate exactly where they were. Instead, they had taken off in the direction of the nearest cover.

The trees grew thicker as they progressed deeper into the woods and, other than a few dividing fences and ditches, they encountered few obstacles as the woodlands closed in around them. After half an hour and heaving for breath, deeply camouflaged, they had allowed themselves to stop and consider their next course of action. Apart from their racing hearts and the wind rustling the upper branches above them, all was quiet. They had searched about in the damp gloom, looking for somewhere to hide. None of the men had any food left but finding anything to eat, for the present, seemed out of the question. Only after they had walked a further half a mile and settled in a deep hollow beneath the trunk of a fallen oak did they realise quite how hungry they were.

They had left the A48 road far behind them, cutting south west across farmland, the buildings of Ruddle Court Farm hidden behind a row of trees to their north. Unknowing, they had entered the outer reaches of the Forest of Dean. By the time they had allowed themselves to take refuge under the tree trunk, they were on the western border of the area known locally as Moorland Grove. Had they continued a further few hundred feet they would have broken into open country around

Soudley Brook and the well used road leading to the villages of Upper and Lower Soudley.

As dusk fell and the unfamiliar sounds of the woodlands started to disturb them, they decided to move once again. They calculated they had been heading west but their roughly drawn map proved inadequate to pinpoint their exact position. Although they knew they should be going north east, that route would return them to the area where they had last been spotted. They decided to continue west until they reached a road, then check if it appeared on their map and try to calculate their position.

They didn't have long to wait.

The Forest of Dean had, during the early part of the war, boasted several Home Guard platoons. These had included among their number several dozen gamekeepers and forestry workers who all knew the area well. They had, to a man, now volunteered to act as guides for the search parties of police officers, special constables, fire wardens, local farmers and soldiers. Over a hundred men, many carrying rifles or shotguns, had met at Lydney Board School earlier that day to be briefed by a nervous Chief Inspector. He had seldom seen so many firearms and they made him uneasy, even though he now carried a service issue revolver, conspicuously clipped into a holster strapped round his uniform jacket.

The four escaped prisoners, he had told the assembly, had last been seen heading towards Moorland Grove. He had pointed to a point on a map, unnecessarily as far as the local woodsmen were concerned. The search would start at Lydney and head north towards Soudley, covering the eastern section of the Forest.

Heads nodded as they took in the enormity of their task. Those who didn't know the area had been told that, in the past, people had either hidden or been lost in the Forest of Dean for over a week without being found.

The Chief Inspector assured the men that road blocks had been set up on the A48 to the east and south of the Forest, as well as New Road to the west and the Monmouth Road to the north. An area of some 100 square miles had effectively been cordoned off. Any motorist or pedestrian would be stopped and thoroughly questioned.

The volunteers had set out, organised into search parties of ten, each with local guides who knew the Forest and either an Army officer or senior police officer in charge.

By the time Hans Harzheim and the others had decided to break cover, the search had been going on for several hours. As they crossed Soudley Brook and climbed the shallow slope towards the road leading to Lower Soudley, one of the patrols wheeled into view. Silhouetted against the evening skyline, the fugitives dropped immediately and silently onto the grassy bank. The search party's guide had led them unerringly on the route laid down by the Chief Inspector that morning, and was now looking forward to the final leg of their walk, along Church Road, past St.John's and on to the White Horse where, he was confident, the landlord would unlock his doors early for a group of thirsty searchers.

It was a sensible plan, to search during daylight hours when the escapees were likely to be resting somewhere in the Forest and then allow the road blocks and street patrols to take over after dark. Had they not been busy discussing what they were going to eat and drink when they got to the village they might, as they passed, have checked the surrounding verges. If they had, they might have seen four cold and hungry German officers, lying in thick undergrowth. They might even have felt inclined to provide them with something to eat if they had surrendered quietly.

Harzheim and the others, however, had travelled too far to give up so easily now. Besides, they had seen the search party's armoury. They weren't prepared to take a risk that some over excited farm-hand would loose off a couple of shotgun cartridges if they suddenly revealed themselves. Instead, they lay motionless, face down in wet leaves and waited for the English voices to recede into the distance.

Sunday 11th March 1945, 15:30 hrs.

A little over half a mile south west of the home of Pendri Cord-Evans and his family at Tythegston lies the even smaller community of Wigfach. Shortly after the war, a residential caravan site would emerge; a short term housing solution for those few local families who were bombed out during the war and a smattering of servicemen returning from abroad and in need of low priced homes. Shortly after that, hikers began pitching their tents in a neighbouring field and, later, more affluent holiday makers moved in with touring caravans; an alternative to the caravan sites already expanding in Porthcawl a few miles down the road.

In 1945, however, apart from a few holiday homes and isolated smallholdings, the area was largely turned over to grazing sheep. For a few weeks each year, boy scouts and girl guides used the open pastures to practise their field-craft skills, setting campfires and cooking rudimentary meals which were usually so smoke impregnated to make them almost inedible.

The Third Bridgend Girl Guides Brigade, having spent the coldest winter months honing their talents as knitters, sewers and darners while simultaneously supporting the war effort, had taken the opportunity to embark on their first camping weekend of the year. Never far from home, they could easily make a run for more waterproof accommodation if the weather lived up to its Welsh coastal reputation.

While some of the girls prepared sausages and eggs for an early high tea, others went in search of a supply of milk and fuel. It was while foraging for dry twigs that Jane Morris, Gaynor Edwards and Bethan Griffiths, aged thirteen, fourteen and fifteen respectively, met two young men. They claimed to have been out on a walk when they had become lost. After exchanging a little small-talk about the weather and beauty of the local countryside, they asked for directions to Porthcawl.

Jane, the youngest of the three and eager to demonstrate her adherence to the Guide Law *'to be useful and help others'*, was quick to give directions. She pointed down the hill, explaining there was a path through Danygraig Woods which led into Newton Village and past St.John's Church. She thoughtfully added an appealing description of its mediaeval tower and the pretty village green that surrounded it. Tactfully, she omitted to mention the village's two public houses. New Road, she told them, ran directly from the village into Porthcawl. She smiled and reassured them they really couldn't miss their way, just so long as they kept walking down the hill and kept the sea to their left.

"You really ought to have a map and a compass if you are out walking." She reminded them.

The men thanked her and waved as they moved on, following the girl's pointing finger. As they dropped over the brow of the hill and the Guides lost sight of them, Bethan turned to the younger girl.

"You really are a silly ass. Didn't you hear their voices?"

Jane's face dropped and she shook her head.

"They were obviously foreign. You know, we really should have asked for their identity cards before telling them anything."

Distraught, Jane searched for mitigation. "They might not have been foreign. Anyway, not all foreigners are bad foreigners. My Dad told me lots of them are fighting in the War on our side."

"They sounded German to me." Gaynor waded in with her assessment, siding with the older girl. "You could have just given away a war secret to enemy spies."

Jane's features creased into utter despair. "What war secret? Porthcawl's not a war secret." Tears coursed down her cheeks and she threw the small bundle of twigs to the ground. "It's only got a funfair and a load of smelly old caravans. There's no factory or guns or airfield or anything." She stamped her foot angrily.

"What about Stormy Down, then?" Gaynor folded her arms, gazing triumphantly down at the younger girl.

As the senior Guide present, Bethan felt it incumbent on her to take control. She quickly decided they should return to their Guide Leader and tell her what had happened.

Mrs Harrison listened carefully to the three girls as they explained their encounter. Deciphering their often interrupted and revised account, it seemed to her that, whether the strangers were German or not, the situation called for a swift response. During wartime it was better to adopt a cautious approach to all such matters. If nothing else, the incident could prove an important object lesson in being thorough. As she strode across the field towards her larger 'supply tent', the girls trotting in her wake to keep up with her, she delivered an impromptu lecture on national duty and the need to cooperate with the proper authorities.

Neither the Guide Leader nor any of her Guides had heard the news of the prison camp break-out but she instructed Jane to take two of the bicycles from the main tent. Leaving her deputy in charge with strict instructions that they were not to discuss the matter with any civilians, she and Bethan took the footpath back to Danygraig Hill.

Porthcawl's neat little stone built Police Station, situated half way along the town's main shopping street, was unusually busy for a Sunday. The Sergeant on duty, having been notified of the Bridgend break-out, had summoned every available Constable. He was in the process of briefing them on additional patrols when the panting Guide Leader and teenager reached John Street.

Their arrival was announced by a loud clattering of bicycles as they were pushed hastily against the wall next to the entrance. The two uniformed figures almost fell into the front office where the Police meeting was being held. The officers all turned to gaze at the heavily tweeded woman, red cheeked and barely able to draw breath. She took off her felt Guide's hat, fanning herself and leaning against the nearest Constable.

She was immediately brought a chair and a glass of water while it was left to Bethan to excitedly explain the purpose of their mission. By now, the strangers on Wigfach Hill had become murderous German spies, intent on blowing up the airfield at Stormy Down – despite the fact that they had asked for directions to Porthcawl.

As she spoke, several of the policemen, many of them volunteer Special Constables, grimly placed their hands on their belts, feeling for the smooth metal of their service revolvers. When eventually the girl stopped speaking, all eyes turned on the senior man present. Sergeant Winford Davies nodded with an expression of determination seldom seen in the quiet town's Police Station. It was plain to him that two of the escaped prisoners were on their way into town. For what reason, he could only guess. His senior Constable's suggestion that they could be heading towards the harbour seemed entirely plausible. They had a small fishing fleet at anchor and, when the tide was in, it would be relatively simple for a competent mariner to take one of the boats out to sea. He looked to one of the younger volunteers for guidance. Dewi Morris was skipper of a local trawler and a capable seaman. Before the RNLI had withdrawn from the town in the early 1900's, the young man's father had been a member of the lifeboat crew. There wasn't a family locally that knew the currents, winding channels and sandbanks better.

Dewi glanced at the wall clock. The tide would be high enough to navigate Porthcawl's muddy harbour and over the submerged rocks into the Bristol Channel by about seven o'clock that evening.

Sergeant Davies organised his men swiftly and with an efficiency that surprised even him. When he had been promoted to his present rank in 1942, his Inspector had voiced his concern that the demands of war had prompted his promotion several years too early. Winford was quick to realise his actions over the next few hours could serve to either dispel or confirm those doubts. He swallowed hard.

Three men were sent to the harbour to alert the Harbourmaster to stand ready in case the escapees slipped through the net. While one remained on guard at the narrow track leading to the harbour, the other two followed a path along the line of the beach towards Wigfach. Meanwhile, the remaining men were detailed to spread out across the town, following a course parallel to New Road and up towards Danygraig Woods and the hill leading to the Girl Guides' camp.

As the search party left, and with just ten men at his disposal, the Sergeant telephoned the town's senior Air Raid Precautions Warden to let him know what was happening and try to raise some more volunteers. Next, he alerted the senior officer on duty at RAF Stormy Down. Although the airfield had been deserted by the US Air Force, the RAF maintained a token presence and it was common knowledge that, despite criticism that the grass landing strip was too dangerous for inexperienced pilots, training aircraft were still kept there. Most recently, French aircrew had received initial tuition at the base and the trainers were the most basic and easiest to fly. Sergeant Davies knew little about military aircraft but was aware they were left virtually unguarded for most of the time. Having described his concerns to a seemingly disinterested Squadron Leader, he spent the next few minutes notifying his County Headquarters in Cardiff and the local Army barracks in Bridgend before clambering aboard his Police bicycle and pedalling heavily after the search party.

Even if nothing came of the search, Davies was determined that his Inspector should be given no reason to complain about any lack of attention to detail.

The women had been sent back to their camp with directions to keep all their Guides together and under canvas until the emergency was declared to be over. Reluctantly, Mrs Harrison had returned to her bicycle and the tortuous prospect of a ride back up Danygraig Hill. Meanwhile, each man in the search party had been issued with a stout pole and began beating through undergrowth in search of hidden Germans. She couldn't resist calling a few words of encouragement in the style of a mounted huntsman as she and Bethan wobbled past.

There was little beating to be done for those officers assigned to cover New Road and if local residents were surprised to see policemen climbing over the fences between their back gardens, they didn't show it. They all quickly understood and quietly acquiesced to the need for the search, informed as they had been of the escaped prisoners at their various denominations of Church and Chapel that morning.

The line of men progressed slowly towards Newton, ignoring the twin temptations of *The Jolly Sailor* and *The Ancient Briton*, the dual sweet smells of ale and burning pine logs emanating from their open doors. Pausing only to explain to the Vicar of St.John's what they were about, the party checked the churchyard and began their ascent up Danygraig Hill. On their right wing, four of their number clambered over the hillocks and valleys of Newton Burrows, the sand dunes which bordered the village and protected it, for the most part, from the higher tides of the Bristol Channel.

A few allotment holders glanced up as the uneven string of uniformed men advanced on their oblong patches of soil. Digging for victory was a principal well recognised by many of the policemen and they took care to keep to the narrow pathways between the carefully dug and cultivated earth.

After a perfunctory search of the thin scattering of wooden sheds, the men moved on, beating with their sticks as they reached a thick hedge behind the allotments. Crossing into farmland and starting the climb towards Wigfach, the only sign of movement ahead of them came from a small flock of sheep, moving to avoid them and crossing the field towards a thicket of ancient trees known as Danygraig Wood.

The sheep moved in together, bunching close to one another for protection as they retreated towards the trees. With no immediate obstacles or potential hiding places, the thin blue line advanced swiftly now and in silence, the men gazing up to the horizon above and ahead of them.

One of the Special Constables, a farm labourer named Joseph Hanson, nodded at the distant sheep.

"There's something bothering them." He whispered the words but in the still air the men on either side of him heard and looked up. They noticed for the first time that the sheep had changed the direction of their withdrawal and were now heading at speed across the brow of the hill to the right. Joe sniffed quietly and nodded at the wood. "There's something in them trees." Without another word, the line of men wheeled slightly, towards the copse and almost imperceptibly picked up the pace of their advance. Sergeant Davies, at the centre of the row and now pushing his bicycle, drew his revolver with his free hand and checked it was loaded.

They stopped just short of the first row of trees, each man looking to the Sergeant for instruction. Silently, Davies lowered the bicycle to the grass and looked along the row of men on either side of him. He held his pistol upright in front of his chest, nodding to the other armed men. Replacing his weapon in its holster he drew his truncheon, a stout twelve inch baton which until that morning had been left idle in his desk drawer.

The men began beating their way through the undergrowth, hitting out at outcrops of bramble and hawthorn. With no more reason for stealth, the Sergeant called into the depths of the wood, demanding an immediate surrender. They paused, waiting in silence for a response. None came and they advanced another few steps. One of the Constables smacked his stick against the trunk of a tree, calling into the darkness almost in frustration. Around him, the other men continued their slow advance, gazing intently ahead.

As Sergeant Davies used his boot to thrash another clump of entangled ivy and dead branches, a grim shadow moved in the middle distance. On either side of it, the lower branches of the trees seemed to shiver as, from the darkness, dressed in long woollen overcoats, two men stepped into sight, their hands raised above their heads.

Sunday 11th March 1945, 15:45 hrs.

Elwyn Morris, his wife and their daughter Brenda had closed the bar of their pub promptly at 2 o'clock, settling down for what they had hoped would be a peaceful early afternoon Sunday lunch. The publican's wife had managed to acquire a generous leg of lamb from one of their neighbours whose brother kept a farm and they had been looking forward to their first roast for several weeks. Even news of the Bridgend break-out, which had reached them earlier that morning, broadcast from the pulpit of Laleston Parish Church and carried to the bar by one of their regular customers, had done little to dampen the mood. Even so, their kitchen conversation had consisted of escaped Nazis and little else since they had locked the pub's doors.

As Mrs Morris placed the gleaming repast on the table and Brenda followed with roast potatoes and vegetables, her father was bemoaning the fact that so many of those searching for the escaped prisoners were from outside the area. They were being slowed down by a lack of local knowledge.

"Plenty of local men have volunteered to help", observed Mrs Morris, carefully placing four potatoes on her husband's plate and three on each of the others. Their daughter settled herself at the table and passed her father a jug of thick gravy.

"Well, one thing I do know." Mr Morris beamed at his women-folk. "Those Jerries won't be sitting down to a Sunday roast like this today." He picked up the carving knife and fork, slapping them together in mock knife-sharpening motions.

The family fell to an easy silence as they began eating, punctuated only by Mr Morris' noisy intake of brown ale and murmurs of satisfaction at his wife's culinary skills.

"Mind you," Brenda broke the silence, waving her knife in emphasis. "If I was one of those escaped Nazis, I know what I'd do."

Her mother laughed lightly. "Come now, Bren. You could never be a Nazi." She ignored her daughter's irritation at being interrupted. "You'd look awful in jackboots. All that high-kicking goose-stepping is just nonsense. It can't be good for your legs. It would give you those very-close veins."

"Varicose veins." Her husband, after decades of marriage, still couldn't resist correcting his wife's unconscious errors. "I should know", he justified. "My mother had them." There was a pause before Elwyn's eyebrows rose over his pint glass. "Why's that then, anyway? Why would high-kicking be bad for the legs?"

"Well, honestly, what a question." His wife clicked her tongue at him. "It stands to reason, doesn't it?" She looked at her daughter for support but received only a frown.

Her husband interrupted. "No it doesn't. Not at all. Look at those French Can-Can dancers. They do high kicks and they've got lovely legs."

"Oh they have, have they?" She leaned across the table, flicking her husband's hand playfully with a serving spoon.

Brenda's irritation at her parents' frivolous flirting was obvious. "No, Mam, what I mean is, I know where I'd hide if I were an escaped prisoner on the run."

The girl's parents both looked at their daughter, momentarily silent.

"Given it some thought have you love?" Her father laughed, reluctant to give up the light-hearted mood. "Just in case the Police come wanting to lock you up, is it?"

"Shut up Dad, what I mean is, when I was a kid, me and the others used to play at hiding-out, up in the top fields behind Mr Farrow's tithe barn." She pushed a piece of lamb into her mouth and chewed briefly. "There's a big dip in the ground with a group of old oak trees in the middle."

"I know it, Farrow's Old Copse."

Brenda wrinkled her nose. "Mr Farrow's old corpse? Of course not, he's not dead. I mean the trees up in his top field." She waved her fork, gravy dripping from a piece of roast potato. "There's a big round dip we called the saucer because it's always full of dirty water and stuff. From a distance it looks like it's full of spilled tea and old tea-leaves." Her parents were silent now, listening carefully. "Like I say, when we were kids, we used to make dens up there. We'd bind twigs and branches together then cover them in leaves to make a sort of tent. We could have stayed hidden up there for days and nobody would have had a clue we were there." She returned to her meal.

Edna Morris nodded, chewing hard, impatient to add to the conversation but too polite, even in her relaxed family's company, to speak before swallowing. "That's right, love." She nodded again at her daughter. "Don't you remember, Elwyn? When Iolo Thomas went missing years back, he was found up at the Old Copse. He had been out all night and most of the next day but he was found tucked up safe under a great pile of dry leaves. He couldn't have been more than six at the time." She smiled at the memory. "He said he was being a boy scout like his big brother. Little tinker, he was too."

Elwyn nodded. "Still is, I've heard. I remember it, though. And Constable Hughes was no help. He wouldn't believe it. Said he'd searched the copse himself and swore nobody was there."

"Mind you," his wife added, "that's why they called him Hopeless Hughes."

The small kitchen fell silent as they finished their meals. Unspoken, the family's thought converged on the only possible conclusion.

Placing his knife and fork together with a deep belch of satisfaction, Mr Morris scraped his chair back over the flagstones. As if an argument had been settled, he rose firmly from the table. "Right then. I'll get John. He's got a shotgun."

John Williams had lived and worked in Laleston all his life. A small-holder, greengrocer, horse dealer, volunteer fireman and now a wartime fire warden, he was credited, at the age of fifty five, with knowing the lanes and fields of his small hamlet as well as any man alive.

Elwyn Morris had kept the village pub for almost a decade and there were few men in the area who he didn't know by their first names. The pair would make an effective, if small, search party. Hopeless Hughes had been pensioned off and replaced some years earlier but the latest incumbent was a young and eager Englishman. He had arrived in the village only a few months before and, according to the local gossip, had not yet strayed far enough from his small office and the main street to have worn his boots in. He certainly didn't know his way past the nearby A48 Cardiff Road.

As Elwyn explained his quest to his neighbour, John Williams, they agreed not to trouble the young Constable with their suspicions. They doubted his presence would prove helpful.

With a final instruction to John's wife to stay indoors with the doors locked, the two men set off. They walked the short distance to the nearest road junction and turned right up Rogers Lane, towards Cefn Cribwr. After a few hundred yards, as the lane narrowed, they left the lane, climbing over a broad five bar gate into a rising meadow of thick spring pasture. The occupying heifers and ponies glanced disinterestedly in their direction before continuing to pull at the grass. The men saw no advantage in trying to disguise their approach. The copse was still out of sight over the next rise and, beyond that, behind a thick hedge. In any case, the men they hoped to find would be too busy trying to hide. With any luck they wouldn't be looking out for search parties.

Few words passed between the two men as they tramped across the familiar fields. They made an odd pair; Elwyn Morris stood at over six feet, broad shouldered, with a thick neck and brief tuft of closely shorn grey hair. He strode heavily next to John Williams who, even at his full height, fell short of his companion's shoulder, his diminutive figure lost inside an over-sized olive green waxed jacket.

Only when they approached the final hillock above the Old Copse did they exchange a few muttered sentences to confirm their tactics before turning right and then finally dropping to the damp grass overlooking the copse. Almost immediately, John emitted a brief hiss; barely a whisper, nodding into the shallow valley. At the far edge of the thicket, over a hundred yards away, they both saw the darkened figures of three men shuffling through the shadows. Bending then moving forward in short ponderous steps, they seemed to be working their way across the copse towards them.

Both watchers ducked their heads out of sight. Elwyn turned heavily to his friend. "It looks like they're gathering wood." The other nodded agreement.

"They're either going to light a fire or they're building a hide."

"It's too wet to set a fire. My money would be on a hide. How many did you see?"

"Three."

"Me too. We need to get closer."

The men edged down the slope, away from the copse before half standing and, ducking below the line of sight, moved round the line of the hill. They emerged just fifty yards from the thicket and dropped, half sliding on the wet grass, into a shallow stream. From here, hidden below the level of the surrounding fields, they followed the trickle of running water until they were close to the fringe of trees.

John crawled up the banking, his shotgun wedged between his thin forearm and chest. His dark green cap and jacket seemed to cover him completely and blended perfectly with the surrounding undergrowth as he glanced over the parapet of grass and mud. To Elwyn's surprise, he immediately ducked out of sight again, half turned and rolled down the slope to the brook below. He took a couple of deep breaths. "There are at least half a dozen of the buggers. They're all sitting together there. They've got a great pile of brushwood and leaves."

Elwyn nodded with satisfaction. "Brenda was right then."

"Aye, but we're outnumbered." John caught Elwyn glancing at his shotgun. "Don't be daft, man. I've never shot a man."

Elwyn shrugged his large shoulders. "Fair enough, I suppose." He found it difficult to hide his disappointment. The pair fell silent as they thought about their next move.

Although John Williams was wiry and quick when necessary, they both knew he wouldn't last long if it came to a fight. Furthermore, his shotgun could only take one cartridge at a time. Even if it was fired, they would quickly be overwhelmed by the survivors sheltering in the trees. "Did they look fit?" He jerked his head up the slope.

"God's sake, Elwyn, I didn't ask them to do press-ups. They're bloody trained soldiers." He clutched his shotgun closer to his narrow chest, flapping his free hand aimlessly. "All young German officers. Nazis for God's sake."

Elwyn held his hands out in front of him, making calming motions. "All right, steady now. We'll do nothing rash." He thought again. "And you reckon there are about six of them." John shrugged a nod. "Did you see any weapons?" The other admitted he hadn't, slightly concerned at the way the discussion was turning. "And they certainly don't know how many of us there are, do they?" Elwyn's large face creased into a smile. He nodded encouragingly. "We've just got to give it a go, haven't we." It was more of a statement than a question. Horrified, John watched as Elwyn crawled up the greasy bank towards the crouching Nazis. Reaching the ridge, his thick neck periscoped an inch or so as he peeked through the tufts of grass. He turned, still grinning and beckoned to the smaller man, almost crouching in the water at the bottom of the slope.

Slowly, John left his damp shelter and together, they watched in the slowing dusk the figures of the shadowed Germans. They could almost make out their voices, they were so close. Elwyn nodded once more, his eyebrows raised in an unspoken question. John feigned confusion, shrugging and mouthing *'what?'*

His question was quickly answered. Elwyn coughed loudly and in his best resonating Welsh tenor voice, called over his shoulder.

"All right then. You are surrounded and my men are armed. Surrender now."

As he spoke, John Williams' small frame seemed to contract even further as his head ducked into the hollow between his shoulders and the shotgun visibly shook in his hands. Only his eyes widened as he stared at his friend in disbelief.

"Do you hear me? Put your hands up and surrender now."

They could hear a general commotion from the trees and the large man again glanced over the ridge of grass. The figures beneath the dark canopy were moving now, but not in the way Elwyn had hoped. There were no raised hands or dispirited shuffles of surrender. Instead, the men were moving quickly, gathering fragments of possessions and vanishing deeper into the cover of the trees.

Elwyn grabbed the shotgun from John's clutch, planted the stock firmly on the ground and fired the single barrel into the air.

"Come out now with your hands up." His voice rose in volume, his tone more demanding. It was the voice he reserved for closing time when the slower moving of his customers became reluctant to leave. He pushed the shotgun at John without glancing down and told him to reload it, his eyes fixed on the copse. He could just make out the retreating backs of the final two men as they left the cover of the trees on the far side of the thicket. They were moving fast, bent forward and heading towards the next rise in the fields.

"Bugger." Another pause. "Right, John. You've got to follow them. You know these fields better than me. Keep them in sight. I'll go and get up a search party and we'll ferret the buggers out."

Trembling and still in mild shock, John craned upwards to watch the retreating men. Frightened though he was, he understood enough to know what he had to do. He swallowed hard.

"I suppose, if they were armed, they would have fired back just now."

Elwyn slapped him firmly on the shoulder, all but pushing him back down the grassy bank. "Of course they would. Look at them." He waved his hand vaguely at the horizon. "They're bloody scared witless of us." Grabbing the smaller man by the loose fold in his waterproof jacket with one ham-like fist, he heaved him to his feet and lifted him to the ridge in full view of the copse.

Dutifully, John set off at a marathon runner's jog down the wet slope. He joined a worn path, by-passing the trees and following the line of the Germans' retreat. Elwyn watched the small figure lope into the middle distance and start up the next hill before he pulled himself upright, turned, and started back towards his pub.

It was almost twenty minutes before Elwyn, red faced, slapped the palm of his heavy hand against the door of Constable Havers' office. The small room took up almost a quarter of the building which served as Police Station and accommodation for the lone Constable assigned to serve the village. The young officer had spent most · of the morning reading reports, chiefly with regard to the escape of German Prisoners of War. He had been about to follow his latest order and ask the five former Home Guard volunteers who lived in the village to help set up a road block near the village when the publican's knock interrupted him.

Through gasps and swallows, Elwyn relayed the story of the hide-out at Farrow's Old Copse and John Williams' pursuit.

Inexperienced though he was, Havers picked up the receiver of his office telephone and called Bridgend's Army barracks. He asked for the commanding officer by name and was quickly connected to a young officer who answered the call with a single word.

"Gently."

Taking mild pleasure in the confusion this caused unsuspecting callers, Captain Simon Gently was another recent arrival from England. Unlike the Policeman, however, he had yet to grasp the practical value of local knowledge. He had been temporarily left in charge while his senior officers were liaising with the Police, organising searches and positioning road blocks. He quickly assured the excitable Constable that he would have a patrol mustered to Laleston immediately. Local civilians, he warned sagely, must stay indoors with their doors locked. Vehicles should be immobilised and any weapons made secure. He had read the War Department memo only an hour before and knew the official statement almost by heart.

As he spoke, Gently gazed at the large wall map behind his CO's desk. Apparently reassured and eager to get on with his part of the operation, Constable Havers thanked him and was about to replace the receiver.

"Before you go, Constable." Gently's smooth tones disguised his concern. "Where exactly is Laleston?"

There was a scraping sound at the other end of the line as the Policeman tried to open a map.

"Where exactly are your barracks?" Havers tried in vain to sound well informed.

"For God's sake." Elwyn's large paw grabbed the telephone receiver. He delivered swift, concise directions to the bemused officer at the other end of the line, instructing him to meet him at Laleston Police Station.

"Roger, got that. And who am I speaking to?"

Elwyn had already replaced the receiver and was moving towards the door. He turned briefly. "You'd better get some of your Police mates down here from Bridgend too. I'll get a search party together of men who actually know where they are."

Within half an hour, some forty men in a variety of uniforms had gathered outside the small building. Former Home Guard men, weighing up the urgency of the situation against their desire to look professional, had managed only to pull their uniform tunics on with the civilian trousers they had already been wearing. As if by silent telepathy, three members of the Women's Voluntary Service had appeared with a hand cart laden with tea urn and several dozen thick enamel mugs.

Two open backed Army transport lorries had been parked diagonally, blocking the road while a group of soldiers led by a Corporal made a show of stopping and checking the identity cards of anyone passing. As most of the village's men had already gathered to make up the search party, most of those questioned were women who had emerged from their homes to see what the commotion was about.

Before long, several of the soldiers and policemen were ordered aboard the lorries which grumbled into life and, directed by Elwyn and another local man, set off up Rogers Lane. Another group of soldiers, led by local Home Guard men, cut through the garden of the village Post Office, past the Parish Church and into the lanes behind the village. For Constable Havers, walking with the group, this was unexplored territory. Somewhat ashamed, he hung back and mingled with the local men in case any of the soldiers asked him a question.

Among the women who emerged from their front doors to watch the search party, Miss Jenkins, well known for her extreme and varied forms of patriotism, stood at her garden gate. A Welsh flag displaying a red dragon against a green and white background swung about her frail shoulders like a cape. Waving a smaller Union flag on a short stick, she launched into a surprisingly shrill rendition of Rule Britannia, her warbling soprano continuing unabated until the final man had vanished from sight.

The group being led by Elwyn Morris were the first to spot the small form of John Williams. He was standing atop a long gentle rise which led from the western side of Rogers Lane towards Stormy Down. Following his instinct, Elwyn had directed the leading lorry driver to turn left near the top of Rogers Lane at Langewydd and follow the old farm road towards Haregrove Farm. There they had paused briefly to check the barns and outbuildings, although Elwyn had been confident they would need to travel a little further west before reaching their goal.

As the road narrowed to a gravel track, John could be seen silhouetted against the dim glow of the sunset. He waved his arms at the heavy cloud of diesel fumes visible at the rear of the lorry.

A Sergeant, wedged in the passenger seat between Elwyn and an overweight and sweating driver turned to the publican, concern across his face.

"Is that your mate up there then?"

Elwyn nodded, his satisfaction all too clear.

"And what the bloody 'ell's up there then, apart from him?" The Sergeant's accent stemmed from London's East End and his nearest encounter to countryside had previously been a childhood charabanc journey to Southend.

Elwyn smiled. "It's an old quarry. It's been deserted for years but, fair play to the Jerries, it's the best place to hide for miles."

The Sergeant instructed the driver and the truck strained the final few hundred yards up the gravel slope. It wheezed to a halt as John reached up to the passenger door and pulled it open, his relief clear at seeing both Elwyn and the military reinforcements tumbling from the back of the lorry. Unspeaking, the men gathered at the front of the vehicle, surrounding their NCO. He, in turn, listened closely as John's lilting Welsh accent accelerated through his account of what was happening.

"There were thirteen of the buggers, see. I had to follow five of them right the way from Maes Pen. Sometimes walking they were, then running across the open fields. Tricky, they are too, looking about them all the way."

Elwyn interrupted. "There's more than a dozen of them, now then?"

"No, man. There *were* thirteen. The lot we saw first at Old Copse and another lot that were already hiding out in the quarry. They all met up." He rolled his eyes. "I thought they were going to break into song and have a party, they were so happy to see each other. All shaking hands and hugging and that." John's shoulders dropped. "But then more than half of them moved off, north up Heol Y Sheet towards Kenfig Hill."

"What? Heel of shit?" The Sergeant's frown deepened, frustrated by the suddenly impenetrable language.

Elwyn, who was slightly more used to foreigners, explained. "Not heel of shit. Heol Y Sheet is the name of a road. It's a lane just north of here."

"So there's about five or six of them still in the quarry?" The Sergeant ignored John's explanations of how he couldn't follow the north-bound group for fear that the others would also move on and be lost to them. Silently, the soldier calculated his tactical advantage. They were seventeen, including the civilians and all but Elwyn were armed.

"Have you seen any firearms?" He asked. "Handguns or rifles?" he added helpfully, as if the local man might have difficulty understanding.

The small man shook his head.

The Sergeant beckoned his men closer, unnecessarily repeating that they were dealing with about half a dozen escaped Prisoners of War. His voice dropped to a harsh whisper. "We think they're unarmed, but that don't mean the buggers won't have a weapon or two concealed about theirselves." He looked along the line of young soldiers, searching for signs of uncertainty. "So we don't take no chances. I want your weapons cocked and ready." There was a stifled giggle from the back of the small group. Almost forgetting the covert nature of their mission, the Sergeant's voice rose as he told the man to grow up – he was in the Army now. "Now, me and this 'ere civilian," he jerked his thumb at John, "are going to do a quick rece." He looked optimistically at the bemused young faces. His whisper turned to a saliva ridden hiss. "That's a reconnoitre you thick shits. We're goin' to take a butcher's at the enemy's position." There was another giggle, swiftly silenced by an acid glance. At a nod from the Sergeant, John led the soldier up the final slope to the lip of the quarry.

Within ten minutes they were back. Resuming his stage whisper, the Sergeant confirmed there were five of the enemy in the quarry. He split his men into two groups which he importantly named 'A Troop' and 'B Troop'. There were no other NCO's in the search party and after brief consideration, he pointed at a lanky young Private at the back of the second group. "Henlow, you're about the least useless dollop here. You take charge of B Troop. I'll command A Troop." Henlow grinned sheepishly as his new troop glanced at him uncertainly.

The Sergeant scraped a crescent shaped line in the damp gravel with the heel of his boot. "That's the edge of the quarry, right. We're 'ere." He patted the ground with his toe-cap. "And the enemy is 'ere." He picked up a loose stone and dropped it a few inches within the indented arch. "Henlow, you'll take B Troop this way and I'll take A Troop this way." He scraped two more lines in the dirt. "You will spread out along the edge of the quarry and hold your position, below the ridge. That means out of sight of the enemy, Henlow." He eyed the Private, leaving no doubt as to the disaster that would befall him if he failed to follow instructions. "We will then have encircled the enemy." There was a silence while the Sergeant considered whether his men understood what 'encircled' meant. He decided to take a chance. "I will then blow my whistle once." He held up his small steel whistle in case they weren't sure what it looked like. "I will call upon the enemy to surrender, whereupon you will all stand at the ready, rising to your full and impressive height and holding your weapons, so." He jerked his left foot forward, pulling the stock of his rifle into his shoulder and aiming over Henlow's shoulder. "Except, of course, you will not aim your weapons at no passing pigeons. You will aim your weapons at the enemy." He picked out a stocky young squaddie standing next to the civilians. Even the diminutive John Williams seemed tall next to him. "That should be easy for you, Kelly, 'cos you'll be closer to them than anyone else." The soldiers gazed with blank incomprehension. The Sergeant's shoulders dropped. "Christ almighty. Because they're down in the bottom of the quarry and we'll be up on the edge looking down at them." He pointed the barrel of his rifle at the track in front of the men's boots. "You will not fire unless you are directly ordered by your Troop Commander." He looked up at the lanky Private, now busily checking the bolt action of his rifle. "And Henlow." The man looked up. "*you* will not give the order to fire unless *I* order you. Understood?"

Henlow nodded hastily. The Sergeant inhaled and asked if there were any questions.

"Only one." The NCO looked round. He had quite forgotten about the civilians. "Which Troop do we go with?"

The Sergeant's brow knitted for a moment. "Being as 'ow you're not trained military, you'd better wait in the wagon.

Elwyn pulled himself up to his full height and expanded his chest. "I served in the last lot, in Flanders. I'd take a bet I've seen more action than any of this lot." He nodded at A Troop. They shuffled uncomfortably and collectively in silent acknowledgement.

John grinned at his side. "He's right there. He's seen more action than most, and that's just at closing time on a Saturday night." The Sergeant still seemed unconvinced, despite the large man's obvious physical presence and the smaller man's shotgun.

"And we've got local knowledge." Elwyn added, picking up on something he had heard Captain Gently discussing with one of the police officers.

The NCO inhaled as if finally reaching a difficult decision. "OK then." He pointed at John. "But you keep that pop-gun under control. My orders are that all recaptured prisoners are to be returned in as good condition as we find 'em in." He sniffed. "More's the bloody pity."

At the order, Private Henlow and B Troop, accompanied by Elwyn Morris, bent double and moving as quietly as their heavy boots allowed, doubled up the track and turned on to the northern lip of the quarry. At the same time, the Sergeant led

Sunday 11th March 1945, 18:15 hrs.

It had been a long day and George Charteris had been used to taking a rest day on Sunday while in his last posting in Hampstead. He was quickly learning that life in the provinces was not as quiet or as slow as he had at first suspected.

His ear was still tuning itself to the Welsh accent, although here in Camp 198, the accents were as varied as on any of the London streets he had recently patrolled. The camp guards were drawn, it seemed, from every corner of the United Kingdom and he had detected Geordie, Scouse and a broad range of southern accents which hailed from all parts of London and the Home Counties. That, however, was nearly all that he had detected.

He had been ordered by Inspector Bailey to return to the camp and interview as many prisoners as he could who had been part of the escape plan. He had also been told to interview the guards. He had presented himself to the senior officer on duty, Colonel Darling still being engaged with interviews of his own. All his requests had been turned down. It appeared that a senior figure within Military Intelligence (a contradiction in terms according to the Camp Adjutant) was sending officers who would soon be conducting an investigation of their own. They had insisted that nothing – and nobody – be disturbed prior to their arrival.

Nevertheless, George had managed to gain entry, under escort, to Hut Nine; the building from which the escape tunnel had been constructed. The resident prisoners had been hastily moved out and relocated to other huts around the camp. Finding them quarters had proved simple enough, there now being several dozen vacant beds. Despite this minor triumph, George had learned little. As officers, the prisoners were afforded a degree of comfort, amounting to a small bedroom, shared with one other prisoner and equipped with a pair of bunk beds, simple furniture and two curtained windows. The flooring was constructed of large slabs of concrete and it was beneath one of these that the tunnelling had begun. Each time work had been interrupted, the slab had been quickly returned to its place, the diggers disguising their activity by simply sweeping dust from the surrounding floor into the cracks round the flag and the narrow wooden bunk bed moved so that its feet straddled it.

The Adjutant had been inadvertently helpful when he had praised his Camp Commandant for his prediction that tunnels were almost invariably constructed in threes. Although the earlier discovery of two tunnels had been reported to the Army's Western Command Headquarters and Darling had made no secret of the details during his regular meetings with Superintendent May, the revelation came as news to George.

The young Detective was interested to know how it was that the first two tunnels had been found so easily while the third clearly had not. The Adjutant had shrugged, a tired smile across his face.

"The first two were clearly designed to be discovered, once a respectable time had elapsed. No engineer worth his qualifications could have expected the first tunnel to be sustainable. It was as if they were trying to burrow their way through custard." He grinned, quietly pleased with his description. "The second tunnel, although more promising from the diggers' point of view, had its entrance in full view, in a communal room in Hut 16. It was disguised, of course, and covered with a hearth stone but the walls had very little structural support. They used very little timber and there were no arrangements for ventilation."

"So, destined to deliberate failure, you think?"

"Absolutely. My belief, and that of Colonel Darling, is that their purpose was simply to divert us from the genuine effort." He pointed to the hole at their feet, now exposed by the removal of both the bunk beds and concrete slab. "They hoped we would relax our searches once their earlier work had been discovered. We didn't stop checking, of course, but this third tunnel was disguised far more effectively. They clearly put much more planning and manpower into it, digging faster, using more timber to support the walls and ceiling, building a ventilation shaft. In addition, they must have realised we would discover their excavated soil scattered around the camp but hoped we would put that down to the two tunnels we had already found." The Adjutant sighed. "All in all, a pretty effective scheme." His chin dropped as he gazed down into the hole. Both men knew the camp guards, despite their best efforts and the insight of their commanding officer, had been badly caught out.

The rest of George's tour of inspection revealed how various pieces of timber had been taken from room dividers and beds within the hut. The briefest of explorations into the tunnel (head first; a claustrophobic experience) had identified that, just as the Adjutant had described, they had been used as braces and roof props within the tunnel. It was barely wide enough for a man's shoulders but, George had been told by one of the larger guards, he had managed to negotiate the full length of the tunnel with his arms outstretched before him. The Constable, who took no pleasure whatever from being confined in small spaces, took his word for it. He did, however, note that along the length of the tunnel a long metal tube had been constructed out of what appeared to be food cans. Stretching into the darkened distance, farther than the reach of his torch beam, he was assured it almost reached the tunnel's exit outside the wire.

A series of small metal implements had also been found hidden in various crannies along the length of the hut. A large nail, hammered flat to serve as a chisel had been wedged into a crack beneath the timber frame of one of the prisoners' beds. Another was pushed into a small space above one of the roof joists. A metal tin had been cut and shaped like a coal shovel and pushed deep into a hollow behind a locker. George had been about to place them all in a small box to preserve them as evidence, in accordance with the brief training he had received as a detective. He had been stopped by a quietly spoken Quartermaster Sergeant, tasked to escort him during the remainder of his stay on the camp. Nothing was to be moved until Military Intelligence had conducted an inspection.

It transpired that the Sergeant also hailed from North London and finding common ground, the soldier seemed to relax. They chatted amiably enough as they walked back to the NCO's mess for a cup of tea.

Monday 12ᵗʰ March 1945, 08:30 hrs.

George gathered the newspapers together and carried them into his Inspector's office. He placed them on the desk, leaving the local newspapers at the top of the pile. Inspector Bailey had left home to reach Bridgend Police Station an hour before and hadn't yet had time to assess the outcome of yesterday's press conference.

The Constable watched his superior's face but saw no hint of a reaction.

"Well, George, what are the newspapers saying this morning about our break-out?"

Charteris smiled. "Nearly every newspaper, local and national, is carrying the story, sir." He flipped through the headlines briefly. "The surprising thing is, they are all quoting quite inaccurate figures. The general consensus seems to be that seventy prisoners originally escaped and about thirty of them were recaptured almost immediately."

"Thirty?" The Inspector looked up at the younger man. "Why thirty?"

George picked up one of the newspapers. "*The Daily Herald* has the story on the front page." He read the headline, "*'SS Men in mass jail tunnel getaway. 70 out – 28 back'.*" He looked up at his Inspector. "At least they got the twenty eight recaptured accurately enough. I've been told, sir, that the story has been syndicated by one of the reporters at the press conference. My money would be on the chap from *The South Wales Post*, although they all seem to quote different figures."

He pulled another newspaper from the pile. "*The News Chronicle* is even more creative. They say that of seventy escaped prisoners, thirty four have been recaptured, leaving thirty six still at large. Some of the local papers have got hold of the story about the theft of Dr Milne's car and others say that a twenty two year old woman and her father recaptured five of them."

"What?" The Inspector looked up incredulously.

George started reading. "*'The girl was Miss Brenda Morris of Laleston. Her father, Mr Elwyn Morris told what happened. "Brenda began talking about a sunken copse two fields away from my house where she used to play as a child. It was a fine place to hide in she said and added she wouldn't mind betting there were some prisoners there." '*"

Inspector Bailey shook his head sadly. "What a load of rubbish. Where do they get it from?"

"Probably from talking to Mr and Miss Morris. There's more." He continued to read. "*'Sure enough there was a group of them there. They didn't look very fierce so I called on them to surrender and told them they were surrounded'.*"

Both men laughed quietly. "What a pair of heroes, sir. It just goes to show that reporters don't bother to check the accuracy of these claims. It wouldn't have taken much to establish that half the village also turned out, along with the Police and the Army."

The Inspector sighed. "We shouldn't be surprised. It raises morale to put about that a young woman and her civilian father can capture five of the best fighting men Germany can produce."

"As far as I can tell, sir, the reporters have assumed that when Colonel Darling said sixteen prisoners had been captured at the tunnel exit and then said that more prisoners were rounded up by Sunday morning, they've deducted both those numbers from seventy. None of them have mentioned that eighty six originally broke out so they've assumed the number who actually got away from the area of the camp was only fifty four."

"Good God. Do you think so?"

Charteris failed to identify the less than subtle note of sarcasm in the Inspector's voice. Instead, he shook his head sadly, gazing at the pile of newspapers. "So however many prisoners are recaptured, the press will presumably continue to publish inaccurate figures." He pulled a further page from the pile. "Just to complicate things further, *The Daily Express* has reported that a further twelve were recaptured last night."

The Inspector nodded. "That much, at least, is true."

"Yes sir, but that leaves a total of fifty eight prisoners still free. *The 'Express* calculated there are only forty two."

The older Police Officer smiled gently. "We can't be held responsible for the newspapers' inaccurate reporting, George."

"No sir, except that the press release from Whitehall doesn't make the facts clear either. It simply says a further dozen German Prisoners of War have been returned to captivity. The newspapers have based their reports purely on the number recaptured."

The Inspector shrugged. "I don't suppose there will be much harm in that. People need reassurance, after all."

Charteris sounded cautious. "But what happens when more than forty two more prisoners are rounded up?"

"Let's worry about that when it happens." Bailey gave another reassuring smile.

George wasn't to be put off so easily. "As I remember it, the original figure of seventy was used in order that the Government could continue to claim the break-out from *Stalag Luft III* was the most successful of the war." He gazed at the Inspector. "Won't it become clear we've been lying?" He shrugged expansively. "You know what politicians are like. They'll surely blame the local Police and Camp Commandant for misleading the press." He looked up, his face a mask of horror. "Oh, good God sir. They'll could even accuse us of misleading the Government."

The Inspector thought for a moment. He shrugged again. "We'll put it down to shoddy journalism. Very few people believe anything the newspapers print anyway."

"What about the BBC though? The Home Service reported the break-out this morning. Everyone trusts Alvar Lidell."

"Ah well, that's not our problem. Anything reported by the BBC is the responsibility of the Ministry of Information." He smiled and sat back in his chair. "We are a simple provincial police force in a simple provincial town. We're not authorised to brief the BBC." Bailey leaned the chair backwards, balancing it on its two rear legs. "That doesn't mean that *I* don't want accurate information, though. How did you get on yesterday?"

George settled back in his chair, allowing himself a modicum of comfort during what might well turn into an uncomfortable interview.

"Not very well I'm afraid, sir. The senior officer on the camp allowed me no access to the prisoners and very limited time with the guards. He said Military Intelligence were to have the first stab."

The Inspector nodded and glanced at a page of notes on the desk in front of him. "That would be MI19. They're hush-hush boys on their way from London. Apparently they have responsibility for interrogating enemy Prisoners of War as they're brought ashore from the Continent."

George stifled a grunt of dissent, doubting even before he spoke that he should say anything. "If I had my way, we'd ship the lot of them off to Canada."

The senior officer was not impressed. "Our colonial cousins would be less than grateful, Constable. They have several thousand detainees to contend with already." His tone told George not to pursue his idea further.

"There was a Sergeant, though, who seemed willing to talk to me. It was all very informal, sir, and I don't think he was really on his guard when we were speaking." The Inspector smiled in recognition of a well tried technique, accidental or otherwise, which often yielded results. "He told me the prisoners had been smuggling pebbles from their gardens into the huts. For weeks, they've been tossing them at the fence every night. Apparently the noise they make sounds like wire being cut. It throws the guards into a frenzy, firing their rifles and generally waking up the whole camp with flares going off and dogs barking."

The Inspector scratched his head. "Time wasting tactics?"

"Time wasting, sir, and just plain wearisome. The Sergeant told me that recently some of the guards have simply been ignoring the noises altogether. The Camp Commandant, who incidentally is currently *persona non grata* in the area, had been petitioned by local people complaining they can't sleep at night."

The Inspector frowned. "I wouldn't change places with Colonel Darling at this moment for all the tea in China. He was damned for trying to discourage escape attempts and now he'll no doubt be pilloried for allowing an escape to take place."

"That's rather the impression I get, sir. Having said that, I feel his men are absolutely loyal to him."

Bailey leaned back in his chair again. He linked his fingers together across his waistcoat, taking a few moments to digest the details before speaking again. "From now on, George, I'd like you to report to me each morning with an accurate account of prisoners recaptured and any intelligence gathered along the way. I'm quite sure that at some point the Superintendent, if not the Chief Constable, will want to know how we're getting along." He smiled and returned his seat to the vertical. "That means you will need to interview the detainees as they are released by Military Intelligence and returned to Island Farm. I also need you to interview those men who were recaptured before leaving the vicinity of the escape tunnel. You'd better check in case the MI19 officers want to speak with them first."

George shuffled uncomfortably. "Sir, I think I'm a fairly capable interviewer, but do you really think I'm likely to get any more out of these men than trained interrogators from Military Intelligence?"

The Inspector smiled grimly. "It may just be that the, shall we say, robust interviewing techniques, adopted by MI19 will engender greater resistance than our friendly County Police methods." He smiled encouragingly. "We just want to know how they did it and where they've been. It's unlikely that they will have received outside help but, if that turns out to be the case," the Inspector's face dropped to a pensive frown. "Well, we'll just have to allow Military Intelligence to take whatever measures they deem necessary." His features screwed into a scowl. "Believe me, George, from what I've heard, neither we nor the prisoners would want that."

Monday 12th March 1945, 10:50 hrs

Mrs Ellen Croker had spent the morning in her small home in Elm Crescent, Bryntirion, fussing over her laundry and trying to calculate how much meat and butter her ration cards would allow her to buy.

She seldom listened to the news on the wireless or bothered with newspapers. Like Inspector Bailey, she had long ago concluded that they seldom got their facts right. Besides, there was a paper shortage and she had decided that as part of her contribution to the war effort, she wouldn't buy any more newspapers. It wasn't that she had no interest in the progress of the war but, having lost a brother and two nephews, she was tired of hearing about death, whichever side it was on.

Despite that, she couldn't fail to be interested when a neighbour had told her about some prisoners who had escaped from the Prisoner of War camp down the road. Apparently there were quite a few still on the run and she had followed her neighbour's advice, remaining indoors with her doors locked since the previous morning.

Now, however, she needed to go shopping. Her husband was in the Merchant Marine and would be returning on shore leave tomorrow. He would expect some 'proper food' as he called it and she needed to visit the butcher at which she was registered in Bridgend town centre.

She gathered together her ration cards, purse, handbag, scarf, house keys and shopping bag before pulling on her winter coat. Although a mild spring had been promised, it had yet to materialise. There had been little rain over the previous few days but a bitter easterly wind was blowing up Bryntirion Hill. She would have to walk a clear mile down into the face of the wind to reach the town and, worse, carry her shopping a mile back up the hill to get home again.

She left the house, turning the key carefully in the lock. It was seldom used and the levers creaked and cracked at the unexpected movement. She made a mental note to ask her husband to oil it when he got home.

There were few pedestrians about that morning although Ellen wasn't so surprised. Monday wasn't a popular day for shopping. Most people left it until nearer to pay day. She pulled her collar up, bowed her head into the blustering chill and started to walk. She allowed her mind to wander to happier, more peaceful days when she could walk a few paces to the main road and wait for a bus. There had never been long to wait, but nowadays you could be hanging around for an hour or more. The Council denied it, of course, but the number of buses seemed to have been reduced to a fraction of their peace-time level. Even when they did turn up, they were full to bursting. What's more, they were full of people complaining that they would have preferred to use their cars, but for the petrol ration. If people could afford cars, Mrs Croker argued, they had no business to be riding on buses.

Whatever the reasons, Ellen was now resigned to walking wherever she needed to go. She reminded herself that she should be grateful the Council hadn't housed her and her husband in one of the more distant villages. Some of her friends from Laleston and Cefn Cribwr had no choice but to take the bus, however crowded, when they wanted to get into town.

Her thoughts were interrupted by a feint rustling. She glanced up and, possibly in her imagination, thought she saw a shiver run through the dry laurel hedge that bordered the pavement. Behind it, a wide yard led to a primary school and it crossed her mind that some errant pupils might be skipping classes. More curious than concerned, her pace didn't alter as she approached the hedge.

Something dark and shadowy caught her eye through the dry branches of the hedge and she heard the sound of twigs snapping as the shadow moved, hidden from sight, along the edge of the school yard. In her younger days, Mrs Croker had worked at the school as a cook. Even though pupils' behaviour was undoubtedly better ordered in those days, she had still had reason to issue reprimands on a number of occasions. She wouldn't take any nonsense then and saw no reason to take it now. Stopping, she rolled her hessian shopping bag into a rough tube and grasped it at one end like a club.

"Come on out, then, whoever you are."

Almost obediently, a face appeared briefly over the hedge. It blinked twice and disappeared. The hedge shivered again and three men, all dressed in grey, ran at full speed across the yard and round the corner of the school building.

Ellen shouted something after them which, when later asked by a Police Officer, she shyly declined to repeat. She would comment only that she knew she shouldn't have used bad language, being so close to a school full of young children.

Dropping her rolled up bag, she turned, looking for help – or at least a witness to what she had just seen. Already she was certain nobody would believe her.

She saw a car heading slowly up the hill and almost jumped into its path in her efforts to attract the driver's attention. The car stopped and a spindly man in the driver's seat wound down the window. He peered out at her, irritation creasing his face, and demanded to know what the fuss was. She told him succinctly and with no room for doubt that three escaped Germans had just run through Bryntirion School yard. The man, who was not local to Bridgend and had not heard of the break-out, pursed his lips in disbelief.

"There was an escape." She was bending forward and almost shouting into his face. "From the Prisoner of War camp just down the way." She pointed over the bonnet of the car. "Three of them, wearing German uniforms just jumped up from behind that hedge and ran for it."

The driver frowned again. "Are you sure they weren't our lads? Some chaps home on leave having a lark?"

Ellen stood upright, gasping with frustration. I've got a son in the bloody Infantry. I know the difference between a green uniform and a grey one."

It was the driver's turn to utter an oath. He swung the door open and ran, following her pointing finger into the school yard.

Twenty minutes later, several teachers and local householders, alerted to the drama, had joined in an impromptu search of the area. A dozen soldiers and police officers arrived, one with an Alsatian. While rows of small faces, aghast with wonder, watched from their classroom windows, the men and dog combed the fields behind the school and beyond. Four hours later, with no further sign of the men, the search was called off.

As she was later to explain to her husband, she had to tell everything that had happened, first to a nice young Police Inspector named Bailey then to a less than friendly Army Sergeant whose name she had instantly forgotten, and then to a small huddle of newspaper reporters who had arrived at her front door. Her only disappointment was the absence of a photographer. She would have liked to see her picture in the papers.

Monday 12th March 1945, 11:00 hrs

In the village of Laleston, five miles from Camp 198 and less than a mile from Ellen Croker and her close encounter, Bombardier Richard Makepeace was on patrol. It had now been 37 hours since the first Prisoner of War had crawled his way to freedom under the camp's wire fence.

The repercussions had quickly rumbled through the larger towns and had now moved into the more distant and sleepier villages of Glamorgan. Local residents had locked the doors of their homes for the first time in years. Some had loaded their rabbit guns or sharpened kitchen knives. Even garden scythes and axes had been dragged from garden sheds and ground to a shine in the interests of self-defence.

Bombardier Makepeace had already suffered the indignity of a public, and quite unjustified, reprimand. A local woman had bustled down the front path leading from her cottage door. Standing at her garden gate overlooking the main road through Laleston, she had shouted venomously that it was the likes of him and his stupid, lazy, lack of care that had led to "this terrifying state of affairs". He had tried to explain he was stationed in Pontypridd, nearly twenty miles away. He wasn't a camp guard. The woman had been unimpressed and had stamped back towards the safety of her parlour. She shouted meanly that she was not interested in his "lame excuses" and slammed her front door.

Adding injury to insult, a small boy had thrown a soft tomato at him, catching him neatly on the cheek, as he pedalled by on his bicycle. Richard had sworn after him but again, the boy hadn't seemed bothered.

The Bombardier entered the village churchyard, smearing tomato juice across his face with his sleeve and lifting his rifle slightly as he approached the nearest gravestones. It seemed unlikely that an escaped German would still be so close to the camp and even less likely that they would hide in a graveyard. Privately, he hoped they were all far away by now. Cantankerous women and small boys were enough of a challenge and he had no wish to go head to head with a Nazi combat officer.

His Company Commander, an Artillery Captain with less than three years experience, had briefed his NCO's early that morning and his words were still clear in Richard's memory. The escaped prisoners were all highly trained killers. They were desperate and might very well have found ways of arming themselves. The soldiers searching for them were to take no chances and on no account should a Nazis be given any opportunity to harm a member of the civilian population. Makepeace had barely listened to the rest of the Captain's instructions about recapturing the prisoners alive. He had been too wrapped up in his own imaginings of snarling SS officers unleashing a hail of bullets on innocent women and children. Having said that, he could now think of at least one woman and child he wouldn't mind a few bullets hailing on. He decided to concentrate on defending himself instead.

Tentatively, he peered round the corner of the nearest memorial. Styled as a weeping angel standing atop a large stone plinth, it afforded plenty of cover for an enemy ambush. In the event, he found nothing more dangerous than a stray bunch of dandelions, missed by the volunteer who tended the churchyard.

The Bombardier crept on, glancing left and right, his rifle now at the ready. So stealthy was his approach that the church cat, dozing near a corner of the porch which had been momentarily splashed with a little sunlight, remained undisturbed as the soldier crept past.

Finally satisfied that there were no Nazis hidden among the gravestones, he made his way in rather more relaxed style back to the road. Standing by the lych-gate, the same small boy who had launched the tomato observed the soldier with mild curiosity. He had acquired a wooden rifle from somewhere and now slung it over his shoulder. His jacket was patched at the elbows and he wore a dark green peaked cap, pushed back on his head. He looked up as the soldier approached so he could see his face from beneath the peak.

"'Morning Corp." The boy smiled and nodded as if in recognition of a comrade.

Makepeace eyed him carefully. He tapped his shoulder flash. "Bombardier. I'm with the Artillery." He sniffed. "What are you up to now, anyway? Got any more rotten vegetables, have you?"

The boy came to attention. "No Bomb. Looking for escaped Germans." He swung an exaggerated salute, knocking the cap off his head and quickly bending to retrieve it.

Makepeace frowned slightly. He wasn't used to small boys and was unsure of his ground. "How old are you, son?"

The boy straightened. "Ten." There was defiance in his tone, as if challenging the soldier to contradict him.

"Does your Mum know you're looking for Germans?"

The boy shrugged. "She won't mind. She said she's busy today anyway and I had to get out from under her feet."

Makepeace nodded in recognition of his own distant childhood. "All the same, I think you'd better be off home. I wouldn't like to see you get hurt."

The boy was about to explain the need for the Germans to be caught quickly when a car drew up at the kerbside next to them. The passenger window lowered and a man wearing a grey Macintosh leaned out. A large camera protruded briefly, a flashgun exploded, causing the soldier and the boy on the pavement to blink and turn quickly away. The car left at speed, leaving them coughing in an oily cloud.

The following day, on page four of *The Western Mail* there appeared an extended article about the escape and a photograph taken outside Laleston Parish Church. It showed a Bombardier talking intently to a small boy who carried a wooden rifle over his shoulder. The caption beneath the photograph read *'Soldier recruits help in search for escaped prisoners'*.

Monday 12th March 1945, 11:30 hrs.

Juliette Jenkins had recently celebrated her seventeenth birthday. She was the daughter of a Cardiff solicitor and enjoyed a happy and relatively affluent existence in the small village of Bonvilston in the Vale of Glamorgan. Half way between Cowbridge and Cardiff, she had no doubt of the relative thrills and excitement offered by the towns which flanked her own small hamlet. The news of the prison break-out had served only to confirm her suspicion that Bridgend was a seedy and second grade town that was best avoided.

Over the last few months she had turned her attention to Cardiff and was examining the opportunities it had to offer. She had attended school in Cowbridge and now had no wish to spend any more time there. Having been her class prefect during her final school term, she had lost any small popularity she may have previously enjoyed. That and the demands being made of young women to play their part in the war effort had decided her to leave school and find some form of employment. There were surely types of war work which carried a degree of glamour and excitement.

It was, she had convinced herself, the nobility of cause which now motivated her. She had used this newly discovered need to serve her nation to explain her announcement that she would not be attending church that morning. Her parents were profoundly religious yet, for various reasons, had not been able to attend church the day before. Now, despite being a Monday when her father would normally have been at work, they were attending Matins. Almost as a form of penance, it seemed, they had made the four mile trek to Cowbridge, their own small parish church serving too small a congregation to warrant week-day services. Juliette had announced firmly that she would spend the day scanning the local newspaper for work vacancies and writing letters of introduction to prospective employers. Her father had disapproved strongly, informing her that they would 'have words' when they came home. It was no coincidence that Juliette had waited until her parents were about to leave before making her announcement.

She had been at her father's desk for less than thirty minutes before boredom had forced her into the kitchen and her mother's kettle. Normally, cups of tea would be produced by her parents' housekeeper. However, today was Monday and the housekeeper's day off. She picked up the kettle, shook it and noted with dismay that it was both cold and empty.

Her school cookery lessons had been short lived, having been noteworthy only for their total lack of success. However, she remained confident that she could make tea. She filled the kettle and placed it on the gas stove, lighting the ring only after spending several minutes looking for matches.

By late morning, she was seated again in her father's study, enjoying the solitude of the empty house and once again searching the back pages of the newspaper. She grimaced, glancing at the ceiling as the silence was interrupted by the low drone of an aircraft overhead.

Had this been 1939, such a sound would have immediately driven her outdoors to crane up at the sky along with her parents and neighbours. Six years on, however, the novelty of seeing a military aircraft had passed. An entire squadron could roar by at an altitude of fifty feet and generate nothing more than an irate letter to the local RAF base.

The aircraft in question was a Hawker Hind; a simple, single engine reconnaissance plane with no weaponry and an open cockpit. They had been retired from their duty of patrolling England's coasts some years before but were still useful for search and rescue operations in airspace no longer disputed by enemy fighters.

On this occasion, the pilot and his observer were looking for escaped Germans. There were four such aircraft criss-crossing the skies over Glamorgan between Swansea in the west and Cardiff in the east. They were of limited use over the larger towns where fugitives, whether alone or in small groups, could easily blend into a crowd or shelter in damaged and deserted buildings. Over open countryside, however, and before the advent of the helicopter, the Hind was one the best available; capable of slow flight and easily manoeuvrable, even in the hands of an inexperienced pilot, it was able to turn in a tight circle and take off or land in a small field.

The aircraft had been flying for several hours, following the track of the A48 repeatedly in each direction. Despite that, two hours earlier the observer and his pilot had failed to identify a condensed caravan of four men moving swiftly on foot, following the line of a high stone wall on the outskirts of Cowbridge. There, after briefly sheltering from the passing aircraft, they had agreed to split up and meet on the other side of the town, on the road they confidently predicted would lead them to Cardiff and its sea port.

One of the men, Kurt Rheinspier, decided to skirt around the relatively busy shopping street in the town centre and headed down a side road next to a small parish church. The large houses which surrounded it soon diminished to a string of terraced cottages and these, in turn, to a sports field, now turned over to allotments, and a small farm. Beyond that lay open fields, scattered with hedges and shallow ditches. Kurt turned off the road and skirted swiftly round the edge of the pasture, his dark coat blending with the hedge at his side.

Judging that he was far enough from the town to go undisturbed, he stepped into the shallow valley of a ditch and sat down. He reached inside his pocket and pulled out a small fold of flimsy paper. Wrapped inside was a small block of wood, shaped like a thick domino, one side of which was hollowed out at the centre so the wood was no more than a few millimetres thick. In the centre of the bowl a small hole had been bored which, at a casual glance, might have been mistaken for an ink spot. Resting the tablet of wood on the palm of his hand, Kurt pulled a short pin from the lapel of his coat. He stuck it firmly into the hole so it stood like a miniature mast in the centre of a raft. Next, he unfolded the paper further and carefully picked out a sliver of shining metal.

Until a few days earlier, this had been part of his shaving kit. He had snapped a thin triangular sliver of the blade from his razor using a stone as a hammer and, with a magnet borrowed from one of the other officers, had painstakingly magnetised the slender steel tip. Now balancing it on the pin head, he nudged it to and fro until he found its centre of gravity.

Kurt watched the splinter of metal as it floated and turned slowly to point to magnetic north.

He nodded in satisfaction, took a bearing against a distant group of trees and pushed the three parts of the apparatus carefully back into his pocket. He spread the paper across his knees and bent low over it to study the feint pencil lines drawn across it. There, Bridgend, Cowbridge and Cardiff were all clearly marked, strung along the line that was the A48 road.

He folded the fragile piece of paper again and rose slowly from his niche in the landscape. He scanned about him with a full 360 degree turn then set out to the east.

He waited for as long as he dared on the far side of the town for his travelling companions but none appeared. He had seen and heard nothing to suggest they had been caught, but nevertheless concluded he couldn't risk waiting any longer. It was almost certain that patrols were searching the area.

A little over an hour later, keeping to the fields with the main Cardiff road to his right, he came across a small village. A terrace of small cottages crowded the pavement at the side of the road but beyond them he could just make out a group of larger buildings.

He by-passed the small rectangular strips of garden behind the cottages and crossed a narrow side lane. He could now make out larger gardens and smart, middle-class dwellings, surrounded by tall fir and poplar trees. The nearest house had a neatly trimmed lawn and all were set back from the road, their privacy protected by high surrounding fences and hedges overhanging the pavement. Here, Kurt realised, was the type of neighbourhood which might yield some means of useful transport.

He moved to the rear of the first garden and glanced over the fence, assessing the unlit windows of the large detached house and those of the garage at its side.

He would need to check out the front of the house before making his move. Shuffling towards the main road, he followed the hedge until he found a driveway. There was nobody about and he edged his way up the gravel until he could peer through the small panes of grimy glass in the garage doors. Although dark, he could make out the clear contours of a car. He glanced over his shoulder to the road behind him. All seemed quiet and he took a step further, reaching out and checking the handle of the nearest double door. They were locked but the rattle of the metal hasp which held them made him take a step back to the edge of the drive.

He stood in the shelter of the hedge, half hidden from the road but acutely aware that anyone passing by would instantly suspect he was up to no good. Another quick glance and he hurried down the side of the garage, looking for another way in. There was a door at the back of the building but, again, this was firmly locked and he cast about for some means of forcing an entry.

At a distance of some eighty feet, Kurt spotted a timber shed at the opposite corner of the lawn and sheltering beneath an elm tree. There, he guessed, he might find some garden tools which could be used to force one of the doors quickly enough to get into the garage unseen. Again, he checked his surroundings and made out across the damp grass.

At the window of her father's study, Juliette could barely believe what she saw. A man wearing a long raincoat, bending low, was trotting about on the lawn. She stared, jaw open, before edging backwards towards the hallway. Keeping her eyes on the scene outside the study window, she reached for the telephone and dialled a single digit. The reply, when it came, sounded irritated.

"Quickly, please. I'm in a hurry."

The operator noted the voice at the other end of the line was that of a young girl. Her tone became even more fractious.

"It is Monday, you know." She spoke as if this should be explanation enough. "It's our busiest day and we're very short staffed."

Juliette knew the pinch faced telephone operator well. She also knew that the back room of the village Post Office had only ever had a staff of one. She let it pass. "Please, quickly, I need the Police."

The tone changed to the incredulous. "The Police? Are you sure dear?"

"Yes, absolutely sure. Hurry, please."

"Be it on your own head, dear. They're very busy, you know, with all these escaped Prisoners of War about."

"Oh my God, of course. Hurry, for Christ's sake."

The operator made clicking noises with the tip of her tongue. "Well, really. There's no call for language like that." There was a pause while the operator clucked over her lines. "I know your parents, you know." Her voice sounded a triumphant note. "They wouldn't be happy to know you were using profanity on their telephone, that's for sure." The line went dead briefly as the call was disconnected before Juliette heard the ringing tone return.

A tired male voice answered after a few seconds. Juliette launched into a hurried account of events, ending with "Can you get here quickly? He's still in the garden." She carried the 'phone to the full length of its cord and strained to see through the study window. "I think he's in the shed."

The Policeman's tone at the other end of the line barely rose above his habitual monotone.

"Right you are, Miss. Well now, I can't get anyone out to you as things stand."

"What? Why on Earth not? He could be one of the German Prisoners of War."

"That's right, Miss, he could be. I still can't get anyone out to you. Not until you tell me your address."

She breathed out in a long sigh and quickly gave it. "Right you are, Miss. Now, I must ask you to stay indoors and make no attempt to approach the man. He could be dangerous. Do you understand that? We've heard rumours, unconfirmed mind, that these men may be armed." In Cowbridge Police Station, the Sergeant gazed wearily at the telephone receiver. The line had gone dead. He shook his head, laboriously tore the sheet of notepaper from his pad and stalked across the room. He put on his helmet and called to two constables drinking tea by the station's enquiry desk.

Back in her father's study, Juliette Jenkins peered nervously into the garden. She could just make out a dark silhouette moving behind the shed window. It wouldn't take the man long, she realised, to find whatever it was he was looking for. Whatever that was, the Policeman's warning had made her realise it would probably be used as a weapon. She glanced at her watch. If they were living in Cardiff, she grumbled quietly, the Police would respond far quicker. Cowbridge moved at such a slow pace, she wouldn't have been surprised if they didn't turn up until tomorrow morning.

She made a decision. Armed Nazi or not, she wasn't about to allow a disreputable looking trespasser escape. She quickly grabbed a broom from the kitchen and left the house by the back door. Following the line of the hedge, she advanced holding her broom in front of her like a rifle.

She could hear the man stumbling about in the darkness of the shed and knew that if she was going to act, she must make her move quickly. The shed door had a small but heavy metal loop handle fitted by her father. He had taken it from an old wardrobe and fitted a second handle next to it on the door-frame. On the odd occasion that he had stored anything of value in the shed, he had wrapped a padlocked chain round the two handles to secure it.

Juliette deftly slipped the broom handle horizontally through the two handles until the head of the broom rested against the metal. She took a step back. For almost a minute, nothing happened and the girl remained transfixed, her heart pumping. When the door was suddenly pushed open, Juliette jumped a full step backwards. The broom handle rattled but held. Twice more the door closed then opened sharply, hammering against the wooden pole. The broom bucked and rocked, but held firm.

In silence, Juliette backed slowly towards the safety of the house. She wished she had brought a kitchen knife with her. On reconsideration, she decided perhaps a tea-tray might provide a better defence. Better still, she had won the 100 yard sprint at her school sports day for the last three years. She eyed the back door and mentally rehearsed slamming the door and pushing home the bolt.

She could barely contain her relief when she heard the gate next to the garage click open. A voice that was ponderously slow but which she immediately identified as that of authority, called her name.

Sergeant Harris strolled to her side, placed his hands on his hips and gazed at the rattling garden shed. "I take it you would be Miss Jenkins?

The girl nodded, keeping her eyes fixed on the bucking broom handle.

"And that's our friend in there is it?"

Juliette nodded and pointed with a badly controlled shaking finger, explaining unnecessarily, "I jammed the door shut. I didn't know how long you were going to be."

The Sergeant nodded. "We got here as quickly as we could, but the other van is out looking for these escaped prisoners." He looked round at the two constables at his side. "And so is the rest of the shift, so we'd better get chummy back to the station as quick as possible. We've left the front desk unattended." He grinned. "We don't want our tea money pinched now, do we?" He took a couple of paces towards the shed, reaching under his uniform jacket and pulling a revolver from its holster.

Like many of his colleagues, Sergeant Harris wasn't entirely at ease carrying a firearm. Before 1939, very few British police officers had handled a pistol, let alone routinely carried or fired one.

"You'd better go back inside the house Miss, and lock the door. I'm not at all sure how this thing works." He nodded at the revolver, catching her look of uncertainty. "I am joking. Just a precaution." He jerked his head towards the back door and nodded again in an attempt to appear reassuring.

Harris beckoned to the two younger constables, hovering nervously in his considerable shadow. Sergeant Harris was a large man; well over six feet and barrel-chested. He had played Rugby Union as a youth but no level of fitness or physical size would help him if the man currently locked in the shed was carrying a firearm.

"Careful Sergeant." The constables both moved further behind their Sergeant.

Harris stopped in his tracks and stood upright, a pained expression across his broad face. "Thank you Constable, for your advice." He motioned with his free hand. "Now get yourselves up here and stop hiding behind me." The three men edged closer to the shed door. "Let's not give him a chance to make a bolt for it." The Sergeant made a circular movement with his free hand. The two constables glanced uncertainly at each other. "Well go on then. Surround him." Reluctantly, the younger men moved forward by a short pace. "Ready?" They all crouched forward slightly, like cricketers in the slips.

Harris placed his hand on the broom handle and cleared his throat. He tried to control his voice, raising the revolver to chest height and pointing it at the centre of the door.

"Right then, you in there. This is the Police. You are surrounded and you are under arrest. Do you understand?"

There was a silence as the three men on the lawn leaned further towards the shed, listening for a response.

"Do you suppose he left before we got here, Sarg?"

The Sergeant shot him a grimace. "You should wish. He's in there all right." He addressed the shed door again. "Now we don't want any trouble. I am armed but you'll come to no harm if you do as you're told." He held the revolver up as if in confirmation. Another pause. "Do you understand?" The officers waited for a reply. "I repeat, I am armed. I am going to open the door now. You will come out with your hands raised.

Is that clear?" There was a shuffling noise from within the shed as if a small pile of timber had slipped to the ground. The two constables took a step back. Harris waited until they had resumed their positions before speaking again. "I'll take that as a 'yes'. I'm opening the door so put your hands up now."

He pulled the broom handle to one side, throwing it aside as it came free and grasping the stock of his revolver in both hands. He took a step back. The gun all but disappeared within his large palms but he hoped his business-like stance, feet apart and firmly planted on the ground, knees slightly bent, would give the appearance of confidence. As if to reinforce the image, he called into the darkness of the shed. "Come on, now. Let's have no nonsense." The men stood in silence, gazing at the dark chasm and open door. It swung listlessly on its hinges. To add to the moment, a light drizzle started to fall.

From deep within the gloom, a seed box fell to the hard cement floor with a rattle that jerked the two constables into animation. As one, they leapt forward, flattening themselves against the timber side of the shed. The Sergeant glared briefly at them then stiffened, his shoulders dropping several inches. His knees bent further and he leant forward into the open doorway. The constables moved from their hiding place, each struggling to use the other as cover.

From within the house, Juliette backed away from the window of her father's study, involuntarily reaching behind her for the telephone.

To the surprise of everyone present, Kurt Rheinspier appeared, blinking, in the shed doorway. He glanced skywards, squinting at the thick cover of clouds and, feeling the rain, pulled his collar around his ears. Recovering his composure, Sergeant Harris jerked the barrel of his revolver upwards as the prisoner raised his hands above his head. As Rheinspier came to a halt before him, Harris nodded approval. "Right then. That's better. That wasn't too difficult now, was it?" The constables, attempting belated bravery, moved to either side of their prisoner. "Well, come on then," the Sergeant instructed, "get a proper hold of him." The German pulled himself up to his full height and placed his hands on the back of his head. Almost apologetically, the constables took an arm each and moved his hands until they joined in the small of his back. A pair of handcuffs was produced and placed around his wrists.

One of the constables, feeling his courage return, grinned at the prisoner.

"Now then, Fritz. Forward march."

The Sergeant returned his revolver to its holster. "Less of the cheek, Constable. Chances are this man is an officer in the German Army. He may even be an aristocrat, for all we know. He deserves a little respect, at least."

Rheinspier smiled and offered a slight bow to the senior Policeman. "Thank you Sergeant. You are most gracious."

The constables stared at the man standing between them and the Sergeant uttered a quiet oath. Again, he looked the man up and down, taking in more detail of his shabby appearance, aware that he couldn't disguise his disbelief. They were about to escort their prisoner away when a polite coughing noise attracted their attention. All but the German prisoner turned and gazed again at the shed. In the doorway, a small man, dressed in a tweed sports jacket and grey worsted trousers, slowly raised his hands. He smiled apologetically before slowly moving his hands down, offering his wrists for another pair of handcuffs. Rheinspier smiled and turned back to the Sergeant.

"Gentlemen, may I introduce *Hauptmann* Ewald von Kleist. You suggested that I may be of aristocratic descent. I regret that I am not, but my friend and comrade, von Kleist here, most certainly is." He beamed fondly at the other prisoner as if reunited with an old friend. "Unfortunately, he is far too aristocratic to have learned English. He speaks impeccable French and Italian, but he regards English as a language which is too... inelegant. Too plebeian, you understand?" The German shrugged apologetically.

Monday 12th March 1945, 16:00 hrs.

Pen Castell Farm stood to the south of the main road which leads in a straight line from west to east between Kenfig Hill and Cefn Cribwr. Named after ancient earthworks perched atop a gently sloping hill, in 1945 it was occupied by William Jones and his extended family.

William, his wife Esme, a peculiarly gaunt woman from Cumbrian farming stock, his elderly mother and their three sons were all wedged into a five roomed cottage which clung to the southern edge of their small farm. Fortunately, the boys spent the majority of their days in school and William seldom remained indoors during daylight hours. Mrs Jones and her mother-in-law therefore found they had time to spread themselves through the small kitchen and back parlour, cooking, washing and generally keeping their modest household in order.

Esme Jones' own mother had been born in the nearby Afan Valley but had moved to Cumbria in the early 1900's after her sheep farming parents' flock had been blighted by a series of fatal epidemics. At the time, it had been concluded that the animals had contracted 'Pulpy Kidney'; a condition for which there was no cure. Years later, it was discovered that the disease, which remains fatal to infected animals, is caused by a rapid multiplication of Clostridial Perfringens spores. These produce a lethal toxin in the small intestine, although it is doubtful that even that knowledge would have helped Esme's parents. Ironically often caused by a sudden improvement in the animals' diet, the first sign that anything is amiss is the lamb's sudden death.

Convinced they were farming on 'poisoned land' (a suspicion oddly founded in fact, as the spore-forming organisms which cause the disease are frequently found in the soil) they sold up and moved north to a dairy farm in the Cumbrian Lake District.

Unable to raise much cash from the sale of their 'poisoned' farm, they were forced to become tenants in Cumbria until Esme's small family was all but destroyed by the Great War.

Early in the hostilities, her father had found himself the subject of local whispers and rumours. He was accused of being a shirker; a coward who held back from volunteering for the forces. Later, in November 1915 agricultural workers were given reserved occupation status and exempt from military service, but her father had already volunteered.

He was accepted into the 9th Battalion of the Lancashire Fusiliers and was sent to Gallipoli. On the moonless night of 6th August 1915, wading ashore through chest deep water, Esme's father had been shot in the shoulder. Left unattended, he had died, alongside several hundred others, on the beach of Suvla.

Her mother never fully recovered from the shock of receiving the War Department's telegram. She died three years later, it was said from grief. Aged just sixteen and an only child, Esme used her meagre inheritance to move back to the valleys of South Wales. There she met and married William Jones, recently returned from the Western Front. It was largely thanks to his experiences of claustrophobic dugouts and front-line trenches that he decided to decline his father's offer to get him a job in the mines. Instead, he looked for a job that offered him fresh air and open spaces.

Funded by Esme's savings and a mortgage, they managed to buy the small farm at Pen Castell in Kenfig Hill.

William and Esme worked hard and, to a modest extent, prospered. The despair of another declaration of war with Germany in 1939 had reminded William of his experiences in Northern France. He had occasionally met up with old Army friends and had learned of the horror of the treatment some had suffered in the Prisoner of War camps in Flanders and Belgium.

When he had read early reports of the Bridgend Germans' rowdy behaviour; their raucous singing, frequent fights and disruption at the prison camp, his stocky frame fairly shook with anger. When William sat down for breakfast and opened his newspaper, Esme and his mother invariably found themselves obliged to shepherd their boys out of the kitchen, even though they might have been too early for school. The women would tut around him, quietly chiding him for his bad language. They would offer suggestions that he 'ignore the silly stories' or try to divert his attention to the string of tasks he had earmarked for the day.

When he heard and read of the escape of no fewer than seventy prisoners from Island Farm Camp over the weekend, no amount of reasoning would deflate his fury. He should have enjoyed his afternoon cup of tea and a few minutes rest before returning to his sheep. Instead he had swung his rolled up newspaper, angrily swatting the kitchen table in a snowstorm of shredded newspaper. He had grasped the paper as if it had been the neck of an absconder and twisted until his powerful hands tore the paper in two. Throwing it aside, he had stormed from the house, pausing only to grab his stick and slam the door closed behind him.

Timorously, Glen and Heather, the family's two border collies, fell in step at his heels. Eager only to please and with no concept of war or human conflict, they instinctively knew when their master was upset.

In Jones' mind, the lax behaviour of the guards was clearly to blame. He had seen the Army men, off duty, in the local pubs. To him, they appeared slovenly, undisciplined and almost always drunk. The prisoners' bad behaviour was invariably a topic of discussion when he visited the livestock market in Bridgend. There had been complaints from the Chairman of the Chamber of Commerce, a local butcher who regularly attended the market, about the loud singing of the officers and the tardiness of the German junior ranks when they were on work details at local farms. He had twice been approached to take prison labour onto his farm and, despite risking the anger of several local committees, had flatly refused.

It was clear from the disrespect the prisoners showed for their guards that an escape would be attempted. More dangerously, civilians would be put at risk from attack as the fleeing Nazis tried to put distance between themselves and the camp.

Jones now regretted shredding his newspaper before he had finished reading all the details. He couldn't recall whether the report said the escapees had any weapons. A question which might prove pertinent as he never carried a firearm himself. He had an old rusting shotgun locked away in the attic somewhere but it hadn't been touched in twenty years. Unconsciously, his grip tightened on the heavy staff he habitually used when out in the fields.

Entering his top meadow, Pen Maes, leading up to the old earthworks marking the site of an ancient fort, the farmer placed two fingers into the corners of his mouth and emitted two shrill whistles. Obediently, Glen and Heather broke into a crouching run. Heading to left and right of the hilltop, they encircled the flock of ewes which stood unperturbed between them.

It was a peaceful afternoon with little wind and only the slightest hint of a chill in the air. William tried to settle into finishing his day's work and to forget about the problems away in Bridgend.

The collies should have settled on their haunches a few yards either side of the sheep but instead, first Glen then Heather seemed to become distracted, moving further up the rise than necessary and then disappearing from view altogether. William could only guess they were heading for a clump of trees that stood a short distance from the earthworks. He could only see the top half of the trees from where he stood and assumed they had spotted a stray ewe that had wandered from the flock. He whistled again, recalling them. In reply, from beyond the hillock, he heard Glen utter two loud barks. He whistled again, more urgently, the signal to retrieve. Still the dogs did not return. By now, the other sheep had raised their heads from the thick grass and were looking idly about for the source of the disturbance. William strode through the flock and, though familiar with his presence, the animals cautiously moved aside, bleating a mild protest.

Reaching the apex of the hill, William shielded his eyes from the receding sun and saw both his dogs crouched, tongues lolling, their eyes fixed on the clump of trees to his right. Catching sight of his master, Glen barked again, rising slightly on his haunches. He took two paces forward towards the trees and crouched again.

He had trained his dogs never to bark at a ewe and instinctively, William opened his mouth to shout a reprimand. He held back just in time. Flattened against the trunk of a broad elm, the dark figure of a man turned his head in William's direction and the low sun glowed briefly against the pale skin of his face. Muttering a quiet oath and with renewed resolve, the farmer increased his pace, striding across the meadow. He lifted his staff and held it in both hands across his chest like the shaft of an ancient weapon. The man, his eyes rolling towards the dogs, managed to utter a few words.

"Please, you help. Please."

A few more paces and William came to a halt a little over ten feet from the man. He raised an index finger and both collies immediately came to his side. They sat, waiting to receive a congratulatory pat. The farmer grinned first at the man, still hugging the tree trunk and then at his dogs. He fondled the velvet of their ears briefly before pointing his staff at the man's chest.

"You'd better come along with me."

"Yes, yes. But the dogs, please." He glanced nervously again at Glen and Heather. "They do not like me."

William thought for a moment. "You just behave yourself. No funny business. Understand?" The man nodded energetically. "And I'll keep the dogs off. All right?" He nodded again.

William waved his stick towards the bottom of the hill. Cautiously at first, the man edged away from his tree and, hands incongruously raised above his head, began to follow the narrow path down the slope.

They made a strange procession; the shabbily dressed prisoner, hands aloft, followed by Jones and his stick, the two collies trotting happily at his side.

They reached Kenfig Hill Police Station within twenty minutes having exchanged no conversation whatever. As he guided the man through the double doors, William quietly wondered how he would explain himself if it transpired that the man wasn't actually an escaped German Prisoner of War after all.

The Desk Sergeant, freshly briefed on procedure in relation to recaptured Nazis, was quick to grasp the situation and locked the man in an interview room at the back of his Police Station. Returning to the front desk, he pulled a sheet of paper from a shallow drawer and licked the tip of his pencil.

"Now then, sir. I need your name and address."

"Don't be so bloody foolish, Davey."

The Sergeant sniffed. "Sorry, Bill. Force of habit." Carefully, he wrote William's name at the head of the form followed by his address. "I don't suppose there's any point asking for your identity card, is there?"

William shook his head. "You need to be asking that Nazi these questions, not me." He nodded in the direction of the back office.

"Fair point, Bill. Fair point." He put the pencil down. "One thing though; these escaped prisoners have been travelling about in groups of two and three. I don't suppose you saw any others when you were out and about?" The big man shook his head. "Then I think we need to go a-searching for a while. You doing anything for the next hour or two?" William shook his head again.

The prisoner was moved to the safer confines of the Police Station's only cell and four constables were drawn reluctantly from the tea room. They had been about to go off shift but, as their Sergeant reminded them, there was a war on. Two special constables were due to come on duty shortly and in the meantime, he left a further lone Constable in charge of the front desk. The young man had glanced at his senior officer doubtfully, reminding him he had an injured foot and had been granted light duties only.

"Injured foot be buggered," the Sergeant had intoned to William as they left the station. "He's got an in-growing toenail. And if I'd suggested he go plodding over your fields, he'd have been the first to complain." The older men both snorted in mutual understanding. "Kids today. They don't know what proper work is."

The search party, accompanied by Glen and Heather, turned off Kenfig Hill's main street and headed up the footpath towards the earthworks. The Sergeant nodded down at the dogs. "You know the Army is going to bring in trained tracker dogs to help with the search."

The farmer grunted. "Trained or not, they'd better not worry my sheep."

"From what I've heard, they wouldn't worry a tabby cat." The Policeman touched the revolver he had strapped to his uniform. "My guess is that most Jerries understand a gun barrel better than any dog."

William said nothing but fingered Glen and Heather's ears as if reassuring them of their value.

They were approaching the peak of the hill and William pointed out the copse of trees where he had found the prisoner. The party stopped and looked about the wide fields, shielding their eyes as they turned to the west, down the valley towards Port Talbot. William glanced by habit to check his flock of ewes. They were coming into lamb and he couldn't afford to lose any animals.

"That's strange." His brow furrowed as he scanned the ridge of his pastures. "The flock should be lower down the field by now." He explained to the Policeman, unfamiliar with all but the rudiments of farming, that sheep were creatures of habit. Each evening, they were rounded up by the dogs and moved to the bottom field, nearer the house, where they were given a bit of extra feed to supplement their grass diet. "That's where they would have been heading when the dogs discovered that German". He had expected them to make their own way down the slope by now. Instead, they had moved to the opposite end of the field, beyond the earthworks. They were crowded into a corner, enclosed on two sides by a stone wall. William nodded in their direction. "That's not right. They're not feeding. Something has pushed them down there."

William scanned the horizon again, checking for anything else in his familiar surroundings that might be out of place. "If my ewes are over there," he nodded in their direction, "then something or somebody is over there." He nodded down the slope towards the bottom field and the path that led to his small cottage.

Quickly understanding, the policemen spread out across the contour of the hill and moved in line towards a post marked out by William's pointing staff. A distant gate marked the exit from the fields and his eyes remained fixed on it as they progressed down the slope.

As they closed in, a ragged figure broke cover from a hedge to their right and ran towards the gate. The Sergeant blew his whistle and enthusiastically Glen and Heather bounded off across the field. Two constables followed, somewhat slower, one of them struggling to hold his helmet on his head.

Heather reached the man first and gleefully grabbed his trouser leg between her teeth as he tried to climb over the gate. He lifted his foot and she swung free of the ground. Delighted at the game, she wagged her tail and tried to bark through clenched teeth. One of the constables drew his pistol and shouted a command. Whether the fugitive understood English or not, the old Sergeant had been right in his assertion that he would understand the meaning of a pointing barrel. He raised his hands so quickly he fell from the top bar of the gate. He landed in thick mud with Heather excitedly jumping on his chest and licking his face.

A further two prisoners were found shortly afterwards, given away by the indignant cries of Mrs Jones' flock of hens. They had been trying to liberate a few eggs, unaware that the hen house had been emptied of eggs a few hours before.

The policemen marched their prisoners down the main road back to the Police Station at Kenfig Hill, the younger constables smirking loftily at the glances of passing civilians. The Sergeant could think only of the pages of paperwork the afternoon's work would generate. He would be unlikely to see his fireside for several hours.

Monday 12th March 1945, 18:30 hrs.

For some weeks, following instructions from their senior officers, *Luftwaffe* pilots and navigators imprisoned at Camp 198 had been lying back on makeshift mattresses and groundsheets, gazing at the sky. Mistaking their inactivity for either lethargy, acquiescence or both, the camp guards had paid them little attention. They had failed to identify the apparently idle prisoners as the more senior and experienced pilots and navigators in the camp. They hadn't noticed the carefully drawn plans and notes the prisoners had been writing on scraps of paper each time an allied aircraft had flown overhead. Neither had they heard the whispered late-night discussions between the airmen and their senior officers, nor found the cache of papers carefully collected, sorted and hidden behind a locker in one of the pilot's rooms.

Had they noticed any of these things, the guards may have deduced that the prisoners had been planning an escape, as their observations could only possibly be of use to them if they were free of the camp.

The airmen had been able to ascertain that at least a dozen small military aircraft were making short sorties in the area. They seemed to regularly leave a nearby airfield, returning within thirty to sixty minutes. The flights had been made every day, starting shortly after sunrise and seldom continuing after dark. The aircraft had all been small, single engine planes, some of which the German pilots had never seen before.

One of the more readily recognisable aircraft had been a Miles M14 'Magister'. Resplendent in yellow livery, it had been easy to spot from the ground. One of the officers, not a pilot but invited into the tight circle of plane-spotters in recognition of his knowledge of civilian aircraft, had been able to confirm the M14 was widely used before the war by amateur and other civilian pilots. It had gone out of production in 1941.

Another aircraft seen regularly had been the Avro 626 biplane which had also been out of production for several years. There seemed to be only one example buzzing through the Glamorgan skies but it gave an important clue to the silent watchers on the ground.

The spotters had enjoyed their days, gazing into the steel grey skies above the camp and noting their observations for later collation and discussion. On the morning of 26th February, however, they had all heard a sound which had set their pulses skipping. Overhead somewhere, a small fleet of far more powerful, faster aircraft was approaching. Men who had no knowledge of the work being done by the spotters had emerged from their huts. Prisoners and guards alike had gazed at the clouds, searching for the source of the noise.

The throaty gurgle of engines had grown in volume until one of the officers on the ground had let out an incoherent yelp and pointed. Breaking cover to their north and heading west, first two, then four and eventually six small aircraft flashed their silver grey wingtips before plunging once more, as if dancing a Conga, behind a cloth of grey cloud. Moments later, the silver posse had been spotted again, flying in a tight crocodile, dropping out of the clouds and banking to the left. Like so many of the other light aircraft they had watched, they sank gently towards the western horizon before vanishing behind a row of trees.

Two of the German airmen had glanced at each other. One of them nodded imperceptibly and, as if the moment of interest had passed, they had wandered casually to their hut.

The aircraft they had seen were all North American T-6 Texans. The neat little fighters had finally removed any doubt that had been lingering in their minds.

Later that afternoon, the *Luftwaffe* men had gathered in Hut Nineteen. With their own sentries posted at the door and at three windows with different outlooks, they could speak openly, confident they would not be overheard.

What they had been watching, they had all agreed, were (with the exception of today's flight of Texans) simple, lightweight primary trainers. The Texans however were used by American and Canadian military flyers as advanced trainers. More importantly, they were also used as swift attack fighters. They had a relatively slow cruise speed of about 230 kilometres per hour but, significantly, were known to have a range of over 1,100 kilometres on a full tank of fuel. Although none of the men present had previously been aware of it, somewhere nearby there must be a military airfield.

They had concluded, accurately, that the airfield must be used principally to train new pilots. The aircraft they had seen were all twin seat, simple, light aircraft that would be quick to manoeuvre on the ground and easy to operate in the air. Would a training base this far west be as heavily guarded, they speculated, as a fully operational RAF base?

They had spent the following twelve days carefully plotting take-off and landing paths, triangulating as closely as they could where the airfield could be.

At least four men included in the escape plan became determined to make for the airfield. They had agreed to be led by a *Luftwaffe* officer whose job it would be to find the airfield and then pilot one of the non-flyers out. An *Oberfeldwebel* or Flight Sergeant, one of only two NCO's included in the entire escape plan, was chosen to pilot a second purloined aircraft with the fourth member of the group as his passenger. They had decided to keep their plan to themselves, telling only their Commanding Officer. Although it might have been useful to have others accompany them to help force an entry to the airfield, they had decided they would make the attempt without additional help. It was possible that there wouldn't be enough aircraft for more than four men and, more importantly, a larger flight of aircraft might attract unwanted attention, if not from the RAF then from their own fighters and anti-aircraft gunners.

At the designated time, in the early hours of Sunday morning, the men had crawled the length of the escape tunnel and, as planned, gathered under a group of trees at the edge of the nearest field. They knew they had to go west and the obvious route to follow was the A48 road heading towards Swansea. As the sun rose, they had crossed a shallow ditch to gain the cover of a hedge lining the edge of a field. The men had squatted in the shadows, discussing their tactics. They would carry on until traffic started to move along the road. It was likely that search parties would be out soon, combing the roads and fields. They all understood the importance of getting as far from the camp as possible. One of the men had peered over the hedge, quickly withdrawing and reporting that he could see no patrols or vehicles. Ahead of them and to their right he had seen thin grey trails of smoke rising into the moist air. There was apparently a village nearby.

They had decided to split up. The Flight Sergeant or *Oberfeldwebel* and his accompanying Panzer officer, a Captain or *Rittmeister*, would take a more southerly route, away from the road, cutting across the field they were hiding in before circling round to the right to regain their westerly course. The Flight Lieutenant or *Hauptmann* Eric Shaef, would travel with the fourth member of the party, a *Wehrmacht* First Lieutenant or *Oberleutnant*, and cross the road to the north west across the fields behind the village.

Shaef's travelling companion was a bespectacled, tall and spidery infantry officer in his mid thirties named Eitzinger. He had been taken prisoner within a few hours of the Allies' Normandy landing not far from the small village of Bény-sur-Mer. Captured by an infantry patrol, it was rumoured that he had been found lying face down in a ditch, covered in mud and shaking with fear. His reputation had not been helped when it was suggested that his captors were French. His indignity at being captured being utterly crushed beneath the belief that he had been taken prisoner by a force that his fellow officers had written off as vanquished. The patrol, in fact, belonged to the French speaking *Régiment de la Chaudière* of the 3rd Canadian Infantry Division. Such niceties were lost, however, on Shaef and his pro-Nazi brother officers. Nevertheless, Eitzinger was senior to Shaef and was, until proved unworthy of it, entitled to the respect his rank demanded. Another factor which Shaef had to admit might prove helpful to him was the *Oberleutnant's* exemplary command of English.

They had crossed the broad A48 road without a hitch. There were few vehicles about in any case due to petrol rationing and even fewer at that early hour of a Sunday morning.

Shaef and the *Oberleutnant* had bent as low as his lanky form would allow as they ran across the ploughed field away from the road. The taller man's boots had quickly become covered in clods of mud and he had stumbled, almost falling in his clumsy attempts to shake them clear. Glancing over his shoulder, Shaef had slowed briefly, grabbed the senior officer by the shoulder and pulled him towards a large open sided tithe barn. There, they had clambered over several bales of hay before, panting and sweating despite the chill wind. Falling forwards, they had dropped into a deep pile of loose hay, hidden deep within the barn.

They had eaten a few biscuits, saved from Red Cross parcels received at the camp a fortnight earlier and, pulling more loose hay over themselves, had fallen asleep.

When Shaef awoke next, he had had to squint and hold his wrist free of the shadows in order to read his watch. It was six o'clock. Apart from the *Oberleutnant's* heavy breathing, all around was darkness and silence.

The men had remained, either dozing or searching the skies in vain for tell-tale traces of aircraft until well into the night. Lying on his back in their hiding place Shaef had concluded, quite reasonably, that any training flights would have been suspended while effort was being put into locating escaped prisoners. He had grinned in the darkness, reminding his travelling companion that this was part of the reason they had a duty to escape; to confuse the enemy and use up his resources on search parties instead of placing men in the field of conflict.

At around midnight the men had broken cover, moving slowly and following the shadowed lines of trees and hedges until they had reached the village of Laleston. They had crossed the High Street unnoticed and had scrambled painfully over a blackthorn hedge, following the line of a narrow lane leading north from the village. The night sky had been shrouded in thick cloud that night and, despite his skill as a navigator, Shaef could only guess at the direction they were taking. They were hungry, thirsty and Eitzinger complained of pain in his calf where the thorny hedge had inflicted a deep cut.

He had asked the junior man whether they could look for a farm or a village store somewhere; anywhere, in fact, where they might find supplies. The *Hauptmann* had considered the request, reminded of his own empty stomach, and agreed that if such an opportunity presented itself, they would investigate the possibility of committing a bit of necessary larceny.

No such opportunity had arisen, despite the fact that they had crossed another main road through a village. Before a shop or farm presented them with any opportunities for plunder, they both tripped in the dark and somersaulted down a steep embankment. They came to rest on the far side of a row of neat cottage gardens, bruised and shaken.

Eitzinger had landed squarely on his backside, his thin legs spread in a 'V' shape before him. Shaking his head, he had grabbed the young flyer's shoulder, pointing at a neatly planted row of carrots. They were lined up with military precision beyond a low picket fence. He had nodded encouragingly at his guide. Even raw carrot was better than nothing.

Shaef had looked cautiously over the fence and, leaning forward, had reached towards the nearest plant, its lush green fronds waving almost imperceptibly in the morning breeze. A sharp rattle arrested his progress. A shaft of light from the back door of the cottage illuminated his hand, frozen in mid theft. He pulled back with a jerk, the carrot teasingly and suddenly beyond his reach.

At her kitchen door, ignorant of the vegetable patch drama, Mrs Gwladys Jenkins of High Street, Cefn Cribwr tipped a tray of coal ash into a large metal bin, clattering the lid firmly over it and withdrawing to her warm fire and kettle. She had risen from her bed at her customary early hour to see her daughter off to her job at The Arsenal and unseen, the Germans had watched her silhouette through a net curtain as she had busied herself over her stove. They may have imagined it, but the aroma of frying sausages and eggs seemed to permeate the air.

As the sun had risen, illuminating Monday morning with the first watery rays of dawn, Shaef had reached once more into Mrs Jenkins' garden, grasped the nearest fountain of foliage and pulled.

He had been rewarded with two medium sized muddy carrots and the two men had rolled away from the fence down the slope and out of sight.

As the flyer lay on his back once more, he noted the direction of the long morning shadows and realised they had been travelling north. Pocketing their stolen meal, they moved, bent double again to the bottom of the slope and through a gap in a farm hedge. They had turned left, heading west and, they judged, towards the airfield.

In the surprising morning glare, they needed to find cover. They had crouched in the shadows of a group of trees, sufficiently clear of roads and houses to be safe. They had been lucky, so far, to avoid any search parties or patrols. In fact, there had seemed to be no military presence in the area at all.

Eitzinger had leaned back against the trunk of an elm tree and started to rub the soil from his breakfast with the sleeve of his coat. He had sniffed the vegetable for contaminants, commenting that, had they been in Germany, the place would have been swarming with every conceivable uniform from the SS to the Hitler Youth.

Shaef had gently reproached the senior man, assuring him that he for one would have greatly preferred to be back in the

Fatherland. Taking a firm bite from his carrot he had immediately spat, ejecting mud and grit. The British, he had declared, couldn't even grow a decent vegetable.

They had rested for the remainder of the day, escaping detection among trees and fallen leaves. As the sun had finally sunk over the hills to the west, Shaef had once again taken a compass bearing and, kicking Eitzinger's leg, roused him from sleep. Not for the first time, he had accused the senior man of complacency, questioning how he could sleep at such a time. Eitzinger had smiled back, unconcerned. As any infantryman would have told him, soldiers in the front line quickly learn to grab sleep at any time they can.

The two men pulled themselves stiffly to their feet, stretched and headed off in the direction of the setting sun. Their new route took them diagonally back up the hill and inevitably, their path soon converged with the main road. Finding themselves surrounded by densely packed rows of terraced cottages, they resigned themselves to the reality that Britain was not entirely made up of green fields and isolated barns. The road ahead of them was clearly leading them west and, unaware that the airfield they were seeking was now a little over a mile and a half due south, they continued walking.

A few cars plodded cautiously by, their headlights all but obscured by the blackout regulations. Cyclists had wearily peddled past, heads down and intent on getting home after what had no doubt been an exhausting day at work. Pedestrians hunched below the early signs of a light shower turned up their collars and passed without a word or second glance.

Ahead, the wide main road angled down a long, curving hill, bordered on either side by shops, small houses and a shabby stone built chapel. The two men could see in the gloom through an industrial mist and at a distance of several miles, the outstretched arms of Port Talbot's dockside cranes. A thick deep grey blanket hung over a coke washery and a purple-grey cloud belched from the town's steel works. Eitzinger had nudged his companion. If they couldn't find the airfield, they might have a crack at boarding a ship at the docks. The younger man shot him a glance, hissing in no uncertain terms that they were going to fly out. He had been planning for too long to change direction now.

Five hundred yards further down the street, Special Constables Ernie Johns and Des Williams were preparing to start their shift. The clock on the wall of the mess room at the rear of Kenfig Hill Police Station read twenty past six. They had arrived early for a briefing from their Sergeant on the latest situation regarding the escaped prisoners from Bridgend and had just had time for a bacon roll and a cup of tea. They were due on patrol at six thirty. Ernie Johns belched happily and grinned. He cast a fond glance at the short, rotund woman busying herself in the adjoining kitchen. Even his missus didn't make a bacon roll like Mrs Helston. One of the very few advantages of being a voluntary policeman was the extra ration the Police canteen miraculously provided at the start and end of every shift.

Constable Williams rose from his seat, nodded at the clock, and walked ponderously towards the door. Ernie joined him as both men pulled their coats and Police helmets into place.

"What would you do," Ernie was asking the other as they reached the door, "if you came face to face with a Nazi?"

Des Williams had no time to answer. As they stepped down to the pavement, they found themselves face to face with *Oberleutnant* Gerd Eitzinger and *Hauptmann* Eric Shaef. It is difficult to say definitively who was more surprised. Instinctively, however, both pairs of men recognised their natural enemy and reacted.

Ernie answered his own question by reaching into his voluminous coat. Misinterpreting the gesture as a move for a firearm, Eric thrust his hands into the air just as Ernie held up his police whistle. Gerd jabbed the younger man in the ribs and smiled innocently at the other Constable.

"Good evening Constable. Please excuse my friend. He has a strange sense of humour." He laughed, nudging the pilot again. Eric slowly lowered his hands and joined in with a forced giggle of his own.

Ernie Johns released the whistle and as it dangled at the end of its chain, instead produced his notebook. "May I see your identity papers, gentlemen?"

The German looked abashed. "I am so sorry. We both left our papers at our lodgings. We are working at one of the farms." He jerked his thumb up the hill behind them.

The constables glanced at each other.

"Oh, are you now?" PC Williams folded his arms, his feet planted firmly apart. "Don't you know the regulations, then?"

Gerd shook his head, still smiling. "We are Dutch. We haven't been very long in England, you see." Too late, he realised his mistake.

"England is it? Bugger me, you boys are confused aren't you." Each of the policemen took a firm hold of the man in front of him. "I think we'd better step indoors. It's time we had a proper chat." Guiding them firmly by the arm, they led each of the prisoners up the shallow steps into the Police Station.

Ernie smacked the brass dome on the desk, sending a sonorous chime through the building. He called into the back office.

"Sergeant. We have customers."

Monday 12th March 1945, 19:10 hrs

As Eric Shaef and Gerd Eitzinger were being gently but firmly shepherded into Kenfig Hill Police Station, three of their fellow officers were lying in a pile of leaf-mould, some seven miles away to the east.

Standing in a far corner of a large suburban garden, a large rhododendron bush, left chiefly untended for sixty years, had grown into a large umbrella of thick green foliage harbouring a sheltered void within.

At least three generations of small boys and girls had played games beneath that same bush which, at different times had been a subterranean cave, a coalmine, a nursery for teddy bears and, most recently, the perfect site from which to ambush Jerry storm-troopers.

On the evening of 12th March 1945, however, with a drizzling rain patting the leaves above them, it had taken on an entirely serious role.

Although young and fit, the three occupants had spent the previous forty two hours alternately walking and sheltering until, with aching legs and ankles, they had found themselves on the outskirts of Bridgend. This, they knew, was the nearest town. At least two of the men recognised the area from their march to the camp four months earlier and it dawned on them that, somehow, they had managed to cover no more than four kilometres in almost two days. Brazenly, they had struck out across the town, in full view, in a bid to make up time. Perhaps, they had reasoned, their presence in the middle of the day would cause less suspicion than moving about under cover of night. They weren't entirely sure, even, if there was a curfew in operation in Britain.

At some point, they had come across the town centre and a row of neatly kept shops. Modest offerings of basic vegetables, fruit and ironmongery lay displayed on make-shift benches in front of their windows. While two of the men provided cover, standing in the street as nonchalantly as their present circumstances and acting skills would allow, the third member of the group had managed to push a couple of apples into the pocket of his coat.

At another shop, they had stolen a large potato and at a third, a rabbit. How they expected to deal with these latter commodities was yet to be decided.

Their greatest discovery, however, was made later that afternoon. Easily identifiable as being militarily important by its high barbed wire fence and armed guard, they had stumbled across Number 38 Royal Ordnance Factory, Waterton.

The sign outside had given scant details of its exact purpose but the men had been happy to believe it was likely to be an arms depot of some sort. They immediately resolved to break in and take whatever weapons and ammunition they could before striking out towards Cardiff or Newport docks.

If it turned out to be a factory or store which held nothing of any use to them, they would satisfy themselves by searching for cash and causing as much damage as they could before making their escape.

As they sheltered beneath their rhododendron bush, finishing off the last of their apples, the plan seemed faultless. The three were all aged in their early twenties. Two were members of the *Luftwaffe*; a pilot and a gunner. The third member of the group was a young *SS* officer. Other than their age, they had in common an upbringing indoctrinated in Hitler's Germany which had left them in no doubt that the German people were the master race. As fit and feted young members of the Hitler Youth, it was their destiny to join the military and, ultimately, when the Fuhrer accepted the Allies' surrender, the ruling class of the new German Empire.

Shortly after seven o'clock that evening, leaving the rabbit and potato discarded on a damp carpet of leaves, they left their shelter. With rather more direction than before, they moved towards their target.

They were approaching the factory along a different route than earlier which took them unexpectedly along a wide stretch of highway. They didn't spot the guard post, set back from the road and obscured by trees, until it was too late to change tack.

Former Home Guard Private Harold Francis held his rifle, barrel forward, with purpose and determination. He had received a severe reprimand from his platoon Sergeant that morning for failing to hold his rifle at the ready when challenging a civilian. The civilian in question had been a local parson, well known to Harold who believed him to be quite harmless. That, however, as had been pointed out by the red faced Sergeant, was irrelevant. The platoon possessed only two rifles and, the senior man had threatened, if he didn't use it properly someone else would be given a go with it.

"Halt and identify yourselves." Knowing his Corporal was lurking a few feet away, he hoped his tone of voice sounded properly stern. He had spent several hours in the kitchen of his family home, practicing the same routine on his sixteen year old niece and receiving only a shower of girlish giggles in reply. If the awkward looking men in front of him gave the same reaction, he would go home and hang up his uniform for the last time. They seemed to be no older than him, which should have given him some small degree of confidence. Something about the men's demeanour, however, made him uneasy. They weren't talking, either to him or to each other. In fact, their expressions seemed oddly frozen. They weren't searching their pockets for their identity papers; a wartime habit which had become second nature when confronted by any sort of uniform.

Private Francis repeated the order, aware that his voice had lost its edge of authority. One of the three men took a step forward. His hands folding into tight fists. The other two men, realising what was in his mind, followed suit.

"Halt!" The voice startled Harold, let alone the three escaped prisoners. "You heard the soldier, you horrible shower!" The three turned, meeting the concentrated glare of a large, middle-aged Corporal and recognising in an instant the unmistakable authority carried by seasoned warrant officers.

Two more soldiers appeared from heavy foliage at the side of the road, large sticks held firmly and twitching at the small group. As one, the Germans raised their hands in surrender.

As they were being marched back towards Bridgend's town centre Police Station, and not for the first time, they reminded each other that they could not have served Germany if they had been shot while trying to escape. They couldn't have known that, between the four Home Guard men, their two rifles remained empty of ammunition.

Frustratingly for the Corporal and his men, as they were nearing the centre of town, a car pulled up alongside them. With much engine revving and door slamming, four men, dressed in the dark blue uniform of War Reserve Police Constables, scrambled excitedly onto the pavement, blocking the other men's path. During the course of some heated discussion and the production of various pieces of official paper, they claimed possession of the prisoners. The Home Guard, it was vociferously argued, had been 'stood down' in December of the previous year. The part-time soldiers, claimed the part-time constables, had no official status when it came to the arrest of suspected enemies of the state.

Besides, the Police had been given the responsibility of patrolling the area surrounding the Ordnance Factory and the War Reserve Constables had, less than an hour earlier, been detailed to arrest anyone of military age who couldn't account for their presence there.

Volunteers of any description are often the most enthusiastic in the performance of their duty and by the time the matter was settled, the prisoners had convinced themselves they were about to be handed over to Britain's version of the Gestapo. One of the Germans had caught and recognised the phrase 'enemy of the state'. He had rapidly translated his fears to the other two who in turn began debating their chances of survival if they were to make a run for it. They noted the soldiers' two rifles and suspected the policemen would probably be armed as well. They needn't have worried on either account.

They were still discussing their situation when, with great reluctance, the volunteer soldiers finally gave way to the volunteer policemen.

Disgruntled, the men in khaki returned to their makeshift guard post while three of the men in blue marched the prisoners on their way, the fourth driving the car slowly alongside in the gutter.

Monday 12ᵗʰ March 1945, 20:15 hrs.

Albert Coleman was in no hurry to get home. He had been driving for most of the evening having completed an arduous, and completely unproductive, day in Newport, South Wales. Monmouthshire formed part of his 'patch' and he had been unhappily attempting to sell poorly made household appliances to the town's unwilling housewives. The mischievous music-hall jests regarding travelling salesmen and bored housewives certainly carried no ring of truth for Albert Coleman.

He presented an untidy figure at the best of times and while many of his bright young colleagues managed to look smart in their neatly pressed double breasted suits, when he had left his narrow terraced home in Cheltenham that morning, Albert's wife had compared him unfavourably to a half empty sack of potatoes slumped against her kitchen wall. By the time he had driven eighty miles into Wales, even his Mackintosh, spread out on the back seat, looked crumpled.

He had stopped in Monmouth for an early supper on his way home and had enjoyed a meat pie in a friendly pub near the town centre. He had also enjoyed the company of the landlord who had shared rather too many beers with him before he had finally slid from his stool at the bar and wheeled his way back to his car.

As he had driven through the northern reaches of The Forest of Dean, near Brierley, Albert had seen in the dim glow of his blinkered headlights a group of red lights in the road ahead of him. He recognised the signs of a Police roadblock and, unwilling to enter into a discussion regarding his recent bout of drinking, had pulled off the main road, following a narrow lane until he reached Ruardean Hill.

Annoyed with himself for his weakness of will at the bar and poor sense of direction, he concluded that he was lost. Surrounded by a dense curtain of trees, he pulled up on a wide bend where the undergrowth had been flattened enough to provide a rudimentary lay-by. He sighed heavily and switched off the ignition before reaching into the car's glove compartment.

His hand fumbled ineffectually for his copy of the AA Road Atlas before he remembered leaving it on his kitchen table the evening before. He had been planning his visits for the week and, being familiar with the route into Monmouthshire, hadn't bothered to put it back in his briefcase.

He sighed again, slumped back in the driver's seat, yawned and closed his eyes. He hated Mondays. He wriggled his shoulders, trying to find a comfortable position in the stiff leather. It wouldn't yield, the back of the seat remaining stubbornly upright. With another sigh, he opened the driver's door and pulled himself into the chill night air. He shuddered as a distant creature, unidentifiable to Albert's entirely untrained ear, called out in the dark. The sky, heavy with cloud, allowed no light through to his canopy of trees and he couldn't even see the small silver emblem on the snout of his car's bonnet. Feeling his way along the cold metal, he opened the rear door and gratefully crawled onto the back seat. He pulled the door shut and, arranging his Mackintosh over himself, lay down on his side, knees bent. With another shiver, he closed his eyes again.

Albert was close to sleep when an unexpected sensation brought him quickly back to full consciousness. He heard a light metallic click, a breeze caught the right side of his neck and his temporary bed seemed to sway slightly. He opened his eyes and focussed uncertainly on a surprised, unshaven male face. It had mud smeared down one cheek and was poking into the car, hovering over the driver's seat. The man had one hand on the back of the seat, the other floating in mid air, reaching towards the steering wheel. Albert's instant reaction was to utter an incoherent honking sound.

He managed to blurt out, "What in Hell are you doing?" before the grimy hand quickly disappeared. The face turned with a grunt and a whirl of heavy worsted cloth. It withdrew and Albert heard the sound of rapid footsteps receding into the shadows. By the time the alcohol soaked salesman had managed to sit upright, the curtain of deep shadows had fallen once more. If there had been any movement in the clearing, Albert was unable to see it. Nevertheless, he froze, confused and frightened, straining his eyes and ears for clues. Somewhere in the darkness, he thought he could hear voices shouting to each other. The words were indistinct but they echoed in a way Albert found all too sinister.

Although too old to be called up by the military, he had never contemplated joining the Home Guard or any other wartime force which might have placed him at any physical risk. He would have been the first to recognise he had never been a brave man and this cold, dark woodland was not the right place to contemplate changing. He scrambled out of the car, moving as quickly as his wobbling legs allowed, grabbing the pillar of the open driver's door and pulling himself into the front seat.

He slammed the door and turned the ignition key, still in the lock. Starting the engine and ramming the car into gear, he let the clutch pedal slip from beneath his foot with a jerk. The rear wheels spun, firing pebbles and pinecones into the darkness before they reached the solid surface of the road. As he drove, blindly as in his haste he hadn't turned on the meagre headlights, he remembered his conversation with the Gloucester pub landlord and the item on the front page of a newspaper left on the bar. The headline had read *'Big Nazi Camp Break: Planes Join Search'*. The newspaper had been the *Daily Worker* and as he believed many recent strikes had been stirred up by its rhetoric, he would normally have ignored it. A heading half way down the article, however, had caught his interest. It read, simply, *'Forest of Dean'*. There followed a lurid account of four escaped Nazis, probably armed, driving a stolen car from Bridgend to Newnham-on-Severn and now believed to be rampaging loose through the Forest.

For the first time in as long as he could remember, Albert Coleman wished he could find a policeman.

Monday 12th March 1945, 21:00 hrs

Wyatt "Dash" Smith sat in his office, leaning back in a heavily upholstered chair, balancing it idly on its rear legs and gazing at the ceiling. As usual, Major Smith was bored and despite having little to do in his office, he knew he would have even less to occupy his mind if he returned to his billet. Comfortable though it was, the King's Head Hotel in Salisbury offered little by way of entertainment. The dusty drawing room, which retained many of its Victorian decor and architectural features, had no wireless set and, it seemed, the small upright piano had been closed for the duration of the hostilities. His small bedroom contained even fewer diversions and so he had taken to spending his evenings in the solitude of his office where, at least, he could listen to the American Forces Network. Even this, however, had lost its edge, not least because of the untimely loss of Glenn Miller. He had been reported missing in action while flying from an airfield in Bedfordshire to France in December of the previous year.

Since then, the D-Day invasion had meant the US broadcasters had moved their operations south with the troops. Instead, Wyatt now struggled with the confusing humour and rapid-fire delivery of Tommy Handley and the cast of 'It's That Man Again'. Some of the cultural references still evaded him, even after a year of what the US Army laughingly called 'familiarisation' with the United Kingdom.

He had, in civilian life, operated his own busy transport company, commanding a fleet of a dozen articulated heavy goods vehicles. Based in Cincinnati, his trucks had, and still did, criss-cross middle America ferrying goods as diverse as the latest electric washing machines, giant rolls of paper for the newspaper industry and agricultural tractor parts.

In 1941, however, Wyatt had heard the call to arms – and stoutly ignored it. He was a man who had reached middle age without an ounce of military inclination or ambition. In 1943, however, the US Government had decided otherwise.

He had been drafted to join the Army Transportation Corps; a unit created in July of the previous year in response to the growing need to transport unprecedented numbers of men and materials across the globe.

Dragged from his family and the familiarity of his transport yard, he had been sent to Fort Eustis in Virginia. There, he had spent three months in a classroom re-learning a trade he had believed he was already master of. Throughout the painful process, he had been assured that Uncle Sam would find a place for him on home soil. The need to transport military paraphernalia and personnel between his nation's complex network of bases could only increase until the war in Europe was settled.

Wyatt had been promoted to Captain and stationed to a small transport depot in New York State. There, he had expected to remain until inadvertent success had him promoted again to Major. Informed that he was now in command, he was responsible for seeing vehicles shipped across the North Atlantic to Great Britain. These were followed, to his growing unease, by many thousands of men.

Early in 1944, to his horror, he had received an order which resulted in him joining one of his own shipments. On 15th January he began his long transatlantic journey, contained in the depths of a US Navy transport, along with nearly 2,000 perplexed young soldiers and a few dozen officers who, on the surface at least, gave the appearance of knowing what to expect.

By mid February 1944, Major Wyatt Smith had received word that he was being posted to southern England. His orders had told him to report to a US Army base in a place called Salisbury, Wiltshire. He had known of towns named Salisbury in Maryland, in North Carolina and even in Connecticut. Had he thought about it, he might have come to realise that each of these fine townships may have been named after a mother city in the old world. As he hadn't given the subject much thought, however, he had no idea where he might be heading.

A few days before making landfall, he had asked his clerk to find a map of Wiltshire, adding helpfully that it was in England. When this had proved too difficult, he had asked for a European atlas and, finally, had been provided with a high-school atlas of the world. There, on page sixty eight, he had found a full page map of southern England and, deep within the green background, a small dot representing Wiltshire's only city.

By March 1945, his view of England and all things English had dramatically changed. His primary task of ensuring that men and machinery were promptly moved from disembarkation ports to temporary bases had gone largely without a hitch. The later move to training camps in South Wales and the area known mysteriously as 'The West Country' had not been so easy, pock-marked as it was by local opposition and dissent from those who were displaced from their homes.

With extra fire-power supplied by the British Civil Service and War Office in particular, however, the locals were left with little choice but to pack up their belongings and yield to the greater needs of the war effort. The US Army's final British migration, which he had been given partial responsibility for, to the D-Day embarkation towns of Plymouth, Portsmouth and Falmouth had gone without a hitch. After 6th June 1944, Wyatt had found himself at something of a loose end.

In the relative calm which followed, he had begun to appreciate the relaxed, almost rural, pace of life. To his greater surprise, he had discovered that he was even enjoying the frugal British diet allowed by rationing. Where roast beef was available he would add large portions of Yorkshire pudding and lashings of thick, brown gravy. Potatoes seemed to be in plentiful supply and he invariably opted to have these roasted where the supply of cooking fat allowed.

When the cafes and hotels dotted around Salisbury were unable to provide, the US Army more than sufficiently supplied his needs with large tins of bully-beef, pork and bacon. These were complimented by crates of exotic fruit, many varieties of which had scarcely been seen in British shops even before rationing began. Most important, however, purely as a commodity, were the stores' many thousands of chocolate bars and small blocks of chewing gum. In the absence of more pressing duties, Major Smith became more proactive in his role as the official US Army Liaison Officer for the South West and in this capacity found it prudent to liberally 'donate' these latter items to various worthy members of the local community. The children of an orphans' home in Devizes were the delighted recipient of a hundred Hershey Bars. Teenagers at a dance in Salisbury's Regal Hall were surprised and thrilled in equal measure to be offered a seemingly unlimited supply of Wrigley's chewing gum. A church bring-and-buy sale in Corsham near Chippenham, organised to raise funds to build a Spitfire, benefited greatly from the US Army's donation of a side of lamb and several joints of prime Argentinean beef.

Wyatt revelled in his magnanimity-by-proxy and wrote home frequently to his wife, to her ill-tempered disquiet, that he felt thoroughly at home in this quiet back-water of the English speaking world. Perhaps, he wrote, when the war was over, she and their two children would consider a move to Britain. The boys would benefit from the fresh air of the English countryside and she would quickly find friends within the many women's circles. She could take up knitting and jam making... His enthusiasm for his wife's future domestic happiness had not been well received in Cincinnati, Ohio. His ideas had so far been met with a silence which Wyatt mistakenly took to indicate that she was quietly preparing their sons for the journey to Europe.

In short, Major Wyatt Smith was slowly but inexorably being turned into an Anglophile, imbued and surrounded by provincial middle class values. It had been explained to him quite succinctly by the wife of one of Salisbury's more respected medical practitioners that it had essentially been the middle classes who had kept Britain's chin up during the darkest days of the war. Without them, no funds would have been raised to build Spitfires, no socks would have been knitted for the men at the front and absolutely nobody would have volunteered for the Women's Voluntary Service or the Red Cross. Few would have dug for victory and, goodness knows, the black market would have simply spiralled out of control.

This did little to aid his understanding of the British social class system, although his confusion had finally given way to amusement when a more seasoned US Army colleague had provided an explanation. He could, it seemed, define an Englishman's class quite simply by the type of headgear he wore.

From that moment, Wyatt became an ardent 'people-watcher', strolling the streets of Salisbury, mentally identifying and categorising his surrounding pedestrians. The man with the Bowler hat was unassailably middle-class; the manager of a small branch of a bank, perhaps, or a solicitor, accountant or factory manager. The Trilby wearer was almost certainly one to be wary of – one of the lower order of used automobile dealers or insurance salesmen; perpetrators of shady back street deals or door-to-door purveyors of dustpans, brooms and household appliances. A music-hall comic's dream.

Occasionally, to Wyatt's delight, he spied a gentleman approaching or leaving the town's main-line railway station wearing a 'Topper'. These rare creatures, he had been informed, were most certainly of the upper or ruling class. Safely defined as 'City Gents' they were invariably the product of the uniquely British public school and university system which produced the nation's steady flow of senior politicians, diplomats and civil servants.

Although he had been told that in the towns of Eton and Harrow, top hats abounded on the heads of oddly attired adolescents, when worn by an adult they were almost exclusively confined to Central London. In the suburbs, they would only be spotted when en-route to or from important engagements in the capital. It was enough to draw Wyatt on most evenings to a particular tea-room close to the railway station at around six o'clock in order that he could watch the small parade of these upper class craniums disembarking and walking briskly from the station portals to their waiting taxis.

At the other end of the spectrum, and in the majority by far, working class men favoured the flat cap. Often pulled low over the eyes, the peak provided some sort of shelter from all but the heaviest rain. It also seemed to shade the face into anonymity, allowing its wearer to move, hunched and unnoticed, through the crowded pavements between their terraced houses and factory work-benches or council depots.

More confusing, however, were the hat wearers' off-duty hours. In these off-peak times, top hats were replaced by soft cotton sun hats, like bleached, shapeless Trilbies, as the men beneath them lounged on deck-chairs, taking tea and watching afternoon cricket (a game which Wyatt recognised would take several summers spent in tuition to properly understand).

The bowler hats, once removed, were seldom replaced by anything so far as Wyatt could see, throwing his identification system into dissembled chaos. (Another problem area was created as many hat wearers removed their headgear when indoors, unless the subject kept his hat close by and readily visible). More reassuringly, Wyatt assessed that the shifty Trilby group seldom doffed their headgear, even when indoors although the flat cap wearers frequently and hastily removed their hats, even outdoors, clutching them to their stomachs when faced with a Bowler or, more rarely, a Topper.

Wyatt likened the system to the military habit of saluting senior officers. If the senior officer was wearing his cap, one would salute. If not, no salute was necessary. Similarly, he guessed, etiquette demanded that when indoors, the Bowler or Topper would have to be removed. Therefore, the flat cap wearer would, in his turn, be excused the need to remove his headgear. He doubted the average Trilby wearer would ever be caught in the same room as a Bowler or Topper and therefore the same rule would not apply.

He was yet to resolve the issue of female hat wearing. British women seemed to have adopted a different and infinitely more complex system to that of their men. Unless standing next to their hat-wearing husbands, it was virtually impossible to classify a British woman. It was necessary, he had concluded, to cross-reference her headgear to the remainder of her clothing, the occasion she was attending and the weather. As this seemed to vary almost by the hour, Wyatt had all but given the subject up. The chances are, he had concluded, these same women were the backbone of the British cipher breaking teams which he had heard rumours of.

His entire hat-identification theory, however, seemed at risk of being shot down in flames after a chance meeting with one of the senior officers from the Wiltshire Regiment. He had taken to exploring the surrounding countryside, driving his Jeep to various villages before taking to the surrounding paths and fields on foot. On this occasion, he had been enjoying a leisurely stroll across a corn field near Coombe Bissett, a few miles south west of Salisbury, when he saw a group of figures some fifty yards away, apparently examining a hedge. Such was his relaxed state of mind that the sight of a double barrelled shotgun slung over one of the men's arms did nothing to alarm him and he continued his stroll at the same leisurely pace.

As he grew closer, a spark of recognition ignited in his mind. The man at the centre of the group, dressed in what seemed to be an unusually heavy woollen twill jacket and corduroy trousers, stood a clear four inches taller than those around him. As he turned towards the approaching American, Wyatt could clearly identify a broad, grey moustache and, to his immediate consternation, atop a neatly cropped head of matching hair, a subtle tartan confection in fine Harris Tweed.

The Major had previously met with Brigadier Sir George Willis-Henby on a number of occasions as part of his official liaison duty but this was the first time he had seen him out of uniform. The Brigadier was surely of the Top-Hat class. Wyatt's eyes fixed accusingly on his flat cap.

The Brigadier's face broadened and he immediately strode towards him, his hand extended in greeting. A genuine smile spread beneath the moustache as he gripped the Major by the hand.

"Major Smith. What the blue blazes are you doing out here? Not looking for me are you?"

The American stammered his reply, apparently unsure of his ground. "No sir, not at all. I was just taking a stroll."

The Brigadier glanced up at the small clumps of white cloud and calm blue of the summer sky. "And why not? Damn fine day for it, what!" He turned briskly to the other men in his group and beckoned them forward. He introduced them by surname and job title. There was Willard, Estate Manager; Johnson, Gamekeeper and Bates, Head Beater.

Wyatt's eyes widened. "Head-beater?" He swallowed hard. "Whose head is it, exactly, that you beat?" The other men laughed aloud and he wished his voice had sounded less timid.

"Bless you, I do enjoy your American sense of humour." The Brigadier's smile broadened even further. The laughter trailed away in the face of Wyatt's blank features.

Bates took half a pace forward and touched his cap with a curved forefinger.

"A beater flies the game, sir." Wyatt's expression didn't change. "He beats the ground, making the birds take to the air, sir, so the shooting party can take a proper pot." He smiled ingenuously. He could tell from his uniform that the stranger was an American but surely even he would understand so simple an explanation.

As if spotting the dawning light, Wyatt's eyes widened and his jaw dropped open in sudden comprehension.

"I see. You're a hunting party."

The Brigadier corrected him. "Shooting party, Major. The English only hunt on horseback, you know." He gave him a condescending pat on the shoulder. "Can't expect you chaps to pick it all up straight away."

Wyatt nodded gratefully suddenly realising that each of the four men were wearing almost identical flat caps. Yet surely,

Bates the Head-beater couldn't be of the same social class as Brigadier Sir George Willis-Henby.

"Tell you what, old chap." The Brigadier's booming enthusiasm shook the American from his silent confusion and he slapped him again, harder this time, on the shoulder. "You must join us for our next shoot. It's all been arranged for this weekend." The other three men smiled and nodded encouragement. Privately and quite independently of each other, they were each looking forward to watching the over-dressed Yank make a fool of himself. "I'm sure we can find you a firearm if you don't have your own."

The Major eyed the shotgun, leaning over Johnson's forearm. He shook his head shyly. "I don't believe the US Military supply such weapons, sir. I have a Calibre .30 M1 and I believe my unit has an M3 submachine gun somewhere." he glanced at the shotgun again. "But I don't suppose either of them would be allowed."

The others laughed again.

The Brigadier leaned back, his hand still grasping the American's shoulder. He looked him up and down. "I think we may have to kit you out with some proper togs as well."

"Togs, sir?" More confusion creased Wyatt's face. Internally, he realised he should be getting used to this strange language. In the interests of harmonizing with the local population, as his commanding officer had instructed him, he should try not to show confusion when faced with the incomprehensible.

"Yes, togs, you know; an outfit for the occasion. Can't have a gun dressed in uniform. Just wouldn't be the done thing." Another slap on the shoulder. "Good. That's settled then. Come up to Bissett Grange at about nine on Saturday morning and we'll get you properly kitted out. Should be a good day even if the only game we're likely to see is duck or partridge. Couldn't pot a grouse even if there were any; not before the twelfth, what." The Brigadier ignored the American's obvious and deepening confusion. "Of course, we're bound to find rabbit or hare." He shrugged almost apologetically. "I normally leave them for the chaps from the village but needs must and all that, eh?"

With that, the group moved away, the Brigadier signalling a final farewell with a backward wave of his hand. "Enjoy your walk, Major. Don't forget, Saturday at nine."

Wyatt watched their slow progress down the field in silence. As if in a moment of revelation, he came to a decision and turning, strode with renewed determination back towards his Jeep.

Monday 12ᵗʰ March 1945, 23:00 hrs.

After the shock of their encounter with travelling salesman, Albert Coleman, Steffi Ehlert and Hans Harzheim had led their two companions north from Ruardean Hill, through the remaining borders of the Forest of Dean. Albert had chosen the highest hill in the Forest to take his rest and they ran quickly, if not easily, down the slopes until they reached another road and, beyond that, open fields.

Conveniently shielded from the road by a final line of trees, they turned west, walking more cautiously now and constantly alert for patrols or other activity on the road that ran alongside their path. Constantly glancing over their shoulders, they stumbled on until they reached a village. A few cottages still burned lights in their windows and the four men settled down to watch and wait.

Gradually, the patchwork of dimly lit squares diminished as lights were extinguished and the householders retired to bed. Within an hour, the final glimmer had died and the men stirred once more. They had been discussing, in low whispers, the last time they had enjoyed a satisfying meal and their hunger pangs had grown with every mouth-watering description of their favourite dishes.

One of the men, Werner Zielasko, volunteered to explore the village. He was a small, wiry man in his early thirties and well used to skirmishes in similar countryside both in his native Germany and Normandy. He took a final glance round and crept from his hiding place behind a hawthorn bush. He had been scratched across his hands and face but the cold had numbed them to the extent that he felt nothing.

A few hundred feet from their hiding place, Werner found what he was looking for. Sealed for the night, isolated from its neighbouring cottages by a yard, which in turn was surrounded by a simple fence, the village shop made a perfect target for larceny. To the rear of the yard, a timber gate stood obligingly open and, without breaking step, Werner slipped inside. Sheltered by the fence, he worked quickly and silently, checking a pile of wooden boxes before moving towards the back door of the building.

Gently, he tested the door handle. It was locked. Werner glanced over his shoulder again, holding his breath. Other than a quiet wisp of breeze in the surrounding trees, the entire village seemed to be asleep. He placed his shoulder against the timber panel above the handle and applied a little pressure. He felt the door give a little and he turned the handle once again. With a firm, swift shove, the door bowed away from the doorframe. He wasn't a heavy man, but with a slight increase in effort and with a single crack, the timber splintered and the door swung open. The metal latch which had held the bolt in place on the doorframe chimed like a dulled bell as it swung impotently on the bolt and Werner quickly stifled the sound with his hand. He froze in mid stride, listening once again for any signs that he had been detected. There were none. He stepped slowly into the cramped space beyond the door, gently closing it behind him.

He pulled a box of matches from his pocket and immediately returned them. The box was so damp that attempts to light one would have been pointless. He decided not to look for a light switch and instead felt his way deeper into the room, immediately jarring his thigh on something hard and pointed. He cursed under his breath and reached cautiously down in the direction of the obstruction. It was a tea chest, one corner reinforced with a strip of metal pointing awkwardly into the space left down the middle of the room. Sitting astride the chest, a cardboard box had been opened and, with the little light available, Werner could make out a dozen or more metal cans. He pulled the nearest one out of the box and held it close to his face, inspecting the label. He could make out some blue print on a white background but no helpful pictures to illustrate what it might contain. He held the can up to the only source of light; a small window next to the door and squinted again, just able to make out the word 'casserole'.

"*Kasserolle?*" He smiled in recognition and dropped the tin into his coat pocket before returning to the box and picking out a further three.

Emboldened by his success, he crept through the space between the boxes and into the shop area. He found himself behind a long counter and his eyes immediately lit upon the cash register. With something approaching a sense of guilt – he had never contemplated theft as a career, despite what seemed to be a natural aptitude – he experimentally pushed at the drawer of the till. To his surprise, it sprung open. His fingers explored inside but found it was empty. He clicked the drawer gently shut again and continued his search, picking out four pears, four apples and two red cans on which was printed '12 pure dried eggs' and in smaller print below 'in powder form'. He shrugged, unable to translate and, pulling a net bag from a hook behind the counter, slipped it and the fruit inside.

He made his way back towards the store room, pausing only for one final acquisition which joined the other goods in the bag. With a last wistful look round, he silently left the shop.

Within minutes, his three fellow escapees were carefully examining the contents of his shopping bag. Harzheim, whose English was the strongest of the four, shrugged sadly when he saw the red cans.

"*Getrocknet eipulver.*" He translated. The others moaned quietly. They would have greatly enjoyed a few eggs, but there was little they could do with dried egg powder. While the others greedily bit into the fruit, Werner produced his final find from the bag – a metal can opener – and began prizing open the lid of the first can. He dipped his finger into the yellow powder, inspecting it briefly before dabbing it on his tongue. He pulled a face and spat voluminously. He bit into an apple to mask the earth dry taste. They buried both the red cans in shallow graves beneath the hawthorn bush. The fruit quickly consumed, they hid the cores in the same way. As if suddenly remembering, Werner grinned and raised his finger in the air before pulling the four remaining cans from his pockets. He placed them on the damp ground, spreading his hands over them proudly.

"*Kasserolle, meine heren?*" He smiled as the men enthusiastically picked at the tins. It was the first meat they had seen since leaving Bridgend. Even cold, it would be a welcome source of protein. The men admired each of the cans, grinning and nodding their appreciation.

"*Es ist Wal.*" Harzhcim spoke quietly, almost whispering. "*Er sagt 'Walfleisch'.*"

Werner's grin fell. How, he demanded, could whale meat be described in any civilised country as casserole?

The translator shrugged. At least it demonstrated how short of food the enemy were. This would make useful propaganda when they got back to Germany. The others nodded sadly. Three of the tins of *'Taistbest Whalemeat Steak Casserole'* were buried alongside the dried egg powder before the men moved. Travelling north once again, they skirted round the rest of the village, carefully checking for any signs of activity before crossing Highview Road, and into the fields north of the village. Away from the cover of the Forest of Dean, they began to hurry now, anxious to find a hiding place before sunrise. They crossed several fields quickly enough, reaching a large barn set in the corner of a yard and adjoining the apex of a wide bend in a pitted gravel lane.

There they stopped and dropped, panting again, under the branches of a large elm. Steffi Ehlert glanced up at the sky, once more ink black and starless. The bare branches rattled inhospitably and, not for the first time, he wondered silently at the wisdom of making an escape before the spring weather had warmed slightly. It was a doubt he wouldn't have dared voice to any of his senior officers at the camp. Questioning of any senior military decision was seen as dissent and he would have immediately risked losing his place on the list of escapees.

There again, Hans had told him often enough of overheard conversations between the camp guards. It was one of his tasks while in camp to eavesdrop on any British conversation. Even the most casual of remarks could prove helpful both for German morale and to aid an escape. It seemed, however, that the British had an overriding obsession with the weather. Every conversation seemed to begin with a discussion about the climate; the rainfall during the day before, current air temperature and the forecast for the coming day. Every Englishman seemed to have a different opinion of how the day's weather was going to turn out but one thing remained constant: their eternal pessimism that a season which should bring an improvement in the weather would turn out to be as cold and miserable as the last. Perhaps there had been no point waiting for warmer weather after all.

His musing was interrupted by a sharp poke in the ribs from Harzheim. He nodded at the barn. Together, the men approached the shadowy building. Whether it contained food, water, a vehicle or simply a place to rest for the next few hours, they were quickly learning they must make use of every resource they stumbled upon.

In a few hours the sun would be coming up and they would need a place to hide that would remain undisturbed, at least until the following evening.

Tuesday 13th March 1945, 05:40 hrs

Following the success of his outing the previous Sunday morning, Flight Sergeant Jim Thomson had temporarily become a minor celebrity at his RAF base in St.Athan. Although stationed there only to attend a short training course, he had become the base's unofficial search party organiser and leader.

It came as something of a disappointment to learn that he had been outgunned late on Monday evening by a flight lieutenant named MacDawlish who had flown in, quite literally, from Glasgow.

Hearing of the break-out in nearby Bridgend and learning that further searches of the area were still needed, he had immediately asked the base commander for permission to lead the next patrol. He presented his credentials as a pre-war mountain rescue team leader and although the base Wing Commander had laughingly pointed out there were very few mountains in the Vale of Glamorgan, he had expressed his delight with anyone who volunteered for extra duties and had given his agreement.

Shortly before midnight a police despatch rider from Bridgend delivered an order signed on behalf of Superintendent May and a sketch map showing the area they should search. By the early hours of Tuesday morning, Jim had been reduced to the status of second in command but, officer or no officer, had studied the map closely and hand-picked the search party himself. He sensibly chose three local men who knew the area and who also happened to be Military Police dog handlers.

Following the Lieutenant's orders, Sergeant Thomson presented his small group of men and three Alsatians for inspection on the parade ground shortly before sunrise. He had already briefed them on their task over mugs of hot cocoa in the sergeants' mess, although he allowed Flight Lieutenant MacDawlish to feel he was in charge, lecturing them in his thick Glaswegian, which few fully understood. The Lieutenant turned smartly to the Sergeant.

"Right, Sarn't. Move them out."

147

"Sir!" Jim snapped to attention, stamping his foot smartly on the gravel. He winked at the men and, with a jerk of his head, beckoned them to the waiting transport.

At the wheel, Jim had already pulled the heavy truck to the left, steering east towards the Port Road before MacDawlish had calculated which way they should go. Five miles down the road he pulled up, easing the nearside wheels of the vehicle onto a grass verge.

"Why have you stopped?" The Scotsman glanced uncertainly at the map.

Wordlessly, Jim jerked on the handbrake and turned off the ignition. He leant across the officer's shoulder and pointed to the corner of a pencilled square, marked on the map and crossed through with the words 'RAF St.A. search area'. "We're here, sir." He indicated the fields next to the truck. "We start the search here." He pointed again at the corner of the square. "And we move across, there." His finger slid to the opposite corner of the square. He smiled ingenuously at the officer. "At your command, sir."

The Glaswegian coughed. "Right. Of course. Get the men unloaded, then." The Lieutenant jammed his peaked cap on his head. "Don't hang about Sergeant. We don't have all day, you know."

The search proceeded as planned, the men spread across the ploughed field, covering its full width between two ancient hawthorn hedges. The Alsatians appeared to enjoy their early morning walk and although they periodically inhaled the aroma of freshly turned soil, it's unlikely they caught the smell of anything more unusual than a rabbit or two.

The search continued through a second then a third field while the sun began to show itself over the distant docks at Barry. Man and dog progressed and, as they moved through each five bar gate, the officer carefully drew a tick across another field on his map.

Leaving the third field, the party moved onto an open stretch of common land, dotted with patches of rough bracken, scrub and brambles. This was bordered by an area of heavy, unmanaged woodland, punctuated by fallen trees, overgrown and entangled by ivy and thorns. As they passed under the shadow of the branches, one of the dogs started pulling harder on its lead and, despite efforts to pull the animal in, the handler finally slipped the clasp open at the dog's collar and let him run on ahead. The men watched him go with some interest, quickening their step as the Alsatian became hidden amongst the trees. The handler ran forward a few steps, craning to see his dog and catching a glimpse as he bolted fast towards a large patch of brambles.

MacDawlish turned to the man nearest to him. "Probably just wants a wee."

As if in answer, the dog barked, accelerated again and, leaping, disappeared into the tangle of thorns. Almost immediately, the other dogs started barking. They were joined by a sudden, short, human cry. Cut short, it echoed eerily round the damp woodland. From within the thorny pile, a man, then another, followed by three more tumbled, jumped and fell into the path of the search party. One of the men stumbled at the feet of the dog handler, forcing the other two policemen to haul back as their animals strained forward on their hind legs, snarling, their front paws paddling the air.

The five prisoners lay motionless and unbidden on the damp soil, their hands behind their heads. The RAF men crowded round, rifles aimed down at the recaptured Germans. Sergeant Thomson was the first to gather his wits and while the loose Alsatian was gathered up with some difficulty by his handler, he ordered the prisoners to their feet.

The RAF men began to relax, smiling and congratulating themselves on a successful morning's work. A search of the prisoners and their hideout in the brambles, ostensibly for weapons, revealed that the men were armed only with a few apples, two tins of bully-beef bearing the distinctive marks of the Red Cross and a rudimentary map sketched on a sheet of brown paper which would originally have been used to wrap their relief parcels from home.

The Germans were shivering, partly from cold and partly from the shock of being awakened suddenly by a salivating Alsatian. Through several days growth of beard, one of the Germans explained they had been asleep. They had tried to keep one man awake as a look-out, but exhaustion had got the better of all of them.

They began their trudge back across the fields and Jim reached into the pocket of his greatcoat. He pulled out a packet of cigarettes, shaking the white tips through the torn corner of the pack and offering them to each of the prisoners in turn. They each took one, nodding their thanks.

"What in Hell do you think you're doing, Sergeant?" MacDawlish's Scots accent rose indignantly.

Hidden from the officer's view, Jim rolled his eyes. "Offering the prisoners a ciggie, sir."

"Don't be so damn insolent. I can see what you're offering them." He Gasped as Jim held out an illuminated cigarette lighter, igniting each of the cigarettes as the men leaned in towards him. "Those cigarettes are issued by the Government for the use of British service personnel only. They're not for the likes of the enemy."

"Right you are sir." Jim snapped the lighter shut. "I'll bear that in mind, sir."

The German who had spoken earlier smiled appreciatively. "I think your officer is, how is it you say? A stickler for the rules."

"That'll be what it is, I expect." Jim grinned back, inhaling a thick mixture of smoke and early morning air. He rammed his hands in his coat pockets as if enjoying his walk.

"You are making fun of your officer?" He glanced nervously at each of the men, recognising the similarities between British military personnel and his own. Wartime officers were seldom given respect by experienced senior NCO's.

Jim glanced at the German again. "Where did you get your map from?"

The prisoner shrugged his shoulders, releasing a satisfying plume of grey-blue smoke. "That was easy. We were brought to the camp by train. In the carriage there was an advertisement for holidays by the seaside." He took another draw from the cigarette, pausing briefly to enjoy the moment. "There was a map of the south of Wales and England showing the railway lines and all the holiday resorts." Jim found it hard to disguise his surprise. "One of the *Luftwaffe* navigators copied the map onto the back of the shirt of one of the pilots. They wear white shirts, you know."

Jim nodded. "Where were you heading for, anyway?"

"We were looking for a ship. Last night we could see the docks. We didn't mean to sleep for so long."

The Sergeant shook his head. "Sorry we woke you. If we'd known we would have let you have a lie in."

The German laughed aloud, translating for the other prisoners. "Now, I think, it is me you are making fun of."

Tuesday 13th March 1945, 09:00 hrs.

George Charteris tapped on the door marked *'Insp. Lancelot Bailey – Detective Branch'* and waited. It was to become his habit to drive to Port Talbot each morning in order to update his senior officer on the progress of the man-hunt being centred in Bridgend. Thereafter each day, he would return to Island Farm Camp and Colonel Darling's clerks' room where a small desk had been set up for him in a corner.

He had also been promised the services of a translator; an eager young Captain named Donald Donovan who had been a post-graduate student of languages at Cambridge before the war. Other than a brief introduction, however, George had had little opportunity to talk with him. The good Captain had thus far been apparently given more pressing duties elsewhere.

Invited to enter, George moved cautiously at first. He felt he still didn't know his senior officer well enough to risk passing any comments that might be interpreted as being too light-hearted or flippant. He still had embarrassing memories of his remarks about exporting prisoners to Canada and the reported numbers of escapees. He had no intention of revealing further his naiveté regarding the dark arts of propaganda and misinformation.

"Of the original eighty six escapees, sir, fourteen were recaptured at or near the tunnel exit and a further two a short distance away. That left seventy men at large."

"Yes, Constable. I think we became aware of that in the early hours of Sunday morning." The Inspector found it hard to hide his impatience. He had a reputation as one who got things done quickly and didn't like his or his officers' time to be wasted.

"Fourteen more escapees were detained during the course of Sunday, sir. Two in..." He hesitated, squinting at his notebook.

"What's the problem, Charteris? Can't you read your own handwriting?"

George smiled apologetically. "It's not that, sir. I'm just not used to the local place names yet."

The Inspector held out his hand to take the notebook. He glanced at it and passed it back.

"Tythegston. Don't worry. I can't get my tongue round half the place names in Wales, and I was born here."

"Right, sir. Tythegston. It's a little place between -"

Bailey held his hand up. "I know where it is. Just carry on with your report."

"Sorry, sir. Two more were apprehended by police officers in Llan... Llanharan." He glanced up to check whether his pronunciation was going to be corrected. "And three more in St.Athan, picked up by a Royal Air Force patrol. Two were tracked down near Porthcawl and five more on Sunday evening in the Army search operation at a disused quarry near Laleston." The Constable looked up. "That was the incident attributed in the press to a couple of civilians, sir. That's fourteen prisoners recovered on Sunday, sir."

The Inspector nodded. "So you said. Fourteen on Sunday. How about yesterday?"

"Yes sir." He flicked a page over in his notebook. "Eleven more prisoners were recovered on Monday, sir. Two in Bonvilston near Cowbridge, three more by War Reserve Police Officers near a factory in Pencoed and six in Kenfig Hill; four of them with the help of a farmer named William Jones and two by a pair of Specials just outside their own Police Station." He closed his notebook and looked up. "That brings the total recaptured to forty one and forty five still at large." There was a pause as Inspector Bailey wrote a note on the corner of his blotting pad. "But what the newspapers are saying is quite different." He looked down and started flipping through the pages of his notebook again. Inspector Bailey held up both hands.

"I don't care what the newspapers are making of all this, George. That is someone else's problem. Our job is to coordinate the search and glean any intelligence we can from the escapees regarding their methods."

"But the public thinks there are only twenty seven prisoners still free, sir. Won't they soon assume they've all been recaptured and stop providing us with information if they see anything suspicious?"

Bailey sighed. "Just tell me what else you've learned from your investigations."

"Sorry, sir. I asked about Military Intelligence and how I should proceed regarding interviews with the recaptured detainees, but haven't received any clear reply. In any event, I've been permitted to speak with several of the German officers who speak English. So far, there is no indication that they received any help from members of the public outside the camp. I haven't been able to speak with any non-English speaking prisoners because the interpreter, Captain Donovan, has been too busy to help."

"Too busy?" The Inspector sounded incredulous. "I'll have a word with Colonel Darling. It's important you talk to as many detainees as possible." He looked down, momentarily avoiding eye contact. "Particularly as MI19 haven't yet managed to get any of their interrogation experts down here yet."

"I've spoken with the officer who was shot and wounded, sir; a Lieutenant named Tonnsmann. He's still in hospital in Bridgend, but he seemed quite happy to talk, once the doctors let me in to see him. He's asked to be transferred to a different camp. He's afraid of reprisals from the other prisoners." George looked up. "I think he would probably give quite a lot of useful information if he was led to believe we were willing to help with that request."

The Inspector shrugged. "That's really something only the Army can grant him. I'll make a note and pass the information on. What did he have to say?"

"He told me he shouldn't have been in the escape party at all. It seems he hadn't been properly prepared and, according to his own account, gate-crashed his way into the tunnel. It was his light coloured kitbag that gave the game away. All the others had dyed their bags to blend in at night. Tonnsmann was carrying a white bag and was spotted as he made a run for it. The guard who wounded him could only see one man, so took a pot-shot and got him in the shoulder."

"And that's why he wants a transfer to another camp? Because he fears the others will blame him for the escape being discovered?"

"That's right, sir. The irony is, Tonnsmann wasn't the last man out of the tunnel. He just happened to be the one who was visible when the guard fired his rifle. The man who followed him out and who may well have been seen by the guard had his attention not been drawn to the white kitbag was a *Luftwaffe* pilot named Hermann Schallenberg. He was caught almost immediately in the woods close to the camp." George allowed himself a sly grin. "Mind you, sir, I haven't told Tonnsmann there was a man behind him. I thought it might be useful if he continued to think it was all his fault."

The Inspector sighed again. "Very clever, I'm sure, Constable. Let's not get too carried away with cloak and dagger. In the Glamorgan Constabulary, we leave deception and skulduggery to others."

"Yes, sir. I haven't spoken to Herr Schallenberg yet but I understand he is extremely unhappy that he was recaptured so quickly. He realises he was given away by a junior officer who, by rights, shouldn't have been there at all." He looked up to gauge his Inspector's reaction before continuing. "There is another thing which I think will be of interest to the military authorities. I mentioned it to one of the camp officers but I don't think he took me very seriously." George glanced at his notebook again. "The Germans laid curry powder along a stretch of the perimeter fence."

"Curry powder? Are you sure?"

"Yes sir."

"Why on Earth would they do that?"

"Apparently to deter the guard dogs, sir."

Bailey frowned doubtfully. "Who told you this?"

"An officer by the name of Herzler, sir. Heinz Herzler. He was brought in by a Constable Baverstock from Llanharan. Herzler says that each time one of the prisoners went anywhere near the wire fence, the Alsatians picked up their scent and alerted the guards by barking and following their trail. Apparently they experimented by putting a trail of curry powder down, then going over to the fence where the powder had been placed. The next time the dogs were taken past, they failed to pick up the scent. On the night of the escape, the first man out spread curry powder round both ends of the tunnel and along their route to the trees where they rendezvoused."

"Good God. We'll have to hope that bit of intelligence doesn't reach the enemy or the Army will have to re-train all their dogs."

"Or ban the use of curry powder in Prisoner of War camp kitchens." George smiled weakly, hoping the introduction of gentle humour might ease the stilted relationship he still felt existed with his Inspector. Receiving no response, he got up to leave.

"Before you go, George, there is one other thing." The senior officer's tone had mellowed noticeably and George immediately returned to his seat. "There was an incident last night in Porthcawl which has all the appearances of becoming a time-consuming enquiry." Seeing his Constable's back straighten in anticipation, he immediately raised his hands to reassure him. "It's nothing which need take up your time. It simply means that Mr May and I will very probably not be at our desks very much over the next week or so. Should situations arise during your investigation for which you would normally require my guidance, I will expect you, for the time being, to use your own initiative."

George hadn't yet felt the need to call on his Inspector for guidance. He decided to say nothing.

"I will still expect daily reports each morning from you and that will be your opportunity to ask for any advice you require but, for the rest of the time, I will be busy conducting other enquiries or in conference with Mr May."

"Might I know the nature of the incident you'll be investigating, sir?" He caught Bailey's warning glance. "In case something arises during my enquiries which might be relevant, sir."

Bailey looked down at a slip of paper which had arrived on his desk less than an hour earlier.

"Murder, Constable. Mr May and I are dealing with an undoubted case of manslaughter and very possibly murder."

Tuesday 13th March 1945, 10:15 hrs.

Wyatt "Dash" Smith drove the country lanes towards Salisbury, a clear purpose and destination in mind for the first time since his D-Day preparations had concluded nine months earlier.

He had passed the place just off the city centre several times over the previous few months and given it little attention. Now, he parked the Jeep directly outside and closely surveyed the window.

Jarvis and Swayle, Oufitters to Selective Gentlemen had been established, so their sign declared, in 1836. Wyatt climbed from the Jeep and straightened his tunic jacket. He touched the belt, subconsciously checking the buckle lay centrally. He pulled his peaked cap from beneath the seat and tucked it squarely under his left arm. Almost marching, for the first time since his basic training, he crossed the pavement and entered Messrs Jarvis and Swayle's hallowed establishment.

Passing from bright sunlight to the dusty murk of the shop, he pulled up short in the doorway and blinked until a few details of his surroundings emerged. Before him, a glass topped counter displayed a sign advertising varying grades of ready-made shirts, priced at two shillings, two and six and three shillings respectively. Beneath the glass counter top, lay a few pairs of flaccid looking leather gloves. A manikin stood unsteadily next to the counter, one arm bent at the elbow so the hand just failed to touch its jacket lapel in what might have been an attempted Churchillean pose. It wore tweeds and a pair of dusty leather brogues, each garment pinned with a price label and a circle of paper glued to the label giving the number of ration coupons required.

A small, trim man approached the broad figure at the open door. He asked if he could be of any assistance.

The Major smiled, composing himself. Returned to the familiar world of commerce and trade, he felt more at ease.

"Would you be Mr Jarvis or Mr Swayle?" He smiled his best Liaison Officer's smile.

"Dear me, sir. No sir." The small man hid his smile behind the neatly manicured fingers of one hand, the other holding the end of a tape measure draped round his shoulders. "Dear Messrs Jarvis and Swayle are no longer with us, sir. We are now Messrs Hardy and Featherington. My partner and I took over the business some years ago after the late Mr Swayle passed over." The shopkeeper's eyes rolled up to the ceiling as if indicating the late Mr Swayle might be resting in the store-room upstairs. Wyatt's eyes followed his gaze. He coughed awkwardly.

"I'm sorry. My condolences, I'm sure."

"Oh, please don't apologise sir. Mr Hardy and I barely knew the gentleman." He smiled contritely. "Is there anything I can help sir with?" He stepped to one side, allowing the American a clearer view of his wares.

"I'm looking for a hat. Well, more exactly, a cap. A cloth cap of the sort worn... well, worn by country gentlemen."

The little man beamed in understanding. "Certainly, sir." He motioned a little wave of welcome, bowing slightly from the waist as if about to throw his cloak over a muddy puddle. He looked up into the deeper gloom at the rear of the shop. "Mr Hardy." His voice rose slightly as he searched the darkness. "Mr Hardy, can you assist, please? Sir requires a cap."

From the back of the shop emerged a short, broad man in a three piece pin-striped suit and bow tie. His neck overflowed the confines of his collar and wobbled slightly as he walked jauntily into the dim light.

"Sir would like a cap?" He caught sight of the American officer and bowed his head, his eyes briefly closing. "If sir would please follow me." He turned neatly on his heel in a movement that was surprisingly light for so heavily built a man. Obediently, Wyatt followed him into the cavernous recess of the shop until, with a sudden flowing movement, Mr Hardy swept his right hand over a counter and flicked an electric switch. The back of the shop was bathed in a pale light, revealing several shelves stacked with flat caps in varying hues of copper brown, mottled green and grey.

Mr Hardy's right hand waved once more over the rows of caps, his features almost ecstatic with pride.

Wyatt grinned at the shelves and placed his hands on his hips as he absorbed the confusion of choice.

built man wearing an outsized dark grey coat. Another man, taller but similarly clad, was trying to disentangle himself from the Jeep that he had apparently fallen into.

Wyatt grabbed the German's wrist and pinned it to the pavement, surprised that his own hand seemed so large and heavy by comparison. He looked up at the approaching shopkeeper.

"They're Krauts." He yelled the word, forgetting for a moment his own ancestry. "Grab hold of that one." He jerked his head at the second man, now swaying uncertainly after his collision with the Jeep.

The entire incident was over within seconds. A police whistle sounded from further down the street and the next thing Wyatt was aware of was a black wooden truncheon, aimed at but missing the German, splintering on the pavement close to his shoulder. Several pairs of hands reached down, grabbing the hapless prisoner and pulling him unceremoniously from beneath Wyatt's weight.

The American, doing his best to regain his composure and vaguely aware that as a senior officer he might be expected to take control of the situation, clambered to his feet and straightened his jacket. Looking about him, the smaller of the two Germans was being held easily in place by a heavy Police Constable. The other, taller, man was complaining loudly, bent almost double over the side of the Jeep by the greengrocer who was clearly enjoying himself.

A Sergeant from Salisbury Barracks arrived brandishing a rifle and, in the company of two Constables, the German prisoners were marched away to continue their spell of captivity. Both had been unshaven and, in Wyatt's estimation, probably exhausted, thirsty and hungry. In such circumstances, he found it difficult to accept the unanimous congratulations from Brigadier Willis-Henby and his shooting party the following Saturday morning. So immersed was he with his new set of friends that, by the end of the day, he had revealed his nickname of "Dash", a sobriquet conferred upon him while at high school. Not, as Wyatt bashfully admitted, because he was so fleet of foot but rather the opposite. He was known as the slowest full-back in his college football team.

"It was my team-mates' shot at sarcasm." He explained to his entranced and chiefly female audience.

"Oh no." Announced the Brigadier's youngest daughter firmly. "Not sarcasm, surely. *Irony* perhaps, but not sarcasm. That would never do." She released a sharp, horse-like bray of laughter. The few men in the group smiled, nodded and, out of politeness, emitted suppressed chuckles.

Tuesday 13ᵗʰ March 1945, 11:00 hrs.

Deep in the heart of Westminster Palace there lie several long corridors, lined with Victorian hunting scenes and portraits of worthy and long absent parliamentarians. Off these corridors work the myriad civil servants and politicians who operate the mechanism of British government. Along one of these corridors in particular, dozens of heavy oak and leather padded doors lead into a series of cavernous, usually empty and usually darkened rooms. Each of the rooms is lined with fitted walnut book-cases which cover the walls from floor to ceiling. They each contain long forgotten yet worthy tomes from the annals of English literature, the law, British history, the governance of Empire and a dozen other topics ranging from theoretical and Marxist economics to world geography.

In one of the rooms, at least a dozen shelves are taken up by chronologically arranged volumes of *Jane's Defence Review*, superseded as they reach 1984 by *Jane's Defence Weekly*.

In 1945, however, the binders containing the latest and most definitive catalogue of international weaponry had become particularly well thumbed, as had *Jane's Fighting Ships*, first published in 1898 under the title *Jane's All the World's Fighting Ships*, and *Jane's All the World's Aircraft,* published annually since 1909.

The publisher's founder, John 'Fred' T Jane had earned a certain degree of belligerent respect from his Government when, in 1914, he had voluntarily censored his own publication, due to be released shortly after the outbreak of the Great War. At the same time he had successfully calmed a panic stricken British public with reassurances that Germany lacked the capacity to launch large scale air-raids on London.

The publisher's approach had been rather different in 1939 and all that could be published, particularly with regard to the enemy's capacity for war, was given as much space as paper rationing regulations would allow. Such was the respect for the publication's accuracy and detail that numerous defence committees, both political and military, frequently referred to it.

162

For this reason, the entire collection had been removed and transferred in 1939 to the Cabinet War Rooms in Whitehall. Deep beneath buildings occupied by the Treasury and the Foreign and Commonwealth Office, bordered by Horse Guards Road and Parliament Street, the extraordinary complex of offices and operations rooms had been enlarged and reinforced during the 1930's in case the war everyone expected caused damage to the Palace of Westminster or Downing Street.

Whatever befell London at ground level, the work of Government would continue unmolested in a reinforced rabbit warren of subterranean corridors, offices, kitchens, sleeping quarters and even hospital wards.

It remained the work of a small team of civil servants to ensure that the valuable volumes were kept up to date and in good order in the room used for the frequent meetings of, among others, the War Cabinet's Home Defence (Security) Executive.

On 13th March 1945, the 268th such meeting was convened. Senior members of Churchill's War Cabinet and their civil servants squeezed into the narrow space left between concrete walls, now lined with bookshelves. The fine old oak conference table, once the centrepiece of their Westminster committee room, had been carefully cut into sections and brought down to the War Rooms before being reassembled. The work had been completed by carpenters carefully selected for their discretion as much as their skill and all were sworn to secrecy. At the suggestion of the foreman in charge of the job, three feet had been cut from one end of the table in order to allow slightly more room. It was in this confined space that the committee's secretary now perched on a high stool and took notes.

The meetings were invariably arranged to start during the late morning. The Chairman considered it a sensible measure on two accounts; they could commence with a cup of coffee and the canteen stopped serving lunch at one o'clock, making it imperative that the meetings were drawn to a prompt conclusion. He drained his coffee cup, took a final draw on his cigar before extinguishing the glow in a large oval ashtray and adjusted his spectacles. He seldom referred to notes during meetings, preferring instead to wake early and read the overnight reports before rising.

Similarly, he relied on his civil servants to brief him on the latest relevant news immediately prior to each of the meetings he attended during the day. He was known to be quite intolerant of any omissions on this score and several officials had been removed from his personal staff as a result of their failure to provide him with the latest information. In short, the Chairman required of himself that he remained at least as well informed as his most senior military advisors. He did not like to be caught out.

"The Directorate of Prisoners of War has reported that in the seven days ending yesterday, 102 German Prisoners of War and Italian non - co-operators absconded from prison camps and work parties." His bottom lip protruded in a characteristic pause. "There are at present at large, eight Italian non – co-operators, forty three German prisoners from British camps and four Germans from American camps." He eyed the members of his committee, huddled uncomfortably round the table. Nobody present was in any doubt that the figures did not reflect well. The Chairman was not happy.

A Colonel seated at the far end of the table cleared his throat. His latest posting, following a minor wound gained in Northern France, had placed him with the Directorate of Prisoners of War. For the previous six months he had found himself representing his Director at these austere meetings. With an increasing number of escapes from British and American camps, the initial excitement of rubbing shoulders with the nation's most senior politician had swiftly worn off.

"Colonel Sheppard; you have something to say I hope?" The Chairman's voice dropped to an even rougher growl than usual. Several heads turned expectantly in the Colonel's direction.

"Yes, sir. The committee may wish to know that two of the escaped German prisoners absconded from a labour party. They were members of a group which was being transported to a base camp. Security screening had suggested they were likely to pose a risk to the public."

The Chairman looked up quickly before turning to the committee secretary, a young WAAF Lieutenant named Bernice Hudson. "Miss Hudson, you may enter in the minutes that the two German prisoners were considered unsuitable for employment." He returned his attention to the Colonel and waved an unlit cigar to indicate he could continue.

"They escaped, no doubt, because they had no wish to return to a prison camp."

"No doubt." The Chairman grunted.

"Of eighty six German escapees from base camps, seventy were from the officers' camp, Number 198, at Bridgend in South Wales." He glanced surreptitiously at a typed sheet of paper. A capable officer, Colonel Sheppard had never claimed to possess a memory as faultless as the Chairman's. "Two tunnels were discovered at the camp last December. The subsequent discovery of loose soil deposited about the camp was originally assumed to be spoil from those two tunnels." The Colonel took a sip of water, swallowing with some difficulty. "As it now transpires that there was a third tunnel, it appears likely that the loose soil was also generated by the construction of that third and ultimately successful tunnel." He looked up, blinking in the limited light at his fellow committee members. After a few seconds he felt the need to fill the ensuing silence. "Quite clever, really, don't you think?"

Someone coughed lightly and another cleared his throat.

"Mr Ross. Can you add anything to brighten our day?"

Donald Willard-Ross, a tall wisp of a man in a dark suit with a distinct pin-stripe which served only to exaggerate his slim build further, was a Permanent Under-Secretary with the Home Office. Part of his remit was to coordinate the work of county police forces with their neighbouring branches of the armed forces. He was essentially a Police policy maker and disliked what he saw as Army interference. He leant forward languidly, interlacing his fingertips and smiled, nodding graciously at the head of the table.

"Thank you Mr Chairman." He inhaled deeply through his nose, taking his time and privately enjoying the Colonel's obvious discomfort. "Glamorgan County Constabulary, I am pleased to report, have acted extremely effectively. The Chief Constable issued a prompt request to police divisions, councils and parishes in the immediate area on the morning following the break-out. As a result a laudable turn-out of special constables and civilian volunteers including many former Home Guards joined with regular police officers and Army personnel in a widespread comb-out of the fields surrounding the camp." He smiled again. "It is my view that it is largely thanks to these and subsequent efforts that we can now report that so many of the Bridgend prisoners have been recaptured."

The Chairman grunted again. "One must hope, Mr Ross, that by the next time we meet, Colonel Sheppard will be able to report that all our German guests have been safely returned to their proper quarters." It was not the first time the Chairman had abbreviated the Civil Servant's surname, nor was it accidental. He disliked affectation and was aware he had appended his mother's maiden name of Willard on joining the Civil Service in the hope it would assist his career.

Willard-Ross bowed his head obsequiously. "There has been one matter brought to my attention, sir, which the committee may wish to consider."

The Chairman lowered the lighter that had been flickering close to the tip of his cigar.

"The Police have, as the committee will no doubt be aware, been instructed not to use wireless communication when reporting issues relating to escapes by Prisoners of War." There was a general murmur of agreement around the table. It had long been suspected that enemy reconnaissance aircraft might pick up Police messages from the ground and use the information for both propaganda and intelligence purposes.

Privately, senior police officers had told him the only intelligence the enemy were likely to glean from such eavesdropping was the amount of sugar a British bobby liked in his tea. When he was at the committee table, however, Mr Willard-Ross felt more inclined to put on a serious face and talk about risks to national security. Personally, he believed day-to-day talk of Police business was more likely to be of interest to professional criminals than German pilots.

"This being the case, Mr Chairman, one has to express some degree of surprise, on behalf of our police officers, when one heard a BBC announcement regarding the escape from Bridgend."

As Ross had expected, the man sitting opposite him immediately sat up, shuffled his papers and looked to the head of the table, seeking permission to speak. Robert Mears was Donald Ross' opposite number at the Ministry of Information and had responsibility to the Official Censor at the Press Censorship Division.

"Mr Chairman, if I may?"

"If you may what, Mr Mears?" The Chairman disliked prevarication. "Say what you mean if you please. It will save us all a lot of time."

"Indeed, sir. Thank you. The BBC report was very similar in content to the press reports carried by newspapers in the immediate aftermath of the escape. It certainly contained no details or descriptions of the escaped prisoners. However much we might have preferred the BBC not to broadcast the report at all, Mr Chairman, it was not open to objection from the point of view of disclosing secret or confidential information." Mears smiled wanly and raised his eyebrows in silent and insincere apology. Before taking up his post with the Ministry of Information he had been a senior executive with the BBC. It was clear to all within his Department, and those around the table, where his sympathies lay.

"Perhaps," Colonel Sheppard leant forward again. "It would be helpful if the Press Censorship Division would refer any accounts of escapes by Prisoners of War to the DPW before passing them for publication."

"I don't like acronyms, Colonel." The growl from the opposite end of the table reached new depths.

"My apologies, sir. Perhaps press reports could be referred to the Directorate of Prisoners of War before they are passed for publication – which, of course, would include broadcasts by the BBC."

There was silence as all eyes turned to Mr Mears. His irritation was obvious, yet he managed to maintain his outward sanguine calm.

"Thank you Colonel. The committee may be assured I will arrange to have your suggestion looked into."

"Discussions regarding the advantages and disadvantages of Police wireless transmissions and the procedure for press censorship will have to wait gentlemen. I fully expect that by our next meeting you will have reached an accommodation which fully serves the national interests."

The Chairman, with a note of finality, thanked everyone for attending. He scraped his chair back to add a further punctuation point and glared at the wall clock. Muttering about the menu he hoped the canteen would have available, he rose heavily, finally lighting his cigar and leaving the room through a cloud of grey smoke.

Tuesday 13ᵗʰ March 1945, 11:30 hrs.

Jimmy Morgan, or simply 'Jim' to his friends now he had reached the age of eleven, had listened intently to the breakfast table discussion between his mother and aunt. The subject, unsurprisingly, had been the escape of seventy German officers from the Prisoner of War camp, just five miles down the road in Bridgend. He and his friends had been collectively and individually warned by their parents, teachers and guardians to take care when out playing. In particular, they had been told to stay away from neighbouring fields and woodlands as it was widely suspected that it was here the escapees would be most likely to take refuge.

Special constables had been stationed on every street corner in the small village of Pencoed and the Army had set up check-points on the main road out of the village towards Bridgend to the west and Llantrisant to the east.

It was the westerly barricade that the boys visited first. After the initial excitement of inspecting the soldiers and their military paraphernalia, Jim and his friends had reached the conclusion that the Germans wouldn't be stupid enough to travel by road. Like the area's senior military and police officers, they agreed that escaped prisoners would be more likely to move about at night and to keep to the fields and back lanes.

Henry Hanson, a London refugee who, at the age of twelve, claimed an extra year of wisdom over his fellow gang members, had closely questioned the Lance-Corporal in charge of the road block on that very point. The soldier, uneasy in his role of commanding a military position which could become a front line spearhead, had told the boys to 'buzz off and go to school'. Henry had stood squarely in front of the soldiers and placed his hands on his hips.

"Shows how much you know, then." He sniffed contemptuously. "School's closed for the day."

The soldiers clearly weren't convinced and Henry closed his eyes, half turning away. "It's 'cos of the 'present state of alert'."

He quoted from the brief note posted on the school gates the previous afternoon.

"You lot don't look very alert." Jim butted in, causing a round of laughter from the boys. The Lance-Corporal's right hand rose over his shoulder, preparing to take a swat at the boy's head. The laughing ceased as the boys made a swift tactical withdrawal.

They retreated to a safe distance and sat on the pavement behind a dustbin. Jim was a local boy, living with his mother and aunt while his father contributed to the war effort, sailing with the Merchant Marine. Henry had lived in Pencoed for less than four years, having been evacuated from Edgware in Middlesex. His home had been close to the London northbound railway lines and his parents had reluctantly agreed that he should be moved further from the centre of the bombing when the Blitz had been at its height. He would have been returned to his parents by now but for a stray bomb which had struck his family home, rendering his parents and grandparents temporarily homeless.

The third member of the group, also aged eleven, was Toby Morris. The son of one of the village's few career policemen, he had originally been seen as a liability by his friends. Until, that is, an incident involving an empty shop, a brick and several days of fearful suspense had convinced them that Toby could be trusted not to report their misadventures to his father.

Tossing a pebble into the gutter, Jim suggested they go over the fields.

"We could go up to the woods towards Heol Y Cyw." He tossed another pebble, knocking the first one through a drain cover. "Last time, I found a dead bird up there." He looked up as if this latest revelation might encourage the others. Instead, Toby wrinkled his nose but Henry, anxious that his senior age should place him as the group's natural commander, rose decisively to his feet.

"Right, then. Heel a queue, what's its name, it is then." Striding as if they had genuine purpose, the boys moved off towards the far end of the village.

By the time they left the Penybont Road, the main street through Pencoed, they had become Army Commandos on a mission to track down and recapture seventy enemy paratroopers.

169

with something hard and he shuffled a shallow covering of leaves to one side. Nestled in the ground-covering lay a tin, its roughly cut lid discarded a few inches away. The label, dark with damp, bore a familiar red cross. Beneath the cross were some printed words that the boys could not identify. They looked at each other, searching for confirmation before committing themselves to declaring what they believed they had found.

Toby started checking the ground around them, kicking and pushing with his feet at the undergrowth and dead twigs that lay entwined with ivy and layers of brown leaves. At the edge of the small clearing, he stopped. Without taking his eyes from the ground, Toby beckoned to his two friends.

Half buried, half covered with branches and brambles, lay an olive green bundle, its canvas webbing clearly identifying its military origins. Henry pulled gingerly at one of the straps, revealing just enough for the boys to see it was attached to a back-pack. As if afraid they might detonate an explosion, the boys stepped slowly backwards. They turned, Jim's injury forgotten, and ran as fast as they could towards the safety of Pencoed.

It was a full five minutes before Jim's aunt could get any lucid words from any of the boys as they sat at her kitchen table, engulfing glasses of water between gasps. His mother was at work in Waterton at the shell-filling factory and it had perhaps been a subconscious awareness of explosives which had prompted the boys to leave their discovery undisturbed. Whatever, the reason, Jim's aunt was the nearest available adult and the first of many to congratulate them on their common sense. Any thoughts of punishment for leaving the village apparently forgotten, Pencoed's police force, having heard the story, swung into action.

Joined by a unit of Army Sappers and several local volunteers, a search party was quickly formed and headed with determined silence across the fields, retracing the boys' earlier gallop, towards Heol Y Cyw. Each man carried a stout stick and, given any slight reason, swung it briskly through gorse, bracken, brambles or tall grass in a show of flushing out the enemy.

Their efforts were rewarded. By mid afternoon the search party had returned, surrounding four despondent German officers who continued to object to the close handling the escorting men were giving them and insisting they be treated respectfully. Reciting lengthy passages which, they insisted, were direct quotes from the 1929 Geneva Convention, they demanded food, drink, bedding and a change of clothes.

The Police Sergeant taking charge of their temporary incarceration at Pencoed Police Station sighed and shook his head with a thin smile. He was, he explained, a mere civilian. As such, he doubted that he was bound by the worthy and altogether very decent conditions laid down by the Geneva Convention, concerned as it was with the conduct of military personnel. He shrugged and apologised, shaking his head further. They would have to put up with the, admittedly inadequate, facilities afforded by his small Police Station. As he showed the still protesting officers to their cell, he added that, as much as he would like to help, food and other supplies were limited. He slammed the cell door noisily, pushed home a solid iron bolt and turned the key. He grinned, sliding the small shutter from the peep-hole in the door.

"It has something to do with the privations forced upon us by six years of unwanted warfare, gentlemen." He rubbed his chin in exaggerated thought. "Who was it, now, who started the war?"

The Sergeant offered another wide smile as he pushed the shutter closed, cutting out all but the loudest protests from within.

Tuesday 13th March 1945, 13:00 hrs.

Howie Harris, Daniel Williams and George Morgan had lived in the small village of Merthyr Mawr near Bridgend all their lives. Lives which, admittedly, had spanned no more than fifteen years; long enough to have discovered and explored every small and grimy cove along the four mile coastline between Ogmore-by-Sea and Porthcawl.

Their favourite stretch was, without doubt, that which lay closest to their homes. Perched over a sea cliff, the near vertical wall of stone was pock-marked with rugged but secure foot and hand holes, making it ideal for climbing. Even better, a few feet from the base of the cliffs, a series of deep caves punctuated the high water mark. Seen from the Bristol Channel, they appeared on the lip of each receding tide like an irregular series of full stops. Rumoured to have been used by pirates and smugglers for centuries, the draw of the 'Wigfach Caves' had always been too great for the boys to resist, despite (or possibly because of) repeated warnings from their parents.

Over the years, the boys had made camp in them, lit fires and cooked rudimentary meals of smoky sausages and eggs in them. They had hidden contraband of various varieties and value, storing flotsam treasures found washed up on the thin beach below.

The sand and pebble beach was only visible at low tide and seldom exceeded a few yards in depth between the rock strewn foot of the cliff and the yellow-grey foam of the tide. This stretch of coast, in common with the rest of the Bristol Channel, is noted for its unusually high tidal reach. In nearby Porthcawl sea levels can typically rise over nine metres between the extremes of low and high tide. The caves, scattered along the coast, were at varying heights above the beach and many of them regularly disappeared beneath the waves at high tide. Those higher up the cliff which remained relatively dry could best be reached from the fields and coastal path above.

Despite the tide being well down the beach when the boys reached the path, it was one of these higher caves which they scrambled to, placing hands and feet with sure footed confidence as they descended the cliff face. It was a journey they had made many times before and they progressed with practiced ease and an assured disregard of any risks.

They settled down, taking their seats as they had dozens of times before, on rocks worn smooth by the action of wind and rain. Without looking up, Howie reached over his head to a shallow shelf. From the darkness, he produced a crumpled packet of cigarettes and a box of matches. They each took a cigarette, lighting it and inhaling with bravado, suppressing their coughs. They felt at ease in their own private world, as confident as any man might feel in the privacy and security of his own living room. Immune from prying adults, they were also intimately aware of every inch of their surroundings.

What they were not aware of, however, was the presence of two men, shivering with cold and crouching less than twenty yards away. The two Germans, both officers of the German Navy, had lost contact with the other two members of their party quite early after their escape. They had been the group's designated navigator and English speaker but, with the separation they had also lost their sketch map and most of their food.

The original plan of reaching Cardiff Docks had to be quickly aborted and the two remaining men had instead followed their instincts. They had turned in the darkness towards the sea, their natural habitat, crossing fields and narrow lanes until they had come across the River Ogmore. At this time of year a busy froth of a river, it drained out of the Ogmore Valley or, as the Welsh speakers would have it, *Cwm Ogwr* and through the centre of Bridgend. They had followed the widening valley, passing the ruins of a small mediaeval castle and reaching a silt laden delta. Here, at Ogmore-by-Sea and in the rising dawn, they had squinted over the fifteen mile stretch of water to North Devon then along the coast in each direction, assessing which route gave the better chance of escape.

Cardiff, they were well aware, lay to their left. To their right, however, they could just make out the misty headland of Porthcawl. There, they remembered from their lost map, was a small harbour. Where there was a small harbour, there were undoubtedly small boats. Small enough, they hoped, to slip away under cover of night yet large enough to cross the Bristol

Channel. The narrow peninsular to their south, they imagined, would be relatively easy to cross en route to France.

They had turned right from the river, north west, and started walking along the stretch of shallow sloping beach. The sun rising behind them, they had soon realised the flat coastal plain and gentle slope of sand ahead would provide no cover from either reconnaissance aircraft or search parties. They had stopped, discussed briefly their dilemma and had decided to postpone their journey until nightfall. Retracing their steps, they had passed the river towards the rising wall of rock on the other side of its mouth. With increasing anxiety they realised the beach was getting narrower the further they walked, the increasing light making their position ever more conspicuous. It would only take a rambler or a farmer to glance over the edge of the cliff above them and they would be trapped.

The tide was coming in and they were already discovering their boots had lost their waterproofing. They were German Army issue, their Navy rubber soled shoes being deemed unsuitable by Camp 198's senior German officer. The water had already splashed up their trouser legs, soaking them to the knees when, glancing ahead, one of the men had suddenly pointed and quickened his pace, splashing through the waves with renewed vigour. Fifty metres ahead and just above their shoulder level, was a cave, large enough for both men to crawl into.

They had peered into the void, rising onto the tips of their boots. It seemed quite deep enough to shelter them both in darkness.

The first man had helped the other to get a foothold and scramble heavily up the rock before turning awkwardly and pulling the first man up after him.

There they had stayed, sitting in salt-soaked and cold trousers. Crouching and gazing out at the sea, having discussed their plans, they had filled their morning by alternately dozing and chalking marks on the wall of their cave, each mark denoting the sight of a fishing vessel; a potential target for their forthcoming night forage.

They had seen no fewer than fourteen boats, the majority heading towards Porthcawl, by the time hunger drove them to search their pockets for the last of their food. They had between them a tin of corned beef, known almost universally within the armed forces as bully beef, and two wedges of nougat saved from their Red Cross relief parcels.

One of the men picked up the tin of meat and pulled the small metal key from its side. In the darkness, he squinted to find the thin tongue of metal near the lip of the tin, trying to thread it through the slot at the end of the key. Turning it slowly, he glanced up to ask his companion if he had thought to bring one of the metal knives that had regularly gone missing from the officers' canteen. As he spoke, his hand slipped, the thin sliver of metal sunk into his forefinger and he let out a sharp yelp.

Further up the cliff, the three teenagers froze. In silence, they blew the last vestiges of smoke from their lungs and stubbed out their cigarettes. They waved the smoke away, wide eyed and silently daring each other to glance over the edge of their cave.

Cursing, the German thrust his hand under the arm of his coat, sending the tin of bully beef rattling across the floor of the cave. The other man uttered a brief warning, almost falling forward to grab it as it bounced towards the daylight. Retrieving it, he turned, admonishing his companion and needlessly reminding him they had no other rations.

The boys looked quizzically at each other before edging sideways in the direction of the noise.

"Did you hear that?" Daniel asked unnecessarily.

The other two nodded.

"I didn't hear what they said. Was it Welsh?" Howie glanced at his Welsh speaking companion.

Daniel shook his head. "Didn't sound like any Welsh I know."

They fell to silence again, concentrating on the sounds outside for further clues. Hearing nothing but the rattle of waves on gravel and the buffeting wind as it circled and eddied, the boys decided they would have to go and search if they wanted their questions answered.

Daniel Williams was the smallest of the trio and it was agreed he would make least noise disembarking from the cave mouth. Without a word, he rolled up his trouser legs and pulled off his shoes and socks. He slipped soundlessly to the beach and edged along the crest of the beach, hugging the cliff. The water was already up to his knees and he knew only too well that, had the wind whipped the surf up to its normal March ferocity, he could have been pulled off balance and out to sea by the

177

undertow. As it was, the waves barely broke before they struck the cliff face. Even in these conditions, Daniel knew he could only spend a few minutes in the water. The cold was already biting at his legs and the tide was rising fast now.

He found a hand hold above his head and pulled himself up, taking another step up until his feet were clear of the frothing tide. He leaned in to the cliff, listening for noises from the nearest cave, a few yards to his left. Hearing nothing, he edged closer to the gaping black hole, cautiously peering round the lip. It was empty and, with a mixture of relief and disappointment, he moved on to the next.

Crouching in their cave, unaware of the teenager's approach, the two Germans had reconciled their differences over the tin of Spam and were greedily scooping lumps of it into their mouths with crooked fingers. As sailors, they should have had more awareness of their surroundings but all their attention had been absorbed by hunger and tinned meat.

Beneath them, the sea lapped slowly closer. Like a besieging army, confident and unhurried, it slowly climbed the cliff, advancing on their hiding place.

Daniel needed no more than a moment to assess the situation. He had heard about the escape from Island Farm Camp and knew the cave well enough to understand exactly what had to be done. He dropped into the water, the sound of his body hitting the waves insignificant amidst the slapping of the tide against the cliff. Half climbing, half wading, he returned to Howie and George, clambering with renewed agility back into the dry hole in the rock. Rubbing his legs to renew the circulation, he quickly told what he had discovered. It took no more than a few moments for the boys to agree the tide would soon reach and swallow the German's cave. That would be long before it reached its full tidal reach but still the water would be too deep and the waves too violent for any but the strongest swimmer to escape.

Daniel agreed he needed to get moving in order to dry off and Howie was voted their quickest runner. George was elected to stay as lookout to check if the Germans left the cave while the other two boys ran for help.

As Daniel and Howie climbed like spider crabs up the rock face to the grass above them, George arranged himself carefully at the mouth of the cave, one foot wedged against the opposite wall for stability, his eyes firmly fixed on a point in the cliff face a few yards along and below his vantage point.

The two boys reached the cliff top and started trotting along the path. There was a pub half a mile or so down the coast in the village of Southerndown. The landlord had been a member of the local Home Guard and they were sure he would have a sufficient number of customers in the bar at lunchtime to mount a search party.

In the event, they had no need to run so far. Ahead of them, a small fishing boat moved slowly with the rolling surf, the two men on board hauling at lines to bring in their catch of crabs. Howie pointed and shouted.

"It's Alfie and his Dad." He ran on, stopping adjacent to the boat now no more than thirty yards out. He cupped his hands round his mouth and shouted Alfie's name. He waved in a wide arc, almost jumping in his enthusiasm.

The two figures, leaning over the stern of their boat immediately stopped and the slighter of the two men waved back. Alfie Harris was a year or two older than the boys but knew them from their habit of hanging about on the length of beach between Ogmore and Porthcawl. Occasionally the boys had walked as far as Porthcawl's harbour and helped them either prepare for a day at sea or unload their catch. The boys' reward for their casual labour varied, but usually included a handsome clutch of crabs to take home to their mothers.

Today, in the unseasonably calm waters of the Bristol Channel, the small vessel was close enough to shore for their voices to carry. Responding to the boys' urgent hand signals, Mr Harris edged his boat closer to the cliff until they could converse in voices raised just enough to travel over the surf.

Excitedly, Howie abbreviated what they had discovered. The men on the boat listened, nodded, put their thumbs up and issued instructions.

The boys turned and walked back towards the caves, keeping pace with the progress of the small boat as it bobbed alongside. Above the Germans' cave, they stopped and pointed down to where the prisoners lay hidden. Harris nodded slowly, turning his boat to shore and edging closer to the cliff. The sea was now lapping the rocks to within a few inches of the cave's entrance.

Skilfully holding his vessel off the rocks, Harris inhaled and shouted at the cliffs.

"Germans. Show yourselves now." Alfie and his father gazed at the dark void, waiting. A few seconds passed and he repeated the order, louder now and adding "Oi, Fritz" as a precursor. Again, there was no response. Peering over the edge of the cliff, Howie began to wonder if their quarry had moved on. It was then that he saw George Morgan, leaning out from his cave a few yards away, pointing to the prisoners' cave, nodding and giving the thumbs up. The Germans were still holed up in their hiding place.

"Germans, you listen to me. The tide is coming up. Give up or you'll drown. Understand? *Kaputt, Mein Herr.*"

Finally, a shadowy face appeared in the mouth of the cave, glancing first at the boat, then at the rising waves. As he watched, a small wave broke over his knuckles, dampening the sleeve of his coat. He shook the water from his hand, turned and muttered a few inaudible words into the darkness.

It took them a few minutes but the Germans indicated they had decided on the sensible course of action. They squinted from their shadowy hiding place, weighing up the distance between them and the crew of the small fishing boat. There appeared to be only two men and one of them barely more than a boy. The Germans looked at each other. They were both in their mid twenties and, although tired and hungry, they were physically fit. Having followed their commanding officer's orders to follow a regime of daily physical training, they were probably stronger now than they had been before they were captured. They both were naturally athletic and the swim across to the small fishing boat shouldn't cause them any problems. Once on board, they concluded, they could take stock of their situation and decide what could be done. Certainly they would have no difficulty handling the boat themselves and the rustic fisherman and his young assistant could have no way of knowing they were competent seamen.

The first of the two men affected what he confidently believed would pass for a look of fearful submission and beckoned to the men in the boat, urging them to come closer to the cliff. Harris was a skilful skipper but he was not reckless. He knew the waters well enough to understand the unpredictable nature of the local currents. He shouted again, beckoning to the German with a wide sweep of his arm.

"Jump, you bloody nancy. We'll pick you up."

"Don't you mean 'bloody Nazi'?" His son glanced up at the older man, half smiling.

"Aye, boy. A bit of both I expect."

The German had no intention of jumping and he leaned further from the cave, beckoning insistently. It was then that the Bristol Channel proved its reputation for tricky behaviour. A freak wave rose above the others, lifting the boat unexpectedly and crashing directly into the mouth of the cave. The gesticulating German felt his legs pushed from under him. He grappled for a hand hold, his fingers slipping on lichen covered stone. He lost his footing and his balance, falling heavily. His face hit the waves first, his arms flailing impotently.

Harris gazed down at the man, frantically paddling to stay afloat. He turned to his son.

"That's not exactly what I meant, but it'll do." He picked up a boat-hook from the deck and dropped the metal capped end next to the man in the water. The German was a reasonably strong swimmer, but weighed down by a woollen pullover, heavy worsted trousers, full length coat and heavy boots, he now knew he stood little chance against the numbing cold and undercurrents. He had already taken a mouthful of bitter salt water and was choking uncontrollably. He grabbed the pole and allowed himself to be pulled on board, still gagging and regurgitating seawater.

As he lay on the deck, convulsing noisily, his companion, peering from his hiding place, realised their bid to take control of the boat was doomed before it had begun. As Harris and his son called out to him again, he edged towards the mouth of the cave. Instead of dropping into the water, the German began a hazardous climb to the top of the cliff.

The fishermen watched, bemused, as he made hesitant progress towards the grassy bank above. On the deck of the boat, the sodden escapee turned, saw what was happening, choked one more time and tried to cry out a warning. His voice was swallowed by the wind and waves and would have been too late anyway.

The climbing German thrust his right arm over the bank of soil and was preparing to pull himself up. He was surprised to feel several hands grasping at his coat and collar, propelling him rapidly up and forwards, away from the cliff edge. He felt a weight pressing down on his back and shoulders and, lying flat on his stomach, was firmly pinned by the substantial weight of two heavily planted teenage boys.

Triumphantly, the boys turned to the boatmen, grinning and giving them another thumbs up. The boat's engine picked up, Harris pointed to Porthcawl, gave a final wave and started chugging slowly but surely towards the nearest harbour.

It was a surprised publican who, seated in the snug at his Southerndown pub, took custody of the escaped German prisoner and telephoned the Police Station at Ogmore-by-Sea. In the meantime, clutching their reward of pint tankards of mild, the three boys, now reunited, gleefully told and retold their story to a growing group of villagers.

Tuesday 13th March 1945, 14:00 hrs.

There was no denying that, despite the efforts of four perfectly competent officers, they were quite lost. Two of the men had, in the earlier stages of the war, commanded Panzer tanks in the North African desert. They had learned to tell the time of day and their east from their west by means of following the position of the Sun. They were now discovering, however, that on a dank spring day in South Wales with the Sun buried behind a dense grey wall of cloud, there was little opportunity to gauge either.

They had been heading for Port Talbot Docks and had found themselves in the company of another group of escapees. Agreeing that seven men could not continue to travel together unnoticed, their plan had been overruled by the other group's leader who held the senior rank. Reluctantly, they had been forced to change their route and had turned inland. They now intended to bypass Port Talbot and travel on to Neath where they hoped to find transport to carry them on to Swansea, to the small fishing village of Tenby or even the ports of Pembroke Dock or Milford Haven. Their map, painstakingly copied onto a thin sheet of paper and folded into one of the men's left boot, indicated where the towns were and gave enough detail of road and rail routes. The German naval officer was confident he could pilot a small craft out of the winding channels that made up the Cleddau Estuary and the *Luftwaffe* pilot officer remembered enough of his bombing mission briefings to know that the south-westerly corner of Wales was lined with industrial docks dotted with craft of all sizes.

Now, however, the four found themselves in limbo between towns, faced by a broad horizon of green fields which, despite being speckled with landmark church spires and farm buildings, were not marked on their map. In the absence of any better plan, they walked on, following one footpath after another until they reached a canal. Apparently little used, they turned left and followed the string of water believing, correctly, that it would lead eventually to a river and thence to the open sea.

Had they continued on the same route, they would have reached the River Neath which runs into the Bristol Channel a few miles north west of Port Talbot. Instead, their journey was interrupted by a loud clattering noise which drove them to take cover. A wheezing locomotive, belching deep grey smoke, crossed their tracks, struggling its way out of Port Talbot. Taking the time to reassess their tactics, they reasoned, again correctly, that it could guide them to Swansea and beyond. Where there was a railway line, they agreed, there must be trains and, with a bit of luck, they might be able to hitch a ride.

The ancient locomotive had crossed the canal over a Victorian arched bridge and, their leather boots slipping on the damp grass, the men slowly managed to climb the embankment from the canal towpath and turned to follow the tracks.

They followed the rusting metal along a raised embankment and, now exposed to even a casual glance, quickly slid down the grass to follow the tracks from the shadows cast by a line of trees. Walking was difficult, made heavier by their boots and thick clothing and before long the weakest of the four, a young man in his early twenties, had dropped back. He dared not complain, knowing he had overlooked his physical fitness and a breach of conduct charge would be smartly thrown at him. He struggled on, pausing to feign a pull at the heel of one of his boots while the pain in his calf muscles subsided. When the others turned to check his progress, he asserted firmly that the boot was digging into his ankle. He waved the others to press on. He would adjust his boot and catch them up. As his three compatriots vanished behind the curtain of trees, he slumped onto a fallen log and pulled a packet of cigarettes from his pocket. A few minutes respite would make no difference. Unlike the other officers in his group, Friedrich Gossler was not an enthusiastic Nazi. He was not even an enthusiastic soldier. He would never have admitted such a thing during his spell at Island Farm, of course, surrounded by career soldiers. Most had gained their commissions in the *Waffen SS* before war had been declared and knew only a life of military order and combat. Friedrich would have been quite happy to sit out his time and wait for the Armistice which, unlike many of his fellow officers, he was reasonably sure would come sooner rather than later. He was also, almost uniquely, certain that it would be Germany and not the Allies who would be forced to capitulate.

These thoughts, now more rampant in his mind than ever, could never have been repeated out loud and within earshot of his countrymen – at least until he was relieved of the need to wear his uniform.

As a civilian, Friedrich had been an accounts clerk for a small business based a few miles from the southern city of Munich. He had been called up in 1943 and, until a few months earlier, had spent a relatively peaceful and uneventful war, posted well behind the front line. His office in Dusseldorf, where he shuffled papers and passed messages, had been a comfortable, peaceful place. The recipients of his messages in Berlin and the combat unit commanders on the western front, however, considered he had proved himself so adept at paper shuffling that he had been promoted to *Offizier-Bewerber* or Officer Applicant. Such had the need for front-line officers become by the end of 1944 that he had been awarded his commission and the rank of *Leutnant*. Had he been asked for an opinion, he would have readily admitted the promotion had come earlier than his ability warranted.

Friedrich had been drawn into the escape and tunnelling scheme at Island Farm quite early in its planning for no better reason than he was, standing in his thick woollen socks, the smallest man in the camp. The escape committee had singled him out as ideally fitted to dig in the confined space beneath Hut Nine.

He had been happy to help, hoping his cooperation might increase his popularity and associated perks. It had never occurred to him that the British guards would fail to discover the tunnel before it reached the perimeter wire. Even when the engineer in charge of the building work had announced they had reached their goal, Friedrich had remained confident that his junior rank and lack of qualifications in all other relevant matters would deem him unsuitable to join the escape party.

He had been wrong. As an active participant in the preparation of the tunnel, the German sense of fair play had ensured him an early position in the queue. He had taken his place alongside more senior and capable officers considered to have a strong chance of success. Finally, being teamed up with more experienced men had given him a glimmer of confidence that they might keep him relatively safe, at least from being shot. It was a confidence which had quickly evaporated when he began to understand the haphazard standard of forward planning. Once they were free of the camp itself, it became obvious that none of them had a complete knowledge of the area or any clear idea of how they would leave the British coast.

He would have been even more worried, as he sat and pulled on the last vestiges of tobacco smoke, had he been able to see his three travelling companions.

Having reached the River Neath without encountering a railway station or another train, they had been forced back onto the exposed railway line in order to cross the river. Admittedly, they had paused to consider their options and to give *Leutnant* Gossler an opportunity to catch up with them. There were still several hours of daylight remaining and they needed to find a means of making up ground overnight, preferably in the wagon of a goods train.

After five minutes they decided to move on. If Gossler had been captured, there would be nothing to be gained from waiting around or looking for him. If he was on his way, he had only to follow the railway line. If he had somehow become injured, then he would only slow them down and put them all at greater risk. Better that he be sacrificed to the British in order to improve their chances of success.

Now at a steady run, the three officers crossed the steel railway bridge, the River Neath sliding slowly by beneath them. On the western side of the river, the tracks were supported by heavy iron stanchions which carried the line between the upper branches of large trees. Further on, it crossed another bridge over a narrow lane. They stopped, squatted down and quickly ran through their options. Ahead of them was an open stretch of several kilometres of exposed railway track, affording them no cover and still no sign of a railway yard or station. They dropped over a wire fence to the embankment below and made their way onto the lane. Gossler would now have no means of knowing the route they had taken. He would just have to take care of himself.

They dodged quickly to the side of the lane, vaulted over a fence and slid into a large copse. They would wait there, reasonably well hidden, deciding their next move until darkness fell. If they saw the diminutive *Leutnant* they would try to draw his attention but, even as they quietly whispered their doubts, two policemen, barely three metres from their hiding place, strolled into sight pushing bicycles. At least they were sure now they had made the right decision by leaving the railway line. It was clearly visible as it spanned the wide valley and they would certainly have been spotted. Reassuringly, it seemed the two police officers were making no effort to search the area. One of the Germans hissed a suggestion that they could overpower them and steal their bicycles.

By an extraordinary coincidence, at the same moment, one of the constables drew his revolver and aimed it into the banking at the side of the lane. He drew back the hammer and closed one eye. The three fugitives, spying from a tuft of grass a few feet from the pistol's barrel, instinctively flinched. They didn't hear the country policeman, a veteran with over thirty years service, joke to his companion that he had thought he had seen a rabbit for his dinner table. He released the hammer gently and slipped the sidearm back into its holster.

The two constables continued their stroll unmolested, unaware of the crime they had inadvertently prevented. They left the Germans lying on the grass, listening to the occasional sound of traffic passing further up the lane. Perhaps they were close to a main road. In the absence of any rail traffic, they decided to investigate. After a quick glance up and down the lane which confirmed the presence of neither Gossler nor an enemy search party, they emerged from the trees and walked swiftly away from the bridge.

The lane soon joined a wider stretch of road and, despite seeing only one or two vehicles, it wasn't long before they came across a bus stop and, parked obligingly in the shallow lay-by, a bus. Apart from a driver reading a newspaper, it appeared to be empty. The men stopped short, gathering in a circle once again to discuss the possibilities. Trying not to look furtive, one of them pulled out a cigarette packet and shared it around. They could overpower the driver, but on this main road they might easily be seen. The authorities would be alerted immediately and the road was bound to be controlled by Army roadblocks at regular intervals. They could take the driver hostage and force him to drive them to the nearest port, but that would surely create new complications. Not least, one of the men speculated, it would give the British an excuse to shoot them. Far better, they agreed, to remain as inconspicuous as possible.

As they were talking, a man wearing a grey uniform and carrying a satchel over one shoulder crossed the road and boarded the bus. He exchanged a few words with the driver and took a seat close to the front. He glanced at his watch and pulled a package from his pocket. Unwrapping it carefully, he took a bite from a thick sandwich and settled back in his seat.

A woman carrying a shopping basket passed by, barely glancing in their direction, and boarded the bus. She paid her fare, nodded to the driver and took a seat. The Germans silently understood that the kidnap option was now untenable. The driver sniffed noisily, folded his newspaper and wedged it into his jacket pocket. He glanced at his conductor, nodded once and turned the ignition key. The engine rumbled into life and both men glanced out of the window expectantly at the men on the kerbside. The other uniformed man leaned out of the door and spoke a few words of English which only one of them understood.

Quickly, the men boarded the bus and moved to the rear seats. They had not seen the front of the bus or the makeshift sign which showed the towns covered by its route. If they had, they might have realised they would be carried north east, up the Neath Valley and away from the coast.

As part of their preparations for the escape, several of the prisoners had been issued with small amounts of British currency. This had either been smuggled in from outside the camp by work-parties of German prisoners, stolen or given to them by their guards. Several of the prisoners, with time on their hands, had whittled scraps of wood to carve animals or sketched portraits. Impressed, some of the guards had bought them, knowing the war would end soon and intending to keep them as souvenirs. Some had paid with cigarettes or rations of margarine, coffee or powdered egg. Although strictly forbidden, others had paid with cash.

At the back of the bus, the Germans counted the coins. They had no idea of the cost of a bus ride but hoped the small selection of silver and nickel coins would be enough. They watched intently as the uniformed man with the satchel chatted briefly with the woman passenger before zig-zagging his way to the back of the bus, holding the vertical metal poles as he was jolted by the movement of the bus.

He frowned with mock indignation. "You had to sit right at the back, didn't you?" The passengers gazed at him uncomprehendingly. "Where to gents?" He checked his supply of tickets. The German selected for his knowledge of English cleared his throat.

"Swansea, please." He held a collection of coins between his outstretched fingers.

Something in the conductor's mind clicked into place moments before he began to speak. He was about to explain they weren't going to Swansea. Instead, he took the offered coins and made a show of counting out the fares. He returned some change and three tickets.

A few miles up the road, the bus entered the outskirts of the village of Glynneath. A few people had got on board at the intervening stops and were sitting alone and in pairs, unconcerned and apparently unaware of the three men in the rear seats.

The woman with the shopping bag got up and exchanged a few words with the conductor before stepping down to the narrow pavement.

The Germans, reassured by the familiar routine, sat back and waited for the sights and sounds of a seaport town. Privately, they were beginning to congratulate themselves on their smooth progress. They remained unconcerned when the driver seemed to be in no hurry to continue their journey. A man dressed in a dark blue uniform stepped into the bus and took a seat close to the door. Men in uniform were common during wartime and he was too far away for them to determine which of the services he might belong to. A merchant seaman perhaps, returning to his ship? One of the rear seat passengers nudged his neighbour. He could guide them to the docks if they were able to follow him. Holding what appeared to be a coat rolled up under his arm, the man wasn't wearing a cap and they couldn't see any insignia on his cuffs. They concluded he might be a Royal Navy officer; an encouraging sign but they would have to be wary in case he was armed.

The bus pulled away and almost immediately took a sharp left hand turn off the main road. A hundred yards down the narrow side street, it pulled up again. The man in uniform rose from his seat but, instead of alighting, took a few steps towards the back of the bus. With deliberate care, he put his coat down on the seat next to him, revealing a policeman's helmet which he fitted firmly on his head, ducking slightly in the limited headroom of the bus. Reaching down, he pulled something from below the rolled up coat. Only then did he look up at the three men on the back seat. He raised a service revolver and pointed it at the man seated in the middle.

"Would you gentlemen kindly oblige me by walking this way?"

The eyes of every passenger in the bus were now trained on the Policeman. They turned, following a line from the barrel of the pistol and settled their gaze on the three men who, in turn, slowly raised their hands.

Only then did it occur to the others on board, including the escaped prisoners that they had come to a halt directly outside Glynneath Police Station.

As they were escorted through the Police Station doors, the woman with the shopping bag could be seen panting briskly up the street towards them. She paused and nodded at the escorting officer as he passed, a knowing smile passing between them.

Tuesday 13th March 1945, 16:45 hrs.

Friedrich Gossler was now totally lost. Being the most junior member of his party he had not been trusted with a copy of their precious map and neither had he been given any money or the crudely forged identity papers which some had acquired.

Moreover, despite tightening the laces on his boots in pretence that they had been slowing his progress, they had now begun rubbing for real and his ankle was developing a large and painful blister. He had also been unable to find his travelling companions, despite walking as fast as he could tolerate for over an hour.

He had followed the railway line as far as the bridge over the wide stretch of river, clambering up the embankment to gaze along the line for any sign of his fellow officers. Seeing nothing, he had turned right, following the river up the valley. Had he given his situation more thought, he would probably have turned left, following the flow of the river towards the sea. That way, however, seemed to Friedrich to be blocked by dense trees. He had had enough of trudging through woodlands and blamed protruding roots and fallen branches for much of the pain in his aching feet.

The realisation that his comrades had deserted him was quickening his heart rate far more than the exertion of his brisk pace. He hadn't taken to any of the officers he had been matched up with but, he had to reluctantly admit, he would have been safer in their company. He was hungry, tired and felt both hot and cold at the same time. Under his heavy layers of clothing, rivulets of sweat trickled over his torso, chilling his chest and back. No longer thinking rationally, he slowed his pace, unaware that he was following a wide right hand arc in the river, walking at least a mile to cross a field spanning no more than a few hundred yards.

It was beginning to get dark as he found himself approaching a broad open gravel yard and, beyond that, a small but busy town. In one corner of the yard, an unattended lorry was

191

parked. Next to that, a gate leading from the yard had been left open.

Had Friedrich been with the other three prisoners, there is little doubt they would have made every effort to take the vehicle and cover as much ground as possible. Friedrich, however, could not drive. Instead, he crossed the gravel barely glancing at the lorry and passed through the open gate on to a busy street. By contrast to his earlier route, it was churning with humanity; factory workers either heading for home or on their way to start a night shift.

He was too exhausted to feel any fear as he trudged his way through the crowd, ignoring them in the same way that they seemed to be ignoring him. At the far end of the street, the press of urgently moving people became sparser and he found himself in a wide street lined with a terrace of small shops. Despite his hunger, he resisted the temptation to snatch supplies. Although there were vegetables displayed in boxes set out on the pavement and within easy reach, his burning ankle was making him wince at every step. Even if he managed to pocket a few carrots, he wouldn't have been able to run more than a few steps before being caught. Instead, he limped on, his pace slowing.

Finally, he found what he was looking for. He pushed open the stout timber door and entered a stark room, painted in sombre shades of bottle green and brown.

He crossed to the counter and leaned against it, taking the weight off his ankle. Seeing nobody to serve him, he tapped the palm of his hand on the dome of a brass bell. He waited patiently until a door behind the counter slowly opened.

"*Mein name ist Leutnant Friedrich Gossler.*"

The elderly Sergeant pulled his spectacles down his nose, gazing at the unkempt little man across the desk. Gossler spoke slowly and deliberately, emphasising each syllable.

"*Ich bin ein entflohener Häftling.*"

The Sergeant had no idea that he had just been told the man standing before him was an escaped prisoner. Despite that, he was all too aware of the fiasco emanating from Bridgend and he recognised a foreign language when he heard it.

He lifted the hatch separating the public side of the room from his own and beckoned him to follow.

Tuesday 13th March 1945, 18:00 hrs.

Like *Leutnant* Gossler, Dieter Kellerman had followed his party along a railway line. Unlike Gossler, however, they had found and boarded a goods train a short distance from Bridgend. Their leader, an imperious Major or *Sturmbannführer* in the *Waffen SS* Panzer Corps named von Hindermeer, had ordered that they make for Barry Docks. It was, he had argued, closer than Cardiff and being a less important town than Cardiff would not be so well guarded. All three junior officers in the group had nodded enthusiastic agreement. Too many of their peers were also heading for Cardiff. Cardiff Docks would soon look like a *Wehrmacht* reunion with so many German officers lining up to board unsuspecting vessels.

Von Hindermeer had confidently predicted that the port at Barry would be awash with 'common sailors' who would be susceptible to bribes, especially if they were from Spanish or Portuguese ships. Despite being technically neutral and forbidden from assisting either side in the conflict, it was well understood that they were all too willing to profit from the war where they could. There was sufficient sympathy for the Nazi cause within both nations to ensure they would receive fair treatment. It had been the *Sturmbannführer's* experience that, if their ideology or respect for his rank proved inadequate, the lower orders could be bent to his will by the injection of a little cash. Fortunately, he had been able to accumulate several hundred francs and a handful of British silver coins while still serving in France. He had managed to smuggle them through a perfunctory search when he had been taken prisoner and now patted his jacket pocket as if in confirmation.

Dieter Kellerman was a junior officer, having been made a *Leutnant zur See* only six months earlier. In the short time since, his E-Boat had been engaged in two actions against the enemy. During the first, three members of his watch had been killed by shrapnel and during the second, they had run into a minefield. The resultant catastrophic explosion had left him unconscious, without a vessel but fortunately afloat. The majority of his ship's company had not been so fortunate. He had been scooped from the North Sea by a Royal Navy frigate and put ashore with half a dozen others in Hull. He had been warned of the atrocities he was likely to be subjected to if taken prisoner and had slept uneasily, dreaming of being locked in chains and excruciating tortures. When he had woken, however, he had found himself wrapped in a thick blanket and a Royal Navy rating gently nudging him. A wedge of bread and ham shared space with a mug of hot coffee on the tray next to his bunk.

Since becoming a Prisoner of War, Dieter had been instructed by more senior prisoners that, despite the British 'ruse' of offering fair treatment, it remained his duty to escape and rejoin the Fuhrer's crusade. The poor conduct of his own senior officers since his enrolment in the *Kriegsmarine* remained firmly lodged in his consciousness and he had been surprised to have been chosen to join the escape party. Only on the night of the escape had he been told that it was his experience of piloting light sea vessels which had secured his position in the tunnel. He would have happily stayed behind and, now, as it became clear that the train they had boarded had by-passed both Barry and Cardiff, von Hindermeer was coming to the view that Dieter's usefulness to him might have been overstated.

The four men now crouched in their goods van, a match sputtering its final moments of life over the outstretched map as they tried to determine their route. Once more in darkness, their only feint illumination coming in thin slices through gaps between the planking of the carriage walls, Dieter pressed his face to the timber. He peered into the dusk, watching as trees passed at alarming speed, flickering specks of sunset flashing between them. He shook his head, calculating they were travelling east and switched to the other side of the train. He could see water – and it was getting closer. He reported his discovery to the other officers. Immediately, another match was struck and von Hindermeer's elegant index finger traced the line of railway track as it left the eastern suburbs of Cardiff, heading towards Bristol. Between the two cities lay the Bristol Channel. He predicted they would shortly be submerged in a tunnel seven kilometres long.

Already the train was slowing but Dieter's mind was beginning to race. Von Hindermeer leaned back, a satisfied smile spreading across his face. They would, he announced,

194

simply adapt their plans and make for the docks at Bristol. It was well known that there was a port in the city.

Dieter shook his head. Bristol was a major Royal Navy dockyard. The port would be securely guarded. They would have no chance of getting on board a civilian vessel there. The *Sturmbannführer* was not accustomed to being contradicted and said so with a clarity of mind borne of his rank and breeding. He closed his eyes and turned away, the discussion at an end.

Silently, Dieter calculated that if they stayed on the Welsh side of the Bristol Channel, there was a chance they would find a small fishing boat or coastal trading vessel. The train was beginning to brake as it turned a final bend towards the tunnel. He reached towards the handle of the freight car's sliding door. The other two officers looked anxiously from one man to the other, unsure of where their loyalties should fall. Von Hindermeer carried rank over all of them, yet they also appreciated the young naval officer's logic and insight.

One of the men nodded at Dieter, and he jerked the door back, admitting a rush of cold air and noise. Without a second thought, he half fell, half jumped from the wagon, hitting the ground hard and rolling away down a mercifully spongy embankment of grass and dead leaves.

"*Nein!*" Von Hindermeer's conceit was such that he could barely accept any man would disagree with him, let alone disobey. He jammed his foot against the edge of the door, pushing it shut again. The two officers, visibly shaken, simply sat and stared at him.

The first to speak asked timidly whether they should have checked, at least, to see if the *Leutnant zur See* had survived the fall.

The *Sturmbannführer* shook his head firmly. *Leutnant* Kellerman would be reported. If he survived, he would face a court martial on charges of disobeying the direct order of a superior officer and of desertion. He closed his eyes again and folded his arms. The outcome, he concluded, would be death by firing squad. Of that there would be no doubt. The other two men wordlessly glanced at each other. They kept silent.

Only half of the lengthy Severn Tunnel passes below water and the wagon was thrown quickly into darkness as it was plunged underground. The thunder and rattle of the locomotive echoed back at the men from the solid tunnel walls; Victorian engineering at its best coping with mid twentieth century locomotive power. The van slowly filled with the acrid smell of coal smoke and steam. The carriage jerked and swayed. The cacophony rose in tempo and volume and all three men, privately, became immersed in their own thoughts. The *Sturmbannführer* used his time to silently argue, as if justifying himself to a higher authority, that he had made the correct decision. The two junior men merely prayed for safe deliverance.

Tuesday 13ᵗʰ March 1945, 20:00 hrs.

Leutnant zur See Dieter Kellerman lay, flat out, his cheek pressed to the damp earth. With some effort, he drew a deep breath, reassured that he was still alive. He rolled over and crossed his arms across his abdomen. He waited a few moments, blinking up at the sky and waiting for pain to kick in. Experimentally, he raised first one knee, then the other. He was winded and his ribs hurt but other than that, his major limbs seemed to be in reasonable working order.

He glanced over his right shoulder. The dim red light strapped to the back of the guards van had vanished from sight and he could hear only the faintest grumble of the receding engine. He sat up, moving each shoulder in turn then got to his feet. Von Hindermeer hadn't allowed him much time to inspect the map but he was fairly sure that if he followed the tracks until he reached the tunnel before turning right, he would get to the tidal shore of the Severn River. From there, he could turn back on himself, heading west, until he came to a harbour or village. At that point, he would just have to improvise.

He looked up at the embankment carrying the railway track and gave his greatcoat a final pat down to dislodge a few damp leaves. He climbed the steep slope and turned away from the tracks, peering into the darkness in case he was already within sight of the water. He had seldom seen such darkness in so open a space. The mud flats leading down to the Severn were uninterrupted by buildings and either there was no moon that night or it was deeply hidden behind clouds. There were no ships' lights and not a glimmer reflecting off what, at low tide, would have been a smooth mirror of wet sand.

Dieter was about to resume his walk towards the tunnel when a short, metallic, double click immediately changed his prospects. He spread his arms wide, turning slowly towards the sound.

A short, curly haired Corporal, his battledress characteristically bulging untidily about his waist, stood between him and what might have been his route to freedom.

More importantly, the Corporal was holding a .303 rifle and its barrel was pointing at him.

"*Hände hoch.*" The Corporal expended his entire German vocabulary in one brief phrase. It was sufficient, made more so as Dieter's second qualification for joining the escape party – and one which he had purposely kept to himself – was his moderate command of English.

As they made their way to the nearby village of Caldicot, the Corporal was flattered to find the young German was quite prepared to confirm he had escaped from the Prisoner of War camp at Bridgend. He described how he had run across several fields to find shelter before making his way to railway sidings near the town. He told him how he had travelled by goods train through Cardiff and had jumped when he caught sight of the sea.

"I was afraid the train was going to stop and the railway guard might make a search." He waved his hand in a vaguely southerly direction. "There was the sea and I am a sailor. I think I am better with a boat. Yes?"

The Corporal grinned and nodded before pulling a face.

"Personally, I hate the bloody things. Boats, that is." He was about the same age as Dieter and in their short acquaintance had found in him nothing to dislike. "When I was a kid my dad took me over to the Isle of Wight on the ferry." He shook his head at the memory. "Was I sick or what!"

"I don't know. Were you sick?" The German looked concerned.

The other grinned and nodded. "All over my dad. He wasn't too happy, I can tell you."

Both men laughed. The Corporal pulled a cigarette packet from his tunic pocket. The white paper was almost as crumpled as his uniform but the cigarettes seemed mainly intact. He offered one to his prisoner, pulled another between his lips and pushed the pack back into his pocket. To his surprise, the German produced an elegant silver cigarette lighter which he flicked open. The two men stopped, shielding their faces from the breeze. The Corporal, unconcerned, leaned his rifle against his thigh, the stock resting on the path. Dieter lit both cigarettes and they resumed their walk.

On an impulse, Dieter introduced himself, using his first name and without thinking, omitting his military title.

Somehow, this stroll across the rural Welsh borders seemed about as far from his military existence as he could get.

"Harry. Harry Cooper." He slung the strap of his rifle over his shoulder. "My mates call me Barrel."

The German glanced at the soldier's portly torso. "That is not kind of them."

Harry followed the other's glance to his own waistline. He laughed again. "Not because I'm fat." He patted his stomach, inhaling. "It's because my name is Cooper." The German gave a brief shrug. "In English a cooper is someone who makes barrels. You know, beer barrels and stuff."

"Ah." Dieter's eyebrows rose. "This I know. We also have barrel makers in Germany. There, we call them '*der böttcher*'."

Harry shook his head. "I don't fancy being called 'Botcher'. That means something else again over here." He looked up at his companion. "It means someone who makes a mess of things. If you 'botch' something up, it means you make a mess of it; you don't do it properly." He searched for a clearer explanation. "It means you do it jerry fashion." The German glanced uncertainly. "No insult intended." Harry shook his head, "It's just what people say. It's an expression." His voice tailed away. "Sorry about that."

The German nodded with an academic interest that overcame any national pride.

Within minutes they reached Caldicot's small Police Station and Harry had ordered in his mind what he had to do. He handed over his prisoner to the bemused Special Constable behind the desk and asked for the telephone. He was quickly connected to a Sergeant sitting in a small guardhouse a few miles away. The Sergeant had spent the duration of the war supervising a small guard detail in a rural patch of England which, but for an accident of history would have been in Wales. It is neither quite the West Country nor the city metropolis of Bristol. The Sergeant was, at least, grateful for this latter distinction as the city had suffered badly during his tenure in the area. It had been estimated that well over 1,000 people had been killed by *Luftwaffe* bombing which had left ten times that number of buildings either damaged or destroyed.

His posting was, however, a useful line of defence in the eyes of his military masters. For six years, he and his platoon had loyally stood guard over Pilning Halt, a small railway platform on the stretch of line between Cardiff and Bristol. Its significant characteristic being that, although trains seldom stopped there, it could provide the first opportunity for enemy infiltrators to board a train having come ashore on the English side of the Severn Estuary.

The simple timber structure consisted of nothing more than a raised platform of wooden planks, an open shelter and a narrow bench seat. The identifying name plate had long since been painted out and then removed in the interests of confusing the enemy.

Sergeant Trent listened carefully to the Corporal at the other end of the line. The man spoke calmly and concisely. Everything he said which might have been conjecture or guess-work, he supported with logic and reasoning. As their three minute conversation came to a close, the Sergeant knew his war was about to take a new turn. He replaced the receiver and carefully placed his metal helmet on his head. Pulling the strap under his chin and, with a surprising change of pace, he energetically rang a brass hand bell. Shouting as loudly as his lungs would allow, he called out the guard.

Tuesday 13th March 1945, 21:45 hrs.

Sergeant Trent strode at the head of his detail, arms swinging and his steel grey jaw set with a new resolve which had caught his men off-guard. They had been enjoying their habitual cup of tea and game of cards when they had been interrupted by the Sergeant's shouts and his bell. Although they had seldom heard either before, all four men knew what they meant. They had left the guard house at a run, leaving tea mugs and playing cards scattered across the small table and floor.

Now, following the squared shoulders of their leader, they began to learn what had happened. A German, believed to have escaped from the officers' prison camp in South Wales, had been arrested at the other end of the Severn Tunnel. The soldier who had captured him had been placed there as an extra guard only because of the escape, which was fortunate as the prisoner had jumped from a train before it entered the tunnel. He had been captured alone but it was known that the escaped prisoners from Island Farm Camp had arranged themselves into groups of three or four. It was therefore likely that there would be more Germans still on the train. As there had been no trains through Pilning Halt for over half an hour, they had to assume their men were still travelling through the tunnel.

In the darkness, the soldiers heard and felt the quivering rattle of track and train before they saw it approaching. Trent spread his men in an arc with two on either side of the track. As they prepared their rifles, he took up his position between the rails and flicked a switch on the side of a heavy battery powered lantern. It was the sort the Great Western Railway used to mark the end of platforms when the mains electricity failed and it took some effort for the Sergeant to hold it up to chest height. He swung it gently to left and right, silently hoping the driver was paying attention. He shouted at a Lance-Corporal, telling him to pull his whistle out of his tunic pocket.

"Blow the bloody thing as hard as you like as soon as you see the train come round that bend."

The soldier complied without question. Even though trains moved relatively slowly through the tunnel and along the stretch of line at either end, he had known them put on speed as they passed Pilning. It was seen as their duty, according to the managers of the railway, to raise public morale by keeping their trains running on time.

As the straining locomotive approached, steam belching from every valve, the men took their cue from the whistling Lance-Corporal and the sweating Sergeant. They waved their arms and shouted. One of them pointed a metal barrelled torch and flashed a meagre yellow beam down the track. Another, carried away by the excitement of the moment, fired his rifle in the air.

The sharp rapport echoed around them, shocking a few seabirds into flight and silencing the ragged chorus of shouts.

Ahead of them, the train began to wheeze and a thin squeal signalled that the driver had taken the hint and was pulling on the brake. The heavy wagons closed up on each other, their momentum adding to the clamour as they clattered together. The giant boiler finally hissed to a standstill a few yards short. Gratefully, Sergeant Trent dropped the lantern onto the tracks. He took the lead as the men slowly began to move along the length of the train. Through the darkness, they heard the metal on metal scrape of a door being pushed back. Three shadowed figures dropped to the gravel rail-bed. The soldier with the torch pointed it in their direction but the beam was too weak.

Standing next to him, the Lance-Corporal shouted an order into the darkness to stand still. The Sergeant and the other two men were on the other side of the train and the sound of the order was lost in the rush of escaping steam and demands of the train guard to be told why they had been forced to stop.

The German escapees appeared to obey the instruction. They raised their hands, turning slowly to face the approaching soldiers. The Lance-Corporal and young Private relaxed slightly as they began to make out figures in the gloom, apparently doing as they were instructed; two motionless, shabby men, unshaven and looking drawn even in the feint glimmer of torchlight.

Behind them, *Sturmbannführer* von Hindermeer, unseen, slowly lowered his arms. He was slightly taller but of a slimmer build than the other two men. Bending at the knees, he crouched, awaiting his moment. As the two British squaddies stopped and were about to search them, the SS officer pounced forward, pushing with all his force against the Germans standing in front of him. They collided heavily with the British and the four men tumbled in a tangled knot on the gravel. The Lance-Corporal yelled in complaint, firing his weapon loosely and at nobody in particular. The Private swore, convinced their prisoners were attempting escape and hit one of the Germans firmly across the shoulder with his rifle butt. He was the first to scramble up, taking a kneeling position and aiming his rifle down at the injured officer, now clutching his shoulder in pain. The Lance-Corporal, grabbing the other prisoner by the collar and pinning him to the ground, grappled with his rifle to get it in position with his finger on the trigger.

Both felled Germans remained as motionless as their situation allowed, protesting loudly that they were surrendering, their hands still firmly held above their heads. Sergeant Trent and the other two soldiers appeared from beyond the train's boiler and pounded down the track. Between them, they grabbed the prisoners by their coats and pulled them to their feet. It took several minutes of excited pushing with rifles and shouted broken English to establish what had happened.

By the time Trent and his men learned that a third prisoner had made his escape, *Sturmbannführer* von Hindermeer was almost half a mile away. Blindly crossing fields at a run, he had made good headway having quickly removed his restraining greatcoat. Carrying it in a bundle rolled beneath one arm, he still wore his distinctive double-breasted black *SS* Panzer Corps uniform, minus the peaked service cap. He reasoned this was preferable to the unnecessary warmth of his full length coat. He had often expressed his pleasure that when the pre-war black uniform had been withdrawn from the infantry and artillery divisions of the *Waffen SS*, the Panzer Corps had been allowed to keep theirs. It had always been the smartest uniform in the *Wehrmacht* and on such a dark night as this and in these circumstances, it also had certain practical advantages.

Tuesday 13th March 1945, 22:40 hrs.

Charles Heard, proprietor of the curiously named Euroclydon Hotel at Drybrook in Gloucestershire, turned the key in the large iron lock on the double doors to his hotel and slipped the bolts, top and bottom, into place. It was a routine he had followed for several years at the end of each day but, in these troubled times, he had begun to regard it as a patriotic duty. And each evening, with an equal measure of routine, his wife had unnecessarily reminded him.

Today, she had reminded him earlier than usual and with greater force, waving a copy of the *Gloucester Citizen* as she paced the high ceilinged halls and panelled reception rooms. There were escaped Nazis in the Forest of Dean, she had announced loudly. A few guests had looked up from their books or periodicals before relaxing again. There was something about the Euroclydon's ancient grounds and heavy stone walls which gave reassurance. Even the tower at one end of the building, a left-over folly from its original owner, had castellated frills around its vaulted roof, giving it an air of fortitude and solidity. Built in 1866 by a wealthy mine owner, the mansion had been named Euroclydon after a strong wind which blew St.Paul's ship off course during one of his many sea voyages. The story, reproduced on parchment in a large frame in the hotel's drawing room, still tells today how St.Paul was sailing from Palestine to Italy when a storm threw his vessel off course and he was thrown ashore on the island of "Melite" now known as Malta. At least one theologian visiting the hotel had taken issue with the tale, claiming that the Knights of St.John, occupying the island during the 16th century, had concocted this version of events, supporting their claims that Malta was spiritually worthy of them. Conveniently, such a holy connection also made Malta an inviting destination for wealthy pilgrims. Others had claimed, with some force, that St.Paul had been shipwrecked, not in Malta, but on the island of Mljet off the Dalmation Coast which, in antiquity, had been known as "Melita".

Neither version of events detracted from the romance attached to the hotel's name and when Mr Heard and his wife had taken over the hotel some years earlier, they had wisely decided not to change it.

As was their habit, the Heards settled themselves among their guests in the drawing room to enjoy a closing hour or two before retiring to bed. Mr Heard poured a drink for each of those present from the small cocktail bar in the corner of the room and prodded the fire into life with a blackened iron.

The war had largely passed the Euroclydon by, although nobody would pretend that events in Europe and elsewhere weren't supremely important to the security of their future. Nevertheless, Charles felt, with some justification, that he had 'done his bit' during the previous war. His hotel was, to some extent, an indulgence to enjoy in his semi-retirement.

He sat in the armchair nearest the fire, left vacant quite deliberately by his knowing guests, and stretched his legs. He smiled round the room with a proprietary air and was about to open a light conversation on the events of the day. His discourse was cut short by a loud hissing and the unmistakable sound, almost like a series of car horns, of the hotel's flock of geese.

His wife was proud of her geese, and even more so of their generous ability to supply the hotel's guests with daily goose eggs and an occasional roast dinner. Mrs Heard glared at her husband as if he was responsible for the disruption and flipped her hands towards the door, ushering him out of the room.

Since his wife had drawn it to his attention, he had read the newspaper article with some interest earlier that afternoon. He now lost no time gathering a torch and, somewhat perversely, a heavy double edged sword which was normally held, point to the floor, by an empty suit of armour in the hotel's reception hall.

"It's probably just a fox." He reassured the guests who, to a man, had remained unmoved by the commotion.

Charles switched off the lights in the kitchen and rear passageway as he moved to the back of the hotel, easing open the back door in silence. He walked slowly towards the paddock occupied by the geese, switching the torch off as he went. The birds, though crowded strangely into one corner of the pen, seemed relaxed and moved silently towards him as he approached. He was about to switch the torch on again, beginning to believe there might truly be a fox at large, when his progress was arrested by the sound of low voices. He edged to the corner of an outbuilding, resting his shoulder against the brickwork and tried to tune his ear to the voices.

Major Heard seldom used his military title and between 1919 and 1929 he had technically been classed as a civilian, despite serving in Germany, attached to the Army's Special Investigation Branch. His experience had left him with both a natural inclination to investigate the unexplained and a fluency in German which he spoke with a flawless Berlin accent.

Out of the darkness, Charles could discern two voices; those of Steffi Ehlert and Werner Zielasko, although he had no way of knowing that at the time. He would later provide a statement to the local Police that one had complained he was too tired to go any further. The other had told him to be quiet as he had heard someone coming. The first voice had asked where and then another, possibly third voice, had hissed "quickly. This way."

Charles hurried back into the hotel. Once inside, he called to his staff and guests.

While his wife went straight to the telephone and dialled for the Police, Charles, three male guests and the hotel's porter and gardener took to the hotel grounds, sweeping past the goose-run, their paths lit with torchlight.

The four Germans, light on their feet despite their exhaustion, had a few hundred yards head start. They moved north, aiming for another area of cover known as Harechurch Wood.

Short of breath, aching and bleeding from several encounters with gorse, brambles and hawthorn, the four fugitives plunged back into the darkness of the woods, blundering and stumbling blindly on. Several times one or other of the men lost their footing and fell but each time the others stopped long enough to pull him to his feet and urge him forward again. They had never been so near to being captured, the pursuing pack of men so close behind them, they could almost feel their breath on the back of their necks. It seemed to the fleeing Germans that they were heavily outnumbered as well. From the noise the pursuers made as they had poured from the back of the building, there seemed to be at least a dozen.

Werner glanced over his shoulder, asking Hans between gasped breaths whether they had stumbled across an Army billet. Werner shook his head, mouth open in an effort to inhale. Soldiers don't keep geese, was all he could think of saying. Not even British soldiers.

Werner was not convinced. If he were a soldier in a country that fed its population on whale meat, he would most certainly keep geese.

Wednesday 14th March 1945, 08:15 hrs.

A nineteen year old farm worker, Dilwyn Thomas, hurried to leave his parents' home to start work on the family's Oldpark Farm adjacent to Margam Park near Port Talbot. He would normally have left at least ten minutes before but his progress had been delayed by a 'phone call from his cousin. Nancy Thomas farmed nearby at Eglwys Nunydd Farm and had spent the early hours of the morning making telephone calls to impart some potentially alarming news.

Dilwyn ran to the yard where his father and their labourers were moving the last of their dairy cattle into the milking shed. Panting, he held up his hands.

Wheezing through his Asthma, he managed to explain. "Nancy has just been on the 'phone. Some of her boys reckoned their corn rick was slept in last night." The men glanced at each other, unsure whether they should show alarm at this stage. They had all been following the story of the escaped Prisoners of War and, from Dilwyn's urgent tone, expected he had more to tell them. "They saw some men up on the Moor and reckon they were heading this way." He drew breath. "Some of Nancy's boys are coming over now. We're going to try and trap them as they come down the gully." He indicated with a jerk of his thumb the narrow valley which led down from Margam Moor onto a top meadow on Oldpark Farm. He nodded at their two Land Army girls. "You two better get back to the house. Bolt both the doors and don't let anyone in."

Without a further word, the girls dropped the yard brushes they were holding and hurried across the yard. Although he was only nineteen and the youngest of the men present, as the son of the farm's owners, Dilwyn immediately assumed command. He turned to his father's longest serving farmhand.

"Albert, you and me will go back up the culvert towards the Moor. Harry Prince, Eddie Hicks and Willy Evans are on their way down the Moor from Eglwys Nunydd. If there are any Germans up there, we'll flush 'em out."

Albert Jones nodded once and made for the shed they used to store the farm's hand tools.

"Dad, can I borrow your old rabbit gun?" His father nodded and peered round the opening to the milking shed. He had brought it with him that morning as he had seen signs of rats in the corn store the day before. "I think you need to get back to the house. Make sure Mam and the girls don't get all brave and go out hunting Nazis." They grinned at each other, recognising that the farmer's wife would dearly wish to become involved in the hunt.

Albert returned holding a billhook. He made some effort to stand to attention. As a farm labourer, he was in a reserved occupation and excused from military service. However, he had joined the local Home Guard and had often complained that he should be permitted to take his rifle home when not on duty. As his platoon had only been issued with a dozen rounds for their fifteen rifles, however, it would have been of limited use. Now, even those had been recalled by the Army. Not so Mr Thomas' double barrelled shotgun which was now handed over to Dilwyn with a full box of cartridges.

Together, the two men stepped out towards the Moor, their pace quickened by determination.

Twenty minutes later, in the clear light of an almost cloudless day, they saw two figures, bent low and trotting at a slow run down the gully towards them. Dilwyn held Albert's arm and they stood shoulder to shoulder, blocking the narrow path. The younger man cupped his hands round his mouth, forming a megaphone. He shouted a short, direct command up the valley. The two men halted, looked, then turned and ran in the opposite direction. As they increased the distance between them and their pursuers, Dilwyn saw the Eglwys Nunydd men cresting the hill beyond them. One of the men shouted and, once again, the fugitives turned on their heels and headed back down the bath towards Oldpark.

Albert grunted. "They reckon we're the better bet, being as there are only two of us."

Dilwyn grinned with a poor attempt at bravado. "We'll see about that, eh Bert?" He shouted again. "Stop! Stop right there." The men kept coming, bending lower and increasing their pace.

Albert sniffed. "Well, there's a challenge, wouldn't you say?"

Dilwyn nodded, raising the stock of his father's old gun to his shoulder. He aimed carefully, raised the barrels a few degrees and squeezed the first trigger.

The explosion cracked and echoed round the valley. Two of the five men in front of him froze in their tracks, glaring at the man holding the gun.

"I told you, stop!"

With some reluctance, the two Germans stood upright and raised their hands in submission. His shotgun levelled at them, Dilwyn and Albert advanced the fifty yards or so up the valley. Long before they reached them, the three men from Eglwys Nunydd had pinned the Germans' arms behind them and were patting them down for weapons as if they had been conducting body searches all their lives.

The two prisoners were escorted back over the moor to Eglwys Nunydd where a stable served as a temporary jail. One of the men telephoned the Police Station in Port Talbot where an excited posse of constables led by a weary Sergeant were dispatched with a black police van to collect them.

Dilwyn's cousin, Nancy, who ran the farm while her husband was serving in the Army, glanced over the stable door at the two prisoners. Bedraggled and unshaven after three days on the run, they seemed a sorry sight. One in particular, an older man of about forty, apologised in broken English for causing her and her men so much trouble. He shrugged, adding simply, "It is war."

"You're hungry, I expect?" She made knife and fork movements. "You want something to eat? Food?"

The older man smiled weakly. "We have no food, three days." She smiled maternally and left for her kitchen. While she made herself busy, her three labourers hovered over their prisoners, edgily checking and rechecking that they were not attempting a further escape.

Returning with a small tray, Nancy offered the men a cup of tea and some bread and cheese. The farmhand given charge of the shotgun glanced at his employer, impressed by her generosity but not surprised. She had a local reputation for looking after people in need. The older prisoner picked up the mug and plate gratefully thanking her and Nancy turned to the other man, sitting hunched and half turned away from her. He was younger than his compatriot and had so far not uttered a word.

"Something for you too?"

Suddenly and with a savagery that surprised even the other German, the younger man spun round, swinging his fist, knocking the tray and its contents across the stable.

As one, the labourer with the gun levelled it at the man's head as the farm manager, hearing the commotion, swung through the stable door. Seeing his employer backing away, the cup and plate broken on the cement floor, he took a quick pace towards the seated German. The prisoner instinctively stood to meet what he fully expected would be an attack. The move was his second mistake. Despite still being in his early twenties, Harry Prince was tall and powerfully built having spent his teenage and adult years working the family's farms. His eyes narrowed for the briefest of moments as he assessed his opponent before landing a single cracking right hook to the German's cheek. The blow sent the prisoner reeling across the stable and he crumpled into the corner, holding his hands up in front of his face. A thin stream of blood edged its way from his nose, spreading along his upper lip.

Mercifully for the German, the sound of a police bell heralded the arrival of the local constabulary and before further damage could be done, the prisoners were scraped up from the stable and marched firmly to the back of their van.

Wednesday 14th March 1945, 09:00 hrs.

George Charteris entered his Inspector's room with slightly more confidence than previously. He felt, now, that he was beginning to get the measure of his senior officer. As long as he kept to the facts and concentrated on information which the Inspector had no prior knowledge of, he should avoid any criticism.

He reported that he had been able to make a more complete inspection of Hut Nine where the escape tunnel had started. Soil had been discovered wedged into cavities in the walls of the huts. "There's a gap, sir, in the construction of every hut, between the outer bomb-blast layer of concrete and the inner timber panelling. It seems the prisoners cut holes near the roof beams and were shovelling spoil from the tunnel through and into the gap."

Inspector Bailey shook his head slowly. "Here we are, in 1945, struggling to make our homes warmer because for years we didn't build houses with cavity walls and yet we use all our modern technology and latest building techniques to make our enemy detainees comfortable."

The two men sat in silence while George wondered whether he should add that the soil disposal technique hadn't been his discovery. One of the guards had noticed a trickle of brown liquid oozing from one of the skirting boards. His Sergeant had ripped a small section of wall panel away and caused a mud slide that had covered several square yards of flooring in thick glutinous clay.

Bailey jerked his attention away from thoughts of his elderly mother and aunt, chilled and bent over their coal fire. "What else can you tell me?"

"The number of escapees recovered during Tuesday, sir, is..."

"Hang on George." The Inspector leant forward against the desk. "Let's relax a little. I know we're making good progress, so let's just take a little breather first." He picked up a pot of coffee and pouring two cups, passed one across the desk.

"Real coffee, sir?" George inhaled the vapours indulgently before taking a sip.

"Of course, real coffee. Good work deserves some sort of reward, George. Your little tit-bit of information about the Alsatians and their aversion to curry powder has apparently set wheels in motion in high places. I've been told by Colonel Darling that his dog handlers are to be seconded to a special military research establishment. They and their four legged friends are to be the subject of a new investigation into escape and evasion procedures. It is thought your discovery might be helpful for our chaps in German Prisoner of War camps."

"Really, sir?" George thought for a moment. "That doesn't really help us with the Bridgend enquiry, does it sir."

Inspector Bailey smiled his best benevolent smile. "It all goes towards the war effort, George. We have to keep our minds on the broader picture." He put his cup down. "And speaking of which, I have some good news for you. I've received a memo from Superintendent May that, according to the Chief Constable, MI19 recalled their officers before they even managed to reach Bridgend. They were apparently on the platform at Cardiff Central Station on Monday afternoon, waiting for the local train, when an announcement was made over the public address tannoy that they were to report to the Station Master's office. Apparently there's some panic on in London and their services are needed back there." Bailey grinned with the first sign of genuine pleasure that George had seen. "Which means you have free reign to interview anybody you believe could assist with our enquiry." He took a sip from his cup, holding it wrapped between both hands. "Don't forget, George, I'm here to help. If you would like me to join you for any of the interviews, you only have to say the word." He smiled like a benevolent parent offering to help his son with homework. Both men knew that, now the way had been cleared of Military Intelligence, there was nothing he'd like more than to get to grips with some Nazis. "Now then, what you were saying?"

George smiled and nodded swiftly, tearing his thoughts away from a vision of his supervising officer sharing his recent experience of knee deep mud and mocking squaddies. "It's a strange coincidence, sir, that you should mention MI19. During my last interview, with a U-Boat officer, I was accused of belonging to Military Intelligence. Actually, he used the term 'Secret Police'. I told him I was just an ordinary police officer

213

and showed him my warrant card but he just backed away, blubbering something about my not being in uniform."

The Inspector nodded wisely. "I believe they don't have a Detective Branch in the German Police Force. Any officer of the State Police who doesn't wear a uniform is assumed to belong to the Gestapo. They have a less than savoury reputation." The two men paused, absorbing the implications. They looked up simultaneously, both about to add their thoughts to the discussion. Inspector Bailey got in first. "It may be to our advantage if the more timid prisoners believe they are dealing with our equivalent of the Gestapo. Very few men would wish to face their type of interrogation. It may just speed up the process."

Charteris grinned slowly. "I'm not sure I feel altogether comfortable in the role of torturer, sir, but I take your point regarding the need to take their statements quickly." He glanced at his notebook. "Yesterday alone, a further twenty prisoners were recaptured. Five were found during a comb-out by RAF men in the Vale of Glamorgan. Four more in Pencoed and two were hiding in a cave in some cliffs at a place called Merthyr Mawr." He pronounced the last word 'Moor' as if it might have been an area of open marshland.

The Inspector corrected him, pronouncing the word 'Mawer'.

The Constable repeated the word carefully. "Thank you sir. Three others were taken, by bus of all things, to the Police Station in Glynneath and three others were taken close to the Severn Tunnel, one on the Welsh side and two on the English side."

The Inspector frowned. "I suppose it's to be expected that by now, they will have reached further afield. It doesn't look good, though, that some of the prisoners have managed to get out of the Glamorgan County area."

"I'm afraid that's not all, sir. One other Lieutenant named Friedrich Gossler gave himself up in Neath but there were two others caught by a Major Smith."

"Why is that so terrible, Constable?"

"Major Smith, sir, is a United States Army officer and he came across the two German prisoners in the middle of Salisbury."

The Inspector fell silent for a moment. "I'm not too worried about him being an American. That just demonstrates the value of cooperation between allies." He pursed his lips. "I'm not too happy that they got as far as Salisbury, though." He thought again. "I know I said yesterday that I wasn't bothered about what the newspapers have been saying, but since then I've spent quite a bit of time with Superintendent May on the other investigation I mentioned."

George remembered. "The murder, sir."

Bailey nodded absently. "Mr May has been receiving a little bit of flack, apparently. He has enough on his mind at present and is anxious that he isn't put in a difficult position as far as the Army and the press are concerned. The Army's Western Command Headquarters in Chester wishes to issue regular press bulletins about our progress." He rolled a pencil thoughtfully between forefinger and thumb, apparently battling over how much he should tell his junior detective. "It would be better for all concerned if the Superintendent tells Western HQ only what Western HQ would like to hear." He looked up. "Do you understand?"

George nodded dumbly, not at all sure that he did.

"Excellent." Bailey put his pencil down. "So, in the case of this morning's report, for instance, I think we can safely inform Mr May that a further twenty detainees have been returned to custody and that the Police have been ably assisted in this by officers and men of the Army, the Royal Air Force and the United States Army." He smiled broadly.

"And some children, sir."

"Children?"

"Yes sir. And some fishermen."

"Fishermen?"

"Yes sir. Some boys were playing at cowboys and Indians, apparently -"

"Please, George, spare me the details. Let's just say we were acting on information received from members of the public. That normally covers it."

"There is one more thing, I'm afraid."

"Do you know, George, I had thought this morning started unnaturally well. I'm beginning to regret ordering that coffee now."

"We received a report late yesterday evening sir that a hotelier in Gloucestershire believes he saw two German escapees in the grounds of his hotel."

"Gloucestershire? That's rather a long way. How reliable is this hotelier do you think?"

Wednesday 14ᵗʰ March 1945, 20:00 hrs.

Mrs Elizabeth Davies had spent the remainder of her day, having heard from her neighbour, Nancy Thomas that two German Prisoners of War had been found on the Mountain that morning, keeping herself busy with laundry and making flasks of hot, sweet tea for herself and her small workforce of farm labourers.

Along with her husband, Elwyn, she had kept her small hill farm for the last ten years. Perched near the base of Margam Mountain a few miles from Port Talbot, their land boasted the usual South Wales combination of winding rivers, woodlands, rolling meadows and steep fields. The farmhouse itself boasted a mountain view (more correctly, a steep sided hill, but the Welsh are famously proud of their landscape) and a panorama of Port Talbot Docks alongside the industrial landscape of steel works, obese cooling towers and gritty coal washeries.

To Elizabeth, alone since her husband had volunteered to join the infantry in 1940, her idyll of a home now provided her main source of comfort. Indeed, before many decades passed, others would adopt the same opinion. The farm was destined to become a twenty-first century development of executive homes for wealthy professionals prepared to commute daily to Swansea or Cardiff. For the time being, however, it remained a cluster of well managed, smartly maintained farm buildings, built of local stone and topped with Welsh slate as befitting the manorial estate it had once belonged to.

Elizabeth was justly proud of their achievements at the farm, responding rapidly and easily to the Government's periodic calls to increase production of milk, pork or eggs. Their flock of Welsh Hill Speckle Faced sheep, ideally suited to their landscape but kept mainly for wool rather than meat, had been dutifully reduced to make way for Hereford cows and a dozen or more Saddleback and Berkshire pigs.

Elizabeth's only complaint revolved around the paperwork involved. Every animal had to be accounted for and recorded on several official forms. The Ministry of Food insisted on sending

the outset.
The stone s
tractor, an
ploughs and
of any inter
concluded, r

As he crot
hand on the
of metal upo
like a screwc
a small win
squatted low

With no n
dogs again,
piles of wire
and gates. M
inch steel pi
muzzles, ord
rugged timbe
resting the s
clasp and sil
firmly securir

He retrieve
bead of swea
bumping into
brandishing
laughed softly
arms.

Once, in th
her, not on th
and enthusia
years. He h
repeat the exp
had said noth
at her, she r
inches from h
her sides.

It was Geor
"Best we g
Constable dov

a seemingly unending caravan of inspectors with clip-boards, booklets of directives and instructions on how the beasts should be housed and fed. Prior to 1940, animals were routinely sent for slaughter as and when farmers required. For the last five years, however, Elizabeth had almost disappeared beneath the paperwork required by the Ministry to account for the despatch of one animal and the production of another.

Ironically, however, few politicians before or since have managed to achieve the level of personal popularity enjoyed by Lord Woolton, known as "Uncle Fred", the Minister of Food. Across the country, admiration for the work of his Ministry seemed to know no bounds as the public strove to make the most of their rations. Housewives followed to the letter advice doled out on subjects as diverse as the size they should cut a slice of bread and how to make steak and kidney pie without either steak or kidney.

Elizabeth, for one, declined to share their enthusiasm. To her, the war and rationing could not end soon enough. She longed to be surrounded once again by ewes and to have her husband home. Before the War, she would never have believed she would miss the familiar annual routine of lambing and shearing.

Unlike many of his contemporaries Elwyn, and in turn his wife, had flatly refused to dispose of their four sheepdogs. They had bred Border Collies for many years and, in their own minds, had now developed the perfect team to help manage their flock. Elizabeth's private feeling that the dogs were more her pets than her husband's working dogs had been further reinforced since the number of ewes had been so dramatically reduced. Despite being under-worked, the collies held an even greater place in her heart. Although she knew her husband would have stern words to say on the subject when he returned, the dogs had now moved in to the large farmhouse. They could hardly believe their luck, spending each evening curled up at their mistress' feet and sleeping in front of a broad open fire instead of a timber shelter in the corner of the rear paddock.

The dogs had just returned from their exercise on the higher reaches of the mountain and Elizabeth had closed the door to her stone flagged kitchen. As she did every day, she had petted and made a fuss of each of them in turn, checking for any minor injury that might have been picked up during the day.

Satisfied, :
down their
It was a
kitchen si
barking tc
sounded in
The Farɪ
been invite
in order to
billeted in
had spent
over the tel
received fr
He had litt
they had re
He pulle
installed in
time. As I
end of the
enclosed, t
shoulder at
"You've 1
voiced as (
that habitu
back door
almost a y
regulations
"Could 1
didn't keep
and their f
be aware if
giveaway s
dogs, all s
across the
but ran di
outbuilding
them, ramr
snapping tl
shoulder.
Fifteen y;
and crouch
were follow

Elizabeth shook herself free from her heatedly unseemly thoughts. She glanced over the younger man's shoulder at the silent building.

"What do you suppose he was doing in there?"

Her question would be answered a few hours later when, summoned from their beds, Detective Inspector Lancelot Bailey of Port Talbot Police Station and Detective Constable George Charteris of Bridgend Police Station, attended the station at Margam and interviewed two despondent German *Luftwaffe* officers and a disdainful Panzer Captain, *Hauptman* Eric Stiegel.

As the senior officer in the group, and the only one who spoke English, it fell to Stiegel to explain that they had been attempting to make their way to Swansea Docks. He spoke in a way which, in other circumstances for an arrested man, might have appeared inexplicably confident. Seated on the bare wooden chair in the interview room, he half turned, refusing to make eye contact with his interrogators and folded his legs in a display of unconcerned arrogance. For several minutes he declined to give any meaningful replies, repeating only that he regarded their questions as illegal and in breach of the conventions of war. He tried various tactics, insisting he should be interviewed only by a military officer of at least his own rank. He waved their questions away with a backward swat of his hand.

"These are unimportant issues which I cannot be troubled with." He gazed down at his fingernails, incongruously lined by black oil and mud.

Finally, after an hour of exchanges, slices of toast and several cups of tea, the *Hauptman* tired of the game. He let out a long sigh.

"My comrades and I required transport. We located a vehicle in one of the farm outbuildings and decided to requisition it."

"Requisition it?" Bailey interrupted. "You mean steal it?"

The German eyed him distastefully, gazing down his nose at the men on the other side of the desk. "I mean requisition it. This was a military requirement." He shook his head. "I do not expect a simple civilian policeman to understand the principles of what you British refer to as 'spoils of war'." Bailey leant back in his chair, too intrigued to contradict. "It is a well established convention that occupying forces take possession of their defeated enemy's assets."

This was too much for Bailey and he suddenly straightened, spreading his hands on the desk. "But, Herr Stiegel, you are not an occupying force and Britain is not defeated."

Stiegel brushed the objection aside with a silent flick of his fingers.

"No matter. That is a mere technicality and a situation which will soon be corrected."

Bailey shook his head, genuinely impressed by the German's confidence. He turned his hand palm upwards, inviting the officer to continue.

"On inspection of the vehicle, however, we deduced it contained no fuel." Stiegel's lip had curled as he continued to describe the inconvenience this apparent oversight had caused. "We therefore sought and located a supply of fuel. It was in some type of agricultural vehicle. The nature of the vehicle was of no possible interest to us, but its tank appeared to contain some gasoline. We were in the process of requisitioning this when we heard a bolt being slipped on the door to the building."

The *Hauptman* inhaled deeply before releasing his breath with a note of finality. "We were forced to give our surrender as we assumed we had been tracked down by a military search party." He sniffed disdainfully. "I resolved, with regret, to make the surrender personally to the senior enemy officer present." Stiegel's nostrils flared in disgust.

"It was a matter of some disquiet to learn that we had been captured by a country policeman, a common farm labourer and his bawd of an employer." The corner of his mouth twitched. "Nothing more than a serving woman, carrying some type of cooking utensil." He drew in breath through his nose, as if detecting an unpleasant smell. "I distinctly heard her and her great beast of a man-servant laughing at us when they locked us in. As I informed the wretch, when Germany has won this war, I will make it my personal business to request of the Fuhrer that I be appointed as a regional governor of South Wales." He folded his arms. "We will then see who shall be laughing."

Inspector Bailey stopped writing. He screwed the cap carefully onto his fountain pen and returned it to his breast pocket. With a sigh, he rose from his seat, picked up his papers and neatly folded them into his briefcase.

"I honestly believe, Herr Stiegel, whether you care to agree with me or not, that you and Herr Hitler have at least one strong characteristic in common." The German's chest visibly expanded. "You are both whistling in the wind."

The German frowned. "What is this 'whistling in the wind'? I do not know this expression."

"You're pissing in the dark, my friend." He snapped the briefcase closed. "Deluded and pissing in the dark."

Bailey turned and with a nod to Charteris, left the room. The German stared after him, confused yet sure he had been insulted. He glared at George as he too gathered his papers and prepared to leave. Outside, a Corporal and three guards from Camp 198 were waiting to escort the prisoners back to Bridgend.

Wednesday 14th March 1945, 23:15 hrs.

Sturmbannführer von Hindermeer fought an urge to sleep, despite the rough road, uncertain navigation and inherent risk of travelling in a stolen vehicle through enemy territory. On the other side of the cab's bench seat, the *Untersturmführer* (the equivalent of a 2nd Lieutenant) clutched the steering wheel and squinted over it into the dark road ahead. Despite blackout regulations having been relaxed, most vehicles, especially those that were seldom used, still had metal plates with thin slots cut in them bolted crudely over their headlights. The narrow slither of light passing through was enough for a pedestrian to see, and hopefully avoid, an oncoming vehicle but barely enough for its driver to see the road.

Between the two men sat an *Obersturmführer* (1st Lieutenant), wedged uncomfortably and little daring to move his arm for fear of disturbing either his senior officer or the driver's concentration. Both the junior men were members of the 12th SS Panzer Division and, like von Hindermeer, had seen enemy action. Despite the rural peace of their present surroundings, they had no wish to encounter the enemy again, unarmed as they were and likely to be outnumbered.

Every so often, each of the men glanced at the fuel gauge. They had managed to siphon enough petrol to quarter fill the tank and the needle was dropping steadily as the thirsty old engine dragged the lorry along the lanes. As the needle hit zero, the driver pulled up and tapped the gauge. Ahead of them, a crossroads presented them with a further dilemma. Like every road junction across the British Isles, this one had no road signs.

They judged, correctly, that they were somewhere north of Salisbury and the name set alarm bells ringing in von Hindermeer's mind. Salisbury Plain would surely be crawling with enemy troops. The area was well known as a training ground for British infantry and armoured divisions. Despite there being so many allied regiments deployed to Continental Europe, it was almost certain that Salisbury would still be playing host to those held back as reinforcements. They must turn left, travelling east, then maybe south again towards Portsmouth.

They joined the Andover road. This was a wider highway and, had it not been for the late hour, might well have been busy with civilian and military traffic. Ten more minutes passed and they had seen neither pedestrian nor motor vehicle. Von Hindermeer leaned back in his seat, folding his arms and snorting disdainfully. No roadblocks. No checkpoints. How could a nation hope to win a war when it was clearly so devoid of military control?

The driver sat upright and pointed over the wheel. Ahead of them, faintly outlined against the night sky, they could make out a dark, high wall. Behind that, the tall buildings and chimneys of a factory protruded like the fingers of a gnarled hand. He pushed the gear lever forward and moved on a few hundred yards, pulling up just short of a pair of high gates. Where there was a factory, there was likely to be a supply of gasoline. The driver jerked his heel back, tapping a hollow metal fuel can beneath his seat. He felt under the seat, pulling free a snake-like siphon tube taken from the barn.

The gates of the factory yard were reinforced by wide metal plates and attended by a night-watchman. Neither seemed insuperable. The former seemed light-weight with no bolts or chains and the latter, seventy years of age, was soundly sleeping in his wooden hut.

As silently as they could, they alighted from the cab and slipped through the gates, beginning a systematic search of the yard. It didn't take long to find a low shed containing two parked lorries. Twice more they passed silently between the gates, crossing the watchman's hut to refill their petrol can. Twenty minutes after arriving, they were back in the lorry and heading once more towards Andover.

Thursday 15th March 1945, 07:00 hrs.

Wilhelm Schmidt and Klaus Myer had walked from the field next to Camp 198 just after eleven o'clock on the night of the escape. They had been in one of the earliest groups to crawl through the tunnel and, in the company of a *Luftwaffe* navigator and an *SS* officer who spoke faultless English, albeit with an American accent, had walked some eight miles east until they reached the small village of Brynna.

Before their absence had been detected, the four escapees had found a train in a siding and bedded themselves down. They had found an old tarpaulin at the side of the track which they hauled into a roughly folded mattress, pushing it against the corner of the unyielding wooden floor and dropping their kitbags to use as pillows.

The train had jerked them awake at six o'clock in the morning as it left the sidings. It kept them awake until it pulled up again half an hour later in Cardiff. There the men had slipped quietly from their hiding place, crossed several lines of track and had pulled open the door to another goods wagon. It had been full of unmarked tea chests and they had quickly set about searching for food or anything else which might have been of use. To their dismay, they were all empty. The wagon had a sliding door on each side and they had pushed the boxes along the length of the floor, making a space at one end of the wagon before settling down again to wait and rest.

The train had remained stationary for several hours and they were arguing their way towards leaving and finding alternative transport when they heard the engine being fired up. It jolted, eased forward and finally pulled out of Cardiff Central Station just after four o'clock on the Sunday afternoon.

The train took them as far as Wolverhampton where again they disembarked. Several unguided changes later, they found themselves in Swindon and, again without knowing where they were heading, switched trains once more.

They had no way of knowing, but this time their destination could not have been planned better. Six hours later the train pulled into a siding at Eastleigh in the coastal county of Hampshire. Blinking in the daylight, the men assessed their situation. Railway station name plates and other identifying signs had been removed at the start of the war as a way of confusing potential invaders. As a result, and somewhat obtusely, rail company staff called out the name of the station each time a passenger train pulled in. Luck seemed to be running the Germans' way and they quickly learned where they were. Moments later, a postal worker collected mail from their train, shouting above the clamour of the rolling stock that he was heading for Southampton and should be there in about twenty minutes.

The men quickly surmised they could be no more than ten kilometres from Southampton Docks. They concluded that they would stand a better chance of avoiding detection if they split up into two pairs. Each pair would make for the docks and try to stow away aboard a ship. If their luck held, they could make it to a neutral country such as Ireland, Spain or Portugal. Wherever they ended up, they would be one step closer to reaching German occupied territory.

Wilhelm and Klaus formed one pair. Although neither spoke English well, they felt confident enough having already travelled several hundred miles without being challenged.

They had solemnly shaken hands with the other two officers and wished them good luck. By mutual agreement, they had decided that the second pair should leave the goods wagon thirty minutes after the first.

Wilhelm checked his watch and nodded as Klaus straightened up painfully, rubbing his shoulders. He slipped from the wagon to the gravel below, bending and massaging his knees. Five days spent lying on a hard floor and being jolted at every turn had left all four men bruised and stiff. Klaus was over forty and had suspected for some time that he was suffering from Arthritis. A few winter months in a damp Prisoner of War camp and many hours spent digging an underground tunnel had done nothing to cure him.

Wilhelm dropped to the ground next to him. They looked about, calculating where south lay, and started to move away. Aware that railway stations were likely to be heavily guarded and now out in the open in broad daylight, they needed to move quickly.

A low wire fence formed the only barrier between them and a narrow service road. Still rubbing his knees, Klaus followed his compatriot. They crossed the rails, climbed a shallow embankment and squatted next to the fence, watching the road for signs of danger.

Despite their caution, they were tired, hungry and their concentration levels were falling. For almost a minute, they failed to notice the small patrol of former Home Guard volunteers approaching, checking each of the small huts which lined the siding. Hearing a door being rattled closed and catching sight of the soldiers, they clambered aboard the nearest wagon. They tumbled into an open trailer which they rapidly discovered was full of fine cement. Almost liquid, it quickly absorbed them like quicksand. Their movements had been clumsy even before they had landed in the soft powder and a rising cloud of asphyxiating dust soon had Klaus choking and scratching for a hand-hold on the side of the wagon.

When the order came, they were quick to surrender and submitted to being hauled out of their pit by the wrists.

One of the Home Guard men strolled up to the prisoners, now being held at gunpoint. He dropped a kitbag at the German's feet. On it in stencilled ink were printed a name, *Schmidt W.* and a service number.

"Herr Schmidt?" He looked expectantly at each of the men in turn. Wilhelm glanced at him miserably, nodding almost imperceptibly. "I think this is yours." The soldier grinned triumphantly.

It was seven o'clock in the morning of Thursday 15th March.

Thursday 15ᵗʰ March 1945, 07:30 hrs.

Sturmbannführer von Hindermeer had managed to sleep for a few hours and woke when the sun, although deeply covered by grey clouds, glimmered across the horizon ahead of them. He asked where they were. The two junior officers had swapped places and *Obersturmführer* Krause was now driving. Beside him, the junior man, *Untersturmführer* Gruenewald, was snoring noisily in the left hand seat, his mouth open and head rolling back. The lorry hit a hole in the road and the young man's head glanced painfully against the window, waking him with a jolt. He rubbed his temple and repeated von Hindermeer's question. The driver shrugged.

Before sunrise they had risked driving through any darkened towns and villages on their route. They had crossed Basingstoke, Farnham, Guildford and Reigate without incident, each town being scratched out with a pencilled mark on the map as it was passed.

As the horizon had gradually brightened and with all three men awake, the lorry had been steered off the main roads. For an hour they navigated their way east as best they could by narrow lanes, some of them no wider than cart tracks. Eventually, all three men had to admit they had no idea where they were. All they could be reasonably sure of was that London lay to the north and they were travelling east. Von Hindermeer had determined that they should head for Dover, the closest British port to France and therefore the swiftest possible Channel crossing.

Despite their prodigious progress, however, the men felt unable to stop. Their chicken and eggs remained uncooked and, as the lorry took a broad right hand bend, the *Sturmbannführer* rolled down his window and flung them onto the grass verge. Ahead of them, an ancient five-bar gate hung heavily open, almost inviting travellers onto a wide driveway. The senior officer waved his hand at the driver, indicating him to slow down.

Von Hindermeer gazed carefully up the drive, assessing rusting hinges on the gate, the mud strewn yard and surrounding ramshackle outbuildings. His eyes moved up to a thatched farmhouse. Peeling paintwork and a patchwork of corrugated iron hen-coops and pigsties told him all that was required. He felt in his pocket, fingering the small cache of coins he had kept hidden from the camp guards. With a single gesture of his index finger, he directed the driver to steer into the farmyard.

Von Hindermeer had never regarded himself as an actor. In any normal situation, a man of his standing found no need for artifice. This, however, was not a normal situation. His English was tolerable and before the break-out he had discussed several times with other escapers the feasibility of passing themselves off as Dutchmen. The lorry pulled up close to one of the barns, the driver clearly expecting to siphon more petrol. He reached below his seat for the rubber hose but von Hindermeer shook his head firmly.

They were here, he explained, to get food. He jerked a single nod at the house. This was clearly a poorly run farm with little income and the farmer would be happy to sell them some bread and cheese. They might even manage to persuade the farmer's wife to cook them some breakfast. The two junior men grinned hungrily. Von Hindermeer glanced at his watch, noting the early hour. He shrugged and pulled the cab door open. Farmers usually rose early.

Straightening his coat to ensure it fully covered his uniform, he approached the front door and knocked loudly. He took a step back and cleared his throat, mentally preparing his opening speech. Nothing happened. He edged forward slightly, trying to detect sounds of movement from within. Other than a brief clucking noise from the hen house, he heard nothing. He knocked again, even louder.

This time, a window above him was thrown open and a tousled head sporting a shot of ginger hair appeared. It nudged aside a pair of grey and worn curtains and demanded to know what the caller wanted.

"Good morning, farmer." Von Hindermeer applied his friendliest smile. "We are, I'm afraid, a little lost." He paused for a moment. "And also a little hungry."

"Well that's tough on you, isn't it." The farmer's tone hardly inspired confidence but von Hindermeer was not a man to be easily discouraged.

"We are sailors from Holland, trying to return to our ship at Dover."

The man's arm shot out of the window, pointing to the farm gate. "Dover's that way." He grasped the window catch and started to close it.

"But please, sir, we need food." For the first time, von Hindermeer's voice changed from imperious to somewhere closer to pleading. He opened his hand to reveal the small pile of coins. "I have money."

The window immediately opened again and the farmer's small eyes squinted as he attempted to assess the visitor's potential value. He told him to wait and withdrew behind the tattered curtains. A few moments later, the German heard the steady thump of heavy footfalls on the stairs and the front door was noisily unbolted.

As the door swung open it became apparent the man had still been in bed. He had stuffed his nightshirt into a hastily assembled pair of poorly patched trousers. A pair of braces hung limply from his waist. His bare feet were almost as grey as his clothes, coloured only by yellow nails and angry looking red calluses. Von Hindermeer had seen better looking feet pulled from ill-fitting Army boots after a thirty mile march. He tried to hide his disgust as he asked whether he would be able to buy some bread and cheese.

The farmer grunted unhappily. "Where's your rations, then? I thought you seamen were well provided for." He turned his head sideways, squinting as if searching for any sign of honesty.

Von Hindermeer shook his head sadly. "Ach, yes but you see, my friends and I were robbed."

"Robbed?" The ginger head jerked back in surprise. "Three grown men robbed of your food rations?" He squinted again. "And how did that happen then?"

Von Hindermeer shrugged apologetically. "I know, it was very bad. We were asleep and someone took our parcels – our food rations."

The farmer grunted, unsure whether to believe the story but conscious of the sailor's cash. "Right, then. You'd better come in." He glanced over von Hindermeer's shoulder at the lorry. "Just you, mind. I don't want the place over-run with foreigners." He hesitated. "No insult meant," adding: "You can't be too careful these days."

The *Sturmbannführer* glanced over his shoulder and nodded briefly at the two men watching through the cab windscreen. He followed the man into the darkened hallway of the farmhouse and through to a small kitchen.

A duck, still wearing its feathers, lay prostrate on a wooden board, a large cleaver ominously lying close by. A few muddy potatoes lay in a cracked Belfast sink, a single tap hanging loosely above them. A bunch of carrots sprawled on the small pine scrub-table at the centre of the room and a black kettle hung from a hook close to the kitchen range. Pieces of yellowing newspaper had been spread across the linoleum floor. Apart from that, the room displayed no signs that its occupier had any leanings towards domestication or home decor.

The farmer lifted the lid from an enamel bucket and withdrew half a crusty loaf of white bread. He slapped it heavily onto the table before withdrawing to a darkened alcove in the corner of the room. Von Hindermeer tried to take in more of his surroundings, his eyes slowly adjusting to the gloom. The man reappeared holding a large block of pale cheese which he placed next to the bread before rattling open a drawer in the side of the table. Pulling out an unnecessarily large knife, he held it upright in front of his chest.

"Right then." He sniffed noisily. "You wants bread and cheese. How much are you prepared to pay?" He eyed the pocket where he assumed the money was being held.

The German pursed his lips, getting the measure of his man. "How much for half the cheese and all the bread?"

The farmer inhaled deeply. "That's a lot of bread and cheese. I have to eat too, you know."

"And have you any fruit? Some apples perhaps?"

The man let out a short snort of a laugh. "Apples? Where would I get apples in March? Are you mad?"

The German shrugged, almost apologetically. "I am not a farmer, just a sailor."

"Bloody right, boy." His voice dropped slightly. "You certainly aren't a farmer." He paused for a moment. "Let's say six bob for the lot; what's left of the loaf and all the cheese." He laid his grimy palm heavily over the bread. He knew he was taking a chance. He had paid just under a shilling the day before at the neighbouring village shops, and had eaten half the bread since then. He had also traded several eggs and a small basket of vegetables but wouldn't miss them as he produced both in abundance. Although bread wasn't rationed, he had heard that people in the towns were complaining at the Government's insistence of producing only soft wholemeal bread and not selling it until the day after it was baked. The theory, he had been told, was that people wouldn't be tempted to eat it so quickly if it wasn't still warm or have that 'just baked' flavour. Fortunately, his local baker gave as scant attention to official regulations as the farmer did to his ration card, which told him he was allowed two ounces of cheese per week. The block of Cheddar now sitting on the table was at least five times that weight.

Von Hindermeer's brow furrowed. He was about to ask who Bob was and what he had to do with the negotiation when the farmer interrupted him. Misinterpreting the German's frown for dissent and not wishing to lose a sale or enter into a dispute with a man who had two companions outside, he simply shrugged and smiled.

"All right then. In the interests of friendship between allies, let's call it five shillings."

Von Hindermeer scratched his chin, mentally tallying up the coins in his pocket and trying to remember what the large silver half crowns were worth in shillings. He took the coins out and inspected them again, hoping to glean some extra clue.

The farmer took a pace forward and quickly plucked two half crowns from the German's open palm. "There we are. Five bob on the nose." He swept his free hand over the bread and cheese as he pushed the cash firmly into his own pocket.

Taken aback but in no position to argue, the German simply nodded once, picked up the food and made for the door. He had a notion he had been swindled but didn't stop to offer an opinion. Instead, he left the house and without glancing back, clambered into the lorry's passenger seat. Had he been in his own country, he would probably have given the man a smart back-hander for his insolence or, if the price had been reasonable, he would have clicked his heels neatly together and given a slight nod of the head. Neither would have been appropriate today.

Thursday 15th March 1945, 08:30 hrs.

Lars Koertig, Stefan Unger and Hugo Bauer had readily admitted to each other within hours of leaving Island Farm that they had no idea of where they were. They had been selected late in the escape preparations and were lamentably ill equipped for the many tests which lay ahead. Their only qualification for inclusion, so far as they could tell, was their contribution to the tunnel building, and even that had been relatively small.

Lars had taken his turn at the entrance to the tunnel in Hut Nine, pumping air into the make-shift ventilation system. He had also helped collect food tins, slotting and squeezing them together to extend the pipe as the tunnel progressed. Hugo had carried more tins full of the excavated earth, suspended on string which he held through holes cut in his trouser pockets. These were taken to various corners of the camp, emptied and kicked away to blend in with the soil.

Later, as the excavators encountered seams of thick red clay, the material was pressed into globes the size of cricket balls and spirited away. It would be several decades before the discovery was made that prisoners had built a false wall between a washroom and lavatories in Hut Nine using bricks and building materials left behind by the original work party. This formed a conveniently sealed cell with a small gap left near the top of the wall through which the clay balls were posted. Camp guards regularly patrolled outside and searched inside the building but the false wall and the gap remained undiscovered.

Stefan's contribution had been to join the raucous choir which belted out loud Amy marching songs. Their rendition of *"We Are Marching to England"* proved a particular irritant to both guards and the surrounding population. Performed in a makeshift theatre close to the escape hut, it successfully smothered the sound of digging and, on the night of the escape, the noise of the door to the guards' mess-room stores being wrenched from its hinges.

Despite their supplies being supplemented by pilfered British rations, the three prisoners had left with little food and had eaten nothing for two days. Although Hugo's surname means 'farmer' he, like his two travelling companions, had little knowledge of rural matters. This was unfortunate as, having found themselves on the northern fringes of Bridgend, they had travelled almost exclusively across woodlands and open farmland. Since then, without map or compass, they had been travelling blind, guided only by isolated buildings and the hope of finding food. The only nourishment they had scavenged had been discovered when, in the early hours, they had come across a cow shed. They had managed to extract a little over two pints of milk from a bemused cow. Although the farmer later reported his cow had been dry, the Special Constable who took the report failed to appreciate the significance of the incident and it was some days before his supervising officers were informed.

The prisoners had no identity papers, forged or otherwise and one of the men still had the letters 'PW' sewn onto the back of his greatcoat. As a result he had been wearing it inside out for the last four days. Unlike the other groups, they had not been teamed up with an airman or naval officer who could navigate and none of them spoke good English.

They had been travelling by night and resting wherever they could find shelter by day. It seemed that their journey had taken them inexorably up hill. They had no idea that they had been travelling almost due north, into the heart of the Welsh valleys and away from any swift means of escape.

Late on the night of Wednesday 14th March, however, as rain pounded their route up another relentless Welsh hillside, they had been forced to take cover. The three men had woken early on the Thursday morning, wet and cold but with a renewed determination. They left the soaking thicket of brambles where they had attempted to sleep, looked about briefly to get some sense of where they should be heading and recommenced their walk.

An hour later they came across a long, straight road. Devoid of traffic at that time of the morning, it ran from west to east over a high ridge which separates the Rhondda and Cynon Valleys. Looking to their right, down the length of road they could just make out the roofs and church steeples of a town. They had no way of knowing that they were looking down on the town of Aberdare, twenty five miles north of Cardiff.

They pulled their coats tighter about them, the chill wind whipping up and over the hilltop. Wearily, they started pacing.

Stefan, a former member of his cathedral choir, even began a gentle rendition of an old song he had learned during his early days in the Army. First heard in the trenches of the Somme during the last war, it wasn't a marching song and did nothing to encourage them along their way. Far from the rousing choruses he had endured at Camp 198, this was a lilting melody; a lament almost, to the fall of comrades and the casualties of war. It seemed to fit their mood and, as the road took a downward turn into the Cynon Valley, a light drizzle resumed to cloud their state of mind even further.

A mile further down the valley they found what they had been expecting all morning. A black saloon car, parked diagonally across the road, barred their way. Bolted to the boot a simple metal plate identified it as a police patrol car and leaning against it, two constables draped in oilskin capes and dripping miserably. As they saw the bedraggled group approaching, they both checked their service revolvers, hidden below the all-weather uniforms. Their Sergeant, an older and wiser man who had been sitting in the dry interior of the car, now slowly opened the door and moved to stand in front of his men. He murmured a brief instruction to act calmly and took up an authoritative pose with feet apart and hands on hips, his right hand resting invisibly beneath his rain-cape on his revolver.

Even before he raised his voice to speak, the men had raised their hands and surrendered. Lars Koertig, who spoke a little English, acted as spokesman and without being asked, reported that they were escaped prisoners from Bridgend. Pathetically, he folded his arms across his chest, shivered and asked for help.

The Sergeant nodded in silence. The local Police Division had recently been issued with two way car radios but in the overcast weather conditions he could raise no more than a static crackle from his control room in the town below. In any event, he would not have been permitted, under current regulations, to mention the Prisoners of War. Unable to summon another vehicle to transport the prisoners, the six large and wet men squeezed into the Police Austin and made their way heavily down the mountain road.

Within an hour, the Germans had been fed, given a hot drink and a change of dry clothes. Despite being back in captivity, it was clear to all who saw them that they were perfectly content that their ordeal was now over.

Thursday 15th March 1945, 09:00 hrs.

George Charteris settled again in the chair opposite his Inspector. He sipped his cup of tea and glanced at his notebook before closing it and replacing it in his pocket.

The regular meetings had eased the tension he had felt with his supervising officer and he now relaxed sufficiently to summarise the salient points in his report without the need to check his notes.

"The wounded officer, Tonnsmann, asked me for a further interview yesterday evening. It appears he is still eager to keep in favour with us."

"Presumably in the interests of winning a move away from his erstwhile friends?"

"Yes sir. Almost certainly." Inspector Bailey nodded, his lips pursed in thought as the Constable continued. "He told me some of the prisoners were in the habit of throwing scraps of paper through the wire fence onto the road outside."

"Scraps of paper?"

"I checked it out with a Lieutenant who has immediate command of the guards. He confirmed some of the papers had been found to contain messages." The Inspector leaned forward, resting his chin on his hands. "They were written in broken English and German, sir. Some referred to a break-out that was to be attempted."

"They were warnings?" The Inspector sat up.

"I thought that as well, sir, at first. There again, if any of the prisoners wanted to warn the authorities of an impending break-out, there would have been far simpler and more reliable ways of getting the information to them. Why would they pass messages through the wire when the guards were all inside the camp?"

"And how does Herr Tonnsmann feature in this?"

Charteris shrugged. "He says he simply heard about it a few days before the break-out. After all, at the time, he was all set to escape. He would have had no wish to damage the plan." The Constable took another sip of tea. "Tonnsmann now

240

believes they were diversionary tactics; simply distractions to occupy the guards."

Bailey leaned forward again. "What? Keeping them busy picking up litter?"

"Not entirely, sir. Every message had to be investigated in case they were attempting to pass messages to collaborators. It's true that a few paper aeroplanes were thrown over the wire during the early days which turned out to be made of blank paper. Nevertheless, the guards had to spend time picking them up to investigate what they were. It is only in the last few weeks that they have increasingly contained messages." There was a silence as both men mulled over the possibilities. "I understand Colonel Darling ordered that Military Police keep a secret watch on the fence where the notes were found. Several more were thrown but none were picked up. After eight hours the officers gave up their surveillance. Despite that, Darling also ordered regular patrols outside the perimeter fence to check for any more messages." George sighed slightly. "If Tonnsmann is right, the prisoners' tactics succeeded. The guards' attention was almost certainly distracted. It may be no coincidence that the tunnel was dug on the opposite side of the camp to where the scraps of paper were thrown."

"Does Tonnsmann suggest we have a nest of fifth columnists in Glamorgan?" The question was voiced quietly and the Inspector immediately wondered at the wisdom of asking it. To his relief, Charteris firmly shook his head.

"Absolutely not, sir. He doesn't believe any of the escapees had plans to meet up with anyone outside the camp. He didn't recall any discussion about sympathisers among the local population. The nearest he came to suggesting anything of the sort was a conversation with a junior NCO who has been working on a farm in Laleston. He's been boasting apparently that a local girl has taken a shine to him." He watched for his senior officer's reaction. "But hardly an infatuation that would lead her to betray her country."

The Inspector took in what he had just heard, weighing up the need to talk to Military Intelligence. Messages being passed which related to Prisoner of War escapes certainly seemed to be as much a military matter as they were of concern to the Police. He would shortly be meeting again with the Divisional Commander, Superintendent May. He would discuss it with him. He glanced at his watch, reminded of his next appointment. "And what are the latest figures regarding the detainees?"

"Yesterday, sir, was a slow day." He waited for a reaction but received nothing more than a fractionally raised eyebrow. "Just five more prisoners recaptured." The Inspector nodded. "Found on Margam Mountain, sir." He smiled optimistically. "That's encouraging, don't you think, sir? Being found locally, I mean."

The Inspector inhaled deeply. "I heard. Mrs Davies and Mrs Thomas over at Eglwys Nunydd." He slid a piece of paper across his desk, glancing at it for the fourth time that morning. "It seems the Ministry of Food is correct. We can't manage without our women farmers these days. Today, however, promises to be a busier one for us. I've already received a preliminary report from Aberdare that three prisoners gave themselves up in the early hours of this morning. I'm still waiting for the details, but it seems almost certain they are Bridgend men."

"I'll get on to it right away, sir. That takes the total to sixty nine prisoners recovered." He glanced up. "Assuming the Aberdare three are our men. And we now have just seventeen left to find." He scribbled in his notebook briefly, hesitating for a moment. "It isn't strictly a part of the investigation, sir, but I hear there have been complaints made by Colonel Llewellyn."

Bailey cocked his head to one side. The former commander of Bridgend's Home Guard was not given to causing trouble.

"Apparently he told a newspaper reporter that had he and his opposite numbers in Port Talbot and Cowbridge been allowed sufficient petrol, they could have deployed up to 2,000 men to cordon off the entire Glamorgan area within six hours of the escape being discovered." The Inspector inhaled deeply before releasing a wordless sigh. "Do you want to hear what else the newspapers have to say this morning, sir?"

The senior man nodded. That morning, in particular, he was being reluctantly pushed into allowing the press to occupy the forefront of his mind.

"Most of last night's regional evening 'papers had it that nineteen prisoners were still free but by this morning, the number had dropped to sixteen. They seem to be just deducting numbers from their previous total." The Inspector nodded, adding a further note to the file open in front of him.

"Not that I normally read the Socialist press particularly, sir, but *The Daily Worker* reported yesterday that the Chairman of the Bridgend Trades Council has made an official complaint about the behaviour of German prisoners when they are taken on work parties outside the camp."

The Inspector smiled grimly. "I'm not sure what he expects anyone to do about that."

"He's complaining at the laxity of the guards, sir. And the Secretary of the local Communist Party has complained to the Mayor and the Camp Commandant, insisting they take stricter control of Nazis in the camp."

Bailey snorted, unable to hide his contempt. "He's a bit bloody late with that one. Perhaps he should have had a word with Herr Hitler in 1939. He could have asked him to tone down the way he intended to conduct the war."

Thursday 15th March 1945, 12:00 hrs.

"As promised, gentlemen, we are now able to provide an *accurate* update to the situation regarding the absconders from Island Farm Camp." Superintendent May stressed the word 'accurate', pausing and gazing at the assembled press men over the top of his spectacles.

He had been speaking to a few contacts in the Ministry of Information, picking up hints on how to deal with representatives of the press. He had been told he should speak slowly and carefully. Watch every word and, if in doubt, repeat important points several times. This would also provide him with time to think and fill in the silences, discouraging any awkward questions. He had formulated a simple strategy based on this advice. If asked how many prisoners were still at large, he would stick to giving vague assurances regarding the recaptured men. Let the reporters do their own mathematics.

"Police officers from South Wales, Gloucestershire and beyond have been working round the clock to secure the safe recovery of the escaped Prisoners of War. Throughout this exercise they have been very ably assisted by members of several former Home Guard platoons, Civil Defence Volunteers, RAF personnel and soldiers based throughout South Wales and the South of England."

A hand in the front row of press reporters was raised. Following the advice, the Superintendent raised his hand in response. "I'll take any questions later, gentlemen." He smiled patronisingly at his audience, beginning to feel far more comfortable than he had at their last meeting. "I assure you, there will be plenty of opportunity to put your questions." He settled in his seat and glanced at a sheet of paper. "Reconnaissance aircraft have been deployed to assist with the search with great success across the Vale of Glamorgan. Police and Army road blocks have been maintained to create a cordon around the area and this has proved extremely effective. Several members of the public have also helped by providing the Police with details of sightings made across the area." He glanced up to ensure he was keeping his audience's attention. "The task has been made more difficult as the escaped detainees are believed to have divided into small parties, dispersing themselves in different directions in order to prolong the search." May frowned sternly at the front row of reporters as if they were ill behaved children placed at the front of the class. "This will not deter us. Senior officers of Glamorgan County Constabulary are confident that every escaped prisoner will soon be returned to custody." He leant back, his fingers joining over his broad stomach. "It has been reported to me that on Tuesday morning a United States Army officer assisted police officers in Salisbury to apprehend two of the escapees." He scanned the lines of reporters again, checking that they were still writing. He paused a few seconds until they returned their attention to him. He smiled with what he hoped would come across as reassuring confidence. "Such has been the efficiency of the Police and military personnel, it is quite possible that more of the prisoners are being rounded up even as we speak."

He paused again, a little too long this time for the reporters to contain their thirst for information. A voice cut through the silence, asking at least one question that everyone in the room wished to have answered.

"How many Nazis are still at large, Superintendent? Should the public be concerned that so many prisoners were allowed to escape?"

The Policeman smiled again, despite a slight rise in his blood pressure. "I am pleased to report, gentlemen, that the great majority of the detainees have already been apprehended and returned to custody."

Another voice interrupted him. "Can you comment on the report that one of the German officers was shot while trying to escape?"

At his side, Colonel Darling edged forward, preparing to answer. May denied him the opportunity by an almost imperceptible movement of his hand. "It is correct that one of the Prisoners of War was wounded during his attempt to escape, while he was a few hundred yards outside the camp's perimeter fence. He was not seriously hurt and is being treated for his wound."

"What should we tell our readers about the danger, Superintendent, that these escaped Nazis pose? Do you know if they are armed?"

"My advice to members of the public is that they should not, under any circumstances, approach anyone they suspect of being an escaped Prisoner of War. They should immediately report their suspicions to the proper authorities; that is, to a police officer."

"So they are dangerous, then."

"Gentlemen, please. We have no reports that any of the escapees have been armed in any way or have attempted to harm any civilians. There have been no reports of any stolen firearms in the area and vigorous checks within the camp have shown that no military weapons are missing. When properly challenged by uniformed officers they have all surrendered peacefully."

"Where do you think the Nazi prisoners might be? We hear they have travelled as far as Southampton and Birmingham before being recaptured."

Superintendent May sighed. "It is true we have extended the area of our search but, make no mistake, every seaport and airfield in the country was placed on alert within an hour of the break-out being reported."

There was an immediate murmur among the reporters. Another voice rose over the general hum. "So RAF bases are at risk?"

May leaned forward again. "We have to take account of the fact that some of the escapees are *Luftwaffe* pilots. We therefore have to assume that some of them may attempt to take aircraft in order to escape the country. We have taken every precaution to ensure that this will not happen." He stood, prompting Colonel Darling and the other uniformed men at the top table to follow suit. "That is all for now. Thank you for your attention, gentlemen."

Amid a flurry of further questions, the crocodile of uniforms filed away and left the room.

Despite the *Daily Express* story of a few days earlier claiming that twenty seven prisoners were still at large, the following morning's edition reported confidently that following the continued operation to round up the remaining escapees, described as *'all rabid young Nazis'* the number still free was just three.

It was only in the Commandant's office at Camp 198, in Superintendent May's office and along a few deeply hidden corridors in Whitehall that the true figure was understood to be seventeen.

Thursday 15th March 1945, 14:40 hrs.

The centre of Canterbury was busy that Thursday afternoon. The good people of the famous Kentish cathedral city were going about their business in their normal matter-of-fact manner and paid scant attention to a nondescript open-backed lorry as it wheezed to a halt near the corner of Guildhall Street and Sun Yard. Neither did they think it particularly unusual when three shabbily dressed workmen, clearly tired and unkempt, dropped from the cab and made their way into the Sun Cafe. It was common enough in towns close to the coast for lorry drivers to stop on their way to deliver or collect goods from the docks. A casual onlooker might well have assumed, correctly as it happened, that they had driven a long way across country in order to be there. They might equally have shown no surprise that the men wore overcoats buttoned to the neck. The chill March wind, blowing strongly from the east that afternoon, would have seemed particularly cold after several hours in the stuffy confines of a lorry's cab.

The men gathered briefly round a blackboard propped up outside the cafe's door and studied the menu. One of them, slightly older than the other two, muttered something under his breath and shook his head imperceptibly.

Having carefully counted his remaining coins, von Hindermeer calculated he had a little less than two shillings left in his pocket. The blackboard announced a choice of main courses followed by an array of desserts, the origins of which they could only guess at, all priced at one and sixpence.

Despite their repast of bread and cheese, it had proved inadequate after four days of fasting and the sight of a cafe had been too good an opportunity to miss. Even now, the waft of cooked meats and gravy drew them in, despite von Hindermeer's warning that they could only afford one meal between them.

They took their seats at a table close to the door and made an affectation of intently reading the menu. Only von Hindermeer could understand English and he had no intention of translating the list of dishes. He would order what he had a taste for and the junior men could either share a small part of it or go without.

The young waitress pulled her dress down below the belt and smoothed her apron. They didn't appear to be in uniform but they might just be Yanks, despite their rough exterior. She sighed quietly to herself. She had often been accused of being a dreamer and her imagination allowed her to believe the newcomers might be smart GI's under the layers of grime. It was becoming quite common for soldiers to pass through the city on their way back from a spell of heroic fighting in France.

She fussed briefly over her blonde hair and drew a notebook from her apron pocket. Approaching the table she gave the customers her best professional smile. She wished them a good afternoon.

"What can I get for you gentlemen? Everything's on except the chicken pie and rabbit stew."

The oldest of the customers nodded and returned to the menu with a sigh as if the two deleted dishes had been the only ones he had been interested in.

"I will have the mutton with vegetables if you please."

The girl's eyebrows rose slightly but she made a show of writing the order carefully on her pad.

"And for you, sir?" She turned to the customer sitting to von Hindermeer's left. *Obersturmführer* Krause opened his mouth to speak but was cut short.

"My friends are not hungry. They require nothing, thank you."

The girl seemed confused. "Nothing at all? Not even a nice cup of tea?"

"Nothing, thank you waitress."

There was something in the man's tone which told her his companions wouldn't argue with him. She retreated from the table, writing again briefly before tearing the page from her note pad and handing it to the cafe manageress.

Krause leant forward. He was no longer afraid of the man's rank or lofty status. He had persuaded himself that, in their present predicament, they should all be considered equal; fellow soldiers on the run in enemy territory and with a common foe. Under his breath, Krause repeated his belief that they should have overpowered the cheat of a farmer and taken whatever they needed. There had been no need to part with any money. That way they could all have had a meal. He glanced about the almost deserted cafe and suggested they ordered three meals. All they had to do when they had finished was get up and leave without paying. What could the girl or the old woman behind the counter do?

Von Hindermeer didn't like his judgement being questioned. He too leaned forward, closing the gap between himself and the two junior men. A farmer who had been assaulted might just kick up a fuss. A dead farmer could possibly give cause for suspicion – even in this God-forsaken country. The officer's tone was heavy with sarcasm. Stealing food from a cheap cafe was not only tantamount to setting off an alarm bell; it was beneath the dignity of a German officer.

The words *'Deutsch offizier'* hissed across the table rather more loudly than von Hindermeer had intended. All three men glanced about for prying ears. A large poster adorned the wall next to the counter. It showed a simple line cartoon, unmistakably of Adolf Hitler. He was sitting precariously on a series of telegraph wires with one hand cupped to his ear. The caption beneath him read *'Be careful what you say'*.

Von Hindermeer glanced at the poster and stiffened. He turned away, muttering so quietly that even the men at his table failed to hear him. He placed his hands, palms downwards on the tablecloth, indicating they should all keep quiet.

The *Obersturmführer* quietly repeated his complaint that they were all hungry, adding that the ship they boarded had better be friendly enough to feed them or they would all arrive back in Berlin too ill to return to the struggle.

The remark was too much for the aristocratic Major. He placed his elbow firmly in the middle of the table, extending his index finger so it almost touched the younger officer's nose. He would tolerate no talk of struggle. Germany was on the brink of the most glorious and spectacular victory in the history of modern warfare. The Fuhrer would soon be supreme commander of every Army in Europe and they; his finger spiralled round the table, as men who had tasted victory over the British, would be senior members his elite officer corps.

He nodded once, a single jerk of his head. All three men froze, suddenly aware that the cafe had fallen silent. Barely daring to move, they slowly looked up. In the deathly hush, the other customers hovered over their meals, gazing at the table next to the door. On the far side of the cafe, two British soldiers stood at the counter, staring in their direction.

As one, the Germans jumped from their table, swung the door open and bolted across the street towards the waiting lorry. Falling over each other in their haste, they clambered aboard and the man who found himself in the driver's seat started the engine. The gearbox screamed in complaint as the engine roared and the old wagon jerked off the pavement and down the road.

Behind it, the two Tommies ran hopelessly after them. One had the presence of mind to scribble the registration number on a scrap of paper but they had no means of giving chase.

Hurriedly, they returned to the cafe and while one of the soldiers checked for details with the waitress and manageress, the other telephoned his barracks, breathlessly asking for the Adjutant's office.

A search party was quickly organised and the port authorities at Dover and Folkestone were notified. The Kent Police established that the lorry had been stolen and its owner was carefully questioned by local detectives for any indication of collusion. They found none.

Information from the cafe staff and customers confirmed that several words of German had been spoken between the three men although nobody present had quite summoned the courage to challenge them. It was thought, suggested one apologist, that the men might have been Dutch. At the same time and at a remote desk located at the end of a lengthy corridor in Whitehall a telephone was ringing. When the suited junior Civil Servant answered the call it was confirmed that the only Prisoner of War camp currently missing any prisoners was that at Bridgend. The young man glided silently into the neighbouring office of his Principal Officer and placed a slip of paper on his desk. On it was written simply 'Canterbury 3 confirmed as Bridgend PW's.'

The following day, Henry Stowe, a retired council official and former soldier visited Canterbury Central Police Station. He had, he said, been in the cafe when the three men had arrived. His suspicions had been aroused and he had quietly left with the intention of finding a policeman. Moments later, as the lorry had made its headlong escape, he had narrowly avoided being run down. When questioned over why he had become suspicious, his answer was simple and assured. He was certain he had glimpsed a black uniform beneath one of the men's coats. It had a silver badge of some sort on the collar. He knew of no British or Allied military uniform that it could be mistaken for. He clearly believed he had seen the black uniform of a *Waffen SS* Panzer officer.

Thursday 15th March 1945, 18:30 hrs.

George Arkwright had worked on the London Midland and Scottish Railway for twenty two years. During that time he had been employed as a ticket office clerk before becoming a supervisor and, nine years ago, accepting a job as a guard. Since then he had run the routes between London and the West Midlands, taking pride in the occasional incidents of punctuality which his company made such capital of in their advertising. He had gained even greater satisfaction from his record of catching fare dodgers. Since war had broken out, however, there had been more of a demand for goods trains and he had been employed far less on passenger services. He saw no reason, however, for that to prevent him from exercising the diligence demanded of his position to protect company revenue.

As he left his guards' van at the end of his shift in Castle Bromwich near Manchester, he glanced at his pocket watch and made a note on his pad of time sheets. They had arrived on schedule and within a few minutes he intended to reach his favourite corner of the bar in The Railway Tavern and order a pint of dark mild.

As he headed towards the station office to sign his clock card, however, he caught sight of something unusual which at once stirred his adrenalin. The pub would have to wait. In the shadows near the rear of the train, behind the final goods wagon, a shadow shifted against the dim glow beyond the rail shed doors. The sidings should be empty of engineers by now and the area was certainly off limits to the public. George moved hastily to the staff office and eased the door open. Six of his fellow guards were sitting at a circular table in the middle of the room, shoulders hunched over cups of tea and an intense card game.

"Quick, boys. I've got a freeloader on the Liverpool freight."

The other men rose as one, following wordlessly as George walked quickly across the platform. He pointed in the direction of the train. Clearly visible, four heavily clad men were moving along the length of the train. George half turned to the others, keeping his eyes on the stealthy caravan of darkly covered men. "They just got off my train. They must have been on since Gloucester." The others nodded knowingly.

Three of the men peeled away to the left while the other three moved right. It was a manoeuvre which any skirmisher would have recognised, closing in on their prey in a pincer movement. As they closed in, George straightened and crossed the tracks towards the train. He shouted an order at the men to stop.

Hans Harzheim was the first to see they had been spotted and to react. He waved and put on his warmest smile. He was about to explain that they had become lost looking for the ticket office. Any effort to explain their way out of trouble, however, was rendered pointless by Werner Zielasko. Without another thought, he turned and fled, his slight frame leaping first to the right then left, avoiding the outspread arms of the oncoming guards. One of the railwaymen lurched forward but he was no Rugby player and his tackle missed his man completely.

Oswald Prior and Steffi Ehlert ran in the opposite direction and seeing three officials fanning out in front of them, swerved to their left. Their escape route was blocked by the goods train and they dropped to the gravel, rolling uncomfortably across the tracks. With George closing in to their rear, they had nowhere else to go. Outnumbered, their only options were to flee or to surrender. They came to a halt and, to the guards' surprise, raised their hands.

The railwaymen stopped, glancing at each other in speculative silence. In the moment that followed, as nobody moved, something in Oswald's mind clicked into place. He lowered his hands, tapped Steffi on the elbow and together, they turned and ran.

Ahead of them, a high wire fence seemed no obstacle at all after all they had been through and they quickly scaled it, ignoring the barbed wire as it nipped through their thick clothing.

They kept running beyond the wire, ignoring the rising voices and obvious anger of their pursuers. In the gathering gloom of a Midlands evening, the men pounded down narrow urban streets, their boots echoing between the terraced houses until they reached a lane that narrowed to a single footpath overhung with trees. Grateful for the extra cover this provided, they pounded on, conscious of their own failing stamina but also aware that nobody seemed to be following them. They slowed to a walk as the bath broadened out onto a canal towpath.

Ahead of them, sitting on a bench and apparently gazing into the water, they could see two men. From where they were sheltering, although there seemed to be something familiar about the two hunched figures, neither Oswald nor Steffi could make out whether the men were in uniform or carrying rifles. They decided to take a chance and, all attempt at camouflage abandoned, began strolling down the canal path towards them.

The men on the bench suddenly rose, turned towards them, pointed and walked briskly towards them.

Hans Harzheim and Werner Zielasko embraced the other two men and, through laughter borne out of relief, the four of them exchanged details of their escape from the goods yard. They ambled on, following the line of the canal, with no sense of direction or particular destination now in mind.

The canal left the urban streets of Castle Bromwich and rows of narrow houses were soon replaced by open fields. Their animated conversation punctuated only by a brief silence as they crept past a brightly illuminated lock-keeper's cottage. By the time they were out of earshot, their increasing hunger had become their most pressing concern.

Beyond the next field, a trickle of smoke rose from a single chimney and they could make out the scattered buildings of a farm. They speculated that they might find food there. If their luck held, they might even be able to persuade the occupants to give them a meal if they could devise a convincing story. They were too far from the coast now to claim they were marooned merchant seamen.

As they considered the options, the dull drone of a low flying aircraft passed slowly overhead. Immediately, Steffi announced he had a plan. He watched carefully as the 'plane gradually dropped in altitude, circling to its left and vanished beyond a covering of trees. They heard the tone of the engine drop almost dead ahead of them, as if it was going to use the canal as a runway. There must be an airfield close by. They would cut across the field and try their luck for food at the farm. They could say they were Polish bomber crew and had brought in a new Lancaster to the airfield. They were on a twenty four hour pass but had got lost. Whether they were given food or not, they would ask for directions to the airfield.

Steffi grinned. The next step would take even more nerve. If they couldn't find any other way in, they would try to talk their way onto the airfield through the main gate. They would then persuade the ground crew they had orders to requisition an aircraft. If that failed, they would take one by force.

Werner shrugged. The worst that could happen is that they could be shot down by their own side. Eventually they would be recognised as heroes even if the iron crosses were awarded posthumously.

Whether it was bravado or mild hysteria brought on by exhaustion and hunger, the four men laughed at Werner's bleak humour. They left the towpath and cut across the fields towards the farmhouse. The powerful crack of a gunshot brought their progress and apparent hilarity to an abrupt halt.

A flurry of noisy crows took off from a newly ploughed patch of field and the men turned towards the sound of the echoing explosion. A human shape emerged from a shadowed corner of trees. It strode towards them with an assurance which held the men rooted to the spot. As the figure drew closer they identified the features of a heavily built man, a shotgun held lazily over one arm. At his hip, a brace of rabbits tied by lengths of string to his belt swung and bounced with the motion of his quickened pace.

Once again, Hans adopted his open smile, his eyebrows rising in friendly enquiry.

"Good evening. I'm afraid we are lost."

The farmer showed no surprise. "Are you now? Where would you be looking to go then?"

"We are with the Polish Airforce. We are trying to find the airfield." Another innocent smile.

"Well this is no airfield. This is my land. And you're trespassing on it."

Hans spread his arms wide in an ingenuous shrug. "I am so sorry, sir. We have been on leave today and we became lost."

The farmer still seemed unimpressed. "Lost you may be. As for the rest, I think you're telling a pack of lies." He lifted the shotgun to point into the centre of the group. "I've just been talking to some mates of mine. Soldiers, from the infantry garrison, they are. Funnily enough they've been looking for four blokes, just like you." The twin barrels jerked up and down.

Hans Harzheim, Werner Zielasko, Oswald Prior and Steffi Ehlert glanced mutely at each other. As one, they raised their hands.

During their subsequent interviews with the local Police, two of the four Germans were to admit that they had thought the railway employees might have been armed police officers; an admission that caused more than a little mirth in the interview room. The Sergeant taking Ehlert's statement grinned across the table. He had been in the Royal Naval Air Service during the previous war and had decided he liked the young *Luftwaffe* pilot. He chuckled softly.

"Dear me. You Jerries really should do your homework better. British train drivers don't carry firearms, you know." He shook his head and picked up his pen to start writing.

No less surprised were the railway guards who had confidently reported to the Railway Police that they had caught a group they believed were either fare dodgers, pilferers or, worse, deserters. They had concluded the strange accents were probably either Polish or Dutch. Although they had seen the newspaper reports of escaped prisoners and heard the BBC news, they had failed to associate the break-out in South Wales, well over 100 miles away, with their stowaways.

Friday 16th March 1945, 09:00 hrs.

George Charteris leaned forward, placing his forearms on the Inspector's desk and cupped the mug of hot tea between his hands. He had delivered his daily report, updating the numbers and discussing the latest newspaper reports. A total of seventy five prisoners had now been taken back into custody, leaving eleven still at large.

Inspector Bailey nodded. "Superintendent May managed to evade questions from the press yesterday about the numbers." He made a clicking noise with his tongue. "But the Army's Western Command HQ at Chester issued a press release quoting a figure of sixty seven. It's no surprise that this morning's newspapers are saying there are just three more at large." Both men fell silent with the simultaneous conclusion that the actual number of recaptured prisoners now exceeded the number who had supposedly escaped.

Further up the Police hierarchy, seated in an office at County Police Headquarters in the Cardiff suburb of Canton, senior officers were also huddled over a desk and discussing the events emanating from Bridgend.

They had been made aware that the day before, during a late session in the House of Commons, an announcement had been made which referred to *'an escape by sixty seven German Prisoners of War'* who had escaped from Bridgend. The officers, like Superintendent May in Bridgend, were optimistic that the inadvertent slip of the tongue, if that's what it was, would be overlooked by the press. With this in mind they had chosen not to refer to the incident or the number quoted again.

In lowered tones, they darkly imagined the scene being acted out behind Westminster's closed doors. Small clutches of senior civil servants would also be meeting. Permanent Secretaries and Under Secretaries would mutually be congratulating each other on their decision to order reports regarding the escape be particularly carefully vetted. Their only regret would be that the D-Notice had not touched on the recovery of prisoners which, after all, should be seen as good for morale. They would surely be lamenting that newspapers across the country had taken such a close interest in the escape. Nobody in those ivory towers had expected the hunger for news of German officers on the loose to spread so far beyond South Wales.

In reality, the Westminster mandarins all agreed that the story had to be brought back under proper control. It would otherwise soon become apparent to one of Fleet Street's troublesome hacks that the numbers didn't add up.

Permanent Under Secretaries from the Ministry of Information were well acquainted with the techniques of propaganda and persuasion; the sort of pithy message which encouraged housewives to make do and mend. They were less comfortable with misinformation and subterfuge.

In league with their opposite numbers from the War Office, however, they agreed to bury the Bridgend story. They would adopt the well tested and simple tactic of emphasising alternative items of news. By releasing greater detail of other recent events, escaped Germans might soon become unworthy of mention.

Most recently, there had been a number of V-2 rocket attacks, with some quite horrendous casualties, in and around London. That was really not the type of story, they all agreed, that the press should give space to.

In the last twenty four hours, the Americans had launched a devastating fire-bomb attack, using B-29 bombers, on the city of Nagoya in Japan. Given an appropriate slant, that might fill a few paragraphs in a positive way. Nevertheless, to capture the public's attention, they really needed a story of military heroism closer to home. Ideally, they needed a British success in the European theatre.

The US Third Army had captured Kochem on the Lower Moselle River, crossing the Moselle near Koblenz. Although undoubtedly good news militarily, it was hardly likely to set the public imagination aflame.

"Couldn't we invent the foiling of a German plot to, say, introduce forged fivers into Britain?"

The Permanent Secretary from The Treasury sighed. "Unfortunately that's rather old news." The other men looked up in surprise. "And, of course, it never happened." He, more than most, remembered all too well his Ministry's greatest challenge of 1943. It had taken his staff, along with a small army of men from various Military Intelligence branches several weeks to bury that story.

"We could release a little about the preparation for Operation Plunder."

The other men frowned. It was a dangerous tactic, discussing plans for future military manoeuvres. The plans for 30 Corps and 12 Corps to cross the Rhine were surely off limits.

Another Permanent Secretary coughed. "Let's wait for signs of success before we release details about that one."

"There was a successful crossing of the River Mass by a Scots Division on Wednesday, wasn't there?"

The senior man shook his head. "Wednesday's successful assault was a rehearsal for the offensive on The Rhine. As I understand it, the main advance won't be attempted for several days yet."

"Surely we need not refer to the Mass crossing as being a preparation for another assault. Can't it simply be seen as another British success in Europe?"

"Enough to fill a few front page paragraphs, I would imagine."

The men stood upright from the pile of papers they had been bowing over. They watched for each other's reaction before beginning to slowly nod.

It was agreed. The crossing of the River Mass would become the primary news item to be released to the BBC and news agencies in the War Ministry's next press release.

Friday 16th March 1945, 09:30 hrs.

He was responding to a telephone call from an excited citizen of Port Talbot when Police Inspector Edwin J Hunter pulled on his overcoat and peaked cap. He glanced out of his office window before leaving the building and was quietly gratified yet unsurprised that so many men had answered his request for help.

In the small vehicle yard behind Port Talbot Police Station some twenty men stamped their feet against the cold as they awaited his instructions. Police constables and a couple of sergeants, ARP wardens and Home Guard volunteers, their uniforms less unkempt than usual after several months of careful storage, all looked up as Hunter strode onto the yard. Some even came to attention. Few had rifles but held broom handles or garden rakes and one or two old soldiers brought these smartly but almost comically to their sides.

Edwin wasted no time in informing the assembled search-party that four men, possibly escapees from Island Farm Camp, had been seen in the early hours of the morning in the area of Cymmer. Situated at the confluence of the Afan and the Llynfi valleys, Cymmer's small community sat at a geographical crossroads. Despite being closer to the town of Maesteg, local politics and the tradition of demarcation between valleys determined that Port Talbot acted as its administrative centre.

The men split into two groups and clambered aboard two vans. One, the property of Port Talbot Police, was a plain regulation black box of a vehicle normally used to transport prisoners to and from court. The other, painted in smudged camouflage green, was a former furniture van appropriated in 1940 from a local removal company. The van's interior had been thoughtfully fitted out by the Home Guard with slatted wooden seats running down each side but it remained even less comfortable for its rear passengers than the prisoner transport. Nobody complained.

Hunter took his place next to the driver of the police van and, checking nobody had been left in the yard, waved the short convoy to move out.

It was a cold morning which was following an even colder night and as the vans progressed slowly up the Afan Valley, the outside temperature dropped even further. A thickening storm blustered over the ridges, nudging the heavy vehicles left and right as their high sides caught the wind. Hunter instinctively pressed his hand against the dashboard, steadying himself against the van's rocking movement. The driver switched on his windscreen wipers, ineffectual against the large irregular splashes of rain and stretched a cold hand over the wheel. He wiped condensation from the glass with the cuff of his jacket.

Cymmer lay ten difficult miles from Port Talbot and much of the road was surrounded by high, forested hillsides which threw the road into even deeper gloom. After some thirty minutes, Hunter told the driver to pull in at the side of a wide bend just beyond a row of labourers' cottages. Known as Duffryn Rhondda, the modest little houses provided homes for a handful of farm and mine workers. The men disembarked, rubbing their backs and stretching against the pain of unforgiving timber seats as Hunter directed one of the constables to call at each of the houses. He wanted to check how many local men might be out on the hillsides – and to ensure that those who weren't, remained indoors. Stray civilians could easily lead to confusion and they had no wish to go chasing after the wrong people.

"Unless anyone wants to volunteer to join the search party, of course." He added as the Constable made his way towards the first front door.

Once again, the volunteers gathered round the Inspector and his two sergeants.

"For those who don't know the area, he began, "this is the Brytwn Road. It runs up to Cymmer." He swept his left arm to the east. "But it's in this area that we have been told four men were seen crossing fields in the early hours of this morning."

He instructed half the men to search north of the road, led by one of the sergeants while he took the other party south. "We will spread out in a line, about twenty yards between each man, and comb out, moving directly north and south respectively." He looked about for any lack of understanding. "Where there is scrub or any form of cover where a man might hide, I want at least two men to beat through it using their sticks." He glanced at the few Home Guard men who were clutching rifles to their chests. "You men who are armed, by all means use your rifle butts to beat through any cover but please," his voice slowed for emphasis, "keep the safety catches on. I want no accidents and no casualties." There was a significant pause as the soldiers made a show of checking their weapons. Few were loaded. "Not even a Nazi casualty." There was a ripple of nervous laughter as the more skittish members of the party were reminded of the seriousness of their task.

Obediently, the group separated into two search parties and clambered over the ditches on either side of the road. They stood facing their target countryside, their backs to the road and, choreographed by the sergeants, shuffled left and right to give each neighbouring man his predetermined space.

As one, the lines of men began trudging across the wet fields, their boots already sinking into several inches of mud. Edwin quickly realised the morning was not going to pass pleasantly. He wasn't alone in his hope for a quick resolution.

They were guided south by the line of a path which, had they a map to study, would have been shown to follow a shallow valley before petering out in the depths of a boggy area of marshland. Alongside the path a thin stream wound round outcrops of bare rock before vanishing, its constant supply of rainwater soaking into the soil. Beyond that, the land rose in a broad bank, hiding from view the next deep valley which led down to the sizeable town of Maesteg.

At this time of year, the deep, rich soil quickly became saturated and it was only in high summer that the local man who counted the area as part of his farm could use it for grazing his sheep.

Hunter checked left and right that his party was keeping a straight line and, satisfied, returned his attention to the area ahead. There was little cover for any absconding German to use as a hiding place. At each end of the search line, the outermost men were walking close to the ridges which ran either side of the shallow valley. The Inspector knew this area well and he was satisfied they would have a clear view east and west across several miles of open country. Having grown up in Cymmer, as a boy he had roamed, against his parents' wishes, along this very path. Often returning home soaking wet and covered in mud, he knew all too well what lay beyond the next hilltop.

As they crested the next rise, Hunter first heard the cries of men to his right and then followed the line of their extended arms and pointing fingers. Several hundred yards ahead and to the west, four men stood, apparently frozen in horror, observing the emerging and apparently disciplined line of uniformed men advancing on them. They cannot have failed to notice that several of the men were dressed in military uniforms and carried rifles. Despite this, they broke from their reverie, turned and with strangely long, slow steps, began to retreat. Beyond them, a thick covering of trees provided a dark backdrop which, if they reached it, could become an instant camouflage.

One of the men on Hunter's right flank broke into a run, his heavy boots moving with commendable speed through the mud. Hunter called out to hold his position and, raising his voice further, repeated the instruction for the benefit of the rest of the search party.

The line of men moved quicker now, travelling down the shallow south facing slope. Their feet were becoming heavier, picking up clods of thick rich mud, but in the adrenalin driven heat of the moment, none of them noticed. The line turned to face the four fleeing men, closing in from both sides as they advanced. Hunter became aware that they were making up ground, the distance between them and the escaped prisoners diminishing. There could only be one reason and when the last of the four men ahead of them stopped completely, he instructed his team to halt.

He held his arms out along the line then cupped his hands round his mouth.

"Do you speak English?" The words, partly lost in the driving wind, were apparently clear enough. One of the men immediately replied that he did. "You must walk towards us. You are in danger." The men raised their hands and their spokesman shouted again.

"Do not shoot. We are not armed."

Hunter heard a snigger from the man standing nearest to him and the distinctive double click of a rifle being cocked.

Hunter curtly warned him to be careful and returned his attention to the men fifty yards ahead of them. "I mean you are in danger of the marsh." The German appeared not to understand. "You are standing in a marsh. In a bog." He beckoned them forward. "You've strayed off the path. This area is dangerous."

The German muttered something to his companions and all four looked down, trying to pull their boots precariously from the mud. They wobbled unsteadily and then, with painful effort, managed a few slow, glutinous steps forward.

The men of the search party watched in silent amusement as the enemy officers strenuously moved, at a snail's pace, towards their surrender. Once on firmer ground, Hunter took a small pace forward. He introduced himself.

"May I take it that you gentlemen have until recently been guests of His Majesty at Camp 198, Bridgend?"

The English speaking German nodded with as much dignity as he could muster. "That is so, Inspector Hunter."

"In which case, I would like to extend to you a further invitation to join me and my men at our police station." He smiled as a father might greet his son leaving the pitch after a cold and wet game of rugby. "I think I can promise a nice hot cup of tea and a few warm blankets."

The German shivered and spoke briefly to his three comrades. They exchanged a few words and nodded. "That would be most welcome. We thank you, Inspector. I think we have seen enough of the Welsh countryside for the present."

Saturday 17th March 1945, 17:30 hrs.

John Hopkins sat at the rough pine table in his kitchen and watched his wife poke into the open door of the range. The scraps of wood gathered from about his farm burned well and served to heat their comfortable home as well as cook their breakfast. He inhaled deeply, enjoying the aroma of frying bacon. Life had been kind to John over the previous few years. His wife, Maygwen, had expressed only contentment since they had moved from the Swansea suburb of Morriston to the open pastures surrounding their farmhouse a few miles north in the village of Glais.

His mother, Annie, had been widowed in 1940. Some say her husband's end had been hurried by the shock of the *Luftwaffe* damaging his beloved city. Whatever the truth, John had determined to leave his job and take over the running of the family farm. It had, all agreed, been the best decision of his professional life. Although a well regarded policeman for nearly twenty years with a steady, if unspectacular, flow of promotions behind him, he had no doubt that he was better suited to a life on the land.

In his early years as a beat bobby he had patrolled the northern fringes of Swansea happily enough, earning the respect of local business people and making sufficient numbers of arrests to satisfy both his superiors and the law abiding element within the area of his beat. Promoted to Sergeant, however, he found more of his time was taken up with paperwork, collating reports and calculating work rotas for his section. Only occasionally did he manage to venture onto the streets and his time was then usually spent introducing new constables to their beats.

Nevertheless, he was good at his job and through steady perseverance and attention to detail, passed his Police examinations to become an Inspector. That was when things started to pale for him. He spent eight hours a day behind his desk, reading interminable memos from the Chief Constable's office about budgets, staffing levels and the rising tide of politicians who wished to involve themselves in police business. When he wasn't reading or writing reports, he sat in meetings with even more senior officers who seemed to have more interest in the next bulk purchase of police boots than in the disturbingly swift increase in violent crime.

When his mother had suggested to him that he should inherit the farm, he had leapt at the opportunity. It was a decision he had never regretted.

Now, as if to provide further reassurance, Maygwen placed a broad plate of fried bacon, eggs, sausages, lava bread, mushrooms and toast on the table before him. A large woman with a healthy appetite of her own, she saw it as a perk of their occupation that she could indulge his passion for a full cooked breakfast at any time of day. This was the third such meal she had served him today and one he would never tire of. She lifted the old enamel teapot from its rest by the range and refilled his mug.

Maygwen smiled and took her seat at his side, carving a thick slice of home baked bread for herself. She would have none of this 'National Loaf' she had heard so much about. A compliant soul by nature, she drew the line at politicians dictating to her what she should eat. She slathered a generous portion of butter across her bread and reached for a block of cheese.

It was bad enough having to register with the village shops and carry a ration card. Few of the farming community needed to fulfil their official ration from shops as they produced eggs, butter and milk aplenty but, as far as Maygwen was concerned, it was the principle of being told how much she should eat that she objected to. Two ounces of butter a week would, in her view, barely feed a babe in arms, let alone a hard working man like her husband.

She reasoned that he worked long hours to provide for his family and politicians should be grateful for the surplus he was able to supply to the rest of the country.

Above them, they heard shuffling steps passing across the floorboards of her mother-in-law's bedroom. Maygwen nodded with another smile. Annie had taken to having afternoon naps recently and these seemed to enhance her appetite and energy levels well into the evening. She poured another cup of tea and sliced a further doorstep of bread in preparation.

Later, refreshed by their early evening meal, the two women set out to tend their hens before the evening light disappeared altogether. They had a flock of over sixty Buff Sussex hens from which they earned a steady income from both eggs and, occasionally, meat. Their three cockerels ensured the flock remained buoyant and it was these which the women heard first as they walked up the long sloping garden towards the hen run.

"The boys are feisty tonight." Annie commented, wondering privately whether one of the local dogs was causing trouble.

Maygwen was having similar thoughts and wondered whether she should have brought her husband's shotgun. She was about to put voice to her concerns when, from the corner of her eye, she saw something move. A rhododendron bush rustled, apparently blown by the wind and before either woman could comment, they found themselves confronted by three men. They had the collars of their coats turned up to cover their faces and one of them carried a length of wood which both women recognised as the handle to an old shovel that had been in one of the farm's outbuildings.

"Who the devil are you?" Maygwen spread her ample figure across the narrow path, protectively standing between the men and her mother-in-law.

"You will give us food please." The man spoke with a heavy Bavarian accent although neither woman had any experience of foreigners to draw on. Annie was later to describe his voice as 'Sort of foreign. Just odd really.' She didn't care to mention that he also sounded menacing and demanding. Well after the event, neither she nor Annie would admit they felt any fear.

"Food?" Maygwen repeated. "This isn't some cafe, you know." She tried to make her indignation register louder than her nervousness.

The man lifted his shovel handle slightly. His coat collar shifted with the movement and she could make out the features of a young man in his twenties, unshaven and with deep set dark eyes. "You women will give us food to eat. You will please not argue."

"I'll be buggered if we will." Annie's voice rose shrilly from behind her daughter-in-law's broad shoulders. "Now you just bugger off. Get off this land this minute."

The three men took half a pace forward, the lump of wood rising to be used as a weapon.

"What's going on here then?"

All five turned as the large frame of John Hopkins appeared at a gate set in the garden wall. He strode firmly across the

268

grass towards them. In an instant, he was a burly young Policeman once more, summing up the situation, measuring his men and ignoring the lack of either a truncheon or reinforcements. He stuck his thick hand out. "Let's see your identity papers."

As one, the three men turned. Dropping his piece of wood, the young man who had been their spokesman led the way as they bolted up the path towards the hen run.

He might have been well into his sixth decade, but Hopkins was no slouch. In his earlier years he had played rugby for both Glamorgan County Police and, twice, for his country. He had been known as 'Halt Hopkins' for his unfailing ability to stop an opposing forward in his tracks. Despite his heavy build, he was also a lot quicker on his feet than the younger men could have suspected.

Worn down by a week of sleeping rough and eating little more than raw vegetables and a few eggs, the men were no match for John's strength and natural ability. He soon caught up with them and deftly knocked the right boot of the trailing man sideways against his opposite heel. He tripped and fell heavily, tumbling in an untidy somersault off the path and into a ditch where he lay, winded and bruised, gazing up at the dark sky.

John's hands fell powerfully and simultaneously onto the thick woollen collars of the other two men, pulling them down with all his weight. They had no time to struggle but fell backwards in a panting, protesting pile on the path.

The words *reasonable force* flashed briefly through John's mind before he dismissed the concept. He wasn't a policeman now. He dropped, allowing gravity and his own weight to apply all the force needed, landing his right knee firmly in the centre of the nearest man's chest and pinning him to the ground. He raised his hand, turning it into a fist the size of a sledge hammer and held it over the other man's head.

"Don't make me get nasty, boys." The last remaining man squirmed backwards slightly, hoping to lessen the force of the expected blow. He raised his hands to cover his face.

John heard a movement behind him and quickly looked round, remembering the first man he had felled. Maygwen was standing by the ditch glaring down at the shaking German. She held her husband's double barrelled shotgun and was pointing it squarely at the man's chest.

John burst out laughing, gazing with undiluted affection at his wife, her apron blowing in the breeze. "I do declare, Maygwen Hopkins, I do love every inch of you!"

She smiled fondly at her husband. "Well, John Hopkins, there are quite a lot of inches to choose from, so take your pick."

As the farmers laughed with each other, the fallen Germans simply stared in confusion.

They became even more confused when they were marched back to the Hopkins' farmhouse kitchen. They were told firmly to sit down and behave themselves. Within minutes they were provided with a hot meal of sausages and eggs, fried in goose fat and washed down by several cups of tea.

By the time Hopkins and his wife escorted them from the house, they were smiling and totally compliant, even though it had been made abundantly clear they were being returned to custody.

The nearest police station was a little over half a mile away but they seemed to quite enjoy the walk, albeit accompanied by John's shotgun. They had become quite talkative and the English speaking prisoner provided a running translation, telling their captors they were joking at each others' behaviour over the last few days. One of the men suggested that when they reached the police station they should confess to stealing some slices of bread, taken from an open kitchen window the day before. He pulled a gnawed piece of dried bread from his pocket and asked whether he should return it.

Glais Police Station was no more than an office in the local Constable's terraced cottage and when Maygwen hammered on the front door there was no reply. A neighbour, as inquisitive as any Welsh Valleys 'Mam', glanced round her doorjamb.

"Looking for Constable Morgan are you, love?" She didn't wait for a reply. "He have gone out he have. I dunno how long he'll be, like." She sniffed and looked the three unkempt young men up and down with exaggerated distaste before glancing at the shotgun. "You could try Mrs Donne. She have a lock-up behind her back parlour." The woman withdrew and firmly closed her door.

Mrs Donne ran the village Post Office and, in the absence of anyone in uniform, was the nearest thing to an 'official' in the vicinity. She was also one of the few people in Glais to have the use of a telephone.

Seated in the back room of the Post Office, surrounded by the technical paraphernalia of a GPO telephone operator, the growing group of captives and captors sat in relative comfort while the Postmistress boiled a kettle for yet another cup of tea.

"I hope you don't mind us coming here, Mrs Donne." John remarked, rather belatedly. "I don't know where Willie Morgan has got to."

Mrs Donne smiled as if entertaining escaped Nazis was an everyday occurrence to her.

"He's probably just popped out somewhere. Looking for Germans, I wouldn't wonder."

She served steaming cups of tea all round, apologising that her ration wouldn't stretch to them all taking sugar. They politely waved away her apology as unnecessary.

"I am sure we quite understand." It was the German who spoke for them all, oddly incongruous though it seemed.

After a moment's silence as they sipped their tea, Maygwen began giggling quietly. Her husband gazed at her enquiringly.

"If you'd said to me this morning that I'd be sitting here tonight with Mrs Donne, having a tea party with three Germans, I think I'd have called you stark raving mad." John laughed with her. "All we need now is the vicar to walk through the door and the party would be complete." They all laughed, despite two of the Germans having no understanding as to why.

Mrs Donne edged her way round the crowded little room, moving a sack marked 'Royal Mail' out of her way and pulled a cord from her switchboard. She plugged it into a socket near the top of the board and wound a handle. She glanced over her shoulder. "You don't mind, do you? I've just got to make a call." Her attention was drawn away as a voice crackled at the other end of the line. "Hello, Morriston Police? This is Postmistress Donne at Glais calling. I've got a little job for you."

Sunday 18th March 1945, 09:00 hrs.

"That's eighty two prisoners recovered, sir." George took a sip from his mug of tea, quietly inhaling to dull the scalding ripple across his tongue. "I was up at Glais until ten o'clock last night. I asked one of the Germans why they had all made such efforts to escape when it is so obvious that the Americans and Russians will soon be in Berlin."

The Inspector smiled. He asked what the reply had been, confident the Germans would have denounced the Allied successes as propaganda.

"He told me that during the final one hundred days of the last war, 2,600 allied soldiers were killed every day. He saw no reason for this war to be any different and he wished to play his part."

"Bastard. Was he looking for a way to continue his war on British soil?"

George shook his head. "He said he was heading west and planned to cross to the Irish Republic. Mind you, do you remember that Panzer Captain, Eric Stiegel?" The Inspector nodded. "He reckoned he was destined to become some sort of Regional Governor of South Wales. Some of the fellows I've interviewed still believe absolutely that Germany is going to win the War."

"Let's hope to God they've got that wrong."

The Constable nodded. "I'll drink to that." They both raised their mugs and took another sip of tea. He glanced at the rotating brown swirl. "That reminds me. The prisoners who were held at the Post Office in Glais last night were given tea by Mrs Donne, the Postmistress." Inspector Bailey nodded. "One of them told me it had just dawned on him why Hitler has been supporting the Japanese advance through Asia." He sighed. "The typical German officer absolutely hates the idea of being allied to Japan, you know. They see Japanese officers as being an utter disgrace; totally without honour or decency."

"So why did he think the German High Command formed an alliance with them?"

"Because of this." He raised his mug again. "The Japs are trying to invade India, aren't they. This chap had come to the conclusion that if our supply of tea is cut off, the British Tommy would lose his will to fight."

The Inspector smiled and glanced into his mug. "Now that, George, really is an official secret." He put his mug down, pulling a buff coloured file from a pile of papers balancing on the corner of his desk. He opened it, glancing at the last page to remind himself of a few details. "What about the three men seen in Canterbury. Any news about them?"

George shook his head. "Nothing since the incident in the cafe on Thursday. They took off in a stolen lorry in the direction of Ramsgate. There have been no reported sightings of either them or the lorry for three days."

Epilogue....

Nobody who has studied this small smudge on the history of World War Two doubts that the break-out of Prisoners of War in March 1945 from Camp 198 was one of the largest in history. All agree that, despite the search which immediately followed the escape, several prisoners managed to wriggle through the Police and military cordon thrown round the Bridgend area.

What remains in doubt to this day is the exact number of prisoners who escaped. Although there have been a few accounts published of the escape and subsequent events, none of these has been able to confirm that the number of recovered prisoners equalled the number who escaped.

Despite this, the Chief Constable of the Glamorgan Constabulary, Joseph Jones, was moved to take the unusual step of issuing a general message of congratulations and thanks to all those involved in the search. On 26th March 1945, General Order Number 57 was issued from his office at Canton, Cardiff. It reads as follows.

Mass Escape of German Prisoners of War –
11th March, 1945.

The recent escape of 70 Prisoners of War from the Camp at Bridgend set the Force a task which called for the prompt and energetic attention of all ranks.

At the outset, it was clear from reports which reached the Police that it would be anything but an easy matter to trace and recapture the escaped men, who would take full advantage of what they achieved in getting away from the Camp environments by separating in parties of two, three or four and making their way from the Camp in different directions.

In view of the magnitude of the escape, measures had to be taken to organise the search and maintain keen observations on a far wider scale than could be done by the limited numbers of Service and Police personnel; and, for this purpose, an appeal was made by the Chief Constable for the aid of all available

Special Constables, members of the Home Guard, Wardens, and members of the general public who could give assistance.

The response to this appeal fulfilled all expectations. With the least possible delay search parties were methodically organised and a comb-out was undertaken, which yielded such good results that within the space of six days all of the Prisoners had been recaptured and returned to the Camp. Through the energy and vigilance of the search parties, and the wonderful co-operation of the members of the public who passed on to the Police without delay any information they considered would be helpful, only eight of the escaped Prisoners of War were able to make their way outside the County of Glamorgan; four of whom had taken possession of and driven away in an unattended motor car immediately they escaped from the Camp, and were probably outside Glamorgan before their escape was reported to the Police. It is known that the other four boarded goods trains at isolated spots.

Messages of thanks for the good work done by the Police have been received from both the Officer Commanding, South Wales District, and the Officer Commanding, Severn Sub-District, and the Chief Constable desires to take this opportunity of expressing his personal appreciation, not only of the members of the Force, the Police Auxiliaries and the Special Constables, but also of the invaluable assistance given by the members of the Home Guard, the Air Raid Wardens, members of other branches of the Civil Defence Service, and the very large number of other public spirited citizens who came forward and gave their services so readily at a time when they were so much needed.

It is desired that this expression of thanks for assistance rendered should be conveyed also to the Ministers of Religion, of all denominations, who contributed such useful and material assistance in connection with the search by announcing to their congregations that this large number of Prisoners of War had escaped, and that if any persons resembling them were seen the matter should be reported without delay to the Police. It is impossible to send a personal message of appreciation to all who assisted in the protracted search, and, for this reason, the Chief Constable hopes that the members of the Force in their respective districts will convey this message of thanks to all those persons who co-operated as the source for disseminating the information for the valuable assistance which was so spontaneously given, and proved so very effective.

By Order,
Joseph Jones
Chief Constable

The minutes of the War Cabinet Home Defence (Security) Executive committee meeting for 20th March 1945 reveal that the contentious use of Police wireless sets to discuss Prisoner of War escapes was satisfactorily resolved. By the time it was agreed that the exact location of Prison Camps was no longer a matter of national security, it was too late to assist with the recovery of Island Farm's escapees.

It was not until many years had passed and the police officers involved had all retired that a few of them met with a small group of Bridgend's amateur local historians. They had, with renewed interest in Island Farm and the events surrounding the escape of March 1945, gained access to the site and Hut Nine in particular. There, it was discovered that the prisoners had created a false wall inside a small room used for the prisoners' ablutions. Behind the false wall, several hundredweight of clay balls, about the size of cricket balls, had been stashed; the spoil from the excavated escape tunnel which had been started from the hut. The wall had been carefully sealed when the work was completed and had remained undetected for many years.

The attention of Glamorgan Constabulary's officers in March 1945 was not taken up entirely by the escape from Island Farm. Police interest was also drawn by events in Porthcawl and the actions of an individual who, although unconnected to the escape, decided to take advantage of the unfolding drama for his own ends. I am grateful for Brett Exton's research and the information which appears in his website *islandfarm.fsnet.co.uk* which greatly contributed to the following account.

Superintendent May received a report during the evening of 12th March that one of the escaping Prisoners of War had shot and seriously wounded a woman, Mrs Lily Grossley. She had managed to tell the first police officers who reached the scene that escaped German prisoners had accosted her and demanded she hand over her handbag containing her week's housekeeping money. When she had refused, one of the men had shot her at close range. Her husband, Howard Grossley, had been present but had been unable to prevent the attack or stop the men from running off.

Within a few hours, however, a different version of events had emerged. Howard Grossley, it appeared, was a Canadian soldier, absent without leave from his unit. It also transpired that he had a wife in Canada. His Welsh 'wife' was actually named Lily Griffiths and they had been living together at a guest-house with their two year old son.

Howard gave the Police a statement to the effect that he and Lily had been taking a walk late at night. They had taken a short-cut down a lane returning to the guest-house when they had been confronted by men who they immediately identified as German. They tried to steal Lily's handbag but here, his account differed from his girlfriend's. He told Police that he had drawn a revolver which he had been carrying and threatened the men until they ran off. As they had made their escape, he fired a shot at them but had inadvertently hit Lily by mistake.

Whoever had pulled the trigger, Lily's lung had been punctured by the bullet and as the hours passed, septicaemia set in. Her doctors began to realise they were losing her. Realising her time was limited, she asked for a police officer to take a new statement. She now changed her account again and tried to find excuses for Howard's action. She claimed he was depressed due to terrible burns on his back caused by a phosphorous explosion while on active service. The high dosage of painkillers he was obliged to take had reacted badly with a heavy day of drinking and his judgement had become severely impaired. He was, she said, thoroughly ashamed of his desertion from the Canadian Army and this further depressed him, as did his unhappy marriage in Canada. She said that when the men had run off, he had threatened to shoot himself. In the ensuing struggle, as she tried to wrestle the gun from him, it had gone off.

Lily Griffiths died on 16th March as a result of her wound and Howard Grossley was charged with her murder.

He denied the charge but was convicted on 12th July 1945 at Swansea Assizes. Following an unsuccessful appeal he was hanged on 5th September 1945.

A further conundrum persists, however, concerning the former Royal Canadian Artillery Bombardier, Howard Joseph Grossley whose body was interred in Cardiff Prison Cemetery. There is a memorial to a J H Grossley at Brookwood Memorial

War Cemetery in Surrey, England. The corresponding Commonwealth War Dead Memorial record confirms the similarity to that of the executed man in Cardiff. The man honoured at Brookwood is Bombadier Joseph Howard Grossley of the Royal Canadian Artillery. Extraordinarily, both men are recorded as having the same service number: D-106883. By a cruel coincidence, the Surrey J H Grossley is recorded to have died in combat, exactly two years before the Cardiff hanging. To date, no explanation has been found to either confirm or refute the identity of either man. It is of course possible that a simple clerical error could explain the discrepancy. The late Brookwood Bombardier may simply have been associated to the wrong service number in the memorial records. Alternatively, perhaps the convicted Grossley adopted a war casualty's identity in an effort to hide his own past. Further research will be required if the mystery is to be resolved.

That question aside, it should be no surprise that during the difficult week following the break-out, Superintendent May and his senior officers were somewhat distracted.

More junior police officers carried much of the burden of tracking down, arresting and returning the escaped prisoners to the custody of the Army. They would have recorded these events in 'occurrence books'; simple narrative accounts of daily activity kept by every police station in the country.

During the author's research it became apparent that none of the police stations involved managed to preserve any occurrence books for March 1945.

Newspapers throughout the country published their versions of the unfolding events using information chiefly gleaned from official sources: statements from spokesmen for the Police, the War Office and the Army's Western Command Headquarters at Chester.

Other snippets of detail were contributed by members of the public, by soldiers and others caught off-guard by covert reporters. All reports, of course, had to be passed by the Official Censor before publication but it is doubtless the case that by March 1945 editors, particularly of national newspapers, were prepared to risk an occasional rebuke by the Official Censor in the interests of publishing a headline that would sell more newspapers.

The fact remains that it was widely reported from the start that seventy prisoners had escaped during the night of 10th to 11th March 1945. The same figure was used (or at least recorded in the official minutes) of at least one senior Cabinet committee.

Whether the discrepancy was due to a misunderstanding or a deliberate sleight of hand, the authorities were satisfied to allow the public to believe the figures published in the press.

By the morning of Saturday 17th March the same newspapers had reported no fewer than seventy six prisoners had been recaptured. It is known from other sources that at least a further four and possibly six were captured during that period.

Three others, seen in Canterbury, Kent on Thursday 15th March and identified as German from their conversation and their uniforms, were never accounted for. Eleven men, still at large at the time the 'Canterbury Three' were sighted, were recaptured over the following forty eight hours as far away as Castle Bromwich in Warwickshire, Cymmer near Port Talbot and Glais near Swansea - all at least two hundred miles from Canterbury. No other Prisoner of War camps had reported escapes which might account for the three Canterbury men.

By the time the Canterbury story had reached the press and been published on the following Saturday, it had already been declared that all the escaped Bridgend prisoners had been recaptured. Censorship and Defence (or 'D') Notice number 43 would have ensured, if required, that no awkward questions were raised in the press regarding their current whereabouts.

On the same afternoon that the three men were spotted in Canterbury, the Rt. Hon. Arthur Henderson MP, Financial Secretary to the War Office, answered a question in the House of Commons posed to the Secretary of State for War.

Henderson had been Under Secretary of State for War from 1942 to 1943 and MP for Cardiff South until 1931. There is no reason to suppose he would have been either uninformed or disinterested in the events that had unfolded in South Wales.

In his reply he said *"An escape of sixty seven German Prisoners of War, of whom sixty five were officers, took place at 04:00 hours on 11th March from a camp in South Wales. Forty eight of them have now been recaptured..."*

Perhaps strangely, no question was raised regarding Mr Henderson's contradictory statistics and nobody apparently tallied up the number of prisoners reported as recaptured.

A court of Enquiry was later convened to examine the details of the break-out but this was held in secret. The final report, as provided to the War Cabinet at the time, contained only a list of recommendations regarding changes to prison camp security. These included the provision of perimeter lighting, dog patrols to be made outside the boundary fence and increased daytime roll calls to disrupt illicit work on tunnels. The hope was that any digging would then have to be done at night when the camp was quieter. The Committee also suggested that regular inspections were made of blankets and clothes to check for soiling and closer searches were made around the huts to identify soil deposits from excavated tunnels. Inventories should be kept of the contents of each hut to enable guards to quickly identify when items which could be used for tunnel building went missing.

Suggesting that basic precautions at Camp 198 had been overlooked, the report also recommended that a roll call should be taken after lights-out and that new Prisoner of War camps should be thoroughly cleared of building materials before prisoners were moved in.

Colonel Darling, either by choice or under orders, kept silent. Although no criticism was voiced officially regarding the management of the camp, an assumption that the Camp Commandant carried much of the responsibility for the escape was inevitable. Despite the fact that Colonel Darling had repeatedly asked for extra guards, search-lights and materials to build guard towers, the press had already made their feelings known.

The Sunday Express of 18th March 1945 carried an article, attributed only to a 'Sunday Express Reporter' that the camp authorities had ignored a warning, in the form of a note thrown through the fence, apparently by a prisoner with anti-Nazi feelings. While extra guards and flares were deployed, the reporter asserted that the escaping Germans simply continued to tunnel their way to freedom on the opposite side of the compound.

Although it is now clear the 'warning' was simply a diversion, the mood of the press was changing. During the earlier years of the War it had been seen as an editor's patriotic duty to publish only positive, morale boosting stories. By 1945, however, as the tide of the Allies' genuine successes grew, many newspaper proprietors and editors allowed items to appear which mocked or even criticised the management of the war.

The junior guards certainly felt aggrieved that they were being blamed locally for allowing the escape to take place, particularly as they too had made representations regarding under-manning and lack of materials and equipment.

Darling and his men were not alone. Colonel William Llewellyn, the Company Commander of Bridgend's Home Guard also complained. Although his unit had been stood down in December 1944, they had been among the first to volunteer to join the Police search once the alarm had been raised. Although permitted to join in, they were refused extra petrol supplies and the reissue of many of the rifles they had reluctantly returned to the local Infantry Battalion's armoury the previous December. Llewellyn wrote in vain to the Divisional Commander and his MP explaining how, with sufficient petrol, he could have mobilised up to 2,000 former Home Guard men within hours of the escape, effectively searching and cordoning off a far greater area of the county. With more rifles, he argued, his men would have quickly gained the upper hand in any encounter with the enemy. By the time his complaints were considered, it was too late.

It also emerged that, within a few hours of the escape being reported, Colonel Llewellyn had found regular soldiers and police officers combing through the woodlands of his estate at Court Colman Manor, a few miles north of Island Farm. He had, of course, voiced no objection at the time but was later heard to comment, with some rancour, that had he been informed promptly rather than carried to Bridgend Police Station for a meeting, he could have organised an efficient search of the estate himself. His ground staff were, he pointed out, far better acquainted with the local geography and most were former members of the Home Guard.

Inevitably, some of the recaptured German officers complained about the treatment they received on being returned to captivity. The official line remained solid: the prisoners were not punished for the very practical reason that there were fears of retaliation against British prisoners being held in Germany. A few of the guards, however, speaking privately after the events of March 1945 admitted they might have been less than gentle with some of their prisoners who failed to comply with their orders.

Karl Ludwig, the *SS* officer who had been one of the first to be recaptured, complained that he had been forced to stand against a wall with his hands raised for an unnecessarily long time. He told a delegation from the Swiss Red Cross that a guard, shouting curses at him, had accidentally fired a shot which had narrowly missed his head. The Swiss, apparently, found no reason to take any further action and made no formal complaints.

There is no evidence that the Military Intelligence Service became actively involved with the recaptured Prisoners of War, despite having a branch of the Intelligence Service, MI19, set up for exactly the purpose of interrogating and extracting useful information from captured enemy servicemen.

It is certainly the case that in March 1945 MI19 officers were being kept unusually busy due to the increasing influx of German prisoners captured in mainland Europe. During the week of the escape, for example, they produced reports of interviews with German officers relating to *Feldwerkstatt 511*, a branch of the German *6th Batterie* responsible for servicing and maintaining V-2 Rockets. The report runs to thirty three pages; a hundred paragraphs of narrative and dozens of diagrams, ground plans, tables and appendixes including lists of names of personnel and their functions within the unit.

Another report concerns the interrogation of a senior metallurgical engineer formerly based at an armaments factory in Braunschweig. The factory was surrounded by others supplying aircraft parts and tanks which, according to the prisoner, were to be packed with explosives and driven at Allied installations by remote-control. Even more disturbingly, the report also tells of experiments being made with chemical weapons.

Other reports gave details of anti-aircraft defences in various locations and of the *Miag Ammewerk* tank factory which was designing and building a new *Pantherjager* or *Jagdpanther*. The project was regarded as so valuable that since its inception in April 1944, standing orders were issued that should there be a danger of one of the prototypes falling into Allied hands, it should be destroyed, even if this meant the crew would lose their lives. The captured prisoner, being politically disaffected by the extremes of the Nazi regime, seemed happy to disclose enough technical detail to fill over thirty pages, including detailed plans, lists of stores and equipment held at the factory.

A further report was compiled from information given by a former Austrian skiing champion and holder of a world ski record. He provided details regarding power stations and railway installations as well as labour camps, training units and Army garrisons along the frontier with Switzerland.

Captured Austrian cooks and photographers provided information regarding *Abwehr* and *Luftwaffe* bases, giving their interrogators sufficient material to fill a further six pages. Another report describes a series of interviews with a prisoner whose first language, unusually, was English. Captured in September 1944 in Hildesheim, the unhappy prisoner was captured wearing his German *Abwehr* uniform, complete with *SS* motif on the right collar patch and three lions on the left. Near the cuff of his left jacket sleeve he wore a band with the words *'English Free Corps'*. He confirmed that many of the men in his unit were either English, Australian or New Zealanders. Their officers were all German. His main revelation concerned the Burgermeister of Breslau who, in January 1945, was one of the first to evacuate the town which was under attack by the Russians. He was arrested at Frankenstein while attempting to reach Berlin and returned under guard to Breslau. There, he was summarily executed by firing squad at the feet of the statue of Frederick the Great.

Shortly after the final recovered prisoners were returned to Bridgend from Glais, Colonel Darling was quietly removed from his post as Commandant of Camp 198. Days after the escape, an operation had been started to ship the prisoners out to other locations around the country. Within three weeks, more than 1,600 German officers and most of the other ranks had been transferred.

During the Spring of 1946 the barbed wire fencing was removed although, by September 1946, the Prisoner of War population in Britain had reached an all-time high of over 400,000. Camp 198 itself was transformed, in the closing months of the War, into Special Camp 11. There, it is well documented, were housed Germany's most senior field officers, cared for by their batmen and a few remaining German NCO's left over from the former Camp 198.

Many of these senior men were held in preparation for trial for war crimes while others were guarded as potential witnesses. Now, at last, MI19 provided a team of interrogators and interpreters to interview and gather evidence before indictments could be drawn up. The fascinating account of how these investigations were conducted is included in 'The London Cage' by Lieut. Col. A P Scotland OBE, (Evans Bros., London, 1957).

It was announced on 13th July 1948 that all German Prisoners of War had been repatriated. The announcement made no mention of the many German former prisoners who had elected to remain in Britain and the number from Camp 198 who chose to remain has never been assimilated. Some may have settled to work on the farms they had been introduced to as prison labourers and others, perhaps, with British girlfriends. It had been illegal for British nationals to marry German citizens until Clement Attlee controversially lifted the ban on fraternisation and marriage in August 1947.

The Royal Arsenal's shell-filling factories at Bridgend were systematically closed, the staff disbanded and the plant dismantled. The sites were sold off, in time, and today form the basis of two industrial estates. The fine collection of brick built buildings which housed the Arsenal offices were offered to Glamorgan Constabulary. They had long since outgrown their accommodation in Canton, Cardiff and the site in Bridgend seemed a satisfactory solution to all concerned. It was certainly larger and positioned far more centrally within the County. Today, the buildings still serve as the Headquarters for South Wales Police.

Glamorgan Constabulary's Chief Constable Jones continued in his post with a degree of success and acclaim until his retirement in 1951.

In his General Order of 26th March 1945, he chose not to mention that certain aspects of the escape made the task of recapture easier. Although some efforts were made to disguise their clothes, the majority of the escapees chose to continue wearing their German uniforms. The prospect of freedom was broadly eclipsed by the fear of being shot as a spy; a rumour put about by German Intelligence to discourage escaping officers from giving themselves up. Similarly, some effort had gone into producing forged identity papers although anything more than a perfunctory glance would have easily identified them as fakes.

In the turmoil that was Northern France following D-Day, many of the German prisoners, when captured, had mislaid various parts of their kit. The British Army supplied many of them with officers' overcoats and the embossed brass buttons, when dipped in home-made ink, made passable stamps for forged documents.

The journalist who, in 2005, carefully prepared his account of the escape, completed his piece and filed it with his editor in good time before the March anniversary. It was never published. The story, he was told, was of less interest than current news and was 'spiked' in favour of an item concerning the much delayed regeneration of Porthcawl's Eastern Promenade and harbour.

For the Girl Guide leader, Mrs Harrison and her troupe, an unexpected by-product of their camping expedition near Danygraig Woods made itself apparent the following Tuesday. As she opened their regular weekly meeting, she noticed her company had swollen by a further five girls. Conspicuous if only because they were not in uniform, Mrs Harrison asked them to introduce themselves. This done, she asked one of them to share with the group her reasons for wishing to join the Guides.

It transpired that, having heard of the previous weekend's excitement, they had each determined to join up. To their credit, they all had the honesty to admit they were hungry for adventure and now saw the Guide movement as a promising conduit.

In the immediate aftermath of the emergency, Detective Constable George Charteris felt it his duty to follow the instruction given in his Chief Constable's General Order Number 57. He had read the order carefully, especially the part which reads: '...the Chief Constable hopes that the members of the Force in their respective districts will convey this message of thanks to all those persons who co-operated...'

He had checked back on his carefully maintained notebook, searching for the names and addresses of those members of the public who had helped by providing information. His eyes had settled on an entry dated Sunday 11th March. Asking permission of the Duty Sergeant, he had borrowed the keys for one of Bridgend's patrol cars and driven the five miles to the estate of Tythegston Court near Porthcawl.

It was by pure chance that Helena Cord-Evans had been given a few days leave from the ATS and was at home to answer the door. She had smiled with undisguised pleasure at seeing the smartly dressed and softly spoken young detective, quickly inviting him in and settling him in the parlour. Within minutes, she had carried in a tray with a large teapot, two cups and a plate of home-made biscuits, seating herself on the sofa next to him.

Four hours later, they were still chatting, blissfully unaware of the passage of time. Helena's mother had passed the parlour door and, hearing voices, had glanced into the room. Recognising the expression on her daughter's face which all mothers wait for in their daughters, she silently crept away and went for a walk.

George Charteris and Helena Cord-Evans were married at St.Tydwd's Church in Tythegston on 11th March 1946, exactly one year after their first meeting. Afterwards, Pendri Cord-Evans, in his speech as father of the bride, admitted to the complete surprise of all who knew him, that the wedding service had prompted him to shed a tear for the first time since his boyhood.

George's police career took him and Helena to several corners of England and Wales, seeing him promoted to the rank of Chief Inspector before his retirement at the age of 55. By the late 1970's, he had seen a creeping incursion of policing methods that left him feeling uncomfortable and, at times, quite ashamed. By the time his retirement became due George had been posted to a busy police station in one of the less savoury parts of South London. He and Helena had been more than ready to hand in his warrant card.

They retired to a small seaside town on the south coast of England and settled in a comfortable home overlooking the beach. Helena was often heard to repeat contentedly that it reminded her of Porthcawl.

His brief meeting at Hut Nine early in 2005 signalled George's first visit to South Wales for many years. It was also his last.

Only occasionally did George speak of his experiences in wartime Glamorgan, exchanging his thoughts with Helena who patiently listened before adding her own memories of the events.

They both agreed that it was strange that there remained so glaring an unanswered question. The lack of challenge to the official yet blatantly inaccurate numbers was stranger, even, than the Howard Grossley murder or the fate of the 'Canterbury Three'; the German officers unaccounted for since their undignified dash from a small corner cafe in Kent.

Perhaps, they concluded, the official silence was not so strange...

Archive resources researched

Individual national newspapers
Titles published March 1945:
>Daily Express
>Daily Herald
>Daily Mail
>Daily Worker
>News Chronicle
>Sunday Express

British Newspaper Archives
Titles published March 1945:
>Aberdeen Press & Journal
>Dundee Courier & Advertiser
>Derby Daily Telegraph
>Derby Evening Telegraph
>Dundee Evening Telegraph
>Gloucester Citizen
>Gloucestershire Echo
>Hull Daily Mail
>Nottingham Evening Post
>Western Daily Press
>Western Morning News
>Yorkshire Post

Glamorgan Archives
file references:
DCON/276/7
DCON/274/8

National Archives
file references:
CAB 114/23
DEFE 53/4
WO 208/3529
WO 208/3614

16367926R00160

Printed in Great Britain
by Amazon